A Series of Lists
Book 1

The Back-Up List

Miriam Brady & Amber Best

 *Perfect Fit Publishing*

Visit our website for further information- thebackuplist.blogspot.com

First Edition- April 2012

The characters and events portrayed in this book are fictitious. Any similarity to real persons, living or dead, is coincidental and not intended by the authors.

(If you suspect you are a character in this book, or you are a rock star who thinks this is about you, please contact your mental health care provider immediately, but take the book with you for you will be waiting a very long while, and you might want something to read in your delusional state of mind.)

ISBN 10- 061563740X

ISBN 13- 9780615637402

Cover design and editing by Ruby Lowe

Interior art by Cillian Cubstead

Library of Congress Control Number: Pending

Printed in the United States of America

Perfect Fit Publishing

Dedication

For Mike- The love of my life, and the
stitch in my side- Mir

For Jeff- May our love always float
like a feather, love you baby- Ambie

Contents

Contents Continued

Prologue Part One- The Spork

Damn. If only he'd had a Nostradamus-like ability to see into the future or a personal advisor in all things *love* related. Ah, hindsight can be cruel. It was one of those full-circle, it's-a-wonderful-life kind of moments when it all comes back to you, Cal thought. Unfortunately, he had been no hero in his life's flashback. Instead, he could see every single stupid decision which had brought him to this point, and it wasn't pretty. He looked out at the skyline of Tokyo from his opulent hotel suite with a bitter frown on his face. If only he didn't need to perform in a concert later at the Saitama Super Arena. His band- Murder of Crows- would not be thrilled if he ditched them. A jagged view of skyscrapers did not distract him from the aggravating jaunt into his memories. They were all there, every damned, seemingly insignificant, decision he'd made, the decisions which had led him here and now threatened to bite him in the ass. He sorted through them until he pinpointed the one *she'd* used against him.

Lindsey Bell- a mistake if there ever was one- floated to the forefront of his mind. He never thought a slap on the face could so alter his existence, or be used as evidence against him. Oh man, he could practically still feel the sting- if only he'd reacted differently maybe *she* wouldn't have cut him off. Everyone else thought he was a hero, but no, not *her*. Cal had tried texting her best friend the simple words- *Help Me*- followed by the phrase- *everything is not as it seems*. He'd lost her too; her return text had been haunting him for the better part of an hour. *Cal, I'm so sorry. I would give anything to fix this, but she refuses...she says I'm* FORBIDDEN *to talk to you.* What the hell? Was she not a grown woman with a mind of her own? He let his mind drift back to the slap heard round the world by all the women he'd victimized. Cal flopped back on the leather sofa in his suite, closing his eyes; he was taken back to how it all began.

Cal recalled feeling the impact of Lindsey's manicured hand make contact with his cheek, quickly followed by the sensation of blood rushing beneath the surface of his skin into the exact shape of a handprint. He'd wryly smiled in return, hoping the cameras captured his dignified response. See! Right there, he thought, *that* was the moment he should have changed. He could still hear her nasally voice as his mind replayed the incident with clarity. "Liar." Must her voice be so whiney and grating? He listened as her strident scream invasively intruded into his introspective monologue. "Is *she* the one?" He felt his jaw drop. Was she actually accusing him of cheating while cameras rolled unobtrusively in the background? A crowd had begun to form. He turned to see who this mystery woman was, the one he'd supposedly cheated with, and he laughed. He knew it looked bad, but he honestly couldn't help himself. She was no one he knew, pretty, but not familiar in the least. He was tempted to grab the unknown woman and kiss her just to prove the accusation correct, but was uncertain if he had to turn the other cheek and prepare for another slap.

He decided pulling out of the situation was the only thing to do. He drew away, skulking off to the elevator, escaping the well-populated hotel lobby. It had never been easy being famous, or infamous. It brought on a unique set of problems, one being a girlfriend who loved drama. She didn't love drama the way normal women loved drama; she was more of a drama junkie, sucking it up the way some snorted cocaine. He had no idea why cameras were following her around, but it didn't seem to be out of place in San Francisco. No one milling about even noticed, or spared a passing glance. She managed to reach the elevator before the doors closed. He sighed, "What do you want now?"

"To make up." She blinked her long false eyelashes his way, causing him to briefly wonder what he'd seen in her. His eyes swept over her, taking in the platinum hair, fake-baked bronzed body from heaven, stopping at her wide eyed -trying to appear innocent- expression. Innocence was truly eluding her, she had grasped vapid just splendidly though.

"*Uh-huh.*" He backed up to the wall, leaning on the railing in the interior of the elevator. "Where are the cameras? We wouldn't want them to miss anything."

She smelled like bottled sunshine as she pulled herself up around his neck. He pried her free before the doors opened with a ding. She followed him along the corridor, her high heeled sandals clunking noisily along the way. "Cal, baby, it was just a publicity stunt for my new reality show. It's going to be called *Lindsey Lovin'*. Isn't that a great title? I came up with it. My publicist told me to give him a scene, I had to have you act surprised."

He was walking quickly, longing to break out into a full-on marathon run. "So you want to make up on camera?" he asked, his voice filled with sarcasm. He found his key card. "I can't do this, Lindsey. I just can't."

"What does that even mean?" she asked, once again appearing idiotically simple.

He opened the suite door. "I think it means we're breaking up."

She stood there, astonished; her jewel encrusted tank top, hot pink against her tan. "But.." He just shut the door before she could say anything else.

"Why?" He allowed himself to ask it out loud as he leaned breathless against the closed door. He hadn't expected an answer.

"Because you're a moron," his brother shouted out from the sofa. He knew this was an accurate observation, of course. He sat down on the sofa next to his brother, who appeared to be carefree. What was his secret? Rory just stared back at him, "So tell me you ditched the b…"

"Now, now," he interrupted, "no name calling." He relaxed as Rory handed him a beer with the top popped free, the bottle ice cold and frosty. "I can't seem to catch a break in my love life." Cal formed air quotes around the phrase 'love life'. He stretched out and looked over at his brother. Although they weren't twins, they did rather resemble each other. His brother's hair was a blond mess on top of his head, his blue eyes full of mischief, his tall muscular body only slightly shorter than his own. At six foot five, most everyone was shorter.

"Love life?" Rory snorted. He coughed something that sounded like "sex life". Rory chuckled before taking a swig of his own beer. "No one could love that girl, not even her mother."

"I didn't love her, so what?"

"One day you'll have to grow up and settle down. I suppose you can wait until you're in your sixties or seventies." Rory laughed heartily, while Cal inwardly winced. His brother thought it should be easy to find someone. It just wasn't so simple. He wasn't in a position to settle down, meet the proverbial girl next door and raise a family. The women he met were not so nice, more on the naughty side. He wasn't certain he even wanted that life. "You know, Cal, you're bound to run out of those wild oats you've been sowing."

Cal rolled his eyes, "I'm not ready to settle down, okay?"

"You know, I went to KFC today." Where the hell was this going? "And I have discovered I hate the utensil known as the spork." Here we go again, random Rory.

"What the hell are you talking about?" he asked.

"I mean, really, it's neither successful as a spoon or fork. It has all of these little jagged teeth; I might as well be spooning mashed potatoes into my mouth with a spagger," Rory commented.

"Spagger?"

"Spoon dagger. Seriously, you take a mouthful of what you hope will be potatoes and gravy, you gouge a chunk out of your cheek, next thing you know you're eating potatoes and blood."

"Rory, we were talking about my love life, I don't know where you're going with this."

Rory laughed again. He had to be drunk. Cal laughed after he thought about it for a moment, "Spagger?" Rory cracked up, leaning over his faded jeans to catch his breath. "Maybe at our next concert we should announce the potential dangers of eating with sporks. Boycott the spork, save a cheek." He stared out past his brother, to the open doors on the balcony. Was she out there? Would she like his idiot brother? She'd have to get past all of his faults first. Could she? Whoever she was she'd have to be amazing, because not just any woman could follow a conversation about sporks and be willing to stick around. How precisely would he find her in a never ending sea of hoes? He leaned back into the couch and closed his eyes, letting the beer carry his stresses away. He remembered thinking that such a woman couldn't possibly exist.

Prologue Part Two- Conspiracy

"I hate the smell of roses," she said to no one in particular. Her best friend was busy in the next room emptying her townhouse of all of the roses which had been delivered nonstop for days. Roses. They only mean one of two things- someone screwed up or somebody died. At least that was her experience with roses, a flower she had learned to hate. She felt ridiculous to have fallen for *him* in the first place. She tried to recall the last time she'd been happy, desperate to tap into the happiness which now eluded her. Kinley returned to stuff more roses into more garbage bags, while a light musical tone told Madison that Kinley had just received a text.

"Oh, Maddy!" Kinley had a triumphant look which Madison felt her duty to erase.

"If it's Cal you'd better shut him down, you are *forbidden* to talk to him." Kinley stared at her, disbelief etched on her face as she mouthed the word 'forbidden', Madison only nodded grimly in response. "Or you could give me the phone and let *me* do it," Madison grumbled as she stretched out her hand in order to confiscate the cell phone. Kinley stepped back, effectively pulling the phone out of Madison's reach.

"Fine, I'll shut him down, just let me do it in my own way." Kinley morosely typed out a message and sighed. "Maddy, what are you thinking? You look positively sinister." Kinley was trying desperately to change the topic of conversation, which wasn't a bad thing for once.

"I want to kill him, or at least stab him. Maybe we could stage a hunting accident." Her voice drifted away, as she fantasized about walking through the wilds of Manitoba with a hunting rifle. "Actually, I was just thinking about that one GNO, you know before…"

"The Coach bags?" Kinley asked as Madison nodded. "Yeah, how fun was that?"

"The best," Madison sighed.

"Yeah, but once you start the proverbial trip down memory lane you're going to relive the good and the bad. Are you sure you want to go there?" Kinley asked tentatively.

"I'm not sure I can help it," Madison muttered.

"Well, while you're reminiscing I'm going to be tossing roses into trash bags, and I'm afraid it's going to be awhile, since it looks like FTD threw up in your living room. So, my dear, reflect away, while I erase him with the great floral removal." She was sadly shaking her head, tossing her red curls about in the air. Madison knew she wanted to fix things, but it was impossible.

Madison closed her eyes, her head pounding; she could hear her friends chatting around her, her last amazing day before her life was nearly destroyed. Madison felt as though she were reliving it all. She wanted this for some inexplicable, masochistic reason. Her memories rushed at her causing her to feel as though she were reliving them.

She'd always loved girl's nights; it constantly meant a night full of laughter and that night had been no different. She recalled how she'd felt run ragged at the time, four kids on summer break with an endless need for entertainment, had made her feel close to insane. She had a lovely golden tan from all of the time they'd been spending at the beach lately. Her friend, sitting beside her in the passenger seat had been with her every time, and yet, Kinley was just as creamy white as ever. Redheads seldomly tanned. Their friends Megan and Kate sat in the minivan's two middle seats, they were not quite as golden as she was, but they all made Kin look as though she might be a ghost who'd recently decided to haunt them.

It was their typical GNO, dinner and movie, which was always nice. She inwardly sighed; it was a deeply contented sigh. She was also looking forward to tomorrow. She'd have the entire day to herself. "What has you smiling such a ginormous smile, Maddy?" Kate asked from the back seat. It was practically two kid-free days.

"I was just contemplating the idea of alone time; Jack is taking the kiddos to the beach tomorrow. I'll have the entire day to myself." Madison grinned as she drove.

"I'm so jealous," Kinley muttered, "I don't think I've had a Saturday alone in ages. What would it be like to think and hear your own thoughts?"

"Or to pee without interruption?" Meg whined dramatically for their entertainment.

"Or take a bath without someone climbing into it with you," Kate said with a hint of reflection. Her kids were older now, requiring the need of a chauffeur instead of a constant caregiver. "Meg, I know what you mean, the other day I sat down around two in the afternoon and I realized I'd been so busy all day that I'd forgotten to pee at all." The minivan filled with laughter.

"Is it possible to see a later show?" Megan brushed her white-blond hair away from her face, all the while looking like a teen asking her parent if she could borrow the family car. Madison turned and spotted the mall on the other side of the freeway. She knew Meg well enough to know what her question was concerning. She was a shopaholic, and had located her favorite -Nordstrom's. She had a personal shopper there, people knew her by her first name, it was almost embarrassing.

Kate looked down at the times she'd jotted down, "If we see a later one, we can squeeze in an hour of shopping before dinner." Meg never just wanted an hour.

"I'll take Kate with me, she'll keep me in line, then we can meet for dinner in an hour. There is a CPK at the end of the mall; would it be fine if we met there? Please?" Meg's green eyes were pleading and sparkling with the prospect of shopping kid-free in her favorite store for an hour. This meant no Outback Steakhouse, like they'd planned. Madison had to wonder if this had been her agenda all the while, but she only turned into the parking lot without further discussion. Not everyone could be kid free for an entire day; she decided to share the luck. Why not?

"Oh Maddy, bless you, may your life be filled with nothing but perpetual joy and happiness," Megan flattered. Kate had a look of exasperation on her face, as Meg grabbed her hand and began to drag her to the department store. "Oh Nordy, I've missed you," Meg called out.

"Yeah yeah, just be quick," Kate moaned.

"What are *we* going to do for an hour, Maddy, oh great *bestower* of time?" Kinley asked when they were alone.

"Is *bestower* even a word?"

"I'm fairly certain it isn't, but we can throw it into our own personal dictionary." Kinley climbed out of the van. "Now, seriously, what the hell are we going to do?"

"I'm sure we can window shop..." Madison suggested.

"You know us, we never just admire things- cash and credit, first born children and organ donations have all occurred when we go shopping." Madison laughed. She *did* know Kinley, they'd been friends since junior high, and were truthfully, more like sisters than anything else. They walked silently for only a moment through the mall until Madison accidentally found her salvation.

"Do you see it?"

"More importantly, do you hear it?" Kinley asked in reply.

"The heavenly choirs of angels singing? Oh I hear it." They reached the display window of the Coach store and stared into it, salivating over the bags. There were very few things Madison and Kinley loved more than purses, bags, and wallets. Those things would be husbands and kids. "The black bag in the back has a halo around it, as though the world has gone dark where it does not sit."

"I feel the brown bag here in the front has the same heavenly illumination. It would be the long lost match to my new brown boots. Do you think it would hurt to have a closer look?"

"No one was ever hurt taking a look at anything," Madison giggled.

"Except for that Bible lady, who turned into a pillar of salt..." Kinley teased. They easily found the bags they liked, propped up on a table just inside the door. "Oh, breathe it in, Maddy."

"I know." They both loved the smell of Coach leather. "We should try them on, just to see if they hang right, and you know..." Madison suggested to her friend.

"I agree."

They both picked up the purses, examining them closely, trying them on, seeing where they fell naturally against their hips. "It is back to school soon."

"I have a question then. Are you worried about our kids going back on Monday? Are you trying to convince me that we each need new bags to assist us in our stylishness?" Kinley asked.

"No, I was thinking we need these for *our* school." Madison watched her friend's eyes light up. "I know we're in the middle of a session, and we don't start the new one until the end of next month, but don't you think we could use these bags as... I don't know. I can't think of a proper temptation to persuade you. Oh wait, I know, I am going to buy this bag and Kin, you will be filled with unbelievable regret every time you see it on my shoulder, you shall bite your lip and long for that bag." Madison pointed to the bag draped over Kinley's pale arm.

"Maddy!" Kinley groaned. "You are mean."

"Let's at least take a long look in the mirror." She led her friend over to the mirror. "See how sensational it looks on you?" She stared at her own reflection, her dark eyes twinkling with wicked humor, her long dark hair hung in loose curls the way Kinley's red hair did. "I must say- this bag seems to have been designed for me." Kinley chuckled. "Do you have *it* with you?" Madison asked her friend. Many times they didn't need to explain further, they practically read each other's minds.

"I do...but *it's* for emergencies..." Kinley gritted her teeth, whispering. Madison knew she had her.

"If this isn't an emergency, I don't know what is. An even greater emergency might be your propensity to obsess over the bag, and when you return it won't be here." Madison easily won this, she watched her friend's shoulders slump. "We're in this together."

"Yeah, okay," Kinley conceded as she fished around in her purse for the hidden secret credit card, the existence of which was concealed from her husband. "You know I don't think I can live without it now."

They made their purchases, and proceeded to sit on a bench in the center of the mall to switch things out; everything was going from their former bags into the much newer, shining, glorious bags. They were now running late. They raced through the mall on foot, nearly knocking over fellow pedestrians, shouting out, "Pardon me, excuse me," all along the way.

They made it, panting, bags in tow, stitches in their sides. Madison found Megan and Kate seated just inside. They both scooted into the booth, shoving their shopping bags into the corner with Megan's pile. "I told you they were running on K-time," Kate commented.

Madison ignored the snide comment and addressed Megan, "So, how is Nordy doing?" she asked politely, as she perused the menu left for her.

"Sensational. I love seeing my old friend, Nordy. He had things on sale today; it seems they were put on sale just for me."

"If Nordy is such a good friend, why does he charge you? Why not give you everything you want for free?" Kate asked with a sideways grin. "He's using you. I think you've become a victim, you're in an unhealthy relationship, it's terribly codependent."

Megan waved the comment away, while Madison ordered two *Diet* Cokes for her and Kinley. "Why do you order her drinks?"

"I can't help it, and it is what she wanted. She'll sit there and look at the menu, hem and haw over it, lead the waiter on, when finally she'll pick what we all know she'll pick. Like she drinks anything other than a diet," Madison told Kate, who just shrugged.

Megan laughed. "You guys are so funny together. You're the bossy, uptight one and Kinley is all relaxed and easy going. Nothing ruffles her feathers. Don't you care that she's bossy with you, Kin?"

"She's more particular than I am, it's fine. I don't care." Kinley was terribly easy going. "She's been like this for years."

"Speaking of bossy, we have only forty-five minutes to finish dinner if we want to get good seats at the movies, I'm not happy when we have to sit too close," Madison informed everyone.

"We'll scarf our food quickly then." Kinley grinned broadly, "More importantly, who wants to see our new bags?"

Kate shook her head disapprovingly, "I should have gone with *you*. What are you going to tell your husbands?"

"I'm going with the- this is a knock off, got it on the street corner for twenty bucks. What do you think?" Kinley took a sip of her newly arrived

Diet Coke, enjoying the nods of approval. "Maddy is implementing a far more complicated plan."

"The slow reveal." The women nodded their heads again. "It will hang it in the back of my closet, only slightly peeking out, then little by little it will become more prominent in my closet, until at last, I can answer the question honestly- where did that come from? He'll ask me all gruffly, and I can say -what? This old thing? I've had it in my closet for ages. I got it on sale."

They laughed throughout their hurried dinner, while sharing exotic flavored pizzas and a dessert. Dinner came to an abrupt end in order to get to the movie on time. Kinley, who was late to everything, didn't mind missing previews, while Kate couldn't stand it. One might as well miss the entire movie if they missed the previews, according to Kate. Megan couldn't care about such things. The dinner and movie was just the break Madison had been in need of. She'd felt too exhausted lately to be a good mom. One more day of rest should do it, she thought.

All of the girls talked on the way home, laughing, discussing the highlights of the romantic comedy until one by one she dropped everyone off. Kin was the exception; she had parked her car in Madison's driveway behind Jack's SUV. "Oh, no, Maddy, I can't take the Coach shopping bag home. It's supposed to be a knock-off."

Madison replied, "I can't have it here, Jack will think...wait I have an idea."

"Your brown eyes look all silver in the moonlight, silver with that evil gleam." Kinley followed her in, with the shopping bags. "What are you doing?"

"We're going to have a little bonfire, get rid of the evidence." She turned the key on the gas fireplace, and tossed their receipts in, watching the flames engulf the small slivers of paper, she then tossed the boxes, bags, and tissue paper into the roaring blaze. "Why didn't we think to dispose of these things before we came home? Logically, we make no sense." Madison kept her laughter light, soft, as her husband was sleeping in the other room. How ironic that her house phone started ringing, which sounded incredibly loud in the dead silence of the night. Who calls someone at one in the morning? She was agitated, looking for the phone which had not been replaced on the charging base after the last use. Kinley was crawling along the floor searching under furniture while Madison was searching the sofa cushions.

It stopped ringing; only to start up again, the flurry of impatient searching continued until it stopped ringing again, leaving the two friends breathless on the floor. "They're gonna wake your whole family up," Kinley complained in a harsh whisper.

"Looking for this?" Jack was standing there, leaning against the wall, phone in hand. "Darren just got off work, and happened to notice smoke coming up from our house. He was concerned, and so was I…I wondered who would be having a fire in the middle of a hot August night. What evidence of your shopping trip are you two burning? Bags or shoes?"

"You know, Jack, Ryan isn't quite as understanding as *you* are." Kinley smiled at him. "It was all mine." Kinley took the bullet, he seemed to accept it with an easy grin on his handsome face, but Madison knew he didn't truly buy it.

"Yeah, whatever, I'm going back to bed," he yawned, his dark hair disheveled, his blue eyes blurring with lack of sleep. Madison and Kinley giggled into each other. "Goodnight you two conspirators," he called out to them before shutting the bedroom door.

Madison saw Kinley to the door, yawning, "Text me when you get home, let me know you're safe."

"Will do, ya worry wart." Kinley giggled on her way out to the car.

Madison climbed into bed, yawning again, and snuggled into Jack. He pulled her closer. "I love you, Jackie."

"I love you too, my Maddy. I still wish you wouldn't make my name sound girly," he told her, eyes closed, smile spread across his face. She loved him. What a wonderful evening. She was looking forward to tomorrow, and her alone time.

1. Taking Denial to a Whole New Level

Why couldn't she move? She wasn't even breathing. No, she was drowning in the sea of her children's screams, unable to reach them, to twist her body around and hold onto them as the glass and metal compacted all around them. She'd thought her children's screaming was the worst sound she'd ever heard but it wasn't. No, the worst sound was silence. Scream some more, she wanted to yell, let me know you're still there. She couldn't speak to call out to them; darkness had become her living, breathing shroud. Inside of her mind she screamed their names until her mind shut down and she could no longer think of anything. She just was. "Madison?" Someone was shaking her, pulling her back.

Her eyes flew open; she sat up too quickly and fell back again onto her pillow. "Kinley? Why are you here? Where's Jack?" Madison sat up once again, her head throbbing just at the temples, her vision blurred at the edges. Kinley's vivid fiery hair assaulted her eyes there in the cool dark room.

"*What*?" Kinley squinted at her.

"Are you hiding out here, did Ry find out about the purse? You look nice." She yawned, stretching her arms out. "Are you going somewhere?"

"*What*?" Her friend was obviously perplexed.

"I'm glad you're here, you woke me up from the worst nightmare ever. My kids were screaming…" She shuddered.

"You're not even ready. Come on, get up." Kinley opened the shutters and let light spill into the depressingly dark bedroom. Madison shielded her eyes, eyes now used to darkness.

"Where are the kids?" she questioned. Kinley appeared to be looking through her, seeing something beyond her. Kinley's words were finally sinking in. "What am I getting ready for?" she asked as she dragged herself out of bed.

"You don't remember?" Kinley turned away. It was too quiet.

She must have used her key to let herself in. Where was the constant noise of her children? It was disconcerting. Silence was still the worst sound. She walked out to the kitchen; it was full to overflowing with flowers. "Where did all of these flowers come from? *Ugh*, it smells like a funeral in here." She noticed Kinley bristle at the comment. What had she said?

"Maddy, come get ready. We have so much to do." Kinley was deliberately being vague. She wandered back into her room to get ready. Her mysterious friend had chosen her clothing; she picked up the dress gingerly, turning over the soft fabric in her hand, letting it spill through her fingers like water. She never wore all black. What possessed Kinley to choose all black? She didn't argue, couldn't argue. Silence was all powerful and unyielding.

"So, did Jack get the kids ready? Where are they?" She pulled her shoes onto her feet. "Are we meeting them somewhere?"

"Jack has the kids. I think you should hurry so we can go see them." Kinley was purposefully avoiding her gaze, dropping her line of vision to the floor. Why did Kinley's tone chill her? She frowned; she was missing something.

Madison looked into the mirror above her bathroom sink and began pulling a brush through her nearly black tresses. Why was Kinley being so damned silent? "Okay, what time do we have to be there?" Madison couldn't stand any more cryptic behavior from her friend. Something, a weighted feeling in the air was causing her to feel closer to insanity than she would have liked to be.

Apparently, this was a question Kinley could answer, "10:30." Kinley was sitting down in Jack's lazy-boy flipping through the pages of a magazine, trying hard to appear casual when all the while her body was rigid, except for her nervously tapping foot. "You have thirty minutes. I assumed you'd be ready. Maybe I should have stayed with you last night. I really wasn't expecting this." Kinley said this more to herself as she leaned back in the chair and closed her chocolate-brown eyes. "I don't know what to do," she whispered again to herself. Kinley's auburn hair usually spilled over her head in corkscrew curls. Not today. She had it twisted up in a chignon and pinned down into submission.

"Really? We should have had a sleepover? What would Jack and Ryan think?" Madison giggled but instantly felt she'd done something wrong. The laughter was an intruder. She shrugged it away. There was something painful about it. She curled her dark hair, twisting the hot iron delicately through her glossy strands. Something inside of her shuddered with discomfort. Too quiet. She quickly applied her makeup, trying to hurry enough for Kinley, who was by all accounts growing impatient as she was now pacing in her black stilettos.

Kinley drove quickly. She was still too quiet, not answering questions and now that Madison noticed, Kinley was wearing black too. The stereo was usually blaring with their favorite music, but today, even it was silent. Madison felt her chest tighten. They were going to a funeral. When Kinley pulled her car up to the mortuary chapel, Madison felt the pieces of her heart sink within her. Someone had died. That was why Kinley wouldn't answer her. She was too upset. Madison wanted to comfort her friend, but she couldn't think of what to say. Then there was the uncomfortable feeling she should have known who had died. Her family must be waiting for her. Was it Kinley's husband? She should be more supportive. Why couldn't she remember? How could Madison forget her friend's grief? Unnerved she got out of the car.

Her mother-in-law's car was parked beside Kinley's SUV. Her head turned, so many cars, most of them familiar. "Kin, who died?" she murmured as they walked up to the stone building, with pillars supporting the intricate brickwork above. Ivy crawled over the alcove dripping down and winding along the columns. Kinley's lips tightened into a fine line, but her eyes; the look inside her eyes would haunt Madison for years to come.

"I didn't know this would happen," she began, "Maddy, I don't know how to tell you…"

"Tell me what?" Madison sighed. "I should know it. I know. I can't remember anything. I don't understand..." Her words trailed off as they walked into a large chapel. Five coffins. Five! The coffins varied in size, each one overflowing with flowers. "Oh my..." She couldn't finish the sentence. She could feel her knees begin to give out; she swayed and dropped down to sitting on the back pew. The chapel spilled over with mourners; so many familiar faces stared at her. Her memory was coming back. The policemen at her door, the quiet home, the overwhelming grief. It had been too much. It was all rushing at her, the realization a crushing force. Had she shut it all out when it became too much?

People were staring; she could feel it even though she was looking down. Her sense of reality was off. She stood and grabbed Kinley's hand before dragging her back out into the hall. "I can't do this," she whispered vehemently.

Kinley's dark eyes were filling up rapidly with tears. Kinley was the friend who did not hug and had issues with personal space. She wrapped her arms around Madison and let her sob onto her shoulder. "I should be in there with them. I can't do this." Shallow breathing was causing her to feel dizzy and faint. The nightmare was her life. "I should be with them." She clung to Kinley desperately, feeling wild with fright and grief. "I can't do this," she sobbed.

"You don't have to..." Kinley began, "I'll take you home right now if you want."

"Yes she does. You can't take her home. What would people say?" The shrill voice she'd hated for years echoed through the empty hall.

"With all due respect, Debbie, it isn't about what people will think. It's about Maddy. I'm not sure she can handle this...you don't know how she shut down..." Kin was defending her, standing up to Debbie, which was very unlike her.

Debbie's eyes narrowed, "Kinley, it is about *me* too. Those are my babies in there too; *my* son and *my* grandbabies, and I need Maddy. Do you understand?" She cried, as Kinley nodded, consenting when she did not wish to. Debbie turned toward her, "Maddy, are you coming in? It's your duty, you know." Her mother-in-law loomed before her with pursed lips and hands on her hips, fake fingernails tapping impatiently. Duty, it was always about duty. Madison gave in, defeated and let her mother-in-law lead her back into the chapel. She stared up at the photos on easels. Her children's smiling faces stared out at her. Their ghostly laughter haunted her memories, echoing eerily through the chambers of her mind. She couldn't recall what happened. Had it been like her dream, rather nightmare? Had she been the only one to survive? Someone started to speak, but she couldn't really hear it. How was it possible to recover from this? She couldn't do it. Was there music playing? Darkness encroached upon her. She blinked her eyes to steady herself. A voice was reaching out to her, "God has called them home." The darkness grew more intense, more vivid, and in that moment, she gave in and let herself fall.

2. Nightmares and Idyllic Dreams

She knew she was dreaming. She knew, but she couldn't wake and didn't want to. She watched herself, *was* her former self 'the' Madison Grey who enjoyed her life in the center of chaos. She lived for her family; it was her identity- Mom. Her son Jackson was pulling at her shorts. "Did you make me a sandwich?" She loved his high clear voice.

"Yes sweetie, peanut butter and honey for you." She bent to kiss her four year old son on the top of the head, which was the only place he received kisses from her any longer. His dark hair and eyes, his deep olive skin, his wicked little smile always off to the right, melted her. His twin was blond, fair, hazel eyed, and very much a little girl. Alex was standing beside him to make certain only strawberry jelly went onto her sandwich and the crusts were removed completely. She wanted to scream to herself, hug them, hold them, breathe them in, but she had no power.

"You're sure you're not coming?" Jack called out. She needed the break. Sometimes she didn't like the feeling that her family was her entire world, and her sole identity. Sometimes she just wanted to be Madison. Were her feelings wrong? Yes, she wanted to scream. Go with them.

"Nope, I need some alone time." He bent lower to her and kissed her, sending exquisite shivers up her spine. "Well, we could take a few moments for ourselves..." she offered with a sly grin. How she missed the nearness of him now, but she couldn't tell this to her dream self. Her dream self was oblivious and desperate to be alone!

He chuckled, "Yeah, we better save that for later. The kids are anxious."

"Dad, can I pull the *Expedition* out of the driveway?" Their eldest son Jonathan was clearly impatient.

Jack threw him the keys. "Not past the mailbox," she called out to his retreating back. "Damn it, Jack! He's only twelve; I don't want this becoming a habit."

"Oh, relax Maddy, you only live once, come on. What harm is there? I did the same thing when I was twelve." Those words haunted her every waking moment.

One by one, she said goodbye to them all, Jonathan, Riley, Jackson and Alex. Such a family! She'd never expected to have four! The third pregnancy had been something of a shock in the first place, then she'd found out there were two. She never would have believed she could do it, but she loved every one of them so much. She loved them- they were part of her and Jack. Jack. His handsome face forever etched into her memory. She watched as her husband switched seats with Jonathan, and he drove away, off to the beach.

She went inside to study for a test coming up next week. The kids had school starting on Monday; this was their last Saturday before vacation ended. She got several things done around the house, and only had two phone calls from her kids. One from Alex to tell her that Jonathan was an ass, like a donkey, and the second from Jonathan to see if she wanted Dad to order pizza. It was a pretty average day. Pizza sounded great. She got ready for them to come home, tossed a salad, set the table, and pulled her last load of laundry from the dryer. It had been a productive day. One can get a lot done without kids running around beneath their feet. Don't enjoy it, she wanted to cry, it will be your life.

Time kept ticking away. Jack was over an hour late and she couldn't reach him on the phone. Maybe he didn't have his Bluetooth with him; he'd already gotten a ticket for talking on his cell phone while driving. She'd warned him not to do it again. She paced, and called, paced and called. There was a nervous feeling, anxious, growing within her. She tried to relax and watch the television but it was no use. She couldn't sit still. She called up her best friend Kinley, who wasn't answering. She hung up just in time to hear the doorbell ring. Why was Jack ringing the doorbell?

"It's about time- I was so worried…" She stared into the solemn faces of two police officers as her voice trailed away into nothingness. They stood there, not wanting to speak. She could see it clearly. She looked around them having no idea what she was looking for. The night was falling fast.

"Are you Mrs. Jack Grey, Madison Grey?" the first officer asked. She nodded. She could feel her legs wobble slightly. "We need to speak to you, may we come inside?" She nodded again. She wouldn't make it to the sofa; she collapsed onto the floor. The two gentlemen helped her up, but she still felt as though she were falling. She awoke with a start, her breathing shallow and too rapid. She'd forced herself to wake; she couldn't bear to hear those words again. That wasn't how it happened- it hadn't been so idyllic, we'd been fighting, she thought sadly. But they would have made up…damn it, she missed him. Jack, her best friend. She missed the smell of his cologne, which sometimes she would breathe in just to feel near him. She missed her children. The ache was too large, too massive to get past, too dangerous to linger on.

It hadn't been such a burden cutting off crusts from sandwiches, or making special menus to order. It hadn't been so hard being a mother of four. But her feelings had been exactly as they were in the dream. She had wanted a break. She had wanted 'alone' time. She wept into her pillow. She should have been there. She should be gone with them, not here, not alone. Her entire family was gone. How would she ever move on?

She wanted to die. Was that too much to ask of God? Was he even out there listening to her strangled plea for a swift demise? She got up reluctantly, as she did every morning and let the day begin. In the fading lamplight, Madison Grey poured over her notes from philosophy. She usually kept her house rather dark and gloomy. It wasn't her intention to wallow in self-pity, it just seemed that light was a trespasser. Her highlighter was poised as she heard the knocking at her front door, she usually ignored such things. Whoever it was, banged insistently. "I know you're in there." Kinley's voice filled her empty spaces, resonating off the walls. Walls which no longer held family pictures and painful reminders, they were bare now. She placed the cap onto her highlighter and marched over to the door.

"You have a key, you know…" Kinley wore a bright smile while she carried Chinese take-out. "Oh, your hands were full." Madison moved aside and let Kinley in. Was it lunch time already? Hadn't she just woken up? How long had she been working exactly?

"Wow, it is dark in here." Kinley flipped a switch on the wall artfully with her elbow, flooding the room with light. "I brought your favorite." She was already pulling plates out of the cupboard and setting them onto the table before Madison could protest. "There is no use telling me you're not hungry. I won't hear it." She pulled forks out of the drawer and turned her back toward Madison. What time was it? She'd missed breakfast completely.

"Orange chicken?" she sniffed. "Okay, maybe I was a little hungry." She reluctantly sat down. "But you did catch me in the middle of an important essay on Aristotle and his chauvinistic views on women," she muttered as she opened the aromatic box of take-out. "Oh, this smells divine." Kinley passed her a large spoon. What would she have done without Kinley? She would have been institutionalized or she'd be dead, she thought.

"I know the essay you're talking about and it's due three weeks from now." Kinley brushed her auburn curls away from her alabaster face. "You are an amazing student- dedicated- for certain."

"Oh, get to the point Kin; I know when you are not saying something. Are there a few choice acidic words burning a hole in your tongue?"

"*Ouch*," Kinley replied, feigning heartbreak. "Yes, I'll admit it; I have something to tell you. No use keeping a secret. Girl's night on Friday and we want you there; well actually, it is more of a girl's day. You haven't been to one girl's night in the last six months."

"Was that all?" Madison bit her lip, "I don't think I'm ready. And…don't you dare mention the fact that it has been six months." She knew she was biting Kinley's head off; it wasn't how she'd intended to sound.

"Maddy, I bought you a ticket to see *The Producers*; it's a matinee show so we'll be going early. I know you've always wanted to go. Front row and everything. We're taking you to dinner…and it's gonna be fun. I am so sorry; I didn't mean to bring up the six months thing. I just want you to have something to look forward to in your life." Kinley was pushing her food around on her plate, not daring to look up. Things were not the same in their twenty year friendship. Kinley, who was infamous for being outspoken and equipped with razor-edged biting wit, was being very nearly dull. Madison didn't think she could handle it if Kinley didn't return to normal. Madison sighed as she thought it over. What harm was there?

It was going to be her anniversary, her first anniversary as a widow. Thirteen years. She knew what Kinley was doing. It was a distraction technique Madison couldn't help but admire. She kept thinking she'd do the same for Kinley if their roles had been reversed. She had to at least make some effort; she couldn't stay locked up in her house forever. Living in the darkness she had embraced wasn't the answer. She took a deep breath before answering Kinley.

"I suppose I can go." She deliberately shoved a bite of orange chicken into her mouth to avoid saying something she'd regret. Madison, who had formerly been known as the life of the party, gave her best false grin. She missed her own sense of humor; it had been her favorite attribute. She gave it a whirl, "You'll have to drag me. I recommend duct tape; it's good for anything."

Kinley laughed in reply, "I was thinking we should get mani-pedis and do a little shopping. Look at you. Your cheeks are sunken in, your tan has faded into a nice oatmeal color, and your nails are positively scary. Don't even get me started on your toenails. Have they reached talon status yet? You'd better be careful. You're libel to slice your leg in the night, and kill yourself because you've severed an artery with your too long toenail." Kinley was back for a moment. "But seriously, I know both of us could use some pampering." Madison offered her a weak smile in return. "I don't like being snarky alone. I sound vicious, like I found a wounded animal and I'm attacking it." She frowned as she pushed her rice around the plate. "You're not hurt enough, take that wounded animal." Madison let out a hollow laugh in reply.

"Kin, please don't stop being snarky. I need you to be normal. I'll join you soon, I'm sure I will." Their relationship was categorized as more sister than friend. They'd often spoken to one another with what other people might have supposed to be rudeness. It was just their way. Now, that Madison was a completely different person, she didn't know how to act, and couldn't seem to get in touch with her snarky side. She only managed a melancholy response here and there. It did make Kinley appear to be mean, when she didn't dish it back, but what could she do? Changing Kinley wasn't an option. She didn't want it. Kinley was her anchor right now, whether she knew it or not.

Kinley nodded, "I'll do my best."

≈

Kinley dragged Madison around for the next few days, refusing to give her time to relapse into her despair. They'd shopped for clothes to wear to the play, matching shoes, and several accessories. Madison wondered if Kinley had gotten fed up with watching Madison mope around. By the time Friday morning rolled around she was feeling a little more like herself, at least more than she had in several months. Their friend Kate McKnight picked her up promptly at ten forty-five, in her black Dodge *Magnum*. The Hemi was revved up and ready to go; Madison wished *she* was. Their friend Megan was conspicuously missing but no one mentioned it. This was her first clue. Why were they leaving so early? It didn't quite make sense. She still needed a few moments. She called out to them from her bedroom, and they said they'd wait.

She put the finishing touches on her makeup, sweeping the black mascara over her eyelashes in another layer, her heart deflating inside of her chest. She just didn't know if she could go anywhere. She heard Megan's ringtone, and followed it, but it wasn't her phone, it was Kinley's. "I'm putting you on speaker so Kate can hear you too." Madison didn't want to eavesdrop until she heard Meg biting Kin's head off.

"I don't know what you're doing, Kinley. Perhaps you've gotten all twisted around and don't know your role anymore, but this is ridiculous. You are pushing her and it's too soon! I can't be a part of this." Madison leaned breathless against the other side of the wall.

"I agree," Kate interjected, "but I have to be here in case the whole thing backfires in her face. Kin knows we love her, Meg, but we have to worry for Maddy. None of us really know what we're doing here."

"Thanks for the support you two," Kinley grumbled. "Listen, I know it's too soon. I know. But all she has is school. Don't you realize this? There is *nothing* else. I know it won't really help but it could distract her, and that is something."

"I still don't like it, Kin." Megan's voice had gone up an octave with tension and stress.

"I know, you've made it clear. I have to do *something*," her sweet voice broke, in agony and grief. "She's dying right in front of me, and I can't lose her too. Please understand…I have to do something," Kinley pled.

"Okay, I only hope she doesn't go catatonic on you," Megan sighed. "Good luck, guys."

Madison could see Kinley's efforts to keep her here, to keep her alive, and stop her from slipping into her grief too deeply. If she slipped any further, her own death would be imminent. It wasn't a question. She didn't know what to live for anyway. Kin wanted her to live, and so she'd try. She imagined switching places for a moment, and shuddered with despair. She would try if Kinley had gone to all of this effort. She knew it wouldn't help, but she could at least give in to the proffered distraction.

Madison stared out the window nearly all the way there. She tried to appear giddy, delighted, while in reality her insides felt as though they'd been scooped out much like a pumpkin at Halloween. She shouldn't be going out, not so soon. She thought of her anniversary the previous year. She and Jack had rented a room up in Big Bear. She pushed the memories back, trying to focus on the moment. Kate drove as though she were one of the NASCAR elite, weaving easily through traffic. Kinley was fighting back her nausea from the back seat. Madison eyed the bright red box sitting on her lap. A handmade tag was tied to the package with a bright red bow. Yes, these two are up to something, she thought.

"Hey," she watched as Kate pulled off the freeway at the wrong spot. "This isn't the exit for the Pantages, or is it?" Her companions giggled.

"We both agreed you need some cheering up," Kate told her as she turned onto Figueroa. She smoothed her blond bob down while slowing to a stop. "Look up." Madison looked around trying to figure out what she was supposed to be seeing. She had to admit her curiosity was piqued until she found the marquee ahead on the right. *Murder of Crows*. They drove past the Staples Center, finding a rather scary parking lot. Kate looked a little reluctant about leaving her 'baby' in such a place.

"You two...you didn't!" she practically squealed. They'd bought her concert tickets to see her favorite band? Kate and Kinley were laughing. She knew she did not imagine the emptiness in their laughter. She realized, for the first time since the accident, they were suffering right along with her. She hadn't pulled herself out of her grief long enough to recognize this simple fact. Kinley handed her the box; she fumbled with the ribbon as she loosened it. It was a VIP ticket with a rather large price tag on it. Kinley just grinned. What had she done to make this happen?

Kate smiled. "We've brought you super early so we can stand in line for ages. We were hoping to get you into the front row."

"I can't wait," she told them. If nothing else, this was the biggest distraction she'd ever had. The women walked along, crossed the busy street and found the place where they needed to stand in line. This was going to be a long wait, it was 11:15 and the concert didn't start until 6:00.

≈

Calvin Hunt, who preferred to be called Cal, took his preconcert beer from the outstretched hand of his brother. "I'm such an enabler," Rory mumbled.

"Cheers to the enablers of the world," Cal toasted, clinking his bottle against the one held by his brother. They almost couldn't hear each other. Music from one of their opening bands blared loudly backstage. His band, Murder of Crows, would go on after the band called Sludge. Rory had walked away leaving him to contemplate the last line of a Sludge song. "It was love, love at first sight." His eyes glanced over at his brother and his wife. There it was again, the empty stab, the gnawing feeling he was missing something. An unpleasant feeling, he'd been unsuccessfully trying to suppress, was floating up into his throat.

The band called Sludge was not especially sludge-like. They'd been imported from England, and were quite talented. He could hear their infectious laughter in the now quieter backstage area. "Cal, you ever been tossed anything like this, mate?" The lead singer, Rupert threw a grandmotherly bra at him. "I thought I'd die."

"Can I have it?" Cal watched the impish grin fade from Rupert's childlike face. Rupert nodded; the rest of his band mates had gone quiet.

They were all exchanging puzzled glances. He took the nude colored, offensive lingerie and launched it with the expertise he'd developed playing with slingshots as a boy, hitting his brother in the head. Raucous laughter filled the air.

He turned his attention to the stage. Stage hands were busy setting up for Murder of Crows. The buzz of the fans reached his ears. He did like observing them when they didn't know who he was. Loud music blared over the hum of thousands of voices. He pulled on an extra jacket and ball cap, pulling it down over his eyes. He crept onto the stage and positioned himself behind a rather large speaker. He breathed in the stench of pot, beer, cigarettes, mixed in with some very repellent body odor. He knew, sadly, his nose would become accustomed to it and he would cease to smell all of the acrid odors. A woman caught his eye when she threw her head back, laughing with her friends. Her long, dark hair hung in large soft curls which framed her face. He looked closer, her chocolate colored eyes glittered, her exquisitely shaped mouth curled up into a smile. She didn't look like the women who usually came to these things. Who was she? She was just a person in the crowd, but his stomach contracted as though he'd lied to himself. How to meet her? She'd probably come backstage. But…not everyone had backstage passes. He'd invited women backstage before, hell; he'd invited women to his hotel rooms. She didn't seem the type to invite for a one night stand, however.

Cal tried to figure out what he was going to do. He usually cut down on interaction with the crowd. There was a gap between the stage and the crowd; he normally avoided the area which he now found himself contemplating entering. He found he'd been watching her for a while before his body guard found him. "Cal." Cal jumped as a hand the size of small sled landed on his shoulder. Damn giant man. Gabe towered over him by more than a foot. He guessed it was a Samoan thing. "Are you ready?" Gabe grunted. He reluctantly pulled his eyes away.

"See those three women right in front?"

Gabe stared back at him. Cal could practically hear Gabe's confused thoughts. "The only women who are wearing actual clothes? Are you sure? Are you feeling well?" Gabe blinked, not sharing his precise thoughts, "The blond, redhead, and brunette?"

"Yes," he took one more glance at her. "Invite them backstage." He nearly skipped back to gather his guitar as Rory, Chris, and Shawn passed him on the narrow staircase in the now darkened arena. He heard the intro to their song, "Let's find out." He slipped out of his disguise. He loved screaming fans, especially when the screaming escalated as he entered the stage and the darkness was blasted away in a flash of light. He made his way right to her, singing, as he walked out onto a stack of speakers at the end of the stage and hopped down into space between the stage and the bar the fans clung to, "When I wake up tomorrow, will it be with you?" He reached for her hand, feeling the sizzle of electricity course through his arms. He was telling her he wanted her. As she looked into his eyes, he nearly forgot to sing his next line. There was something there, something he couldn't figure out. Her dark chocolate eyes were open, yet closed somehow. Her soul was hidden from him. He shook it off, reaching for her hand once more, "I can't understand what's happening," he sang. Hands grabbed at him from every direction as Gabe stood by, stressed, and ready to pounce. Security guards flanked his sides, screaming filled his ears, but he saw only her. He eventually would have to touch other hands in order to make it look as though he did this kind of thing all the time.

3. The Womanizer

Madison was still slightly dizzy from the shock of being handed a note during the concert. In the slight space between the stage and the bar holding the fans back, a man the size of a large statue, had made his way toward her, weaving through the stationary security guards at the foot of the stage. He'd tucked a note into her hand. It was a folded piece of paper with three backstage passes wrapped up within. It read- *for the brunette, the blond and the redhead.* They'd giggled, been bewildered, and delighted. Madison and her friends had placed the lanyards around their necks immediately. Women all around them had glared. Regardless, it had been the best concert she'd ever been to. She found herself wishing Jack had been there, cheering next to her, and jealous when Cal had sung to her. He'd loved Murder of Crows. She shoved the thoughts back into the darkest corners of her mind. Focus on now, she thought. She had to try. Kinley and Kate had gone to all this trouble. She stared down at her clothes, and was finding she was grateful Kinley had thought to take her shopping. How embarrassing would it be to meet her favorite singer wearing her old clothes? She could hear Kin's laughter as she spoke, "You've become so tiny. It looks like you're wearing the imploded big top of a circus." How could she help it? Food had lost all appeal in her grief.

Madison, Kinley, and Kate were being shoved along as they'd become part of the crowd assembled to go backstage. It was too loud. She couldn't hear herself think. She wanted to lean over and tell her friends, "We're the only women not dressed like hookers." She would have had to shout it to be heard. Not the best idea when surrounded by all of the hooker impersonators who would hear her. Once they reached the area behind the stage, the chaos had spread out. The members of all the bands were weaving their way through the crowd. Cal Hunt himself was standing a few feet away. "I can't believe this." He was the best distraction she'd ever had. He was posing for a picture with a group of beautiful women. She allowed herself to look more carefully at him. His hair was a mess, slightly spiked, blond. The very tips of his hair had been bleached nearly white. His tan was the tan of a surfer, spending his days on the beach. His cerulean blue eyes found her, gazing right into her. She felt her heart stop working. Could his nose be more perfect or his jaw more chiseled? She didn't think so. He was walking toward her. She had to resist the urge to run. She turned to look over her shoulder. Maybe he wasn't really looking at her, she gulped, feeling stupid.

"Hi." She was looking up at him, feeling dizzy again. He smiled at Kinley, Kate, and then turned to her, "I'm Cal." He cleared his throat. Was he nervous? She was just imagining it. You are a dork, Madison, he wouldn't possibly be nervous, she thought. "You might have already known that," he finished speaking with an easy laugh. She and her friends exchanged nervous glances.

"It's nice to meet you." What was she supposed to say?

He tilted his head, giving her a quizzical grin, "Would you like to sit down?"

"*Uh*, sure." She had no idea what to expect; he grabbed her hand and began leading her away. Her friends were trying to keep up, as he dodged the others in the crowd. Was this typical? He led them to a green sectional sofa in another area away from the crowd. In the more private room, the noise dropped off rather steeply. She looked up to see his brother Rory with his arm around his gorgeous wife. He was staring at Cal with a peculiar expression on his face, which led her to believe that Cal's behavior was not typical.

He'd been so stupid. Hi, I'm Cal. Like they didn't know. He brushed his hand through his slightly damp hair. Say something, he thought. "Would you like something to drink?" Was it something a normal guy would say?

"Sure." The women appeared to timidly exchange glances as the redhead answered his question.

His assistant Joey found him quickly, as he always did. He handed Cal a cooled bottle of water. "Joe, can you bring these women whatever they want to drink." His assistant, young and gangly stared at the women in surprise. He listened as they each ordered a water bottle. Joey scurried away quickly. He knew he was acting bizarrely but it couldn't be stopped, he had no idea what to do with himself.

"I feel I am at a loss. You all know my name, but I haven't heard yours yet." He gazed at the dark haired angel before him. He tried to guess what it would be.

"Madison Grey," she answered as her eyes looked away from him.

"Kinley Brooke." The redhead had an interesting name.

"Kate McKnight," the blond chimed in.

Although they were quiet, the awkwardness was killing him; he knew somehow they were communicating. He would have given almost anything to know what she was thinking, but looking into her eyes gave him no clues. He still didn't know how to act. At this point, innuendos usually had begun to fly, when he'd met someone he'd connected with. The talk would turn suggestive, until he was thinking about how to get her into bed. This was not the standard meeting, not at all. He decided to break the ice, "So, where are you beautiful ladies from?" He turned on the charm, she just turned her head.

"Valencia," the one named Kinley answered. She must have seen the puzzled look on his face. "It's not far from here." He only nodded. It was quiet again, and he had never been more uncertain of what to do. Usually he'd be telling her how to meet up at his room later. He instinctively knew this was the wrong tactic.

"Have you been friends for a while then, Kinley, Madison, and Kate?"

He wanted to know more about Madison; he was thankful when she answered, "Kin and I have been friends for a little over twenty years. We met Kate a few years back." Madison smiled as though the conversation had sparked a pleasant memory. She tilted her head in Kate's direction, "She's one of those people you'd rather have as a friend." He knew this must have been an inside joke, watching the evil grins spread across their beautiful faces. "She'd be a terrible enemy; she might even throw something at your head, if you're not careful." They all burst out laughing.

"Yes, but whatever I am, you two are ten times worse." Kate narrowed her blue-green eyes at them playfully. Cal thought things were going along splendidly until Madison jumped up and answered her phone. Kate followed behind her. Was it his imagination or had she taken a slightly protective stance near her friend? He'd never had a fan answer a phone in his presence. Usually they would hit ignore and just keep talking. Something was disturbingly different about her. Normally, he wouldn't care enough to want to find out. This was not the case. Kinley smiled at him. It wasn't the seductive smile he was used to in a fan; she offered him friendship. He would gladly accept. He didn't know why he was tempted to ask if her friend liked him, but he refrained.

"So, is your friend Madison…is she married?" Oh, he sounded completely idiotic.

"*Um*, no." Her face betrayed a hint of a deeper story. There was no follow up explanation, just awkward silence again. He decided to prod further. This was not normal either. Honestly, people usually shared too much information, telling him things he never wanted to know.

"Does she date much then?" He sounded like a green little school boy who had his first crush. Tell your friend I like her, he was such an imbecile. He leaned in toward her, curiosity overtaking him.

"No, not at all." She looked as though she were taking pity on him which had to be the strangest thing of all. "It might be best to forget about her." Kinley sighed as she leaned forward, her delicate hands resting on her knees. Her dark eyes seemed to be communicating a hidden secret of sorts, "She isn't really available, if you know what I mean."

Never had he been more baffled. He was famous; this was enough for many women. He'd just been voted Sexiest Singer of the Year, in *G-String Magazine*. His smile often left women devastated in his wake. He had more money than he could ever hope to spend, lived in a mansion, could literally give her anything she wanted, and she still wasn't available? He'd met happily married women who were more than available, but she was not? It was striking an unfamiliar chord.

Madison was walking back; he couldn't wait to strike up another conversation. "That was Debbie. She's having a rough night; I have to go." She kept her voice light but a heaviness had come over the conversation. Kinley's smile melted away. She turned to him, "It was really nice meeting you, Cal." Madison's smile melted his heart into a tiny mercurial pool of unknown emotions.

"Can I take your picture with Madison?" Kinley's voice sounded hopeful.

"Anything for you," he told Madison. He was delighted as a light blush colored her cheeks. He slid his arm around her waist and posed as Kinley lifted her phone up and snapped the shutter. "Perfect." He liked how small she felt in his arms. He had a previously unknown desire rise up in his chest. She was so fragile, in need of protection, and alluring all at once. He wondered if she'd give him her number. He wasn't sure how to ask. The idea both frightened and enticed him. His heart hammered against his ribcage at the thought of asking her. What the hell was wrong with him? He was never nervous! In frustration, he watched them walk away, and disappear into the depths of the crowd. His stomach began to shrink as he thought of his decision. Her friend, Kinley's, words echoing through his mind didn't help either. He always seemed to want anything or anyone he couldn't have.

He couldn't sleep. He never slept really well after a concert, but this was different. It was often that he didn't fall asleep until four in the morning. He had given in to the useless emotion known as regret, which kept him awake past six. He sat alone in his empty suite with nothing but the buzz of the television in the background to keep him company. He'd gone over the previous night in his head, a hundred times at least. He knew Rory would be sleeping in, and he also knew how unbelievable awful he was if awoken too early. He waited until after noon before he knocked on the suite opposite his. "Just a minute," he heard his nephew answer in reply. He knew he was being checked out through the peephole.

"Uncle Cal, Dad was just talking about you. Do you want breakfast?" Matthew asked.

"I don't feel hungry." Cal couldn't eat if he tried, he'd drunk plenty though. He walked out onto the balcony and stared across the vast ocean before him. He was trying to clear his mind. What exactly did he want out of life? Meaningless liaisons with women who were easily replaceable? Or did he need something more? The empty feeling he never liked to confront, had returned. He stared out at the water lapping at the shore, doing what it always did. Was he like the ocean? Untamable but ultimately predictable.

"Okay, I'll bite, what is wrong with you?" Rory appeared out of the corner of his eye.

"How did you know Jen was..." This was painful. "The one?"

"Oh." He'd expected shrieking laughter at his expense. His brother had become quiet and reflective, leaning over the edge of the balcony, before lightening up and grinning, "I knew something was up, how often do you jump into the crowd? Never. Risk getting mauled? Not likely, but there you were last night. Does this have anything to do with the PTA MILFs you were getting cozy with on the chesterfield?" Cal punched him in the arm. He watched Rory rub the spot, with twisted satisfaction. "Just kidding. I've never seen you hang out with actual women before. You know, not hookers."

"You didn't answer my question," he persisted.

"Okay, jeez," Rory didn't make eye contact. "I just knew. She wasn't like the others. I had to have her." He smiled to himself, as though he were holding something else back, something only Rory would find amusing. "If you ever tell anyone I'm so Oprah-like, I'll kill you in a vicious way they'll never find your body. There are plenty of hungry bears in Manitoba."

Cal gave him a painful, weary expression in return, "I let her walk away." He paused, "She was so different. She didn't want *anything* from me. They didn't even ask for my autograph. I mean, they were shy about getting a picture! She was just so amazing." He ran his fingers through his hair in obvious frustration. "You should have seen it, they were treating me like I was ordinary." Rory gave him a quizzical look, as if to ask- why would that be interesting?

"I told you, you're a moron. What were you scared of, growing up?" Rory had no compassion on him. He appeared to be contemplating something deeper, "Which one?"

"Which one, what?"

"Well, you had a brunette, a redhead, and a blond. I have to admit I am curious." Rory's face was almost in pain.

"The brunette." Rory seemed to relax instantly, relief flooding his face. "Why?" He wasn't expecting Rory to punch him in reply. He rubbed his arm, "What the hell?"

"Hey, Gabe can find her. He's creepy like that."

"How?" Cal inquired.

They waited for Gabe to arrive, which he did rather quickly. He told Gabe about his predicament, while Gabe merely nodded. "You want me to find the one that got away?" his deep voice responded. Cal watched Rory nod. Something was off with him. If only he cared enough to find out what it was. Gabe busied himself on the laptop.

"Why don't you use your phone?" Cal asked him as he hovered behind Gabe.

"Have you seen the size of my fingers? They're like small stumps." Cal shut up and let him work. He'd given him the name Madison Grey and the city Valencia. "There is a listing for a Jack and Madison Grey."

"She's not married," Cal told him. Gabe stared. "No ring."

"Yeah, that is an indicator, genius," Rory snorted. Cal gave him his best withering glare. Rory shrugged. "Try one of the friends."

"Kinley, she was the redhead, but I can't remember her last name." He was pacing, agitated. He'd actually let her walk away. Gabe was typing again, his fingers nearly flying off the keys. His dark black coffee eyes narrowed as he read the screen.

"Kinley Brooke?" Gabe asked, while Rory appeared to be thoughtful.

"Yes!" He tried to calm down. "Yes, that sounds familiar. How did you find her last name?"

"Three VIP tickets purchased by Kinley Brooke of Valencia, California?"

"Did you hack into the ticket office?" Cal was impressed.

"Might have," Gabe grumbled. "Here you are." He turned the screen to face Cal. All of the information he needed was right in front of him. Now, if he could just grow a pair and call her.

~

Madison typed as Kinley sat next to her pouring over an immensely boring textbook on philosophy. "I hate John Locke." Kinley pushed the book away with a heavy sigh. "Wasn't last night the greatest?" she asked for what felt like the fiftieth time that morning.

Madison leaned forward putting her face into her hands, "It still seems like a dream somehow. Like when Cinderella was given a reprieve from her mundane, depressing existence and was allowed to dance with the womanizing prince all night."

"Exactly," Kinley teased. "And where is your other Jimmy Choo sandal? Do you suppose Cal found it and he is scouring the countryside for the fair maiden who owns it?" They both giggled, though their giggling wasn't as whimsical as it had been in the past. Kinley's phone began singing a Murder of Crows song to them, "Do you suppose it's Cal?"

"Yeah, he's calling *me*, on *your* phone." Madison went back to typing. Between school, Kinley and her mother-in-law Debbie, she was steadily busy enough to keep herself completely distracted. But the nights were something else altogether. She shook her head as if she could shake it away. It was too much sometimes. Two days ago she'd found herself in Jonathan's bed when she awoke. Oh, the scent of him long faded from his pillow. She went into his closet trying to remember, only to breathe him in. Her sweet son. She choked back the tears as she started back to work on the essay on Berkley. Damn philosophy had her questioning everything. She'd never before questioned the existence of God or an afterlife. But...then again, she'd never had her faith in those things shaken so thoroughly before. Never had she lost anyone, with the exception of her father. He'd been nothing to grieve over. She lost focus when Kinley's conversation became more interesting.

"Seriously, who is this?" Kinley yawned. "Yeah, right, and I'm the Pope, the second female Pope. I read a book about Pope Joan who was the first, but many of my Catholic friends have denied the verity of it," Kinley's voice was light with sarcasm, she was having a bit of fun with whoever had called. Who was she talking to? Madison had poised her fingers to type again, when Kinley's sputtering reply caught her off guard. "Hold on, it *is* you." She stepped back a moment from her pacing, "I'm so sorry. Forgive me for inquiring but how did you find my number?" Madison watched as

Kinley nodded. "Oh, he's one resourceful guy. Former navy seal, you don't say." She was staring wide eyed at Madison, gesturing wildly, "So, as it happens, she is right next to me." Madison wanted to laugh as Kinley tripped over herself to get the phone to her. "It was good talking to you too," She pushed the mute button, "It's for you."

Madison took the phone, shaking, her heart palpitating as though she'd begun running for her life in front of a pack of wild dogs. Why was she so nervous? "Hello?"

"It's me, Cal, we met last night." Her head whipped to the right as she stared at Kinley who was shrugging. How had he found her? More importantly, *why* had he found her? She was hardly the sexiest little thing at his concert, in fact, she was positively *ordinary*. She'd seen Lindsey Bell on his arm, the gorgeous actress. She'd seen him with supermodels on his arm at award shows. Solely listening to his song lyrics was enough to know he was more than experienced. What did he want with her?

"Hi Cal." What does one say to a rock star, or stalker? She bit her lip nervously, "So, what are you doing?" Kinley smiled and shook her head.

"No *how did I find you?* It's a great story, but the thing is, I thought you and your friends were really nice, and *uh*, genuine." He coughed, "And I was wondering if you might want to grab dinner with me tonight? You can bring your friends, if you want."

She was wholly taken aback. She stared at the phone in her hand. "Can you hang on a minute?" she asked as she once again muted him. "I think Calvin Hunt just asked me out on a date." She gulped, "What do I do?" Was it wrong to entertain the idea?

"Please." Kinley playfully rolled her eyes, "Maddy, he has another concert tomorrow, he'll be gone. Why don't you go? I can't see any harm in it." Kinley was always level headed and rational when it was Madison's life; she wasn't as talented when it came to her own problems. It was good they had each other.

"He said I could bring my friends. Will you and Ryan come? I can't do this alone." Madison didn't want to sound weak; she needed to crack a joke, "Number six is enough, don't you think?" She thought of his latest album, *Tarred and Feathered*, and his wickedly clever lyric choices. Kinley nodded, giving her the go ahead, "Sure, I'd love to have dinner with you."

She hastily added, "I'm bringing my friend Kinley and her husband." She wanted him to know she was not as vulnerable as she appeared.

"Would it be too inconvenient for you to meet me at my hotel?" She thought of him coming here, to the home she'd once shared with Jack.

"It's no problem at all."

"Great. I'll text Kinley everything she needs." He sounded almost giddy. "What time do you eat?" he added as something of an afterthought. She had to say it was the weirdest question she'd ever been asked.

"Is six okay?"

"Wow, normal people eat early." He laughed. "I can't wait to see you again." After he'd hung up she stared into the phone.

"What would Jack say?" She frowned, feeling worse than any traitor ever had.

"Relax, it's not like it can go anywhere. I have to admit it is a little ironic, but I honestly don't think Jack would mind you hanging out with your favorite rock star for a while. Besides, if I know you, and I do, he's getting nowhere, not even a good-night peck."

"You're hugging me again. This is weird. I am thinking I may have to write it down. I think it's like four hugs in six months," Madison teased. If only they could bring back their humor to the level it had formerly been, maybe everything wouldn't feel so overwhelming.

4. C. Willy

"I can safely say, I've never been to a five star hotel before, except for in Vegas, but those hardly count," Kinley whispered into Madison's ear as they crossed the threshold into another world. The lobby they were standing in had marble floors and a Roman motif with genuine marble sculptures of cherubs and half naked men and women. There was a fountain, and soft music playing in the background which made one think of Italy. "He said we'd have to check in with the front desk. What if this is some mean spirited joke?" Madison gulped.

Ryan, Kinley's husband, was silently observing them with a wry smile playing on his lips. "I'll ask, wouldn't want you two to be embarrassed." He winked one of his green eyes at them.

"He's an ass," Kinley whispered.

"Tell me about it," Madison agreed.

"So, how did he find you anyway? You never said. We've been so busy ever since he called."

"His bodyguard tracked us down, he looked up who bought the tickets and found my name. I have no idea how he proceeded from there."

"Why would he go to all the trouble? Then again, maybe it was no trouble at all," Madison said as Ryan seemingly glided back across the floor toward them.

"Apparently, the Cal thing is for real. We're going up now. Do you think he'll let me touch his guitar?" Ryan smirked. He led them over to the elevator, where a man awaited their instructions. He punched in a numbered code into the elevator, which would allow them access to the floor Cal was staying on.

"Boys," Kinley scoffed. They moved to the glass elevator, which reminded Madison of Willy Wonka. "So the name he gave me was legitimately the name he checked in under?"

Ryan laughed, "Yeah. The hotel has his real name, obviously, but the fake name is to weed out the people who actually know him from people who just want to know him." The name he'd texted made them all believe it had to be some kind of a joke. Rationally, what man in his thirties would call himself C. Willy? But apparently he had a naughty sense of humor. The elevator rose along with the number of butterflies doing karate inside of her chest. This was insanity. What had she been thinking by coming here? The elevator slowed and let them out on the top floor. They walked past a window with the view of the beach. "Wow, what a view," Ryan observed.

"The text says suite number 4," Kinley said checking her text. Four, four children and a husband. Five coffins. Madison blinked several times, as she tried to free the image from her head. "Here we are Maddy, you ready?" She tried to push the image from her mind, but it had invaded swiftly and she'd been caught off guard. Jack was holding her face in his hands, kissing her, telling her he loved her. The image held sway over reality. She missed him; she couldn't do this, not to Jack.

"No, I shouldn't be doing this, I need to go." She twisted around and began to walk back toward the elevator all the while hearing the heels of her shoes tapping against the expensive floor tiles. What had she been thinking? It was a question she couldn't answer. But she was too late.

"Madison? Where are you going?" asked Calvin Hunt. She'd know his voice anywhere. She swallowed the lump in her throat and turned around to face him. Normal looking guy, okay, guy who was so hot he could make you melt, wearing just jeans and a t-shirt. She gulped.

"I forgot my wallet, and if we're ordering food…" She left the words hanging in the air. She felt so stupid, her cheeks were searing. The memory of Jack's touch was still imprinted on her skin.

"Come back, Madison, it's my treat. I insist. You may not believe this, but I do pretty well for myself." She laughed as he tried to make her more comfortable. "Kinley, it's good to see you again. This must be your husband."

"Ryan Brooke." He reached out and shook Cal's outstretched hand. Ryan was a big guy, football coach, muscular and tall. He seemed to be dwarfed by Cal. Cal was huge.

"Good to meet you, Ryan." He sounded sincere. Madison followed after them and found herself in a room as large as her entire house.

"This is incredible," she muttered as she stared around at the extravagant furnishings surrounding her.

He grinned. "It sure beats motel 8, and we stayed in plenty of those in the beginning."

"Yeah, those aren't much fun," she agreed. Did he have to be so freaking handsome and charming too, all the while putting her at ease? They all sat down on the most comfortable, down filled cushions. This was something out of a very tantalizing dream, it couldn't be happening. If only she hadn't lost her family. She would have probably gone to the concert with Jack, and never thought anything more about Calvin Hunt, well nothing that could've really happened.

"Is there some delicacy in California I absolutely need to have?" Cal asked, leaning forward until he was inches from Madison. She grinned, her heart fluttered. Was she flirting? She hoped not.

Ryan asked, "Haven't you been to So Cal before?"

"Yes, but I never get to check things out. It seems I'm always in a hurry. The guys get to explore more than I do." She wanted to ask him why this was, but felt she would appear nosy.

She tried something else. "I wanted to see you but I never had the chance to, Murder of Crows, I mean." She immediately regretted sharing this bit of information with Cal. She'd almost said 'we' wanted to see you. Jack. Did he have to be so devastatingly handsome when he smiled at her?

Madison wondered if he ever stopped smiling the smile that would have any woman drop to her knees and surrender. Ryan was talking; this was good. "In-N-Out Burger, you have to experience it before you go, unless you are a champagne and caviar type of guy."

"Burgers sound fantastic. Let's place an order with my assistant. Although, one of you will have to order for me because I'm not familiar with the menu."

"How hungry are you?" Ryan asked with a wicked glimmer in his bright green eyes.

"Famished," Cal replied

"Then, I know just what to get you."

They all spent the next few minutes deciding what they wanted. A young man of around twenty-three came in. Madison remembered him from backstage. He was plain, ordinary, not someone you would look twice at. He took their orders and returned not twenty minutes later. All the while, she found it impossible not to be mesmerized by Cal. He was hilarious. Everything he said would cause her to laugh until her sides ached. He enjoyed the double-double, large animal style fries, large Coke, and chocolate milk shake Ryan ordered for him. He got along with both Kinley and Ryan, which made him positively endearing. What was one afternoon of fun? What harm could there be if she just enjoyed herself?

He and Ryan jammed together on two of his guitars, while she and Kinley sat on the uber comfortable sofa. "This was too much fun. How will I ever go back to my humdrum life after this?" Kinley asked her softly.

"I know what you mean." Madison sank into the cushions behind her. "It's not real though." Kinley nodded in agreement.

"He likes you."

"Cal?"

"Yep." Kinley glanced at her.

"It doesn't mean anything. As flattering as it is, he probably was followed here by a gazillion slutty women last night, and could've had any of them. I am just your ordinary woman who has too much baggage. He is leaving town tomorrow morning, you heard him. So, this is a one day thing." She doubted whether any man out there could handle *her* baggage.

"Yeah, but it was fun. Glad you had me come along." Kinley pushed one of her stubborn auburn curls away from her face, something she did often, "Something about this day doesn't scream normal rock star date though."

"I don't really think it counts as a date," she began, but Kinley just gave her the look with one raised eyebrow.

Cal and Ryan came back, laughing. "Do you want to do anything else, watch a movie or anything?" Madison could see he didn't want them to go. "This is the most normal afternoon I've had in a while, and I'm not ready for it to end."

"If it's all right with Kinley and Ryan, *they* have kids to get back to." The words hurt her. They foamed at the inside of her mouth making it raw. Bitter poison. Kids. Kinley sensed it and took over. Her children's smiling faces floated to her, but she let her mind go black.

"It's fine, the girls are with friends today. Sleepovers and all that. We're covered. So, what kind of movie?" She was quite adept at changing the subject and forcing the conversation in a new direction. When no one was looking, she squeezed Madison's hand.

Cal couldn't remember a time when he'd enjoyed himself more. So this was what it was like to be normal? To date, or double date with friends? He'd never really experienced this kind of thing before. He'd gone out in groups as a teen, but his adult years had been spent touring and hopping from one hotel to the next. He'd watched as one by one each member of the band was married. He'd watched as one by one each of them had children and their families grew. He'd always known they had something more, just never what it was. They had a sense of normalcy in this whirlwind life and he was living in a fantasy. It was a fantasy none of them desired, and not one of them envied. He was leaving tomorrow, off on the tour to yet another city, but something inside of him wanted to prolong this moment. This moment was a breathtakingly beautiful rose, cut and still exquisite, but rapidly fading. No matter how hard he tried, he couldn't hold on to it. As the petals dropped, the bloom faded, and he would soon be saying goodbye. He didn't want to let Madison go, but how exactly was he going to hold on to her?

5. Celibacy is Crap

Cal finished singing "Down and Dirty" with a great sweeping motion of his arm. He'd sung in the general direction of a fan in the front row who was *no* Madison. He compared every fan he saw to Madison. He saw her face whenever he closed his eyes, imagined her lips and wondered how they might taste. He was losing it. Rory, Chris, and Shawn seemed to be thinking along the same lines. He'd overheard them speaking about some kind of 'intervention'. Normally, he might have been upset, even slightly concerned. Now, he just ached. He'd met the woman twice! He thought of her chocolate brown eyes outlined with kohl and the way the gray on her lids faded into black. He'd seen makeup before, hell; every female fan wore loads of it. Why was hers so special?

He'd tried to kiss her when they'd parted. She'd turned her cheek. That had seriously been a first. It confused him, and was beyond frustrating. Every minute of the day, he found himself analyzing the entire afternoon he'd spent with her. Was it the way he'd found her? Maybe it scared her and she thought of him as a stalker but had been too polite to say so. Or…maybe she couldn't turn him down because he was famous. Either way, he'd been on hold for a hell of a long time while she'd decided if she would go to dinner or not. She was damned irresistible and enigmatic.

He put his feet up backstage on a box sitting across from the vivid blue sofa he was sitting on. Rory plopped down beside him, "Cal, what the hell is your problem?"

"Nothing, I'm just tired," he lied. All he needed was for Rory to find out what was really wrong with him and it would be the beginning of the torture.

"Yeah, okay, pretend for a moment I believe you. You must have had a great night last night. No, wait, Gabe told me you invited *no one* to your room. And since we both know it is *so* like you in every other city…" He was light, teasing. His dark blond hair was tousled like always. Cal enjoyed looking down at his brother of six-four. He loved being the younger brother who could only slightly stare down at his older brother. There may have been three years in between Rory and Cal, but he was taller.

"Sometimes I like to sleep. Maybe I'm coming down with something," he muttered before taking a swig of water from his water bottle.

"*Hmm.* You're never sick. But I think I know what's wrong," Rory mused aloud.

"You tell me then, Nostradamus. Look into your crystal ball."

"Funny. I think you're hung up on the hottie PTA lady." Rory was getting cocky the older he got. Cal slugged him in the arm. Someone needed to bring him down a peg, and Cal should be the one who got that gift in life.

"No…" he lied through tightly gritted teeth.

"Yeah, and you know what else? I think you should just admit it so I can execute a plan."

Cal was curious, "What plan, oh brilliant one?"

"This is how I know you're off your game, weak insults. I know you can do better. Listen, our next stop is Vegas. Vegas isn't far from Los Angeles. It's like a five hour drive or a half an hour flight. Just saying." He got up and slugged Cal back, "Maybe she and her other PTA MILF friends will come and see you? You could send them some tickets… We know people, we're connected. It's just an idea little bro." He disappeared to mingle into the crowd. Cal smiled. Damn Rory, and yet, he'd given him an idea. "Idiot," Cal whispered under his breath.

"I heard that," Rory called out over his shoulder.

It was sometime the next day before he got up enough nerve to call Kinley. She answered in a whisper, "Hello?"

"Kinley?"

"Yes?"

"It's me, Calvin Hunt, again." He could hear background chatter and a tiny swear escape her lips. She put him on hold for a second. What was with these women and putting people on hold?

"Sorry, I was in class. How are you, Cal?"

"Class? I'm sorry, I…"

"Don't worry about it. Professor Skinner understands when we take personal calls." The sarcasm was not lost on him. "Really, it's no big deal. What's up?" She sounded happy to hear from him.

"I, you asked how I was doing." Why was he doing this? He was going to tell her and he couldn't stop himself. "I haven't been doing so well lately." He never felt comfortable enough to just share what he was thinking with a stranger. She didn't feel like a stranger though. This was something of a first for him.

"I saw something about you and your band on the news. You looked great. If you're down… Is there something I can do to help?"

He loved it. Here she was asking if *she* could do something for him. He'd never had that happen since he'd become famous. Most people were all about what he could do for them. "Do you like Vegas?" He realized he'd avoided her question, but in a sense, he was asking her to do something for him, and relying heavily upon her saying yes.

"I'm from Vegas. I can't seem to stay away from Vegas. But, why do you ask? I sense an ulterior motive hiding underneath your question, which is intriguing." She was good.

"We're playing in Vegas, this weekend and I was wondering if you would like to be there, you and *Madison*, I mean." He had never been so clumsy. He was losing his touch.

"Really?" she sounded excited; this could be a good thing. "I would love to drag Maddy to Vegas. She could use a break." Break from what? He wondered.

"I could put you up at the Bellagio and…"

"You don't have to do that" she paused, "my family wouldn't let me hear the end of it. They'd be insulted if I stayed in a hotel."

"How many tickets do you need, I mean for your family too?"

"Maybe one for my sister, my brother would love to go, but he's in New York at the moment. The only other family members in town are my parent's and you're a little too naughty for them."

Kinley was really, actually fun to talk to. "*Me*, naughty? They live in Vegas! Nude bulletin boards are a dime a dozen, not to mention all the free porn they hand out down there. They even teach gambling in the elementary schools, or so I've heard."

"Yeah, I did learn roulette and craps in kindergarten. Seriously, my family is a bit on the religious side. I suppose we can only hope they become naughtier." She laughed, "Well, I best be off to class…" Oh, he was keeping her.

"I will have three tickets for you at Will Call. Can I ask you one more thing?"

"Sure."

"Is Madison a lesbian?"

He heard her gag, and laugh, and snort. "What made you ask that?" She was practically dying.

"I tried to kiss her and she turned her head." She was still laughing, "It's just that….well it's never happened before," he reluctantly admitted. He couldn't think of a single reason why she would turn her head.

"No, she's straight. It's just a bit too soon." Something in Kinley's voice made him not want to ask any more questions. He realized she'd be deliberately playing obtuse.

"Kinley, may I ask you something else?"

"Sure, anything." He could picture her smiling.

"Can you forward me the picture you took backstage of me and Madison?" Cal asked, hoping she wouldn't think he was creepy.

He could hear her pause; "Sure," but it sounded more like a question than an absolute.

"I just want to make sure I don't wear the same outfit next time I see her," Cal teased.

"Okay, I will send it over."

So, Madison was straight, she liked men. Maybe she just didn't find *him* attractive. Nah, that couldn't be it. Too soon? Too soon…maybe she'd had a rough break-up and some bastard had broken her heart. He had to be careful with her. Yes, he'd be careful.

6. Nothing happens in Vegas

Vegas was a place Madison generally avoided although Kinley had talked her into going a few times. She hadn't gone since Jack and the kids…Not good to dwell on it. The flight was relaxing, although downtime usually frightened her. Being alone with her thoughts usually proved to be agonizing. She couldn't believe she was flying out to Vegas. She recalled Kinley answering the phone during a chemistry lecture. It was something no student in the class had ever dared to do. Professor Skinner's name evoked fear in quaking students everywhere.

He'd watched her slink back into the classroom, "Miss Brooke, is your boyfriend more important than this class?" Madison mused over Kinley's youthful appearance, knowing many would find it impossible to believe she was thirty-one. Madison thought of how she'd held her breath, knowing Kinley had been irritable lately. She'd wondered if Kinley would lose it, but she hadn't.

"I apologize, Professor Skinner; it was an emergency and it won't happen again." She'd taken her seat and given Madison a significant look, hinting at needing to tell her something huge.

"What made you answer your phone?" Madison had asked her. She'd been worried something happened to one of Kinley's girls.

"Well, I know I shouldn't have done it, but Cal never blocked his number from me. I assumed he was nervous or some nonsense. I saved his number. I never intended calling it or anything, I only thought it was nice to have it. Then, he called. I about died."

Sitting on the plane, Kinley remembered a funny tidbit she'd forgotten to share. "Oh I forgot, he asked if you were a lesbian." Fellow passengers who may have been casually eavesdropping before, all boldly began to pay attention. Should she be offended? What would give him such an idea?

"Did he say why?" Madison inquired through gritted teeth.

"Apparently, you are a good Christian woman." Madison stared at her. "You know, you turned the other cheek." Kinley laughed at her own joke.

Madison let a laugh slip out, "Did you tell him you're my lover?"

"Nah, it would have been funny though. Maybe I should have said-she's mine, you can't have her." She grinned as Kinley went on, "But... I did tell him you were unavailable when we talked to him backstage," Kinley revealed. "I imagine women don't often turn him down. I told him it was too soon for you but he insisted on flying us out to Vegas. How the man got my address, I'll never know. When the tickets arrived I nearly fainted. First class." She let out a low whistle. "How will I ever fly coach after this?"

"It's been difficult for anything to feel normal since we met him."

"We should nurture the acquaintance; after all, he's at the top of your back-up list." Kinley loved teasing her. The idea of him knowing was beyond mortifying.

"If you ever tell him, I will happily toss you into a wood chipper." Kinley only laughed in reply.

Upon arriving at McCarran airport in Las Vegas, they were greeted by a man with a placard with the words Madison and Kinley printed in big bold letters. They stared at each other. He'd gotten them a chauffeur? It was too much. The Hummer turned stretch limo could have fit another thirty people in it, quite easily too. Kinley looked around in awe, "Usually when I come here I don't come to this side of town. It has changed so much."

"I think the casinos are gorgeous," Madison interjected her opinion.

"Yeah they are." She was distracted, "Did I tell you Cal asked me to forward the picture I took of you guys."

"What? Are you kidding? Why?" Madison paused, "Did I look fat?"

Kinley laughed, "Yeah, if you're fat the rest of the world is in trouble. You looked fabulous. Do you want it, you never asked."

"Yeah, I would like it." Madison studied the picture she'd just received on her phone. "Just think he's even hotter in real life, and that is saying something."

"See, I told you he liked you," Kinley informed her. "Why else would he ask?" Why indeed.

The limo took them next to Kinley's sister Taylor's house. "How does he know?" She peered at the back of the driver's head, "It's creepy, right?" By the time they arrived, Madison had gone over many things in her mind. Why had she come here? What exactly was she expecting? Did he have an idea of where he wanted it to go? She was no one-night-stand type of girl. When he realized it, would he leave her alone? She dreaded him walking away, but also thought it might be for the best. Really, what kind of future could she have with him?

Once they arrived at Taylor's home, it was time to explain some things. She walked out, ogled the limo, and turned to face them, "I thought you were renting a car. What are you two thinking?"

"Miss Madison, I am to pick you back up in one hour." His thick accent left her wondering at first what he'd just said, secondly, why. He was driving away before she could ask what was going on.

"Cal is texting me about dinner," Kinley muttered. She knew Kinley probably wanted Madison to give him her number. Madison suspected Kinley was feeling trapped, stuck in the middle of something. She was feeling hesitant about all of this. She wasn't certain she wanted him to have her number, but then again, maybe he didn't want it. He hadn't asked. Maybe all he wanted was a one night stand.

"Who is Cal? Maddy, what is going on? Have you caught the eye of an oil baron?" Taylor's vivid green eyes glittered with mischief. Her dark hair, long enough to sit on, fluttered in the breeze. They followed her in, toting their bags as they went.

"No, just *G-String's* sexiest singer of the year." Kinley had noticed the color drain from Madison's face. She took her cue and ran with the conversation. She knew Kinley would keep it light and on the surface, which made it feel safe. Madison watched Taylor's son and daughter run around the house, caught up in the excitement of having visitors. She used the excuse of needing to get ready to steal away from them. Her heart beat feebly in her chest at the thought of being near children. She turned her thoughts away, steering them toward Cal. What was he up to? She would have to tell him something soon, but what? *Give up on me, I'm broken*, she thought sadly as she began to touch up her eye shadow. Knocking on the bathroom door let her know Kinley had noticed her absence and had found her. "Come in."

"I know Cal said it's a group thing on the text but maybe you should go alone. I feel awkward. I don't want to be the third wheel." Kinley had put the toilet seat down and was perched on top of it.

"Seriously, you're going to pass up dinner with *Rory*?" Madison inquired.

"Well, Rory is divine…." she sighed dramatically.

"I am not going without you. This isn't a regular relationship. It isn't going anywhere, so you'd better not abandon me. What if he asks me something I can't answer?" Madison could feel her heart rate accelerate dangerously. "Please Kin," she added somewhat desperately. "When we entered into this friendship, it was for better or worse. I know this is the 'worse' part so please hang in there with me."

"When you put it like that…" Kinley answered morosely.

Cal paced nervously inside the door of the restaurant. Rory came up behind him. "Cal, the waitress wants to know when we'll be ready."

"Any minute now," he bit off.

"Easy killer, it's just that the kids are starving. I know; I'll let them order first." He walked away, leaving Cal to his self-abusing thoughts. Maybe she didn't like him. Maybe she thought Rory was the cute one. So many women liked Rory, or even Shawn and Chris. Some women didn't care at all, as long as they slept with someone famous. A limo pulled up just outside the door. It was only a moment before he saw them walking toward the glass doors. Madison was wearing a shirt which was clinging to one shoulder while revealing the other. His breath intake was going to suffer. He watched her walk, admiring her svelte figure in her body-hugging jeans. Hell, she was gorgeous. He was in big trouble.

"Hi, Cal." Her black eyelashes fluttered when she looked up at him. Breathe. He was wondering what her skin felt like, he imagined silk would be envious.

"Hi Madison, Kinley, and…" Cal lingered on the and.

"Taylor Johnson." She reached out and shook his hand. Her straight dark hair reached down her back; she could practically sit on it. He sensed Taylor turned heads with the greatest of ease, and although her beauty was flawless, and admirable, he couldn't help but think of Madison and how he was coming to adore her. He could see the familial resemblance in her face, when she and Kinley smiled.

The room was full of people. There was Shawn, his wife Candace, his three children, Rory, Jennifer, Matthew, Chris, his wife Meredith, and their two kids. Candace introduced herself and led Madison, Kinley and Taylor over the table, which was a dozen tables all shoved together. Cal usually hated these evenings. He often did his own thing. He hated being the odd man out. Everyone here was about family, and he was single. He never truly fit in, though they did their best to make him comfortable. He just couldn't be himself in these situations. He was constantly being asked to censor his behavior or tone his jokes down. He held out the seat next to Rory for Kinley, her sister sat on the other side of her. Then he sat Madison down, so he could be with her. He would have preferred something for just the two of them. Whatever was the expression on Rory's face trying to tell him? He gave him a look back, telling him wordlessly to relax. Rory was shaking his head. He was missing something, but he couldn't exactly take a break and find out what it was. Rory just rolled his eyes in surrender.

He noticed Madison was uneasy too. What was it? She wasn't married, but her best friend was. Had she been married before? Did she have children? The presence of children seemed to bring her discomfort edging on pain. He wanted to speak to her, to know her, but she kept everything light and on the surface. She was something of a mystery; he had to concede. "You want to get some fresh air; we could go for a walk or something? They have this atrium in the back. The ceiling opens up. It's nice."

She nodded, and he sensed once again, she was now relieved. Did she feel like he did? Was she uneasy in these situations because she didn't fit in either? He led her to the atrium, filled with curiosity, but uncertain of what to speak about. He didn't often converse with women past anything shallow. "Was your trip pleasant?" he asked tentatively.

"Yes, thank you so much. Neither of us has ever flown first class. We felt completely spoiled." She looked up at him, and his stomach lurched. He wanted to wrap his arms around her, not just because he wanted to kiss her at the moment either. It was a foreign feeling; he wanted to be the one she turned to, he wanted to protect her, to have her lean on him when she needed someone. Normally, he'd have been frightened by this thought. But being next to her made him think he could do anything.

"I'm glad. Did you like dinner?" Stupid questions! She made him feel uncertain, and like an awkward schoolboy asking a girl to a school dance.

"Yes, Kinley hadn't eaten here before either, but Taylor has. It's lovely." She bit her lip. She wanted to say something, but she was holding back, he knew it. "I love filet mignon, it was perfect."

"I liked it too." Why didn't he just talk about the weather? Think of something interesting already! "Are you excited about seeing our concert again tomorrow?" That was a good starting point, wasn't it?

"Yes, very much, except I didn't bring the right shoes to stand in line for eleven hours. I suppose I can go shopping bright and early in the morning." She smiled up at him. "I sincerely wish I would have thought about it beforehand though."

"What? Eleven hours? Are you exaggerating?" He hoped she was.

"We really wanted to be up front, which meant we had to get there in the morning. It's first come first served, and we wanted the bar." The bar, he knew was the metal barrier separating the crowd from the stage. Once someone was holding onto the bar, they didn't leave, because they'd never get their spot back. She'd been standing all day and night.

"I feel horrible. You're not standing in line. I'll have someone take care of that. I'll have someone do the waiting for you."

"Are you sure? I don't want to be a bother." She really meant it too, he could tell.

"It's no trouble, and you're not a bother," he told her, feeling nervous again, and for no reason he could discern.

Her eyes looked away. Finally, she uttered a question he didn't have an answer to, "Cal, where are we going with this?"

"I, *uh*, want to know you better," Cal stammered like a child. "I like you a lot." Yeah, that one wasn't any better.

"Oh, maybe you shouldn't. I'm really not worth it." She was looking down at her feet. This had gone wrong. He wanted to touch her, to tell her something to make her feel better.

"Maybe you are worth it." He lifted her chin gently and brought his lips to hers. If she was resistant, he didn't feel it. Her arms wrapped around his neck, and she kissed him back almost as eagerly as he kissed her. His chest tightened as he let one hand run over the silkiest shoulder he'd ever touched. He wanted more, so much more, but she pulled away and smiled up at him.

"Maybe I shouldn't have turned my head last time," she shared guiltily.

He shook his head and laughed. "That was a complete surprise or shock rather. Surprise hints at something fantastic, and it wasn't. Although, I did enjoy kissing your cheek immensely."

She lifted one eyebrow, "Why do I not believe you?"

He leaned down and brushed his lips against her cheek, so softly, like the flutter of butterfly wings. "I couldn't wait to kiss your cheek again, see?" He touched her face, the face he'd been dreaming of since he first laid eyes on her. "But, your lips are really spectacular."

She looked up at him, "We should go back; Kin will wonder where I am." Was there guilt in her expression, or something more? And why did he feel like he'd just experienced his first kiss and it was better than he'd ever imagined?

7. An Offer From a Non Gentleman

Backstage was pandemonium. What did Madison expect? Cal was surrounded, and appeared to be enjoying the attention, from scantily clad young women, well, women of every age. She felt a slight twinge of jealousy, but he'd kissed her…and come to think of it….every other slutty little thing who had thrown herself at him in the last ten years or so. She had to admit that he was irresistible in most respects. Her thoughts kept drifting back to that most perfect kiss. There were now other feelings compiling rapidly on top of that single reminiscence.

What would Jack say? Sure, she knew he was not here, but she could practically imagine his words. "Maddy, what the hell, I haven't even been in the grave a year. Give me a year at least!" She smiled to herself, although she couldn't have told anyone why the idea of him speaking to her posthumously would amuse her. Her kids would think it was cool, she was also certain of that. "Way to go Mom, someone famous, will he buy us stuff?" She also smiled at this imagining, because it would have been natural for her children to go in that direction.

What exactly was Cal up to? Did he want a serious relationship? She assumed not. She'd listened to enough of his song lyrics to know what he was interested in. It didn't take a rocket scientist to interpret, "You're no princess; you're a whore..." Like *that* was the kind of man who would respect her? She more than doubted it. At first, the idea of Calvin Hunt, the icon, finding her attractive, was more than flattering. It was something of a wicked little fantasy playing out in the real world.

She could remember the first time she'd heard his somewhat raspy, incredibly sexy voice on the radio, he had made an impression. She'd fallen in love with his music instantly, and so had many other people. When she first saw what he looked like...well, who didn't fantasize about him? In truth, had he shown up on her doorstep naked, when she was happily married, she sincerely would have not done anything with him. She loved her husband more than her own life. And...now that he was gone and Cal was here in real life, it was something of a sick cosmic joke especially with the back-up list.

Cal walked over to her, maneuvering easily through the crowd. He walked and they followed, he moved forward and they parted like the Red Sea. "Would you come with me for a moment?" he asked her. She nodded as she tried to swallow that damned lump in her throat. He walked to his dressing room and let her inside. "Come to my room tonight." He was so unbelievably sexy, her knees were shaking, and she was biting her lip. Jack was there inside her mind; his reproachful glance made her nearly double over in pain.

"I can't," she answered softly, while looking down at her own shoes; Jack's eyes were still boring into her, though only inside of her mind.

"Why? We're both unmarried adults." The words stabbed at her, leaving her already broken heart, completely dysfunctional.

"I-you don't love me. Any one of those women out there would be more than happy to take care of you." She grinned up at him, "*I* would need more." She'd gestured to the door. "I can't, we barely know each other." Oh Jack, what would you think? She couldn't, not even to erase the pain, for a few pleasure filled moments.

"I wouldn't mind knowing you a little better. I'm intrigued with you, fascinated really," he answered her. Oh, what could she do with that? She gulped as she found herself becoming lost in his deep blue eyes. She could say yes, and no one would ever know. What did it matter? Truthfully, he'd become real to her now, she'd be left to pick up the pieces in the morning when he was gone and she couldn't. She didn't have enough of a functioning heart left to deal with that. She shook her head.

"It's not a good idea, Cal. I'm no good for you." Her voice was growing hoarse as he leaned closer and pulled her into his chest. "Just forget about me," she advised.

"I confess, I have always wanted anything or anyone who wasn't good for me. What precisely is bad about you?" His mouth, delicious full lips, was a mere inch away from hers.

"I am damaged. You should find some young thing that has never had her heart broken and…isn't afraid to take another chance." She knew this one evasive sentence would make her sound merely wounded, vulnerable. She couldn't imagine trying to tell him how far off that description really was.

He brought her hands to his lips and kissed them sending shivers up her spine, "I really don't want you to walk away without giving this a chance. I know there is something here, something I've never felt before. I don't want to lose whatever it is." He kissed her tenderly, and for a moment she considered letting it go further, but she stopped him. "At least let me call you sometimes, or email you, hell, we can be Facebook friends."

She laughed and leaned her head on his chest. His arms felt so good around her. She wished she could believe that he would take care of her, and try to fill the gaping hole in her chest, but he was not good for her, just as she wasn't good for him. There really wasn't a point. But, what harm could he be when he was on the road constantly, and he lived in another country the rest of the time. "You're on Facebook?"

"Of course. Who isn't? I'll find you and we'll keep in touch. I'll give you my phone number and you can call me sometimes." He had a look in his eyes, pure, intense. She couldn't say no anymore, and honestly wasn't sure she wanted to. She nodded and laughed.

"Does anyone ever tell you no?"

"No," He chuckled. "But it's interesting. I can see why normal people don't like it."

She laughed again; it felt nice. "Hand me your phone?"

He tilted his head to the side and gave her a scrutinizing glance before pulling his phone out of his pocket, "It may be, *um…*"

"Wet?" She giggled. "Sweaty much?" He grinned sheepishly.

"Those lights are really hot up there. The rest of me is dry now, but my pockets…"

She programmed her cell number into his phone, "I'd love it if you called me, and get to know me, you said that's what you wanted, right? Unless you meant only in the biblical sense…"

He chuckled, "Well, I don't think I'd mind knowing you that way either, but yes, I'd like to know you. I want to know what your favorite color is, and what you do for a living, and if you like my music, and whether or not you like string beans, and how tall are you, and where are you from?" He took a breath.

She held up her hand and laughed heartily. "My favorite color always changes, but right now it's blue and don't ask why. I am a full time student, I love your music, every song in fact, I hate string beans, I'm five foot two and I'm from Oklahoma, no wise cracks please."

He grinned, that sexy yet delicious grin he'd modeled on the cover of *G-String Magazine*. Her knees would soon turn to Jell-O if he didn't stop it. "You are not like any other woman I have ever met. I could sit and talk with you all night, although I'd be far too tempted to do more than talk."

"Well, get to know me first, and then you can decide if I'm worth the trouble." She gave him a cunning smile.

8. The Friendship Card

Madison sat at a round black oak table in Kinley's kitchen with her three dearest friends in the world. They were uneasy, it was clear. "Kinley, you should say something," Kate offered first, brushing back her light colored hair. She knew something was up, their food was untouched and Kinley could really cook up some delectable things. Madison was busy pulling apart a piece of freshly baked bread.

"Why me?"

"You're her best friend," Kate pointed out. Kinley scowled playfully back at her, her pale brown eyes narrowing.

"Oh please," their friend Megan groaned, she pushed her long platinum blond hair away from her face. "We are staging an intervention; we think it's time for you to move out of your house." Megan's delicate face wore an absolutely smug expression. Madison laughed immediately easing the tension in the room.

"Okay, I agree with you, but I'm not sure how to proceed. I've never done this sort of thing on my own before."

The other women sitting at the table each looked decidedly uncomfortable. They exchanged dark looks across the table. Kate piped up,

"What about Mandy?" Simultaneous groans were emitted all around the table. They all began looking down at their plates.

"She'll be okay; we know she gets the job done," Megan interjected.

"Yeah, she does…but so did Hitler," Kinley mumbled.

"It's decided then, we'll call Mandy, and one of you will deal with her for me," Madison put it out there and waited. Still, her friends all stared at one another.

"Kinley should do it," Megan said. Kate nodded vigorously. Kinley had that 'why me' look on her face. "I'm allergic to Mandy, she gives me hives."

"Yeah and I will just punch her," Kate pointed out enthusiastically. They all laughed as they recalled the time they'd played volleyball with her and Kate had the lobbed the ball at the back of Mandy's head, and feigned it to be completely accidental.

"I will not punch her, or break out in hives, true, but I will lash out at her verbally and she will be completely ignorant of it, as always, and make it completely *unrewardable*."

"Is that even a word, *unrewardable*?" Madison laughed.

"No, but it should be added to our dictionary with all the other words we've concocted," Kinley answered her.

Madison pulled her purse over to her, and began to pull out her wallet. Each of her friends shuddered. "She's grabbing it, you're in trouble Kinley, you can't say no."

Kinley began chewing on her lip, "Don't do it," she pled. Madison was already putting it on the table, and sliding the nondescript card across to Kinley, pushing it with her index finger. "You're evil."

"I know." Madison shrugged. Kinley picked up the small laminated, business looking card and held it up, just to be certain. There in fire engine red, big bold letters read the word- Friendship. It was the card they passed around between themselves and there was only one. It meant you could ask your friend for any big outlandish favor and they couldn't say no. Kinley put it into her wallet and grimaced, "Fine, but one of you will be getting this one next." She grinned nastily at Kate and Megan, who grinned tauntingly in return.

"Just so you know…I hate Mandy."

It was the next morning that Amanda (Mandy) Murphy, came over to her house. Kinley was there, looking very agitated. As predicted, Mandy opened her mouth and the first of the ten plagues was released, "It's about time you sold this house. I've been waiting ages for you to call me. You need to clear out the kid's rooms and get on with your life." Madison fought the urge to punch Mandy in that overly made up face.

Mandy was small but always seemed to be a giant. Her personality filled the room, leaving no space for anyone else. Madison noted she'd changed her hair again. The top layers were startlingly blond, while underneath it was a deep black. She tapped her overly long acrylic nails on the side of her coffee cup, while looking around the house for possibilities when staging it. "I'm glad you've pulled all of the kid's pictures off the wall; it will be easier to sell."

Madison bit her tongue, and held her fists clenched at her side, while Mandy remained blissfully unaware of the fact she'd said something socially unacceptable. Kinley gave her a repulsed look behind her back. She took over, "Listen, Mandy, you'll be dealing with me, this is all a bit much for Maddy right now, so if you have anything to ask, I will know the answer."

"What if I need your social security number?" Mandy asked Madison's retreating form.

"She knows it by heart," Madison walked away and called over her shoulder. Kinley shot her a pleading glance, begging her to relent, but there was nothing she could do, the friendship card had been played. She could overhear Mandy whining about how this was very unorthodox.

Mandy groaned, "How would you know anything? This is pretty personal stuff."

Kinley's reply gave Madison a new awareness, "Who do you think went with her for the law suit, who do you think kept her lights on, the mortgage paid, who brought her food? When the funeral was over and everyone went home, who do you think signed her name on her checks? I have access to everything you will need, you will deal with me."

"Well, I'm not having you forge her signature," Mandy huffed.

Within days, the house was on the market, and Kinley was planning an open house. All of her friends were pleased with the idea. Megan took her out to look at condos one day, and Kate took her to a new little housing tract. It was difficult to want to go anywhere. Everywhere she looked there were kids, tons of them. There were playgrounds and schools, places she now wanted nothing to do with. Kinley finally found a place that suited her, so the four of them went one day for lunch. "It's all single people, no children, or pets," Kinley announced as they walked through the first floor plan of the townhouse development. "And it's gated, so there's the security thing. It's very clean." Madison fell in love with the second place they looked at, and made her decision.

She wasn't sure if she was doing the right thing. That night she tossed and turned, unable to sleep. Jack was with her, as he often was in the night. She could feel his strong arms enfold her; she could smell the musky scent of his skin. "Please don't go," she would cry, only to wake up all alone, crying into his pillow, the pillow that no longer smelled like him. Actual memories haunted her in the night. Moments where she could hear his laughter, or hear him snore, even though it was impossible. She was alone in her bed tonight, missing him more than anything, when her phone rang.

9. The Geriatric Moves Like Jagger

Cal put out his cigarette and flicked it into the ashtray. "What are you eating, Gabe?"

"Soy nuts," he answered with his trademark straight face. Gabe was too large to be ignored. He had hair the color of espresso, black eyes, and chocolate skin. This didn't make him unusual, but the fact that he was seven feet four inches tall did. It never failed to amuse Cal how Gabe was into saving the planet, and being a vegetarian. It seemed that giants shouldn't care about things like saving the planet or eating soy nuts.

"How can you say that with no expression whatsoever?" Cal interrogated him. Gabe shrugged and continued watching the game. Cal had waited nearly a week; he wanted to call her. Did he seem too eager though? He got up and left the other guys to watch the game they had recorded earlier. What time was it in California? He checked his phone, which seemed to know what time it was anywhere on earth. It was ten, was that too late? He shrugged and thought he should give it a try. He grew antsy as the phone rang.

"Hello?" When he heard her voice, he realized he'd been holding his breath.

"Hi, it's Cal."

"Hi Cal, how is your tour going?" She sounded pleased to hear from him and she wasn't berating him for not calling earlier. So far, so good. He wondered what she expected of him, he didn't have an answer. He was taking this new experience day by day. He did want it to go somewhere, but where could it go?

"Exhausting," he admitted.

"I often wonder where you get all your energy. I mean, you never stop moving when you're on stage. Then you have to travel after all of that? Wow, I would be wiped out."

"Cigarettes and booze," he told her with a laugh.

"Really? Don't you think vegetables and water would be better? For the love of God, have a pomegranate." No one was ever really so straight with him, not ever. He knew he was living hard, and doing all of the wrong things, but no one ever called him on it.

"What will a pomegranate do for me?"

"Antioxidants, and all, plus it's really a great anti-cancer fruit. You should have a nutritionist or something. Think about it…rock stars do not always age well…look at Mick Jagger…*eww*."

He found himself laughing hard, and then thinking the same thing. Each of the members of the Rolling Stones looked like they were inches away from the grave. Sure, they had energy but they looked like hell. "Oh my…"

"You see my point, don't you? Now, look at Jack Lalanne, he's practically dead and he still looks better." He was still laughing. Who was this woman? She had the ability to capture his attention like no one else could.

"I bet Gabe would help me…although I'm not sure I want his help. He eats soy nuts."

"Those are an acquired taste," she agreed. "Where are you now?"

"Virginia, then we're off to South Carolina, and finally finish off this leg of the tour in Florida."

"That sounds like fun. I've never been beyond Texas. Do you like that part of your job, the travel part?" Madison asked. No one ever talked to him like he was human too. No one ever asked him things about himself that mattered; only things that they cared to know, nosy things. It made him feel, even if only for a second, that she cared for him and what happened to him.

"Yes and no. Yes because we get to see so many amazing places, but no because I don't really have the time to enjoy them." His mind whirred, "Do you like Florida?" He was developing another plan.

"I've never been. You'll have to tell me all about it Cal. I've heard it's really nice this time of year. Kinley says May is the perfect time to go. She has family out there; she used to go all the time."

"Doesn't she miss her family out there? Why would she stop going?" This didn't make sense to him.

"Well, she is a stay-at-home mom, part-time student, married to a school teacher. They just don't have the money to travel, you know?" Madison replied. Was he so shallow that he thought everyone had enough money for whatever they wanted? He felt like such an ass.

"How did she pay for those tickets to our concert? They can be a bit steep."

"She never said, but I imagine it has something to do with a secret credit card. We've all been huge fans of yours for years. She wanted to bring our friend Megan but Megan likes other music. Of course now that we've gone to two concerts, she and Kate feel like they are missing out," she giggled.

"Why would your friend do such a thing? That is one hell of a friend. Was it your birthday?" There had to be something behind the story. He wondered briefly about the secret credit card. From the way Madison had said it, it sounded as though Ryan, the poor school teacher would not be thrilled with a secret credit card.

"My birthday? No. My birthday is in October. She just loves me, what can I say?" That was a deflective comment if he'd ever heard one.

"Would you and your friends want to come out to Florida to see us? I could take care of everything." Was he going to push her away by being too persistent?

"You don't have to do that! No, we're okay."

"I mean if you want to. It would be nice to see you again," he muttered, feeling somewhat foolish. Didn't she see that he wasn't going to go away?

"Who wouldn't love to? But, it would depend on the timing of it all. Kin and I have school and all of the others have husbands and kids and…"

Something about her statement chilled him from the inside out, like being flash frozen. The tone, it made him hesitate.

"It will be next weekend, just a weekend. And it would be all four of you…and hell; they can bring their families if they want. I just want to see you." He was getting desperate.

"You're serious?"

"Never been more so," Cal returned.

"*Um*, I'll talk to them, but no husbands and kids…just us girls. Call me tomorrow; I should have an answer for you by then."

After he hung up the phone with Madison, he just wanted to be alone with his thoughts. Most women would have jumped at the chance to fly everyone they loved out to Florida, or just come by themselves. Wouldn't they? She actually had to think about it? She wasn't caught up in all the rock star hype, but she loved his band. She wasn't shallow. She wanted things to be meaningful and lasting. She wanted love, not just sex. She was witty and hilarious. She called him out on his vices. She made him want to be a better person. He just wanted to be certain she returned his feelings. He didn't think he was wasting his time. Hell, he hadn't enjoyed a phone conversation that much, ever. There was still something odd there though.

"I'm going to bed guys, see you tomorrow." He'd never say see you in the morning, when none of them would be up before noon. He was almost out the door.

"Don't you want to know who wins? There's ten minutes left," Shawn called out. "It's *hockey*." He gave this blanket statement which needed nothing else to back it up.

"He's pining away for Madison," Chris chirped. They all guffawed in unison. He turned and glared at them all.

"Come on Cal, we're only playing. What's wrong?" Rory asked, finally with sincerity.

"I don't know. It's like she's so…secretive." Yeah, that was the word.

Gabe cleared his throat. "Maybe she has a good reason to be." Red flag. He closed the door, and stayed in the room. He walked toward Gabe.

"What do you know, G?"

Gabe shook his head, and wore an unusual smile upon his face. "It's up to her. I did a background check on her when you started looking interested. Had to make sure…anyway, I'm thinking *you* don't deserve *her*." Was he teasing? It was hard to tell with Gabe.

"Of course I don't but it doesn't mean you need to keep secrets from me, Gabe."

"They aren't my secrets to tell." Cal knew that was the end of the matter. He'd never get it out of Gabe unless Gabe wanted to reveal it. Cal just stalked off to his suite and frowned. If they were awful secrets she was keeping then Gabe would have warned him to stay away from her. He'd never told Cal he didn't deserve someone before. It was odd. He tried to fall asleep but he kept hearing her laughter, seeing her kohl lined eyes and kissing her lips, that tasted sweet, but not like anything he'd ever tasted before.

10. Fun In Florida

Madison, Megan, Kate, and Kinley stepped off the plane to see a man with a sign reading-Madison Grey and friends. "Oh, you're like the entrée and we're like boring old side-dishes," muttered Megan as she slung her Coach bag over her arm. "I so can't believe I'm in Florida, isn't this exciting?" she squealed.

Madison walked toward the man holding the sign, "I'm Madison Grey," she spoke to the tan young man who barely could pass for twenty. His teeth looked eye-blindingly white. He drove a hummer-stretch-limo-thing too.

"This is too much fun." Kate leaned back into the cushioned seat. "I will never be able to fly coach again," she sighed dreamily. The sunroof was open whipping Kate's blond bob into a frenzy. Kinley scowled as she pulled her curls back away from her face. Megan glowed as her long straight hair tossed back away from her as though she was starring in a movie. Madison felt surrounded by love in her makeshift family.

The limo-driver brought them to a five-star hotel and began to arrange for their luggage to be transported upstairs. He went through a spiel for Madison about how he was there for her during the entire weekend and gave her a number to call. "I will be here whenever you need me. I'm never more than a few minutes away." She tipped him, thinking it was probably what she was supposed to do, and let him go.

Their room was on the top floor, with a sweeping view of Orlando. Kinley pointed out Disney World to them. "I haven't been there in so long," she told them with a wistful expression on her face.

The suite had four bedrooms, as though four friends who wanted separate sleeping quarters always required separate bedrooms in a suite. There was a fruit basket full of pomegranates. She grinned. There was another basket filled with chocolates and roses were in vases all over the room. Her phone beeped, letting her know she had received an email.

Maddy,

You should arrive by 2:30 in the afternoon, and we will not arrive until 8pm. I can imagine I will be anxious to see you, and you might be sitting there bored, wondering what to do. Well, I have a few ideas. (I am useful sometimes.) Have a massage, all of you. I will be jealous as I sit and play video games with my nephew on our tour bus, or at least I can imagine you covered only by a very thin, nearly transparent sheet. Or, do go to the beach. You said you've never been out this way, the beaches are white sand, and there are actually shells on them. (Like what you see in the movies.) It's quite a drive though.

As I have prepaid for all of you to spend an entire day in the spa, doing whatever it is that people do all day inside of spas, you should at least enjoy it. Tell Kinley and Kate hello from me and Megan that I look forward to meeting her soon. Do be in your room by 8pm, because the first thing I am going to do when I get there is come up to see you. I have a little surprise planned as well. All of you should be ready to go by 8. Can't wait to see you,

Cal

She passed her phone around and listened to the giggles of her friends. "Massages? I don't know," Kate grumbled. The idea was definitely unpleasant to her. "Kin, imagine, that person will be in your body space, and I don't get naked for just anyone..."

"It might be fun; we should at least try it," Kinley encouraged her.

"I'm going to," Megan announced. "I don't mind getting naked for strangers." They all laughed merrily.

Madison picked up the phone and made appointments for them at the spa, and then ordered lunch. Even though she was some place new, it was so relaxing in the hotel room that she didn't even have the slightest inclination to go out and explore the city. A girl's weekend had always been something mentioned, but it had never really happened, not with all four of them. Their real dream had been to go to New York together and see a few plays, eat at fun restaurants and see the statue of liberty, and all of those New York type things. It had been a nice daydream. Never had Florida even entered into the equation, not even in daydream form. Yet, here they were at the top of hotel, two hours from the Atlantic Ocean and it was all because Cal wanted to see her. She smiled to herself as she looked out at the city. Had he done this for other women?

Several hours later each woman had been spoiled and pampered beyond anything any of them had experienced before. "I could so get used to this," Megan said. They were ready for Cal to show up. "I wonder where he's taking us." They all had speculated all day long to no avail. Kinley was the only one who had been to Florida previously and she had shrugged. Cal knocked on the door at 8:20, and Madison felt something she did not want to feel-happy. She quickly brushed it away.

"Cal, come in."

He walked in, that delicious smile he was famous for, upon his face. "Is the room satisfactory; is everything okay, did you get a massage?"

≈

Madison laughed, "It's really extraordinary." He hugged her. He couldn't help it; it had been too long. Her friends were pretending not to stare, but the new one he'd never met was laughing.

He turned to introduce himself, "You must be Megan, I'm Cal."

"No one said you were freakishly tall."

"Wow, you just say what you want don't ya?" Cal teased.

"How tall are *you*?"

"6'5.You are like a pixie, an evil pixie." It was true. Megan was 4'10, and he must have seemed gigantic next to her. Madison, Kate and

Kinley were each around 5'2 and she made them feel tall. She just grinned up at him. "I know I'm going to like you," he told her.

"Are you all ready to go? You all look great." His eyes lingered on Madison. His heart was either hanging on waiting for some instruction to beat, or beating mindlessly like he'd been running in a marathon and just pushed through the finish line. He led them to a limo; this one was rather the idea of what limos should look like. There were four limos lined up in the front. He wore a baseball cap rather low and he slouched as they walked toward the lineup of cars.

"Are you in disguise?" Kate asked as he opened the door for them.

They were driving away before he pulled the cap off and tousled his honey blond hair, making it look as sexy as though he'd just rolled out of bed. "I have to disguise myself a little, or your time here will suck."

Megan leaned over to Kinley, "At least he has a small ego."

"Is she like this with everyone?" he asked Kinley who laughed.

"It's how you know she likes you, if she doesn't like you, you'll know that too." Kinley smiled, her red lips arched playfully, "I think she'd choose poison." They all laughed and exchanged glances. It was as though some form of covert communication was going on in front of him. They all laughed harder. Clearly, it was an inside joke, and something about the way they were made him want to be on the inside. The limos began to pull into a parking lot as they all laughed.

"Disney World!" Kate exclaimed. "I've always wanted to see it." They all exchanged excited glances. "The parking lot is huge!"

"Wow, Disney World." Megan looked over at him, "Thanks Cal, this has been the best weekend of my life; counting the weekend I was married." They all howled with laughter, even Cal. It turned out that the band was having a private after hour's party. They took over the entire park with their families. The children scattered, and so did the adults. Cal was left to entertain the women, who began to whisper amongst themselves. They were an interesting group. Madison was at his side, not part of the devious conversation.

"I want to see how different the Haunted Mansion is," Kate said, "Kinley says there are subtle differences."

Kinley nodded. "I haven't been here since I was a teenager, but I imagine it's still a little different."

They all headed off in that direction armed with maps they took from the entrance. Madison gave Kinley a look that seemed to be somewhat pleading in nature, but Kinley just grinned back. He knew for certain there was a higher level of communication; he only wished he knew what it was.

Within the Mansion, they were all together huddling in a small group. He was left to sit in his "Doom Buggy" with Maddy, while the others paired off. "I fear your friends are up to something nefarious," he muttered.

"Nefarious? An excellent word for it."

"Hah! You know what scheme they're planning and they didn't even talk to you."

"They are planning to ditch us. The Haunted Mansion is different, ha, it's a ruse," she told him with a smile. She was thinking it might not be such a bad thing. And as they got off the ride, she instantly realized they'd done it, somehow. They were gone, vanished into the larger than life park. Thank heaven for cell phones.

11. You're No Led Zeppelin

Kinley leaned over and whispered rather loudly in Madison's ear, "My mother would most certainly be praying for their souls." This was in regard to the women backstage. Madison laughed, knowing Kin's mother, she had to agree. "I'm blushing; I've never seen so much cleavage."

Kate piped up, "Please, it's you talking. You have more cleavage than all of those girls put together."

The four friends laughed with abandon. "Excuse me, I couldn't help but notice you from across the room." The lead singer of Sludge was speaking to Megan, in a cool British accent that seemed to make his words more beautiful. She arched a single brow but he continued, "I've always wanted to meet an angel." Her friends were looking at her, expectantly, all as if holding their breath, waiting to laugh. Truth be told, Megan was no angel, even though she looked like one. True, she'd looked like a Botticelli cherub, but alas, she was nothing of the kind. It was obvious that with her long platinum hair, nearly transparent green eyes, and the prettiest face imaginable, she still looked like a vision from heaven above, but she was not even close to being angelic.

She touched his nose, "Aren't you the cutest little thing. What are you, twelve?" She turned toward her friends, "*Ah*, I've always wanted to be a cougar."

"What would your husband say?" Kinley asked.

Madison chimed in, "He can always share you."

"Cougar, married? You can't be a day over eighteen." The lead singer was clearly flustered.

"It's quite a few days over eighteen. Wow, I am old," she muttered. He looked like he was going to be sick. She touched his cheek, "You are very sweet."

Cal walked over and really shook him up, because he was obviously trying to figure out just how old she could possibly be. "Rupert, she's fourteen years older than you," he pointed out. "It's not going to happen." Rupert stuttered his goodbye and walked away, sulking. Cal turned toward Madison, "I am hoping you've enjoyed the show, but by now you've heard all of my cleverest jokes three times, and endured hearing our songs over and over again."

"It was great." She smiled. "Really."

He turned toward Megan, "And did you like it? I know you're not a fan." He gave her his knee-buckling smile and she couldn't help but respond.

"I admit it was *pretty* good, but…you're no Led Zeppelin."

"Who is?" he agreed.

Madison chimed in, "She's just saying that for me, because she loves good old Led Zeppelin, and I hate them." Megan gave her smuggest grin to Madison. Cal just laughed.

"How can you hate Led Zeppelin?"

Madison and her friends looked like they would die laughing. "I don't want to offend you," she muttered. He noticed instantly that her friends were giving her looks of pure incredulity.

"I insist Maddy." He grinned and something within her realized he actually wanted to know what she was thinking.

"Ok, *to me*, it sounds as though a bunch of guys were jamming, while high, perhaps in a public bathroom, and with no plan whatsoever they recorded whatever crap they came up with while improvising tunes." Cal bent over laughing, holding onto his stomach for fear he would lose it.

"Oh my…" He sighed as his breath came back into his chest, "Don't hold back Maddy." He grinned. "So, changing the subject, what did you guys do today?"

~

Madison smiled up at him, knowing she was getting into trouble, "We went to the beach, it was wonderful. We met Kinley's aunt and had lunch with her. We went shopping and then came back to the hotel to get ready and come here." Something was happening at that moment, something unnamable in the pit of her stomach. She didn't want to fall in love with this man. It was a poor investment on her part. He would break her and she'd never recover. But, as she'd learned, the heart wants things your brain would not necessarily choose. His grin was damned unnerving and it did things to her. But…she concluded…it did the same thing to thousands of other women, why should she be any different? But it was more than just his physical appearance, which would cause angels to weep at the sheer beauty of him, but she adored him, everything about him.

He was thoughtful of her friends; he actually spoke to them. He cared what she thought, or least he was great at pretending. She shouldn't fall for this. This life, his life, was not at all the dream existence she had in mind. She thought it was fun and a great get-away, but it was not normal, or in her world, real. And-could she trust him to remain faithful to her? He was beginning to melt all of her resistance. She thought of walking through Disney World last night. The cool spring air, the scent of rain floating on the breeze, and the way it felt to be kissed by him. It almost felt like a normal date, until some of the workers there in the park began asking for his autograph. She'd been somewhat amused at his sheepish behavior. He hadn't been egotistical in the least, but flattered.

Any other normal person would have let him sweep her away. She wasn't normal. She'd had everything before. Everything, and it had been taken away. Marrying her high school sweetheart during her senior year of high school hadn't exactly been a dream come true. It had been hushed up; due to the fact she was carrying Jonathan at the time. Her parents had forced the marriage, on a Tuesday afternoon, she'd met in the county clerk's office and been married by the justice of the peace. No one had expected it to last, but it had. They'd made it work and she thought they'd been happy. She wasn't likely to share any of this with Cal any time soon.

They all went back to the suite, tired, no exhausted. Cal followed them in, and one by one, her friends deserted her with lame excuses. Cal sat politely across from her on the sofa, and began apologetically, "Maddy, I wish we could date like normal people."

"No worries." She smiled. "I've had a lot of fun with you."

"Really? I'm so glad. I can't quite read you sometimes, and I think you must not be happy, but then you give me a smile that melts my insides and I think I must be imagining it." Her heart quickened as she listened to him speak. "I love talking to you every night. I can't stop thinking about you. I want more than this." He smiled brightly as he spoke.

"What do you want?" She realized she leaned forward as she spoke and was now looking at him directly in the eye. She nearly stopped drawing breath.

"I'm not your average guy, I realize that, and normally I can accept it. But, I'd give anything to be average at this moment, to tell you that I want you, only you. How will you be able to trust me, even though I haven't so much as looked at another woman since I spotted you in the audience?"

"You haven't?"

"No and what's more, I can't ask you to put your life on hold for me...can I?" He sighed, "An average guy wouldn't have to do *that*. He wouldn't be touring Europe; begging a woman, he was certainly falling in love with, to not date anyone and not think of anyone but him," Cal muttered.

"He wouldn't?"

"Damn it, I just want to be with you, all the time, Maddy. I can't think straight, I'm damned distracted." He took her hands into his, "Come with me to Europe. Please? Take three months, and come with me." His heart beat ceased as he awaited her response. He didn't know what she would say; he held his breath, quite frightened.

"I..." She sat back against the sofa and breathed in deeply. "I don't know. I have so much going on. I have school at least until the beginning of summer. I have to do this." She was determined to see this through. No more relying on someone else. If Jack hadn't had life insurance, and insisted on getting insurance on every child, she would've been in serious financial distress. She didn't even like to think of the settlement money. She had hated him at the time, for suggesting that one of the children might die and need insurance. She'd been certain she would have the prettiest grandchildren that were ever seen, and she would have made the best mother-in-law. Who knew she would lose every one of them? And she couldn't just rely on Cal falling helplessly in love with her and placing her right smack dab into the lap of luxury. How far off was that bound to be?

"Okay, are you attending school this summer?" he inquired delicately.

"No," she hesitated. "I am not."

"All right, then maybe you can visit for a couple of weeks." He paused, "Let me think, we'll be in England during the middle of summer. You will love England. Will you at least think about it? Bring Kinley or all of your friends if you want," he added. It wasn't lost on him that she loved to be near her friends, and seemed to need them for support. He didn't care. They were actually some of the funniest women he'd ever met. But that Kinley, he felt as if he'd known her in some previous life, she reminded him of his sister Callie.

"Really?" He always had her. He said invite your friends and she knew, and so did he, that she would just melt. "Well, can you give me a while to think about it?"

"I'll give you exact dates and places; maybe the information will help you decide. I just want you to be there, with me." Cal moved closer, she could feel the incredible warmth of his body. She just nodded as he crushed his lips onto hers. There was something in this kiss, something real and tangible. It frightened her.

After he left, she snuck into Kinley's room. Kinley was on her side, breathing deeply and Madison almost woke her. She couldn't. She just sat down in the armchair next to Kinley's bed. There was something in her friend's expression, something undoubtedly heartbreaking. Madison knew Kinley's grief to be nearly as deep as her own, although it would afford her little or no sympathy, as though she had no right to feel it. She had not been Jack's wife, but she had been close friends with him since junior high. She had not been the mother to Madison's children, but had known each of them since birth. She had seen them nearly every day, loved them as though she were their favorite aunt. She knew Kinley's sorrow ran deep, but could not pull herself up to help. She felt as though they were drowning next to each other, she was the weaker of the two. Kinley kept trying to buoy her up, but she would find herself sliding back beneath the inky waves again and again. She wondered if Kinley's strength was waning. It had to be, but she needed her to hang in there.

Madison thought of Cal's words in order to distract herself. Kinley had wanted to go to England for-forever. It was all she ever talked about. Madison had the opportunity to give it to her. She could. But was that the only tempting thing about it? Cal hadn't made a move to sleep with her this entire time. He'd been on his best behavior. How was it possible to know a person when they were always on their best behavior? She shrugged. Somehow, she felt she did know him, intimately.

She couldn't stop the tears. She leaned her head back and let them come. She wept because she didn't know what to do. She wept for Kinley who was obviously keeping something from her. She wept because she'd been so caught up in her own grief that she hadn't noticed it before. She wept because she tried to justify that her grief must always be greater than Kinley's. She wept because she'd had such a wonderful weekend with her friends, and felt deeply confused, guilty and undeserving. Someone doesn't deserve to have the most happiness they can possibly handle in this lifetime, and lose it, only to have more undeserving happiness thrust upon them. She just wept, because it was all she could do for the time being.

She leaned her head back, closed her eyes, felt her head was too heavy to hold up, and aching from the inside out. Her breathing regulated, as she drifted away. She could feel the poking of a little finger, she'd felt it many times before. "Mom, Mom, Mom, Mom…" The little chant pulled her out of her sleep.

"What?" She sat up and stared into those big hazel eyes. "Thanks Alex for the shortest nap in my life."

"I was just wondering, would you be mad if Jackson killed a bird?"

"What!" She remembered this had actually happened a few weeks before the kids and Jack… were gone. Sunday sand-days, every Sunday it was beach day. She looked around, seeing Kinley's vivid red hair, her alabaster skin in a blue bikini, chasing Jackson who was wielding a small metal shovel, which was nearly as big as he was; he was chasing after a hobbling, terrified seagull.

"Aunt Kinley is mad, so I was thinking you might be too," Alex told her.

"Hey Casper, you'd better catch him," Madison shouted.

"What do you think I am trying to do?" Kin called out as she grabbed the shovel. She sat down panting; shovel in hand. "Jeffery Dahmer over there, killing birds," she sighed as she collapsed back into the beach chair. "You're raising a future serial killer there, Maddy." Jackson crept closer, trying to grab the shovel, "So help me Jax, I swear, you are going to dig with my empty soda cup...go and do not touch the shovel again."

Madison laughed as Jackson innocently replied, "Why are you using your outside voice Aunt Kinley."

"Because we're outside," her voice rose steeply but there was no malice there, she was teasing him. "Go play, *killer*." She winked at him.

"I wasn't trying to kill it; I was trying to help it fly away," Jackson argued.

"Go dig a hole, ya little murderer," Madison told him.

"But Ma-um..." He stalked away, grumbling, "I'll dig a hole, a grave for that bird."

Madison exchanged glances with Kin, Megan, and Kate. "Nice sociopath you're raising there." Kate chuckled.

"I know, he gets it from Jack's side of the family," Madison shared her opinion as a man walked by, wearing a bright yellow Speedo. "Wow. I think he must not have a mirror at home. Do you think he's foreign?" She giggled, "He looks like a European Yeti. Where does he get his self-confidence, I ask you? *Eww*."

Kinley was cracking up. "His chest's all puffed out, puffer fish. Oh my, he's peacocking. Gross," Kin whispered. "Disturbing. Hey, Megan you should go talk to him, I'll give you a nickel."

"Why?" Megan asked.

"So you can put it in his coin slot," Kinley teased.

"There's a nickel you wouldn't want back," Kate chimed in.

Madison watched the scene before her. Kennedy was being buried in the sand by Riley; McKenna was chasing Jonathan, a sand crab wriggling in her hands. Jackson and Alex were making a sand castle, kids were everywhere. Jackson came back, on tiptoe, his dark hair gleaming in the sunlight along with his delightful little smirk. He snuggled into Kinley, who put her arms around him, kissing his forehead. "I love you, Aunt Kinley," he told her with deep sincerity. Madison knew he was there to butter her up, but he did love her.

"*Ah*, my Jax, my darling," she smiled. "I love you too, but you still can't have your bird killing weapon back." Kinley playfully ruffed up his hair. "However, I did bring you some gummy worms…" Madison gasped, forcing herself to wake. It felt as though she'd been submerged under water too long, and needed to breathe. Cal was making her remember, he was making her feel alive again. She breathed in deeply, she'd been happy so long ago. She'd been funny, Kin had been funny. She sighed, it wasn't appropriate to feel happy with all of them gone. The flicker of life she'd felt when near Cal, began to fade again.

12. The Hunt Family Compound

It was something of a family reunion happening at the Hunt house. Even though it was four in the morning, there was a full feast going on. Rory and Cal sat at the big wooden table surrounded by their two sisters, Callie and Michelle, Rory's wife Jennifer, Matthew, Brian and Phillip who were Callie's boys, Cadence and Taryn, who were Michelle's girls, and their mother and father. Not much had changed since they'd been gone. The kids grew almost too quickly, and his sister Michelle was pregnant, and downright massive.

"Real maple syrup. It is so good. Thanks Ma!" Rory mumbled, his mouth filling up with warm buttered griddlecakes.

"Well of course," sniffed their mother, who looked put out that they hadn't been given 'real' maple syrup on the road. She was a petite woman, who had a short blond hair streaked with light lines of silver. Her beauty, her agelessness never failed to impress him. Her bright blue eyes always knew how to see inside of him, which also never failed to astonish him. She could see into him this very minute, gauging him carefully, causing him to wonder what she saw.

Cal's nephew Brian, who had just turned fourteen, was watching him carefully. "Did you meet any girls, Uncle Cal?"

Michelle and Callie screeched, "No!" While his mother said, "He's far too young!" And Rory laughed. Everyone else just looked confused.

"Brian," Rory started delicately, while his mother and his sisters seemed to relax. "I'm afraid, good old Uncle Cal has indeed met someone. He is head over heels in love." Rory, loving to be the one in the know, grinned as he patted his lips with a cloth napkin. All eyes were on Cal who was glaring at Rory fiercely.

"I don't know about love, per se…" he began, sputtering. He felt like an idiot.

"Is she hot, Uncle Cal?" Brian asked with obvious admiration.

"She is smokin' hot," Rory answered for him. Cal was uncomfortable with this, and noticed Jen shoot Rory a look laced with daggers.

"*Uh*, I have a picture here." He'd had someone at Disney World take their picture with Mickey Mouse. He rummaged in his backpack for a moment before emerging with his digital camera. Once he found the picture, he passed it around. Nervously, he held his breath, anxious to hear what each one of them thought about Madison.

"She's an actual woman." His mother's voice was full of surprise, "Not like that whore you took to the awards show last year." There were many shouts of "Mother" but she shrugged. "Well really, she wasn't the type you bring home. But this girl," she pointed to the LCD screen, "she is the type you bring home. How did you meet her? I hope he didn't meet her shooting pictures for that porn magazine he was in."

"Porn? I've never posed for a porn magazine!" Honestly his mother… "What are you talking about?"

"It was thong, no, *G-String*, I think." Everyone laughed, hard.

"*G-String*, like a guitar string, not a thong. It's a music magazine, not porn." He practically choked on his food as she made an O shape with her mouth. He went back to the subject of Maddy, which he couldn't seem to get enough of. "Her friends brought her to one of our concerts," Cal mentioned casually, hoping everyone would pick up where they'd left off.

"And he hasn't been normal since," Rory finished with a wicked grin on his face.

"So," he turned to his sister Michelle. "When are you due?"

"Three months. It's another girl." She rubbed her belly. Wow.

"Bummer," his nephew Matthew grumbled. They all laughed. Cal felt his father's hand clap him on the back. It was good to be home, even if it were only for a couple of weeks.

∾

Madison had been home for three days, and done her best to avoid her friends. She hadn't avoided Cal's nightly phone calls, but she still didn't have an answer for him. It was puzzling. She just couldn't decide, even though she didn't have a very good reason to stay during the summer. He had emailed tour dates, times of concerts, venues, and hotel possibilities to her. She was still undecided, and someone was knocking on her door. She closed her laptop computer with open possibilities before answering the door.

As she opened the door, Mandy stood there, foam cup of steaming coffee in her hand, her French manicured acrylic nails digging into the side of the cup. "Don't just stand there, silly, let me in." Madison moved aside. Where was Kinley? Mandy looked as though she were making herself comfortable. Madison ducked out of the room and texted Kinley. She just knew she couldn't handle Mandy on her own. Knowing Kinley, she'd be right over in less than ten minutes.

"You caught me in the middle of something, I'll be right out," she called from the bathroom.

"Take your time," Mandy hollered back. Great. Just great. Mandy was the type of woman who other women just didn't like. She was too brash, too blunt. Not to mention the fact that she was a former beauty pageant, Miss Runner-Up something or another. She was petite, curvy and turned grown men into Jell-O. She was working on marriage number three, or four, Madison had lost track. Men loved Mandy, or as she called herself more formally, Amanda. Women hated her. Her hair was perfect, her wardrobe amazing, her eyes the pale blue of wild flowers, she was just hate-able. Then she opened her mouth, and women would think "I wouldn't have guessed that I could hate her any more, but I can." She was the PTA president, and president of anything else she could be. Her two daughters won pageants left and right, and were just as irritating as their mother. What amused Madison and Kinley the most was that Mandy thought women hated her from an overwhelming feeling of jealousy. Nothing could have been further off the mark. They hated her because she was a bitch- nothing more.

The ringing at the doorbell told her Kinley had arrived, right on schedule. She could hear polite conversing so she decided it was time to come back in the room. "Kinley, I wasn't expecting you." She tried to sound surprised, "What a coincidence, Mandy just got here too."

Kinley grinned, "Well you know me, I like to keep you on your toes." It seemed she was the one on her toes, wearing yoga pants, flip-flops, and having her curls pulled back into a very messy ponytail.

"Did you all have a girl's weekend? I couldn't get hold of either of you. What were you two up to over the weekend, hiding out at a spa? Spas are great for dealing with grief." Mandy also hated to be left out of anything, but she wasn't the type you'd go out of your way to hang out with. Being near her was well- like work.

Kinley looked positively wicked, "We were in Florida, special guests of Murder of Crows, we hung out with them all weekend, when we weren't at the spa."

"Oh you are too funny, Kinley." Mandy straightened her beige skirt and cleared her throat, "You've had an offer on the house." She shifted weight in her beige stilettos.

Kinley smiled, "Already? Wow that's great."

Madison slipped out of the room for a moment and sighed. She couldn't do this, or could she? She was relieved when Kinley came and found her after Mandy was gone. "Was she just awful?"

"As awful as you can imagine." Kinley plopped down onto the sofa and picked up the remote control. She sighed heavily, "The things that actually come out of her mouth."

"I know." Madison bit her lip, "I'm sorry I was avoiding you."

"It's fine." She flipped through the channels.

"I want to sell everything, Kin, everything. I want to sell my van and the quads and the trailer, and the boat." She took a breath, "Give all of the toys and things to the Good Will. I can't drive around like I'm a mom; I can't be who I was." Kinley nodded, but stayed silent. "Kin, what's wrong? What aren't you telling me?"

"It's not like that Maddy; I can't do this to you right now. You have a lot going on; it's not the time to be leaning on you."

"There *is* something wrong then."

"Of course there is, and yes it sucks. I can't just spill and vent to my best friend like I used to though. But, it's not the time. I know." Kinley looked down into her lap. "I just can't do that to you." She knew Kinley wasn't trying to be passive-aggressive either, she was sincerely holding it all in, not wanting to burden Madison.

"So, you're leaning on?" It was a long drawn out 'on' at the end of her question, dripping with sarcasm. She knew Ryan lost it the moment anything went wrong, and Kinley held it all together constantly shielding him from any real stress or strain. Their marriage, while sweet, was somewhat one-sided at times. Kinley had always leaned on Madison more than she leaned on Ryan. This had to be affecting her.

"No one," Kinley answered softly.

"I feel like our friendship is totally lopsided right now," Madison said. Like Kinley's marriage, she thought.

"Don't say that…" Kinley begged.

Madison was crying. Both Madison and Kinley had never been what you would call, overly sensitive. Neither of them liked to be around crying people. They both had a hard time with it; comedy was their mutual, natural defense. It usually didn't help the crying person though. She tried to wipe the tears away, and stop the stream, but she couldn't. "No, no, don't do this Maddy, I can't, you know I am terrible at this sort of thing…" Madison couldn't stop.

"Okay, I'll tell you what's wrong," she groaned in defeat. Madison jerked her head up. "Don't say I didn't warn you." Kinley leaned back into the microfiber sofa. "It's Kennedy. She misses Riley so much that we've put her in counseling, she's on medication now, and she's pulling away from all of her other friends. I don't know what to do. Both my girls keep asking for you, they miss you. How am I supposed to tell you, or deal with it? I just don't know what to do. I know you avoid all children like the plague." Now Kinley was crying, "Look how awkward we are when we cry, and neither of us can comfort the other." They both burst out laughing, although they were both still crying.

"I'm coming over to your house then," Madison said softly.

"You can't…I don't think it'd be good for you," Kinley sniffed.

"You have to leave in a few minutes to pick up Kennedy from the bus stop. I'll be at your house when you arrive. No arguments." Kinley sighed as she left. They could talk about the house offer later. Mandy would be furious.

Madison arrived a few minutes before Kinley and she sat down on one of Kinley's cherry red sofas. When Kennedy finally walked in, her head hung low, her backpack slung loosely over her shoulders, with such a dejected expression, she didn't even see Madison. Kinley snuck out of the room. "Mom, can I have a cookie?" Kennedy asked.

"Do you really think a cookie is the healthiest choice for an after school snack?" Madison asked her. She looked up, startled. Her sapphire blue eyes had tears clinging to them, to her long black eyelashes. She dropped her bag where she stood and ran into Madison's outstretched arms.

"Aunt Maddy," she sobbed, "I miss Riley sooooo much." Madison could feel the warmth of the sweet little girl's tears. "I can't do this. I've missed you too, but Mommy said..." She broke off into pathetic gut-wrenching sobs. How blind had she been? Madison had been so beleaguered by her own despair that she'd forgotten her dear little favorite Candy Cane, her nickname for Kennedy. She held the little girl tightly. She hadn't wanted to see her knowing she and Riley had been practically sisters. It was too painful for her but she hadn't thought of how painful it might be for Kennedy. She felt horribly self-centered.

"Does it hurt to see me?" Madison asked as the girl held onto her tightly.

"Yes, but not like I thought it would." Her tears were calming. She sat up and brushed them over the top of her cheekbones. "It mostly feels good to see you."

"I was scared to see you," Madison confessed. "I didn't know what I would feel either." Kennedy nodded, even at the age of eight, she understood. She pushed her light blond ringlets out of her face. "It mostly feels good to see you too. Although, there is this little ache." Kennedy understood this too. "Because most of the time when we would see each other Riley was there." Kennedy snuggled into her arms and she could hear a soft 'yes'. "Your mother told me that you're pushing your friends away." Madison hadn't wanted the tears to come, but they were. She would have defied anyone not to cry looking at little Kennedy.

"Yes," Kennedy answered. "They don't understand why I'm so sad. They say I need to stop. But I can't, I just can't. They keep telling me it's been a long time." Kennedy shuddered.

Madison nodded. "I've had people tell me that too. You're right, they don't understand. They don't know that we will never get over it."

"We won't?" Kennedy looked up at her with those innocent big blue eyes.

"No, but I hear it gets easier the more time that goes by. It did hurt a lot more at first didn't it?" Kennedy nodded. "Yes it hurts a lot still, but it's slightly better than it was."

"Yes, I suppose," Kennedy conceded. "Sometimes when I am on the playground I think I hear her, and it's not her. Does that happen to you?"

"All the time," Madison whispered. "I hear them all the time." She leaned her head on the top of that little girl's and wept. It was the first time she'd really truly talked about how she felt.

"My mom said that whatever I feel…you feel a hundred billion, infinity times worse," Kennedy told her. Madison laughed through her tears. "That has to be really bad."

"It really is. Some days I don't want to get out of bed," Madison admitted.

"Me too. A lot of days," Kennedy sighed.

"What do you think Riley would want us to do about that?"

"I don't know," she answered timidly.

"I think you do, you were her best friend in the world."

"She wouldn't want me to be so sad. She would tell me to make new friends, and maybe even a new 'best' friend. But, I can't just have another best friend! She was the best 'best' friend ever!" Kennedy was loyal to the bitter end.

"I have many 'best friends', Candy Cane. I have your mom who is my 'best' best friend, and then there's Kate and Megan. I don't know what I'd do without them."

"So I can have different kinds of best friends?" Kennedy was thoughtful.

"Definitely."

"And Riley wouldn't mind?"

"I know she won't mind," Madison cried softly. "Did you know your mother is really worried about you?"

"Really?"

"Yes, and I was thinking she is worried about me too."

"She is; she always worries about you. All the time," Kennedy answered. "What can we do for her?" Madison hugged the little girl even tighter. Visions of Kennedy and Riley came into her mind. Two of a kind, blond little things, running through her house, giggling, or singing on their American Idol video game. It was heart rending, but the memories were happy ones. Riley had been a happy little girl. Madison kissed the top of Kennedy's head.

"I was hoping you had an idea Kennedy."

"I think we could try to be less sad for her. She cries for you, and she must cry for me too. I think it's like you said, I can have more than one best friend, and so can you. I can find new people to love, that doesn't mean that I have forgotten Riley. She is still my best friend, and she always will be. I'm just adding new people to love, not taking anyone away. It's okay to keep living and to find new people to love," Kennedy spoke softly but her words hit Madison hard. Madison wasn't sure how to digest this information. In her own childlike way, Kennedy had given Madison invaluable advice. And to think....she had come here to help Kennedy.

13. Don't Get So Excited

He was in bed, enveloped in silky sheets, holding Madison in his arms. He pressed his lips to hers and began to envision all of the things he wanted to do to her. "Maddy," he said simply. Not even a second later, he could see his mother's face hovering over him and the woman of his dreams, "Maddy, is that her name?" He awoke with a start, on his mother's chesterfield, looking over at his mother who was in a plush chair sitting across from him, eyeing him over the top of a book she was reading.

"Calvin Kenneth Hunt, what is the matter with you?" He hated when she used all three names.

"Nothing," he lied. What a delicious dream he'd been having, well, at least until it had become disturbing. How quickly dreams can become nightmares.

"Her name is Maddy then?"

"Dear God above was I talking in my sleep?" Cal pulled a pillow onto his face.

"Yes dear, but you don't need to bring God into it, I expect he'd rather not be anywhere near you, especially after number 6." She grinned slyly at him. "Down and dirty, indeed."

"Her name is Madison," he sighed, and sat up. "And I'm not so evil that I can't mention God every now and then. According to you he loves all of his children, even the wayward ones who write carnal lyrics."

"This is true," she mumbled. "Madison is a very pretty name. Is she a nice girl?" Why did he feel like he was in school again, being grilled about a date he'd had. There had been too few back in those days. All he'd cared about was the band- band practice, getting gigs, buying guitars and so on.

"She's not a girl, she's thirty-one."

"Oh, a woman." He knew she knew this already. "How nice." Why did he feel that she was about to drop a bomb on him? "Has she been married before, had any children?"

He truly didn't know and thank heaven his phone rang at that moment. "Hello?"

"I didn't wake you did I?"

"Madison?"

"Yes, I needed to hear your voice." His mouth dropped open in shock.

"This is the first time you've ever called me." He was in awe; he'd have to write the date down somewhere. This was unbelievable. Did it mean she returned his affections? He could only hope. She'd been warm and inviting, but somehow aloof all at the same time.

"Are you sure? I thought I called you before..." Her voice trailed off into uncertainty.

"Positive." He couldn't stop himself from grinning. It was so good to hear her voice. He got up and walked away from his mother, leaving her to guess at what they were discussing. "And you haven't accepted my friendship on Facebook; I'm beginning to think you don't care. Then you call me- it better not be to tell me goodbye- I refuse, if that's the case."

She laughed; it was the sweetest sound. "No- wait who are you on Facebook?"

It was his turn to laugh, "*Um*, Ben A. Longtime." She was cracking up, and he couldn't help but join in.

"I thought it was some kind of joke! It had a picture of a huge beautiful dog." She was still laughing. "I ignored it. I thought Megan was pulling off another brilliant joke, she's a professional jokester; but she's brilliant I'll have you know."

"Megan is funny, but no, that was me. That's my dog, by the way, but I won't tell you his name for fear of upsetting you."

"Now, I'm curious, is it something naughty?" He could hear the intrigue in her voice.

"*Nah*, his name is Zeppelin, but we all call him Zeppy for short." She was laughing again. He realized he enjoyed it more than anything else. "I've only had him a short while."

"I have a confession to make; I called you for a reason." His heart stopped, his breathing stood still. "I want to come to England to see you, and bring Kinley with me. She's always wanted to go, and I don't think I could come without her. I can buy our tickets; it's not a problem, but I wanted you to know, I do want to see you." Now his heart was racing, and he felt giddy, like he could jump around and dance, and sing.

"I can make arrangements for you…" he began.

"That's not necessary. I have a little money and it will be fun, you know?" Madison replied, though her tone was little anxious.

"Maddy, I really want to do this. It would cost me less than it would for you. The sad, but true fact of the matter is, people are always offering me deals, as if I need them. And like I said before, I am doing rather well for myself." He was feeling intoxicated with joy.

"I don't want you to feel obligated…" She had pride; he liked that.

"You an obligation? Ha, I don't think so. You're more of a vision, something unearthly, a woman with ethereal beauty. I can't even sleep without seeing you in my dreams. I want to do this, please allow me the pleasure of doing something for you?"

"Alright," she answered softly. "You really feel that way about me? I'm just your average ordinary woman," Madison replied.

"Then you are not seeing yourself clearly," he told her.

"Cal, thanks for making me feel happy."

Though he could hear the happiness in her voice, he began to hear something else in the background. It was a high, shrill complaining voice. "What's going on here, Madison? Are you on the phone with a *man*?" The voice belonged to an older woman, he was certain. But in previous conversations, she'd told him that she and her mother were estranged. "Who is there with you Maddy?" he asked.

"Cal, I have to go. I will call you later."

She was gone in an instant and he was left to contemplate the voice in the background. Who had she been? He felt a mild irritation. Why did he always have more questions when it came to Maddy?

∾

"Debbie, it's my life; I have to live it," Madison told her mother-in-law as she hung up the phone.

"I ran into Mandy Murphy this morning at Target," Debbie began, and Madison thought-here we go. "She told me you're selling everything, the house, the boat, the trailer, and the quads. Those were Jack's favorite things!"

Madison took a deep breath. She'd secretly been wondering when the glass would shatter and everything would return to normal. Debbie had never liked Madison. She'd never thought Madison was good enough for her only child to marry. She and Debbie had a shallow relationship at best. The one thing that kept Debbie around was the grandkids. She loved them more than life itself. It had been a year and half since she'd lost her husband Jonathan to terminal cancer and now she'd lost her only child and every single grandchild. Madison was the only link to what had been. They'd bonded over the deaths, but Madison knew it was as temporary as a Band-Aid. She knew the feelings Debbie possessed for her ran too deep, and could not be forgotten even through the death of every person she loved.

"And now you're talking to another man!" Debbie cried. "Jack hasn't even been gone a year! What would the kids think? Are you getting rid of all of their things too, or just Jack's? I can't believe this." She was pacing and crying, always a bad sign. "I haven't even cleared out Jonathan's study and here you are, nine months later, selling every possession Jack prized!" She was clearly losing it. Madison hugged her and led her over to the sofa. She also handed her a tissue.

"I *am* grieving. I am far from being over losing Jack, or my children. I can't mourn the way you do. Living in this house, surrounded by these things, it's killing me! Do you understand I am literally dying! It's more than a study, Debbie; it's every damned thing this house stands for. You and Jonathan were retired; you bought a cozy little house, which stood for retirement, living out the rest of your days together. This house," she gestured to all around her, "represents a family. Five bedrooms! Three bathrooms, a living room filled with video games and children's DVDs, everywhere I walk, I see them, I hear them. I can't do this! We bought the van so I could drive around with four children! We bought the boat, the trailer the quads, for vacations! I cannot even imagine doing all of those things without them. I can't live like this; I will either lose my mind to insanity, or die. Those are my two choices…and I know Jack would not want that for me." She finished her tirade nearly breathless. She didn't need to explain speaking to Cal.

Cal was for her alone.

After Debbie was gone Madison fell apart. Her sorrow consumed her, capsizing her like a great ship in the deep. Did Debbie want her to lose her mind? As it was she couldn't stop hearing them, or thinking she saw them in rare moments. Her memories were potent, concentrated, too strong at times. She needed them to be dimmer, faded. It hadn't maybe crossed Debbie's mind that in two weeks Alex and Jackson would be five, would have been five. She couldn't stay here and listen to the ghosts of parties past, the haunting laughter echoing from happier times. She had to get out before that date, even if it meant leaving before everything was settled.

14. Damn Rory The Know-It-All

Cal sat on hold with his assistant Joey; together they were working out the travel arrangements for Maddy and Kinley. He stared out the window, the sun was shining, but it was freezing as hell out there. Movement caught his eye and he glanced up to see Rory and Gabe walking up the drive, deep in conversation. He shrugged and turned around as Joey's voice came through loudly after all of that obnoxious silence. "Okay, Cal, it's all worked out. I can email her the itinerary if you give me her email address."

The door opened, letting a freezing, biting wind enter with his brother and bodyguard Gabe. "I'd rather do it, so forward it to me. I want it to be a little more personal than, 'hey I had my assistant forward travel plans to you', know what I mean?"

"Cal, I know it's not my place but, what do you know about her? She could be after you for your money," Joey's voice quivered. Cal paused to control his temper, reasoning that it had taken all of Joey's will power to say what he had, and he'd done it out of concern. He scowled as Rory came up next to him.

"She's not after my money, Joey, it's not like that, okay. I appreciate your concern but…" Rory had ripped the phone from Cal's grasp, and not lightly either.

"Joe, my man, relax, she is no gold-digger. I can vouch for her personally."

Cal pulled the phone away from his brother, and shoved him for good measure, "Talk to you later, Joey." Cal stared at Rory, "What the hell was that?"

Gabe walked in, snacking on a freshly baked cinnamon roll from the kitchen, "Your mom is amazing." He smiled. "What is going on with you two?"

"I was just telling Joey that Cal's girlfriend is not a gold-digger," Rory told Gabe.

"How would you know, Rory?" Cal fumed.

"Easy, Gabe told me." He walked off. "Mom those cinnamon rolls smell so good," he called out.

Cal was holding onto the phone with enough pressure, he was afraid it might be crushed and rendered useless. "Gabe, I wasn't even worried about that, why would you even check up on her?"

"Because Cal, you're like a brother to me, and you have been for the last ten years. I needed to know, I've never seen you become so serious about anyone. I would have told you if I found anything suspicious."

"Why tell Rory?" Cal glared, knowing that Gabe could easily see through the front.

"Cause he was concerned too, had to put his mind at ease." Gabe patted him on the back and began to walk away, "Can I have another cinnamon roll, Mrs. Hunt?" Cal reluctantly followed after him. Why did he feel there was some circle of information going on, and he was on the outside looking in? The kitchen did smell divine, he sat down on a barstool and his mother passed him a plate, the cinnamon roll was still steaming. He grumbled as he began pulling it apart, watching the cream cheese frosting ooze onto his fingertips. His mother smiled at him, that knowing kind of smile all mothers seemed to possess, before she left the kitchen.

"Rory."

"Yeah?" Rory was devouring a roll with a look of great satisfaction on his face.

"*Um*, I've never done this before…and…I was wondering if you had any advice?" Cal was literally tripping over his words. Rory was going to tease him relentlessly. To his surprise, Rory looked up, interested.

"You never dated anyone seriously before, and you want to know how to?" Rory popped a piece of hot cinnamon roll into his mouth. How did he know? Cal hadn't exactly been eloquent in his plea. Cal nodded. Gabe sat across from Rory and grinned at him. He wished he knew what Gabe knew, but then again, it was probably nothing.

"Well, you have to do things for her. Have you sent her flowers yet?"

"Not exactly. I had them put all over her room in Florida, does that count?" He wasn't too surprised when Rory shook his head, "Is that what normal guys do?"

"Definitely," Rory grinned. "And since you're you, meaning rich and famous, you should do other thoughtful things like, I don't know, send her a CD of your favorite music, or better yet send her one of you singing *her* favorite songs." Cal liked this idea. Rory had some good stuff to share. "*Um*, oh, and show up and surprise her. Make sure the timing is right with her friend first and just take her out on the town. You can do that." Rory shoved the rest of his roll into his mouth before getting up off his seat and looking for another one. "Our mother should be sainted." Cal smiled to himself. How did one send someone flowers? Was this type of thing supposed to be innate? Should he have known all of these things before? He began plotting and thinking about asking her what her favorite songs were. Would she even like something like that? Maybe. But the favorite songs of his were out. She hated Led Zeppelin. Who hates Led Zeppelin? A woman who wasn't afraid to share her opinion, that's who; he smiled.

≈

Madison drove her mini-van down toward LA. Kinley fiddled with her iPod until she got to a song they both liked. "Are you sure I'm doing the right thing?" Madison asked for at least the twelfth time that morning.

"Does it matter what I think? What do you think?" Kinley asked her.

"I think this car says 'soccer mom'," Madison told her.

"Then, you should get something the opposite of 'soccer mom'. Why not look at something you've always wanted to drive?"

"What I've always wanted is ridiculously expensive," she muttered.

"Having looked over your finances, I must say, you can afford it, whatever it is," Kinley countered. She was right. Madison had received money from their insurance and the settlement from the trucking company, and still had it all sitting in a bank account. She should invest it maybe, but she was just not ready to do anything with it. It didn't seem fair to receive money when people died. Sure, it represented a little less than Jack's yearly income multiplied by ten, but that didn't mean she could just spend it. But, selling her house, trading in her car, and selling the boat and all the other things would add up. She didn't like to think of the settlement money ever.

She spotted a row of dealerships with gleaming cars propped up, and sitting in rows. "Look Kinley," Madison pointed at the Porsche dealer-ship with their fair share of gleaming cars in front. "I've always loved Porsches."

"Yeah, me too. Look at the red one."

"I know, but we should keep on driving to the Honda dealership," she muttered, unable to take her eyes off the cherry red *Carrera* just sitting there.

"Let's at least go test drive the thing," Kinley prodded. "It won't hurt."

"No, I couldn't, it's not practical," Madison frowned.

"Maddy, let's just have a little fun. Why not? Just test-drive it. Who cares? It might be entertaining." Kinley had her half-way convinced. Madison gazed wistfully at the dealership. "I brought a bank statement if they need to see it." Kinley's argument was won.

"What the hell." And she drove into the parking lot.

She and Kinley got out and looked around in the front. A saleswoman approached them, teetering on five inch high stilettos and wearing a fake smile. "Can I help you?" It was more of a 'are you two lost?' than a 'can I help you?' as she onced over the minivan with a look of cool disdain. Madison began to speak when the girl cut her off, "Seriously, a minivan? Do you need to use the bathroom or are you lost?"

Kinley hadn't been the same since the accident either. She was always on edge lately, and unfortunately for the sales girl, it didn't take much to push her over. "Are you prejudiced against all of your potential customers? She can afford whatever you're selling." She pointed at Madison, "So find someone without the attitude who will help us, because she is here to buy. We won't be dealing with you any further, now shoo."

Kinley actually shooed her away. She skittered away on her heels, looking both humiliated and very angry. She didn't even try a rebuttal. "Was I too mean?" Kinley asked as regret appeared to be setting in.

"Maybe, but it was too funny!"

"I really need to take it down a notch. Perhaps I should apologize. I just can't stand it when someone gets all snooty like that," Kinley muttered under her breath.

A man came out, obviously having been warned of Kinley's ferocity, and was much friendlier. He must have been 'the guy' to call when someone was disgruntled. "What can I do for you lovely ladies this afternoon?"

"I would like to test drive a *Carrera*," Madison said.

"Did you have a particular one in mind?" he asked, with near reverence.

"The red one in front."

It was nearly two hours later that Madison and Kinley were riding home in Maddy's new Porsche. "I can't believe you told that lady off, and I can't believe I bought this thing! I bet that's the first minivan they ever received on trade in." The two women laughed merrily.

"I'm so glad! It's a solid investment. Ryan's uncle still drives his Porsche from the seventies, it's a classic, and it's super-fast." Their music was pumped up. "I do feel bad about letting that lady have it. Perhaps I should..."

"Let it go, Kin, she was a cow," Madison chuckled. She stared at her hands on the leather steering wheel. "I've never done anything like this before," Madison admitted.

"I know, Maddy, but here's the thing, life is too short. As we both already know." Madison nodded in full agreement. "And now it's time to think of *you*. And...if anyone deserves to have nice things, like Porsches and townhouses it's you."

"What do you think Kate and Megan will say?" Madison wondered aloud.

"They'll probably think you're crazy. Well, I guess you're not driving to girl's night tonight. We can't all fit in here." She glanced at the two seats laughing. The car pulled up to Kate's house. Kate and Megan must have seen them driving up because they were already outside staring in awe at the beautiful cherry red Porsche 911 *Carrera*.

"Madison, what were you thinking?" Kate asked first.

While Megan turned on Kinley, "I thought you went with her! How could you let her do this?"

"Settle down guys, she has the money. It's what she wanted. Now, it's all worked out, can we get going? I'm starving." Kinley grinned. They both stared at her as though snakes were writhing on top of her head instead of windblown curls. Kinley was her constant deflector.

15. Sometimes Life Just Sucks

Madison was wise enough to know some days would be harder than others. Some weeks, were worse than other weeks. This week had been particularly brutal. Perhaps she was changing too much too quickly. Within the week she'd sold her house, (she was now in escrow), sold her husband's boat, and their trailer. She'd had an offer on the quads, which she planned on accepting. That had been exhausting. Now, she was thinking of all the days this week, this one was the hardest. She was driving, in silence with Kinley; they'd carpooled to school. She had gotten a D on her test, while Kinley barely pulled off a low C.

It would have been bad enough knowing it was the twins' birthday, but it had been more than that. She'd tried to distract herself to the point of exhaustion. She'd had dreams where her children asked for specific toys. She thought her wedding anniversary had been hard. This was so much worse, and there were two more birthdays this year, and August the nineteenth, the day they had all been taken from her. This first birthday was enough to put her in the grave with them.

She drove to Fuddruckers, their favorite place for milkshakes. She didn't even have to ask Kinley, she knew Kinley would be up for it. Her day hadn't been so great either. Before Madison started the grueling task of packing, she'd invited Kinley and her two daughters over. In her mind, Riley would have wanted Kennedy to have anything she wanted. So, Madison had offered Kennedy a box and told her to take anything she liked. Kennedy had gone bravely into the room, but they'd found her ten minutes later, curled up into a fetal position sobbing on the floor. It took Kinley a half an hour to pull her out of it. Madison sat in that room and offered her daughter's things to that weeping child.

It had taken everything in her not to drop down on the floor and weep with Kennedy. Then, she didn't know what was worse, Kennedy's little heart breaking so obviously, or the way Kinley's older daughter McKenna tried so hard to put a brave face on and appear stoic, while she was clearly suffering too. McKenna and Jonathan had been close too, but McKenna suffered in silence which made her slightly less noticeable. Kinley had tried hard to comfort both girls. Madison knew if the beyond painful situation had been reversed, Riley wouldn't have handled losing Kennedy very well either. Madison gave McKenna some of Jonathan's video games and comics she'd loved. And as if that weren't enough, they didn't have much time to soothe the girls before dropping them off with Ryan and heading out to school.

They both had studied so hard, and even Kinley who had an exceptional memory for pointless information, hadn't done well. They sat at Fuddruckers; there was no need to talk. They'd both gone through hell and were eating for comfort. She learned, however, that the moment one thinks things can't get any worse, they usually can. "Maddy Leblanc?" She wanted to die. "Oh, wait, it's Grey now, isn't it?" The voice was an old familiar one. Chase Bertram was an old friend from high school. They'd fallen out of touch over the years. "Kinley Michaelson? Of course you're still friends. How are you guys?"

Kinley grimaced as he hugged her, then turned to hug Madison. "You both haven't changed a bit." He was one of those friends who hadn't aged well, his hairline had receded, his waist line had increased, but his smile was completely jovial. His brown hair was cut short; his brown eyes twinkled with delight. "Do you both still live here in town?" They nodded. "It's been so long, I moved to Montana, but I'm back now."

"What brings you back?" Madison asked. She and Kinley always managed to fake interest, she couldn't help her apathy after the day she'd had.

"I got a job back out here. So, you two on a girl's night?" Madison nodded. "How is Jack doing? You probably have kids too!" Oh, Chase, why? She nearly choked on her milkshake. Kinley the deflector was back on the scene.

"Chase, did you ever get married? I heard you were something of a playboy, you wicked thing." Kinley's voice was light and teasing, he would have never known what she was covering up.

"I did, only recently. What about you, are you still married?"

"Of course."

"I always thought you and Maddy were taken off the market way to soon. That Jack was lucky, and so is your husband," Chase flattered. "Well, I'd better be going."

"Look us up on Facebook, don't be a stranger." He walked away, allowing Kinley to lean in and whisper to her, "What a Sharleen." Madison chuckled in her misery. A Sharleen was a person who had once been hot, had their glory days in their youth, only to age very badly.

Madison didn't say a word, couldn't. What if Cal asked her questions? She couldn't be away from Kinley. She realized she was clinging desperately to her friend, but no one would have understood. What would she have done if Kinley hadn't been here? Her phone rang and she stupidly picked it up. "Ms. Grey?" She didn't recognize the voice, but he identified himself quickly, "This is Professor Linden, I wanted to speak to you about your test this evening."

Kinley looked mildly interested, while Madison answered back so Kinley would know exactly what was going on, "Yes, Professor Linden, it was an off day, I will do better next time." Kinley's eyes got bigger, and then she shook her head. Could this day get any worse?

"I heard from a little bird, who overheard you and Ms. Brooke speaking, that you have recently lost a child. I am terribly sorry for your loss." It was the damned proverbial straw breaking the damned proverbial camel's back. Her breath caught. She sobbed, people were staring, and Kinley was pulling the phone away from her.

"Professor Linden, is everything all right? This is Kinley Brooke." Madison could hear as she sobbed into her napkin. "Yes, it's a very delicate situation if you must know." She listened. "Yes," she cleared her throat. "You see, our eldest children are six months apart, and our youngest are two weeks apart. My children are connected to hers, like cousins really." She paused again to listen, "She lost every one of them, all four, and her husband. Yes, that was her in the news..." More soft breathing, she hated curious people. "No, it was just a hard day for both of us." She nodded as she listened, "Thank you Professor, we appreciate it so much. Good night."

"He's letting us make up the tests, although I think crying women freak him out, he said he'd email the details. I'm thinking that was wise," Kinley whispered across the surfboard shaped table. "Today was awful." She finally voiced what they'd both been thinking. "Come on, take me home, and tomorrow will be a better day. Besides we need to be rested for lunch with the girls."

Madison dropped Kinley off before heading out to the cemetery. A monument was under construction, honoring her family, at the top of a hill. She made the climb there in the darkness, using a tiny flashlight on her keychain to guide her. She felt the darkness, as though it were more than just something to look at. It was again her shroud. She touched the stone, smooth and rough granite. People around the city had donated, pulled together for this monument. She leaned against it, and softly sang happy birthday as tears coursed over her cheeks. She hated leaving, cold, and lonely. What if Jack had survived? She often thought of him in moments like this. She needed someone to lean on, but he was gone too. Would their marriage have survived the loss? Oh, Jack, she cried to no one, I need you.

When she got to her new townhouse, she flopped down onto the sofa. She didn't have a new bed yet, but she didn't care. Everything had to be new to this place. She was here, free of old scents, old furniture, old things to be left behind. She didn't want to drag old memories along. She sprawled on the new leather, softest leather ever, sofa and melted into it. Her phone rang, and she debated whether to answer it or not. She gave in, "Hello?"

"You sound terrible," Cal pointed out. Did he know she'd been crying?

"Oh, I just had the worst day ever," she sighed.

"Care to talk about it, or talk around it?" Cal could be so adorable.

"Around it, but I will say one thing, I hate nosy people." She thought of the girl Alyssa, (the little bird on Linden's shoulder) who had been listening to her and Kinley before class.

"Me too. Although, I imagine nosy people are different to each of us. For instance, while we were touring in America, a horrid paparazzi man followed my sister around, and then pasted all over the tabloids that she was pregnant, and Rory and I were to be uncles again. I thought it was obnoxious, but what do I know?"

"That is awful." She sniffed. "I just failed a test, no big deal, and so did Kinley. We both had the crappiest day, and we were talking just before class started. Some little eavesdropping student sat there listening to our conversation. The professor is going to let me and Kin make up the test because he felt sorry for us. I didn't want that, but I'm relieved." She paused, the silence made her nervous, "Sorry, I'm just rambling on." She couldn't bring up running into Chase Bertram without explaining why it had upset her so much. She let that one go.

"No, it's fine. What a bitch…" He laughed. "But hey, you get a second chance."

"True, so does Kinley. If I were feeling happy I would have teased her. Awesome memory and she got a C? What is that about?" She really couldn't share anything else. Oh, there's more, Alex and Jackson would have been five today. Who are they? Just my beautiful little twins who aren't here anymore.

"What happened that has you both so upset?" He actually sounded concerned.

How could she put it? How to word it exactly right? "Kinley's daughters both had a difficult day today. They've recently lost a friend." She didn't have to tell him that they each lost friends, or even that they were related to her, did she? "Little Kennedy could break the heart of a stoic. It was just really hard to see. And McKenna putting on her brave face. It was just painful." It was again the best she could do.

"Kinley has kids," he said the statement with a weird tone. "I guess she's a mom, and I never thought about it. I haven't ever asked her either. And although I always think of her as a kindred spirit, I always find myself more interested in you." Her heart was beating fast, too fast. "Madison, what would cheer you up?" She thought about it, seriously there was nothing coming to mind. That was the thing her friends hated most about helping her. Normally, they could all help one another, but the moment of the accident, they each felt helpless, and powerless. She sighed. "You don't know, do you?"

"Nope, haven't a clue." She laughed a horrid, hollow laugh. She was grateful he didn't feel pity for her. Everyone who knew looked at her with the inevitable pity in their stares. They couldn't help it. He didn't know he was supposed to feel sorry for her, so he didn't. Perhaps it was normalcy she craved desperately. They talked well into the night, until she fell asleep clutching the phone, thinking she could probably fall for this guy, which frightened her nearly to the point of death.

The next morning, closer to afternoon, she moved from the sofa, stiff and sore. She had to buy a bed; that was it. But when would she find time? She refused to bring her marriage bed over to the townhouse. A knock on the door echoed through the eerily empty spaces around her. Wood floors, nothing on the walls, and nothing in the entire place but a sofa, loveseat, a big comfy chair, and a coffee table. There was a lone lamp in the corner of the room. It was sparser than a new student's apartment.

She rubbed her eyes and stumbled blindly toward the door. There stood a man with a dozen sterling roses in a vase. "Are you Madison Grey?" he asked, with an odd little smirk/smile on his face. She nodded. "You are loved, that is all I have to say." He turned his head and called out behind him, "This is her!" He wiped his feet on the welcome mat, "May we come in?"

She moved aside, in a daze, "*We?*" He was followed by half a dozen more men and women each carrying roses, there were red, yellow, pink, white, green, blue, slightly red, redder still, white with pink tips, purple, a golden yellow, black and red, and more. Vases of roses came in like a parade and filled the dull emptiness of her townhouse. Before he left, the main deliveryman handed her a card and asked her to sign for all the roses. There were enough to fill an entire store. Thankfully, there were no lilies; the fragrance sent her over the edge. Roses reminded her of love, while lilies and carnations screamed funeral to her. She looked around and moments later Kinley pulled up to her door.

Kinley smiled as she walked in. "When he does something, he really does it well," she muttered. "Ooh I love the sterling ones," she breathed in.

"I don't know what you told him but flowers arrived for my girls this morning, with gigantic teddy bears and chocolates." Tears welled up in her eyes, "Thank you."

"This is where normal people would hug," Madison pointed out.

Kinley laughed and hugged her. "Thanks Maddy."

"Did he send you flowers too?" Madison inquired.

"Yes."

Madison opened her card and read Cal's sweet words.

> *Maddy,*
>
> *I hope this makes you smile, and surrounds you with beauty. Know that you are adored, and that I am wishing you a wonderful day!*
>
> *From the man who adores you!*
> *Cal*

Kinley snorted, "Adore! *Ha*, doesn't he realize he's in love with you?"

"That's not true, Kin, adore is a good word." Madison shivered as she turned away. "I need to get dressed. I didn't realize how late it was."

"Maddy," Kinley was following her, making a path through the roses, "he's in love with you, if ever anyone was in love with you." Madison didn't want to hear this. "I know you're terrified of having your heart broken, and he's got the potential to do it. I know. But, hear me out for a moment. He also has the potential to make you happy again. Don't you think he might be worth taking a chance on?"

Madison swung around, shaking her head, "Kin, can't you just hear Jack saying, 'Hello, it hasn't even been a year, not even cold in my grave yet!'"

"I so can hear him saying that." She grinned. "But Cal is eventually going to want to know everything, and you're either going to have to spill, or..." she paused, "lie better than you ever have before."

Madison sat down on the edge of her bathtub, while Kinley stood leaning in the doorway, "I don't want to tell him just yet, you know? He doesn't pity me. He doesn't give me *that* look, and it's quite refreshing."

"It sucks. I think the fairytale part is wearing off, and reality is settling in. I wish there was something I could do." Kinley gave her a sad little smile. "I've got to go, Maddy, I'm headed off to the provision depot, do you need anything?"

"Actually, could you pick me up some bleach?"

"No problem, I'll bring it by later when I swing by to pick you up for lunch." Kinley walked away leaving Madison alone with her thoughts, which was a very precarious place to be. Madison spent the rest of the morning deep in thought; her pensiveness had something of a soporific effect on her. She collapsed on the sofa, exhausted from grief. She missed her family, but she also missed herself. She missed her relationship with Kinley, which now felt as though it had somehow evolved into something else entirely. Perhaps it was her longing for the past which put her into the dream, her dreams were often as thought provoking as her waking moments. She was driving her van, reliving an event which had actually happened. It was a silly memory, one without a point, but it felt bittersweet to go through it all again. How carefree they once had been!

"Kin, I'm going to be there in fifteen." She heard her voice, so light and unaffected, ringing in her own ears. She knew what would happen, and yet she went along with it. There was a sort of peaceful, beauty to it, which she felt to be indescribable. It was as if she were able to relive her whimsical past, without pain, for a few brief moments. It was refreshing, delightful, and beautiful, to see Kinley and 'Maddy' as they used to be. The 'Madison' of the past knew no great sorrows.

"Is this K-time or an accurate RETA?"

"Real estimated time of arrival, Kin." K-time meant running fifteen minutes late at least, which was how Kinley did things, all the time. "Be out front."

"My make-up!" Kinley began to argue, but Madison cut her off.

"No one on your back-up list is going to be there! It's the provision depot, in Valencia, on a Thursday morning." Madison raced over to Kinley's house after she stopped by Starbucks on the way, for Chai tea lattes. She was not standing in the pre-appointed spot as previously discussed. Madison leaned on the horn. She came out with her make-up bag. "Seriously, Kin? Where are *you* going? *I'm* going to the depot." The provision depot was what they called the grocery store for their own personal amusement. She and

Kinley had not mentioned the word 'provision' since before the accident occurred, at least not until today. Their goofiness had gone out of both of them.

"Yes, I realize you're in your *go-to* outfit of choice, Uggs, black yoga pants and a sweat shirt." Kinley began to apply make-up as Madison drove away, giving her a dirty look. "I dressed up for *you*, Maddy."

"I'll look like your Sherpa and tragically, I didn't even shower." Madison giggled. "I can't believe we were just at the gym a half an hour ago, and you're ready for a night on the town."

"Unlike you, Maddy, I like to shower right away, rather than stew in my own juices."

Madison scrunched up her nose with disgust. "I was picking up my house," Madison retorted. "I had to take advantage of the quiet time; the twins are only in preschool two days a week." She twisted her lips, before steering left and turning the corner, "Are you going to watch *Grey's* tonight?"

"Only if you watch *Bones*," Kinley offered.

"That's a no then."

They pulled up to the store, Maddy parked, while Kinley put the finishing touches on her makeup, puckering her lips and sweeping her lipstick over them. Madison let the radio play, while the deejay announced, "Here's another five songs to get you over the hump-day."

"Did she say hump-day? Damned Veteran's Day threw me off. I thought it was Thursday." Kinley looked up, screwing the lid onto her mascara back into place. They both grabbed their phones and checked the date, "Oh crap, it's minimum day! Who is going to pick up our kids? It's your turn and we're together," Madison said.

"I'm sorry; I honestly thought it was Thursday. How disappointing, no *Grey's* or *Bones*," Kinley groaned. As they walked in, Madison glanced down at her phone again. Madison couldn't complain, she'd thought it was Thursday too.

"I don't mean to scare you but we have to be back to the bus stop in thirty minutes, and it took twenty minutes to get here," Madison pointed out. "How many items are on your list of provisions?"

"Like thirty-ish. How many on yours?"

"Damn, I only have five. How many provisions can you do without?" Kinley looked over her list, taking out a pen, glancing over it, "Hurry, we can't leave eight year olds outside, unattended with no key…" Madison complained.

"Okay, I can cut it down to ten."

"Ten? Well, okay, it's disappointing but we can make it work. Move it, move it." Madison grabbed a cart and rushed, Kinley barely keeping up. "Kin, we can't run on K-time right now." Kinley teetered in her cute high heeled boots.

"But Maddy, we passed the syrup!" She was pointing backward, "I need that!"

"No you don't," Madison told her as they rounded the corner and she reached out and grabbed a bunch of bananas. "Essential items only."

"What qualifies as essential?" Kinley whined as she threw her arms out, in frustration, trailing behind Madison on the cereal aisle. Their voices were quite loud; people probably heard them from a few aisles over. Other customers were staring, but Madison didn't have time to worry about that now.

"You can't have a stockpile of it at home…"

"But I like to have extras, you never know- and my coupons are going to expire…" Kinley was still behind her, unable to keep up. Madison was about to grab her hand and pull her along as though she were a small child lagging about.

"Kin, if you have it at home you don't *need* it." Madison headed for the check out.

"Fine, I just need to grab a milk," Kinley morosely grumbled.

"Good, cause I only need one more thing- tampons."

"Couldn't tell," Kinley muttered. "But if you 'stockpiled' things like me you would have them already." Kinley reached out and grabbed a gallon of milk. "I can't believe I just cut my list of thirty things, down to one." Madison grabbed her hand and pulled her away from a display of cookies. "Quit rushing me, damn it, you're stressing me out!"

They stood in line, Kinley clicking her tongue with disapproval as she glanced down at her useless list. "Excuse me, but I couldn't help but overhear you both throughout the whole store. You *must* be sisters." A woman behind them had begun to speak to them.

"We're not." Madison hastily barked instructions to the cashier, "Can you just add her milk to my order?" Kin was about to protest, "We don't have time."

"Are you sure you're not related?" Why would the woman behind them not let it go? "Because I only talk to my sister like that," she chuckled.

"We've been best friends for twenty wonderful, fun-filled years," Kinley replied with a small hint of sarcasm leaking out in her words. Madison smiled to the woman before hurrying out to the car with her cart, "Maddy, I'm getting blisters. I can't run in these things." Kinley was, as before, a few feet behind her, now tiptoeing in her boots.

"Who wears shoes like that to the store anyway?" Madison called out. She'd already begun loading groceries into the trunk of the van.

Kinley yelled, "Don't forget the milk, my Sherpa." She climbed into the car, while Madison closed the trunk.

Madison woke up, smiling, worries gone for a single second. How nice it felt. She missed how they were, she'd somehow forgotten. She felt out of touch with who they once had been. She picked up the phone and dialed Kinley's number. "Hello, Maddy," Kinley answered brightly. "Hey impatient one, I'll be there in a minute with your bleach, I only just checked out."

Madison laughed. "It's so good to have your own personal Sherpa."
"What?"
"Do you remember when we went to the store, and I rushed you?"
"Which time?" Kinley playfully asked.
"That one minimum day…"
"Oh yeah, the day I broke my boots in, in ten minutes, what made you think of that?" Kinley inquired.
"You said provisions; we haven't said that since…" Madison didn't finish.
"Oh, you're right," Kinley whispered.
"I miss us, how we used to be, you know?" Madison admitted.
"Me too. But, you're starting to come back; I see it every now and then. However, I never want to go to the store with you while we're in a hurry, again." Kinley giggled. "Wasn't my finest moment, or yours, for that matter. But…I still love you, my Sherpa."

16. Surprise! I'm a Rastafarian Who Loves Guinness

It was late afternoon. Cal looked out the window of his taxicab. He was wearing a ridiculous wig with dread locks, he had the look of one who followed 'The Grateful Dead' from town to town and sold pot brownies to get by. The cab driver never looked twice at him. The cab drove into a suburban area and slowed as it pulled up in front of the quintessential American home. The picket fence was white, the lawn was lush and green, and there was a little walkway up to the red door. So this was where Kinley lived? He felt goofy as he paid the man and grabbed his duffel bag. He was alone, in suburbia. He smiled as he walked to the door.

"Hello," a young girl of around thirteen answered, though she was smiling, her eyes were tremendously sad. She was beautiful with shimmering honey-brown hair and sparkling brown eyes, but she was a mini-Kinley. What to say?

"Hi, is this the Brooke residence?" This was awkward.

"Yes." Okay he was going nowhere with this girl…come to think of it, he probably looked scary.

"Is your mother home?" Her eyes roamed over him, taking in his holey flannel shirt, his t-shirt proclaiming that he loved Guinness beer, and his fading jeans, her scrutinizing glance landed on his dreads. He knew what she was wondering…First…who is this man who thinks my mother is going to talk to *him*? Second…when was the last time he washed his scary hair? He couldn't stop himself from grinning. "I'm her friend Cal; I believe she's expecting me."

Her expression remained incredulous until she put it all together, "You're the one who sent the flowers?" He nodded. "Thank you so much, you especially cheered up Kennedy." She was more thankful for her sister's mood change? Odd. He recalled being her age, and always being thrilled when Rory was down.

"Ma-um!" she screamed at the top of her lungs. He plugged his ears. Wow, the lungs on this girl.

"I'm McKenna; it's very nice to meet you, Cal. Are you hungry?" He briefly wondered if she thought he was a homeless man her mother had taken pity on.

Now that she mentioned it, he *was* starving. The aromas wafting toward him from the kitchen were almost taste-able. He nodded again. The girl either didn't recognize him, or she just treated him like he was part of the family. He watched her curiously, as Kinley came down the stairs, holding onto the oak railing. "Cal, it's so good to see you. What are *you* wearing?"

He pulled his hat off, and his wig, and his glasses and set them down on the coffee table. "It was fun. No one knew who I was." Yep, the girl had not recognized him. Her mouth was hanging open as she dropped what looked like a blob of mashed potatoes onto a plate.

"You're…you're…" Her coloring was waning; she turned to her mother, and pointed, "He's…he's…"

"Yes McKenna, he is, and it's not nice to point, sweetie."

"Calvin Hunt is in my living room, sitting on my sofa…" McKenna gushed. "I'm going to die."

"Don't McKenna, you'll spill the food," Kinley pointed out. She gave her daughter an affectionate side squeeze. She was such a kidder sometimes.

Another girl skipped into the room holding onto a gigantic teddy bear. It was the one he himself had picked out on line just days before. She was going to break his heart; she was absolutely adorable. Her blond ringlets floated down her back, her eyes were bright blue and her smile was genuine. "You must be Kennedy," he stated.

"Yes, are you Mom's friend Cal?" he nodded. Both girls had little noses that turned up ever so slightly, and he had to admit they were both little beauties.

"Thank you for the bear. I asked Momma who sent it and she told me it was her friend Cal, so I named my bear Cal after you." Oh, yes, she was definitely going to break his heart. She sat down on the sofa at the other end, not too close to him, but not too far away either. "Thank you for the bear and the flowers and the chocolates." She smiled, and he melted. He could see aspects of their mother and father in both girls but they had taken different traits from each of them.

"You don't know who he is?" McKenna asked the little girl.

"He's Mom's friend Cal. Duh," Kennedy proclaimed. "She is a bit slow sometimes."

"He's the lead singer of Murder of Crows," McKenna told her with a somewhat exasperated tone.

"Really? Then do you know my Aunt Maddy? She's in love with you."

Kinley who had been silently watching everything began to cough and sputter. She choked, "Kennedy why don't you go clean your room?"

"It is clean," Kennedy grinned.

"Go jump on the trampoline." Kinley placed a plate on the table for him. "Cal, I know you must be starving, come over and eat." He walked over to the table, and though he was hungry, he was more interested in talking to little Kennedy.

"So, your aunt is love with me? Did she tell you that?" He grinned, while Kinley scowled.

"She doesn't have to, she sings your songs all the time with my mom, and they are really silly together. They love you. And…I think you're on her back-up list." Kennedy smiled broadly.

"What's a back-up list?" he asked, intrigued. "Is your mom in love with me too?" He looked up at Kinley, who was just staring at him with an indescribable expression.

"No, she loves the one named Rory," Kennedy answered matter-of-factly. Kinley just put one of her hands to her forehead in exasperation.

He gaped, "Your mom has a crush on my brother?"

"No," she stammered. "He's, and you're…Kennedy, go out and play," Kinley said in a sterner voice.

The little girl jumped up and waved goodbye to him. He looked out the window to see her jumping on the trampoline while holding her giant teddy bear. McKenna had been trying to look innocent while taking several shots of him with her camera phone. Nothing, it seemed, escaped Kinley. "If you publish those I will have to take your cell phone away for the rest of the year."

McKenna sneered at her mother, "I was…"

"Delete them and put it away." Kinley's eyes narrowed murderously and her daughter caved.

"I did want a little peaceful weekend," he told McKenna who grinned sheepishly back at him. "Would she *really* take your phone away?" The girl nodded gravely. "I'll have her take a picture of both of us before I leave, okay?" This seemed to appease her.

"Is Aunt Maddy coming over? She will be in heaven," she slyly whispered, a little louder than she'd anticipated, to her mother. Her mother just laughed.

Ryan came in, whistling, "Hey Cal." Cal couldn't help but think that Ryan looked like a football coach. He towered over his wife while managing to be quite a bit shorter than Cal.

"Dad! Not you too!" McKenna groaned.

"What?" He shook hands with Cal. "It's good to see you again."

"Dad, you and Mom never told us that you know Calvin Hunt?" She was in teenage anguish. Ryan shrugged and gave her a warm hug, but ignored her.

"Oh, dinner looks great my lovely wife." He kissed Kinley, who looked up at Ryan with such love and devotion that he felt as though he were intruding on a personal moment. He'd had many women look at him, but never had any woman looked at him the way Kinley looked at her husband. He suddenly felt as though someone had just pointed out that he had a gaping hole in the center of his chest. The imaginary person was saying 'Hey didn't you know that was missing?' And he was feeling foolish because he'd never noticed it before.

He spent the night in the Brooke's guest bedroom. There was something relaxing about being here. It was a homey little place, and they obviously loved each other very much. It reminded him of his family. In the morning, Kinley made the most heavenly breakfast, homemade waffles with real maple syrup. Dinner, the night before had been mouthwatering. The woman made homemade bread, according to her family, every day, and they had no idea how spoiled they were. He found himself fantasizing about this kind of life, and living it with Madison. Mostly, he wanted her to look at him as though there was no one else she'd rather see, he wanted her eyes to light up. No one had ever looked at him like that, and it nearly broke his heart now because he'd noticed it.

He'd bonded with little Kennedy right away. Now, she was watching some cartoon so he sat down beside her. "So, Kennedy." He knew Madison would arrive any minute to pick up Kinley, but she had no idea that Kinley would not be going. He only had moments with the child.

"Hi. Cal."

"So, what else does Aunt Maddy say about me?"

Kinley was washing dishes, and talking on the phone. "Momma and Aunt Maddy always sing your songs. But they won't sing number six. They always skip it when I'm in the car, and then they joke about it. We don't know why they do that. What is number six anyway?" she asked, her wide blue eyes couldn't have been more innocent. "Will you sing it to me?"

"Twinkle twinkle little star?" he sang to her with a grin on his face.

"Momma says it's naughty." She laughed, but her face turned serious quite suddenly. "How did you know I was sad?"

"Your Aunt Maddy told me you lost a friend recently, and that it was a really hard day for you. It broke her heart," he worded it gently.

"Oh. I did. She was my very best friend in the world. Her name was Riley. We even looked a bit alike." Her little face grew anxious. "I miss her all the time."

"Riley is a pretty name," he told her. "What happened to Riley?"

"She was in a car accident, they all died. All five of them, but Momma says I'm not allowed to talk to you about it. Maybe she thinks you'll be sad too." Before he could pry further, the doorbell rang, then Maddy just walked in not waiting for anyone to answer. Five people died in one accident? She must have known them all. Poor baby.

"Kin, I'm here."

She wasn't looking at him; she dropped her purse onto the hall table. "Kin?"

She looked up and now he was standing, wanting to see the way she looked at him, maybe he could gauge her feelings somehow. Her eyes lit up and a smile spread across her face. "Cal!" She walked a little closer and hugged him tightly. She smelled like spring rain, and honeysuckles and fresh meadows, and just clean. He smiled.

"Surprised?"

"Very, but, does this mean Kinley and I aren't going out today?"

"Yes, I'm afraid it does," he said to her.

Kennedy watched their exchange, and a grin formed on her face. "Aunt Maddy, does he sing number six to you? He wouldn't sing it for me." Kinley was coming down the stairs listening to this.

"I should hope he didn't," Kinley told her.

All the adults laughed, he could see the confusion on little Kennedy's face. McKenna was walking down the stairs, and looked a little disappointed that he was leaving. Madison looked up at him, it wasn't quite the look he was hoping for, but he'd take it. "Are you ready, Madison?" he asked her. "We can just do what you and Kinley were going to do. Don't change your plans for me."

"*Uh*, okay, but you may not like it." Madison had an interesting expression on her face.

He stepped outside with her and saw a gleaming red Porsche in the driveway. It still had stickers in the window, and a dealership license plate. "I really should remove those," she sighed.

As he climbed into the car he grinned, "This is really nice." This woman was an absolute paradox. He couldn't figure her out. "So, what is it we're doing, that you think I won't like?"

"I just moved into a new place," she explained as she backed the car out of the drive carefully. "And I'm afraid I've been sleeping on the sofa the last week or so. I need a bed, so we were going bed shopping." She laughed, "This is the weirdest thing ever. A famous rock star at my friend's house. Did you stay there?"

"I did, and may I say she is one hell of a cook…her bread…I would kill for that bread. The only thing missing is homemade chocolate chip cookies." He grinned.

"Why didn't you stay in a hotel?" she asked as she turned another corner.

He pulled his hat down closer to his sunglasses. "Kinley and I came up with a plan and she offered, so I accepted. It was more secretive this way. I flew in yesterday, and fly out again tomorrow. I actually had a really nice time. They remind me of my family, Kinley reminds me of my sister Callie."

"Your twin?" she blushed.

"So you are a fan? Little Kennedy told me her Aunt Maddy loves me," he teased. "But no one ever lets her listen to number six."

"Can you blame us?" She laughed, "Poor kid. What else did she tell you?" Madison seemed a little edgy for the moment.

"She told me about her friend Riley. Sweet little thing." He looked at Madison, distinctly getting the feeling he needed to change the subject. She must have known Riley too. "Oh just that you and her mom love me and you guys sing along with me, that Kinley is in love with Rory and I'm on a back-up list, whatever that means."

She coughed.

"Just when things got interesting though, Kinley always pulled her away." He frowned. "I have the feeling I would've eventually found out national secrets from Kennedy."

"You just may."

"So what's the back-up list?" he asked, liking to see her slightly unnerved.

"Nothing, oh look we're here." She smiled. He had the feeling it was something good.

They chose a bed together, and he sincerely wished he could sleep in it with her. But he was trying to be good. He'd never been celibate for so long. It was worse when he was near her, and when he kissed her; things became too tense, uncomfortably so. He felt as though he couldn't function. They went to the movies, and out to dinner. It was so wonderfully 'normal', he'd never done anything like it. Occasionally people would stop him and say, "Aren't you...." But he would just shake his head and smile. His hat did little to dissuade those who would recognize him.

She took him all over town in her little Porsche. "Can I drive?" he asked after sitting there all day feeling incredibly envious.

"But, I just got it..." She pressed her lips together.

"Oh please! I could buy you a new one if anything happens…" he told her.

"In that case, but, maybe I should get it in writing…" She beamed at him rather wickedly. He smiled his most charming smile, showcasing his teeth, and looking her in the eyes. "It's that smile…" she said. "That's how no one can say no to you, you just turn on the charm." She laughed as she pulled the car aside, "And look at me, I can barely focus when you smile at me."

He reached for her face and held it in his hands tenderly, before he kissed her. "Stay with me tonight." She gave him a look, "No, not what I meant. I meant we can hang out on Kinley's sofa and talk into the night, but it will be better because we won't be on the phone. I just want to be near you." She dropped the keys into his hand.

"I'll give you directions." She smiled, and he thought he knew how she felt when he smiled at her.

They sat on Kinley's red sofa with the television giving background noise. Her head was resting on his shoulder. He knew she was falling asleep.

"Come to bed with me." He wondered what she'd say. He needed to be with her, he could barely breathe for wanting her so badly.

"I can't Cal." She looked up at him. "I just couldn't." She bit her lip.

"Nothing is stopping you," he muttered, holding her tighter.

"Knowledge is stopping me." She grinned teasingly. What did she mean?

"Because I've been with lots of women?"

She laughed softly, keeping her voice low, as everyone was sleeping at Kinley's house, "It's funny, but that wasn't exactly what I was thinking, but now I have to admit I'm curious."

"Crap, I just opened it right up there, didn't I?" She just smiled and nodded. "Okay, I'll tell you, give you an estimate then you tell me your number." That seemed only fair.

"The number of men I've slept with?" She raised just one eyebrow, as he nodded. "You have a deal." She shook his hand.

Something about this was highly uncomfortable. Rory told him once that one day someone who mattered to him would ask, and he'd have to either lie or be ready to drop the bomb on her. He'd thought Rory was an idiot at the time. He told her the number but her eyes didn't widen like he imagined they would. She looked thoughtful, as she considered his answer then nodded as if to say, okay, I've digested that bit of information. "It's your turn." He grinned evilly.

"One."

"One what? One minute and you'll tell me? That's not fair, I was truthful I'll have you know." He knew he sounded childish. "Besides I won't care if you've had tons of lovers. I mean, look at you, it would be impossible that you haven't."

"No, Cal, I mean one. I've only ever been with one person."

It was his turn to digest this information. It had to be impossible, yes she was lying. But, no, she didn't look like she was teasing; she didn't look ashamed at how small the number was to his. No, there was something in her expression letting him know he was the one who had been missing out on something. She knew what it felt like to 'make love'; it hadn't been 'just sex' for her. He felt reverence for her, and admiration.

"You were married?" he asked, feeling the sting of the words on his tongue.

"Yes, I was married." She looked thoughtful, or as though she was chewing on the inside of her cheek.

"And…when did you stop being married?" What a dumb way to word a question!

"I like the way you asked that." Okay, maybe it wasn't. "I stopped being married last August, the nineteenth." He picked up her left hand and looked at it in the dull light. The faint indentation of a wedding band was all that remained of her marriage. He assumed she'd only recently removed her ring. The bastard had broken her heart. How was he out there living with himself?

"Maddy." She looked into his eyes. "He was the luckiest man who ever lived."

"He used to say so," she sighed wistfully. "But none of it matters now. All that matters is that I'm here with you and I'm happy." She leaned against his shoulder again, leaving him to think about everything she'd said. She'd only ever been with her husband, and he'd thrown it all away. It hadn't even been a year. That was why Kinley had told him it was too soon. It would just take more time, and he was willing to give it. If only she could find it in her heart to let the other man go, and look up at him the way he'd seen Kinley look up at Ryan. It was in that moment, that he realized he wanted to be with her for the rest of forever. He realized as her eyes closed and she drifted off to sleep in his arms, that he loved her.

17. Pensive on a Plane

"What's the problem little brother?" Rory asked Cal as he flopped down on the seat next to him.

"Nothing. How was Yellowstone?" Cal was not as adept as he would have liked, at changing the subject.

"Nice, cold, pretty and all that," Rory yawned.

"Did you have any admirers?"

"A few, thank goodness you weren't there, it's always worse when you're there." Rory wasn't the least bit jealous of Cal being the star of the band. He was only too happy to stand in the background. He'd always been that way. Cal was more of a- center of attention- kind of guy and Rory let him be. "How was California? I realize you've been back for a week, but we just missed each other."

"It was like heaven," Cal groaned.

"Then, what's wrong. Not in heaven anymore?" Rory teased.

"It was perfect, low key, quiet, and normal. It was everything I seem to never have."

"Haven't you been back at home since then? Surely it was quiet enough for you." Rory seemed somewhat interested in Cal's mood.

"I don't know, it's been nice, I guess." He watched as Gabe came onto the private jet last. He was toting a box underneath his arm.

"Box for you Cal," he muttered as he passed it to Cal.

Cal looked at the address. It was written to Gabe, from Madison. He smiled. Before he'd left California, Madison had driven him to the airport, with his scary dreadlock wig back in place. He'd given her Gabe's number in case she wasn't able to reach him. She must have contacted him. Gabe was somehow always 'reachable' even if everyone else wasn't. He pulled at the tape and opened the cardboard flaps. From the inside, Styrofoam packing peanuts burst out everywhere. He dug through them to find a cookie jar? *Hmm.* He opened it and the scent of chocolate chip cookies permeated the entire private jet. The aroma was heaven sent, he was certain. He picked up a card, and pealed the envelope open.

> Cal,
>
> Made these just for you. Kinley would love to say she helped, but mostly she just ate the dough. I'm thinking of you, wish we were together. Hope this makes you feel like 'home'.
>
> Miss you,
> Madison

He smiled as Rory helped himself to a cookie, "These are the best cookies I have ever had, don't tell Mom." He took another bite. Gabe grabbed one too. Cal didn't really feel like sharing, and it was worse after he'd tasted one of them. He wanted to horde them.

Normally, he was happy when the jet hit the air, and he could look out into the blue sky, but something foreign was plaguing him, a feeling he couldn't name. "Cal, what is going on with you? Usually you are playing around, loud and obnoxious, but now you are all, well, pensive."

"What would you have thought if Jen told you that she'd only been with one guy, when you first met her?" Cal asked in a rather low voice. He looked over at Gabe who was falling asleep. Shawn walked by on his way to the bathroom, before Rory answered.

"I don't know. I wouldn't have thought much I guess. I mean, she was only eighteen. We're talking about sex right?" Rory grinned.

"Yeah, I don't get it. Maddy has only been with one guy." Cal stared out the window.

"So, she was married. That means she was faithful to her husband, what's the big deal?" Rory had that look on his face, Cal knew all too well, he was dying to give some advice, but was trying to hold it in.

"You knew she was married?"

"Yeah, and so do you, apparently." Rory shrugged as he stole yet another cookie. "Seriously, these are so good. I have to get Jen the recipe." Jen didn't bake and they both knew it.

"But, just *one*, it made me feel like…" What exactly?

"The man-whore you are?" Rory countered with false innocence. Cal slugged him in the arm, but the term did seem to apply. He groaned as he covered his eyes.

"It's not what you're thinking, Ror, it's the look she gave me. The look that said, *I* was the one who was missing out. Does that make any sense to you? Because it sure as hell makes no sense to me."

"It definitely makes sense to me." Cal gave him a look that bade him to continue. "Well, it's like this- you Cal, are living in a one dimensional, black and white cartoon world. It's not real. The sex you have is great, because you don't know anything different."

"I beg your pardon, but I have an extremely gratifying sex life," he argued. At least until Madison had come along, now it was nonexistent.

"Good to know," Chris walked by and chimed in.

"Whatever." Rory was laughing. "You think it's great because you don't know it's just okay. When you're with the woman you love, you'll see what I mean. Everything around you will become more alive, more beautiful and sex will travel beyond just the physical realm, it will be better than anything you've ever experienced. Madison has obviously had that, and she knows just by talking to you, that you have no idea how amazing things can really be." Rory took another cookie. Cal moved the jar away from Rory.

"How can love make sex better? Sex is physical." Cal was determined not to let Rory one-up him on this.

"That was the most ignorant statement I have ever heard, Cal. Obviously you haven't slept with her yet, or you wouldn't be asking such an idiotic question. Listen, is kissing her just like kissing anyone else?" Rory had his answer just by looking at Cal, watching his mouth twist into a contorted expression. "I didn't think so." Damn Rory. He frowned as he looked out of the window.

The most exasperating part of it was that Rory's words struck a nerve, a raw nerve at that. He couldn't have Madison, not yet. He wanted her more than he'd ever wanted anyone. The things he wanted to do to her- was it possible everything would be better with her? Now, he really did feel like he was missing something. It was that feeling you get when you're a child and an adult smugly discloses that they'll tell you when you're older. He not only wanted her more than ever, he felt an uneasy sense of needing her too. This was not a place he'd been in before.

Madison was relaxing next to Megan's pool. Kate was reading a magazine article to Madison, Megan and Kinley, and they were all laughing. They took turns taking the quiz called, "Are you what he wants in bed?" and each ended up with different results such as –You're a sex goddess, you're a fantasy, you need to learn a bit more, and wow are you a virgin? They were laughing so much that Madison almost felt all of her sorrow somehow siphoned away. It could never truly be gone, but there were moments when it almost disappeared, or at least she forgot to think about it.

She missed Cal. It was a small, dull ache in her chest that caught when she tried to breathe. She didn't want to miss him, which made the ache more like a stab. Was it wrong to want him? Was it wrong to want him to want her? What exactly was the time limit? When was it respectable to go on with your life as a widow? Who knew the answer to that question? Perhaps there was a magazine somewhere with a quiz…How soon is too soon? Were there categories like- that is a respectable amount of time, maybe you're rushing it, and wow, did you kill him or what- she'd like to take that quiz. Were there questions like, how soon after your husband died did you let another man kiss you? She cringed as she thought of how she would have to answer that question.

"Maddy?"

"*Huh*, sorry?"

"Did you want more lemonade?" Megan asked her. She squinted at Madison as though she could read her thoughts. She nodded and took the glass. "Do you think he got the cookies yet?"

"I hope so. I paid a fortune for them to be shipped overnight. Never again," she laughed. Wow, seriously a lot of money to mail a box overnight to another country. Lucky that Canada is at least next to the US. "His bodyguard assured me he'll get them. He will call me tonight." She smiled as she thought of their nightly phone calls and how every night she found herself losing the battle to 'not fall' in love with Cal. She just didn't think she could take it if he broke her heart.

Cal was no longer some celebrity who was just to be adored from afar. He was a person, who had opinions, not just the ones someone could read about in a fan magazine. He had a beautiful soul, and wow, could he kiss. She hated to admit it; she'd never been kissed like that before. He knew what he was doing, alright. But should she take the next step and sleep with him?

As she drove Kinley home later that evening, she was relieved to voice her concerns aloud. "I can't do what he wants me to do." She winced at the idea.

"Why not?"

"Because, I'm not some bronzed Italian sex goddess, swim suit model and I'm no Lindsey Bell," she mumbled as she turned into the residential area.

"Oh, I see," Kinley told her.

"Do you?" Madison wasn't certain that she believed her.

"Well, yes. If I had to start over with this body...*ugh*."

"You look great, what are you talking about?" Madison laughed.

"Okay, I've only had two kids, but still...naked...geez I look much better with clothes on, let's put it that way. For instance, this body will never see the light of day in a bikini, around a love interest again. That was pre-kids, if you know what I mean. And...the stretch marks I've got. It looks like I had a slim escape from a grizzly bear attack and have only the scars to prove it. Ryan has seen it all, they are his children. Who else could love this horrid body the way Ryan does? Nope, I wouldn't want to start all over with this body and a new man. Especially one who didn't have children."

"You wore a bikini today!"

"What's a bikini among friends?" Kinley asked. "You all don't look at me the way a man would." She laughed.

Madison laughed with her as she pulled her car up into the driveway and stopped. "Yeah and that's not all. The boobs are no stranger to gravity." She cupped her breasts, "These babies are real. Is he used to that? I doubt it. And…stretch marks from four kids…I'm terrified of him seeing me like this. I can just imagine him saying 'wow what happened to your stomach? Did an alien break free from just below your rib cage?'"

"You're adorable, perfectly beautiful," Kinley loyally pointed out.

"Yes, once again we all look great with clothes on," Madison grimly observed. "Look at that Lindsey Bell; I hate her. My heaven, have you ever seen such perfect breasts? She's gorgeous, and I'm not even a lesbian."

"Thanks for clarifying that, I was wondering why you never offered…but then again I am married and maybe you respect that sort of thing," Kinley teased.

"I don't know what to do."

"Is that the *real* reason you are taking me to England? You're using me as a chaperone?" Kinley grinned brightly.

"No, you know why I'm taking you. You've always wanted to go. I couldn't go without you," Madison explained to Kinley.

"Very well. But I might not be able to keep you from making that leap into his bed."

"I know. But having you there will dissuade me, don't you think?" Madison asked.

"I don't know." Kinley bit her lip. "Maybe he is one of those men who think it's exciting to have people in the next room. He might be, you never know."

"Well he didn't mind propositioning me at your house. I couldn't-that would be too weird. You're upstairs with Ryan and your girls that would be terribly awkward. I could imagine Kennedy asking why I'd spent the night, but McKenna is old enough to get what was going on and she would be posting it all over Facebook."

"Your imagination knows no limits. I hope McKenna wouldn't pick up on that."

"Please. Don't you remember us at thirteen?" Madison said.

"Good point." Kinley looked around, "Well, come in for dinner. Where else do you have to be?"

"Is there bread?"

"When isn't there bread?" Kinley asked sincerely as Madison shut down her car.

18. The Thin Line Between Nightmares and Dreams

The sky outside was deep velvety twilight, that moment in time where it is both dark and light, and neither. Her children were laughing, and she turned to see Jack driving their SUV down off the highway. "Almost home kids." He smiled at her and reached across to squeeze her hand. They stopped and parked in front of the violent red traffic light. She knew what was coming, and consequently looked for it, before she would hear her daughter Alex scream, "Mommy, look!" There he was, driving the semi-truck, his head lolling to the side as though he were a lifeless doll.

The truck careened over the median, and predictably Alex screamed the words she screamed every single time. The truck driver's head jerked up, and his eyes were wide with terror. It was unavoidable, the collision, she could hear the squeal of breaks, smell the burning in the air, hear the beautiful twilight shatter in the screams. Unearthly sounds, shrieking, metal twisting and snapping gave way to thick, pervasive silence and darkness. Kinley was shaking her awake, pulling her out of it, "Wake up, Maddy," she whispered urgently.

Madison swiveled around to see other passengers on the plane, and two flight attendants staring at her as though she'd just sprouted a hand out of the top of her head. Kinley, defensive as ever, "Hey, it's nothing to worry about, just a nightmare. She hates to fly." Kinley's voice filled the cabin, and seemed to soothe most of the people who went back to quietly chatting.

"Well, you shouldn't fly if it gives you nightmares." A woman across the aisle leaned over and spoke to Madison rather tersely. "It frightens others around you. I, for one, thought the plane would crash."

"Shut up," Kinley told her with a heavy note of exasperation in her voice, drawing it out as she said it. The woman stiffened. Kinley hadn't even tried to reason with her. The agitation in Kinley's voice made Madison slightly concerned; she was defensive, ready to snap.

"Well, I never…" the older uptight woman replied.

"And you never will," Kinley bit off before looking back at Madison with a repentant gaze. The woman across the aisle let out a '*humph*'. Kinley, perhaps ashamed and filled once again with regret, stared out the window until they landed.

It wasn't surprising to find a chauffeur waiting for them at the London Heathrow airport once the plane landed. Cal loved to hire those limousines. This one wasn't a Hummer, but rather the regular old limo one would expect. "Are you all right?" Kinley asked once they were on their way, and the glass was raised by the driver. She never seemed to stop worrying about Madison.

"*Hmm*," she nodded.

"Do you have the nightmare every time you sleep?" she asked tentatively.

Madison nodded in reply. It was different depending on what she might have been contemplating earlier or even if something had happened during the day to trigger it. The nightmare was always there, taunting her with what could have been. She hadn't been in the car. The police officers explained what happened and her mind had clung to the information. Her family was in their SUV on the way home from Long Beach. She had elected to stay home and study, and yes, it nearly killed her knowing that she could have gone. The freeway had been backed up that night. When wasn't it?

Maybe if they'd left earlier…but she always started things this way, and always berated herself later. There was literally nothing she could do about any of it. Jack had pulled the car off the freeway and was stopped at a traffic light. This was what was factual. While the SUV had been idling at the light, across the street a truck driver, taking a shipment of propane had fallen asleep at the wheel, crossed the median and struck the SUV while her family sat there waiting to die. Her mind never truly had grasped it all. She came up with various scenarios always involving her sitting in the passenger seat, where in reality, Jonathan had been. She grieved for the imprudent choice she'd made.

Jack had been on his way to pick up a pizza, while she'd set the table for them and tossed a salad. He'd been literally minutes from home. The medical examiner explained that death had been instant for all involved. This should have comforted her, but it didn't. People told her they were with God, and at least they went quickly. This was not comforting either. Nothing anyone said comforted her. Here she was shivering and their words of advice, and cliché' bits of wisdom were like throwing her some paper towels to make her warm. It did nothing for her. They were gone. God might possibly have them with him, she couldn't be certain of it. If he did, why should it comfort her, when what she really wanted was to have them be with her? She supposed it was the next best thing…but all the words in the world couldn't convince her that her husband and children belonged anywhere but with her.

There was something Kinley could do to help, but at this point; it was beyond her capability to ask. Kinley's potential answer frightened her. Kinley wasn't psychic, nothing like that, but she had weird dreams sometimes. Anytime someone around them died, Kinley would dream about it before it actually happened. Madison wished it would spread to picking lotto numbers or a winning team. But, Kinley wasn't any Madam Cleo; she just had the one quirk with the dreams. Madison knew, deep down, that Kinley had dreamt of her family dying before it happened. Madison wanted to know, but then again, she was frightened. Then there was the possibility that Kinley never had a dream this time.

Kinley just hugged Madison, drawing her out of her thoughts. She knew there was nothing to say to alleviate the sorrow, nothing to wipe out the vivid images her mind had supplied her with. She was relieved when the limo pulled up to the hotel. Kinley was apparently trying to distract her again. "I can't believe this. Remember this hotel in *Notting Hill*?" Madison nodded and laughed. Kinley was practically jumping out of her skin with joy. This alone, made the trip worth if for Madison.

They followed a bellboy up to their suite. The suite was opulent, muted in grandeur but, quite distinctly furnished. The view of London was breathtaking causing Kinley to stare out of the window, transfixed for several minutes. There were vases of roses, baskets of fruit, one of chocolate imported from France, and terry cloth robes in their rooms. "This can't be real," Kinley said in awe.

"You keep saying that, and I'm sure you have scars from all of the times you've pinched yourself, but it's real." Madison heard a knock at the door.

"I know who that is…oh look; I have to go to my room. Bye."

Madison opened the door for Cal, and silently thanked Kinley for disappearing. He held her in his arms, and captured her lips in a tender, yet passionate kiss. At least it started out that way. Her fingers ran through his hair as he pulled her closer. She hadn't realized how much she'd missed him. If she hadn't had the distracting nightmare, she might have noticed her heartbeat had been slightly elevated with fervent longing and anticipation. She shivered as his hands moved over her back, feeling each of his individual fingers spread out and sink into her. "I have missed you," he told her softly. "Where is Kinley?" He looked around.

"Oh, she disappeared when you knocked. She didn't even try to make a lame excuse, she just left." Madison laughed lightly. He looked into her eyes and touched her hair, brushing it back from her face. He had the most amazing deep blue eyes, the ocean was surely filled with envy, and his lips had been made exclusively for kissing, or so it seemed. She could feel the light calluses on the tips of his fingers as he traced a faint invisible line around her lips. This was dangerous, her breath caught in her chest as she locked eyes with him. She wanted him, not just Calvin Hunt the fantasy, but Cal, her Cal. And…looking into his eyes she could see that *he* was hers.

"Maddy." He pressed his face into her hair.

∾

Could she feel him tremble? No one ever made him tremble. What did this woman have that no other woman seemed to possess? He could and would ask himself this question at least a hundred times always with the same inability to answer it. She was a mystery, one he started out wanting to solve, now it was a need, a drive. Rory's words echoed through his mind. He needed her, physically, mentally, emotionally. He wanted to possess her, not in the way of possessions, but in the way of people. The way he saw old people who seemed to be able to communicate telepathically, or the way someone just belonged to someone else. Thoughts had been driving him insane, thoughts of losing her. A hopeless despair would wash over him like a chilled wind, and he would swear he was falling backward while he was standing still. Imagine not hearing her voice, or seeing her face, and he would immediately feel his breath freeze and imagine he could see it emit a heavy mist in the even colder air.

Kinley was sweet enough to give them at least a half an hour alone; when she emerged from her room, it was with great reluctance. "I wanted to give you more time, I'm so sorry," she began as she eyed them snuggled up on the sofa. "But my stomach is growling at me; I'm surprised you didn't hear it out here. I have to eat, or I will be a total witch," she muttered.

Madison laughed and nodded, "It's true, she's evil when she doesn't eat." He got up, not without some small resistance to the idea. "Are you going to wear your Rasta wig?"

"Nope, believe it or not, I'm not really plagued too much here. People are a little more polite and friendly." He shrugged, "Want to go to a pub?"

"Ooh, fish and chips. Fun," Kinley nearly squealed with excitement. "I still can't believe I'm here. Thank you so much, Cal." She ran off, presumably to get herself a little more 'fixed up'.

"It's weird; I thought she was going to hug me for a moment." He sat there, puzzled.

"She doesn't hug. She has issues."

Maddy took a moment too. He stood and began to pace. He'd never been celibate for this long before. His body was betraying him, craving her body, and all of the things he wanted to do to her were skipping, teasingly through his mind. He had to think of something else, not the scent of her skin, honeysuckle-like, or the aroma of her hair, which was some unnamable lusciously enchanting scent. He couldn't think of the way her petite body curved seductively underneath ordinary jeans and a tight fitting shirt. He didn't want to recall the way her body fitted perfectly against his, or how her head was obviously made to fit into that space between his arm and his ribcage. She mesmerized him, thoroughly.

He led them down to a pub, and they seated themselves at a tall table. Kinley looked at the menu and made suggestions to Maddy. They had the communication through telepathy thing down. Kinley would begin a sentence, only to have Madison finish it, and vice versa. It was entertaining to watch the two of them. "You're sure you two aren't related somehow?" he had to ask.

"We get asked that all the time. We don't even look like each other." Kinley smiled. "I can't imagine what it is."

"It's your facial expressions, and the way you seem to read each other's thoughts, and the way you both move. It's the way you speak, the things you say, it's like the girl version of me and Rory, it's like you're sisters."

Madison smiled at him, "It's good to know. We've never quite figured it out."

They ordered dinner, which was when he discovered that Maddy hated fish, but Kinley loved it. He loved fish and chips. She wasn't the type of woman to order something just because he ordered it first. She had her own mind, and wasn't afraid to let him see it. It had happened in the past where women would order the same thing he had, just to impress him, when it had been painfully obvious that they didn't care for what they were eating. This whole relationship felt real, and that had never happened before.

He asked them what they wanted to do while here in England, but Madison looked a little tired. Kinley took over for her, telling him things they'd looked up on the internet. He was just now realizing it, but Kinley did this a lot, as though she were defending Madison. What could she possibly be defending her from? He couldn't quite put his finger on it. It was more likely that he'd imagined it. He didn't like what it meant if he wasn't imagining it. Did she always need Kinley there? Would they never be alone? Kinley seemed to want to leave but it was as though Madison was unable to allow it. It puzzled him. Their relationship was unusual, to say the least.

That night as he flopped over in his bed, he pushed away the desire to have Maddy there with him. Even if he did nothing, she would be there wrapped up safely in his arms. It was a constant ache in his chest, there was a physical pain there. He was used to speaking to her nightly. They'd spoken until she'd drifted off in his arms, on her sofa. He'd hated leaving her. He'd taken a blanket and draped it over her, hating himself all the while for wanting to devour her, but he'd left her to dream, left her to be alone.

19. Giving and Receiving

Was there something she could do for him? She could never repay him. This relationship was slightly off balance! Madison never would have thought he'd be so absolutely, well, thoughtful. Kinley had rambled on at dinner, and he'd been listening, as though he'd recorded the entire conversation. They had toured White Chapel, where Jack the Ripper had rampaged murderously through the poor prostitutes. Kinley was always interested in the macabre. Yet, Madison had to admit the outing had been fascinating.

Kinley had mentioned that she and Madison loved plays. They'd seen *The Producers, Cats, and Les Misérables*. How could she ever thank him enough? Each time, they'd been escorted back stage from the front row, to be introduced to cast members. Kinley was in heaven, and somehow that made Madison more than happy. They had been to Harrods, and shopped till they were more than exhausted, only to see his concert that evening. They toured the Tower of London, and gone over to watch the changing of the guard at Buckingham Palace. Kinley confessed that she felt guilty about having more fun than she'd ever had in her lifetime, without Ryan.

Madison hated that their stay was drawing to an end. Every moment she had with Cal, she fell in deeper. She was losing her will to fight against it, even though there were intrusive thoughts, given Jack's voice, trailing through her thoughts at times. Really? A rock star is what you're replacing me with? Or how could you? Or it hasn't even been a year yet, and you are kissing this guy who has probably kissed hundreds of women…But the most disturbing thought was…What if he breaks your heart? He's certainly capable of it.…These thoughts generally kept her from letting the kisses progress any further than light petting on his part.

She was human after all, with very real desires. He made her blood boil, and yet he also had the power to still it, as if it were a frozen river in her veins. He was not just some icon any longer; he was a person, whose soul she'd been privileged to see. Their time in London was rapidly disappearing, and somehow she felt she needed to do something for him. What could she purchase that he didn't already own? What could she give him that he didn't have or couldn't get for himself? She still felt violently insecure about giving him her body. She'd given birth three times, (there had been twins) and despite the way super models managed to make it look like every woman has elastic skin that bounces back to its' original shape, most normal women are worse for the wear. She was no exception. Kinley tried to tell her that she needed to look in the mirror and see herself as other's saw her, but she felt it was impossible. Kinley told her she was too critical of herself, but she couldn't hear it, she knew what she saw when she stood in front of a mirror.

Their last day in England came too quickly for Kinley. She'd found something she just had to do, but wouldn't take Madison along. She insisted on going out on her own, and so Madison was left, dreading what would happen when Cal came in. He was joyful; practically bouncing he was so giddy. It was contagious, he made her happy. She couldn't be miserable around him, although she was tempted. They ate dinner together, danced in a club, and came back to her sofa. His hypnotic glance sucked her in, and his kisses left her breathless. With Kinley out of sight, his hands slipped underneath the edge of her shirt in the back, and glided up over her bare skin.

She needed to make an excuse, to get away. What would Jack think? He couldn't think anymore. She shivered as she made an excuse to slip into something more comfortable. She was wearing heels. Had it sounded suggestive? He followed her into her room, not with a look of anticipation, but with ease of being near her. He kept talking, smiling, laughing. But she couldn't take it all in. Her heart was pounding nervously. She heard the door to the suite open, and without thinking, she shut her bedroom door. She giggled, as did he, "I don't want Kinley to think…" But what it was, she didn't know. She couldn't finish her sentence. His face was perilously close, there in the dimly lit room. Just the two of them standing there, his lips a hairsbreadth away, the scent of his skin made her quiver. She wanted him. She wanted him to want her.

His lips brushed ever so softly against hers, she needed breath, to exhale. He caught her in mid-gasp, and let his tongue travel along her bottom lip, teasing her, as he explored further. Her heart rate was treading on dangerous ground, soaring as it hadn't in a long time. "Good night, Maddy, see you in the morning," she heard Kinley call to her in a clipped voice through the closed door. Her words were rushed. She wanted to wonder about this but Cal had thoroughly distracted her. His lips soundlessly moved over her neck as his hands moved up underneath her shirt.

"Goodnight," she called, hoping Kinley hadn't noticed the way her voice caught in her throat, as Cal leaned her backward until she dropped onto her bed. "We probably shouldn't, I probably shouldn't…" she began to protest, but her traitorous body was telling him she needed him, more of him. She could feel her back arc as her body pressed against his body. He lowered onto her bed all the while awakening long dormant desire. She wanted to push him away, but she also wanted to slide his clothes from his body and feel his skin against hers. "Please," she began, but she didn't know if she meant 'please stop' or 'please continue'.

"I love you." He kept his voice low, his words were soft, his lips whispered against her ear. Did he mean it? He didn't seem like the type of person to say it just for the sake of saying it. Was he? "I love you so much, Madison," he told her again. She kissed him, tasting his lips, his mouth, in the only way she could reply. They were undressing each other, with an urgency she'd not foreseen. Their bodies tangled together, as his hands moved over her, caressing her, cupping her, lingering. All of her protests remained unspoken, as her body ignored them, beckoning him to continue exploring.

He awoke early, her head resting sweetly on his bare skin. He couldn't believe she was in his arms. Rory had been right. He'd known sex, but it was a completely different thing from 'making love'. It was love, and he'd given his soul to the woman next to him. He kissed the top of her head. Damn it, that this had to happen on their last night in London. They could have been doing this the whole time, although he doubted that Kinley would have approved or enjoyed herself nearly as much. He watched Maddy's face, he traced over her lips, she peacefully breathed in, and twitched a little when he touched her nose.

Her breathing increased, and her body tensed beside him. She twisted around, and shook her head. She was dreaming something unpleasant, but before he could wake her, she was screaming, "No!" she screamed over and over again, until, to his chagrin, Kinley raced in.

"Maddy, wake up!" she shouted, and then became instantly uncomfortable as she noticed Cal entangled in Maddy's sheets. "I…" she stepped backwards, and shut the door as Madison's eyes flew open.

"She saw didn't she?" Madison asked, rather sheepishly.

He nodded. "I'm afraid so." They laughed. She didn't seem to remember that she'd been having a nightmare, her light laughter unnerved him. He wanted never to hear that scream again. It had riveted through his body, sending chills throughout his veins, and pounded wildly inside of him reverberating all through his mind and soul. He'd been helpless to save her, to comfort her. It had been no ordinary nightmare; it had possessed her and taken her prisoner, all within her mind. "Are you all right? You seemed to be having a nightmare?"

"Oh, I'm sorry. I hope I didn't startle you." She was apologizing to him? "I sometimes have this awful dream. I'm sure it will stop one day." She was trying her best to assure him, but he was still uneasy. The same dream over and over again? Did it involve *him*, her ex-husband? He would just have to do his best to combat whatever scars she had, and let her feel safe with him. He would never hurt her the way her ex so clearly had. He would take care of whatever she needed.

20. So...How'd it Go?

Madison had avoided speaking about 'it' most of the way home, in fact, she and Kinley had slept all the way from London to New York, then watched an in-flight movie. Now, inside an airport shuttle, she still didn't feel comfortable speaking about anything, with the little old man sitting next to them. Having a conversation with him was work, but she and Kinley both had a major flaw in their personalities, they both hated unbearably awkward silences. They both felt compelled to delve into the little old man's life, and ask him about his grandchildren and his trip to Boston, despite the fact that neither Madison nor Kinley felt truly interested.

When the shuttle pulled up to the gated complex where Madison lived, she felt a sigh of relief shudder through her body. She knew Kinley was only waiting for the opportune moment to pounce. But, there she was, yawning, asking to be taken home, and not mentioning anything. Finally, frustrated beyond measure Madison piped up, "Why haven't you said anything about 'you know what' yet?"

"I don't know. I figured you'd tell me when you got around to it." Kinley was reluctant to pry this time.

"Seriously?" Madison growled, letting the sentiment drip with sarcasm.

"I know; it's so unlike me."

"Especially after…" She didn't need to finish the sentence. They both laughed. It was December of her senior year in high school. Madison had been seventeen and head-over-heels in love with her darling Jack. She'd lied and told her parents she was sleeping over at Kinley's house but Jack's parents had been out of town. Kinley, of course, had known what she was up to, since she'd been the one to cover for them. The next morning, Kinley called her at Jack's house and started the conversation off with, "So…how'd it go?"

It had been mere curiosity on Kinley's part. She remembered replying that it hadn't been at all what she'd expected but that with time she might enjoy it more. They had laughed so hard that Jack had overheard and therefore become tragically insecure. She'd gotten pregnant that night, but Madison had the last laugh. Kinley seemed to follow her example in nearly everything and just after she'd turned eighteen, got pregnant herself. Madison had called her up and asked the same question months later. Madison had been stressed about Kinley going away to school in New York, but her unexpected pregnancy had stopped her in her tracks. Kinley had stayed, gotten married just like Madison, and they had reared their children side by side. Madison didn't know what she would have done if Kinley had gone off to New York instead. She, truthfully, didn't like to think about it.

She'd expected Kinley to ask, or say something by now. Madison was practically grinding her teeth. "Say something Kin, you're making me nervous."

"Sorry, Maddy. So…How'd it go?" *Ah*, the old line worked well for this situation too.

"He made me feel alive again." She sank into her sofa.

Kinley nodded thoughtfully. "Good, I'm happy for you." She sounded sincere, but then again…

"You are full of lies, Kinley Brooke."

"Okay, so I am a little worried," she muttered before taking a seat at the opposite end of the sofa.

"What about?" She hated, absolutely despised, dragging information out of Kinley. It was worse than having to talk to the little old man in the shuttle who answered every question in monosyllables. "Are you worried about what Jack would think, I am, a little."

"No," Kinley paused, trying to think of a way to be truthful and delicate at the same time. "Jack's opinion shouldn't matter at this juncture. He always wanted you to be happy. I know that. To see you happy would be enough for him. He wouldn't have wanted to see you the way you've been for the past eleven months. It would have hurt him more than anything, as it hurts everyone who loves you." Kinley was doing better than Madison would have predicted. But she knew it was the calm before the proverbial storm. "It's just that he loves you, Maddy."

"Kinley, did you notice something? Maybe, something I didn't see."

"No matter how painful?" she was apprehensive, and it showed.

"No matter what," Madison answered, although inwardly she retained second thoughts.

Kinley shifted uncomfortably, "I don't know why but I think Cal is in this for the long haul, like marriage and kids, the whole thing."

"Please be wrong," Madison choked.

"I am most likely wrong." Kinley smiled painfully, "It happens all the time."

Madison felt all of the breath leave her body, as though she'd been punched in the sternum. She just didn't think she could do the whole 'family' thing again. What if it went really wrong? She didn't know about this. Kinley had more, "Then there is the issue that you haven't told him, it's going to be either no big deal, or a hard thing for him to overcome, even though it will be up to him how he deals with it. He lives in Canada, you live here, there is so much to consider. And, I will remove his beating heart from his chest if he hurts you, but…"

"Do you think he'll hurt me?" Madison asked, with a bit a fright etching her voice. "It's something always lurking in the back of my mind."

"No, truthfully, but…" Kinley faltered.

"What?" she found herself asking rather weakly.

"I think you're more likely to hurt him," Kinley finally shared her reservations. "He loves you."

"He told me so last night," Madison muttered as she stared at her empty ring finger.

Kinley nodded, "Anyone can see he loves you. You love him too, but you have yet to admit it to yourself…and you feel guilty about sleeping with him."

"Damn it Kin, do you need to see through me so clearly? I can't love him. I can't be what he wants. I can't be the little wife and have kids. I have already done it, and I don't know if I have it in me to do it all again. What if he cheats on me? He cheated on that Lindsey girl. Remember it on her television show? He travels all the time. What if he's faithful, and wants a family? What if they all die in some accident? My heart can't handle it."

Kinley just listened thoughtfully. "Maddy, there is nothing I can say to you that will comfort you. I wish there was. I would offer encouragement to pursue the relationship. He's really perfect for you. But who knows, are you even ready for this?"

"I can't tell if I'm ready." Madison barely managed to whisper, "I don't believe in meeting two perfect people in one lifetime."

"Why not? Do you think that Jack wants you to seal yourself up cryogenically rather than remarry? He told you if something ever happened to him, he wanted you to remarry."

"Did he mean it? I said it too, but I wouldn't want to see him with someone else, I wouldn't! What if he meant it so that the kids wouldn't grow up fatherless? It doesn't matter now, don't you see?" Madison cried, and pushed the tears aside with the back of her hand.

"It does matter." Kinley sat up straighter. "Because you *are* all alone. Anyone who loves you, that is me included, finds it painful to watch you go about your life as though everything were fine. It's not. The first time I saw you begin to come back to life was when we went to that concert, when you met Cal, and every time you mention his name, your eyes light up. I know you don't want to put yourself out there, because everyone knows you've been through hell and we don't want to see it happen to you again. The thing is, you have to take a chance, make that leap of faith, or you will be all alone. Nothing will change. Why do you think you are so undeserving of having a second chance? Maddy, I love you like you were my sister, you need to know this…I think if anyone deserves a second chance at happiness, it's you."

"You really believe there can be more than one perfect person for you?"

Kinley gazed at her thoughtfully, "I do, Maddy, I really do."

Cal sat at his home, plucking out random chords on his guitar, when a tune began to come together in his mind. "Cal?" he heard Rory call to him.

"Come in," he yelled out.

"I like the sound of that," Rory told him as he pulled up seat across from the big screen television.

"Thanks," Cal murmured. He looked up to see his brother not quite looking like himself. "What's wrong?"

Rory shrugged, sinking deeper into the cushions. "*Hypothetically*…if you knew something I should know, would you tell me in person or with a note?"

"I don't know." Cal put his guitar down, "I guess I'd tell you right out. Why?"

"I thought you would, no matter how painful." He looked away. "Let's drop it."

"Rory?"

"Let it go, Cal," he groaned. "I have some things to figure out." He grimaced. "Is it a song for Maddy?"

"I don't know yet," Cal answered truthfully. "I was thinking about asking her to marry me. What do you think?" He grinned happily. Rory glanced at him with an indiscernible expression on his face. "What now?"

"It's just that there are certain things you don't know about her…" Rory began delicately.

"What is wrong with you? I'm fine; she'll tell me everything in good time. I know she will. She will let me know about her divorce when she is ready. It must have been awful. From what I've gathered; they were high school sweethearts." His brother had a look of apprehension on his face. He went back to playing the guitar.

"Have you two discussed kids?" Rory was positively nervous.

"Not really. But they seem to make *you* happy, so I think the idea of having kids is great."

"*Uh*…" Rory began, "What if it's more complicated than what you're thinking? Just be careful with her."

"What does it matter? You never cared before, if I had a one night stand or broke someone's heart." Cal was beginning to suspect something, but he wasn't able to put his finger on it.

"This feels more personal somehow," Rory admitted solemnly.

"Well, I was thinking about inviting her up here, you know, just her. I want to spend more time with her, then I will pop the question, and I hope she'll have me."

"You don't deserve her," Rory pointed out, rather rudely, Cal thought.

"I know, but one can always hope she'll say yes anyway. She doesn't care if I have money or not, she has money of her own apparently. She doesn't care if I'm famous. Somehow, I think she'd have me if I were a postal worker, or a clerk somewhere. She actually likes me for *me*. Maybe eventually, she'll fall in love with me too. She hasn't said it yet, but when I'm near her..." he drifted off. He could feel it. It had been only two days, yet, he missed her. There was a constant gnawing ache in his stomach. He'd always felt complete, until she'd come along, and it'd become painfully obvious that he was incomplete without her. He'd been functioning on a basic, primal level, this was new and thrilling, he was *alive*, not merely living.

Rory was ruining it for him; he just wanted him to go away, which he seemed to gather. Rory left him alone to compose, and he searched for his inspiration, her smiling face. He felt ashamed of the way he'd regarded women, somehow he'd objectified them unintentionally. He hadn't meant to, it wasn't until he was with her that he realized what a completely shallow idiot he'd been, and for a long time too. How was it possible that she made him feel incredibly weak, but undeniably strong in a single moment?

And...though he thought he'd known everything there was to know about sex, he'd been more than ignorant about making love. He never knew that a woman who had only been with one man could teach him something...but she had. It felt new, and beautiful, and more sensual than anything he'd ever experienced. Damn Rory for always being right about everything. Cal needed her. Living without her was something he did before, because he didn't know any better. Now, it was utterly painful to be away from her.

He wanted to be curious about Rory's cryptic conversation, but he didn't feel an inclination. He knew she was in pain, he could sense it, see it in her eyes. He wanted to be the one she leaned on, and who she relied on to ease the pain. He wanted to make certain that her nightmares became a thing of the past, and he wanted to make her dreams come true. Did she not want children, or was she unable to have them? That had been a strange thing for Rory to hint at. He strummed several notes on his guitar as he contemplated Rory. There was more to this than the routine painful divorce. If only she'd open up to him about it. Had the high school sweetheart cheated on her? Had they had children? Did the bastard take them away from her? What was going on?

The only thing he could do was to invite her up to Canada for a while. Maybe she would realize she could tell him anything. He loved her. She claimed she was damaged. He wanted her, damaged or not. Contemplating his future, she was in every scene, every fantasy. He wanted to wake up next to her in the mornings, sleep next to her at night. He wanted to make love to her, only her, for the rest of his life. He thought of the moment he'd realized there was no turning back, she was giving herself to him. He had never felt anything like it before. It was almost more pleasure than he could bear, it devoured him, encircled him, a flame it consumed him. Her body fitted perfectly next to his, he needed more time to explore every inch of her. Thinking like this wasn't good for his health.

Sighing heavily he picked up the phone. He needed her here with him, alone. No friends to surround her, no interruptions. Not that he minded her friends, but he wanted her alone, for himself. He realized the selfishness of it all, but he didn't care. He imagined locking himself away with her for a week, and not doing anything but letting his hands roam freely over her body, and tasting her honey sweet kisses, feeling the burning pleasure of her lips on his skin. He shook his head, trying to get his mind cleared of the tempting thoughts pulling him down like leaden weights. Would she accept his invitation? Would she accept his proposal?

21. The Back-Up List

During her flight, Madison thought of her last conversation with Kinley. Kinley could be the most aggravating person in the world at times. "No, I won't go, he doesn't want me there," Kinley had argued. Madison didn't care if Cal wanted Kinley with her or not. She didn't want to be alone with Cal. "We'll end up staying in bed all week…" she'd told Kinley. Her friend had smiled and pointed out that most people wouldn't be complaining about such a thing. Kin had told her she didn't want to be a third wheel anymore. Still, more frustrating was the fact that she had no other alternatives. Megan was in New York on vacation, and Kate was in Hawaii with her family.

When she exited the plane, and found a Rastafarian looking man with a goatee waiting at the exit for her. She grinned broadly, and found herself safely enclosed in his arms. He drove a Jeep. She didn't know what she'd been expecting, but this wasn't it. She realized vaguely that she'd never thought to ask what kind of car he drove, though, when she thought about it further, she realized that he probably owned many cars. So many celebrities did. She couldn't help but think of how she'd pled with Kinley to come with her, but now at this moment, she was happy she'd come alone. They laughed all the way to his home. It had been a long time since she'd let herself lose that constant composure she'd recently centered her life around.

His home wasn't what she'd pictured either. Perhaps it was from living in California for nearly her entire life, but she'd pictured a stately, regal mansion surrounded by woods, simple in splendor. It was a log cabin albeit a mansion sized log cabin. One wall was made up of a large window, when she turned; she realized the reason for this. From where she stood she looked down on a valley of silvery green trees and Cal's personal lake. It was impressive, but not Hollywood at all.

"It's beautiful," she breathed.

"Why thank you. You're the only woman I have ever brought here." Cal grinned.

"You can't be serious."

"Oh, but I am," he replied before kissing her. It was the kind of kiss that left one breathless and tingling all over. She had wanted to wait a few minutes before she fell helplessly into his bed, but apparently, there wasn't time. Her body longed for his touch, while her mind feebly protested, he managed to roll her suitcase, schlep her carry-on tote and show her to his room, all the while kissing her until she needed to come up for air. "This is my room," he muttered in between kisses, he tangled his fingers into her hair and pulled her down into his bed. His skin had a lightly sun-kissed glow as she removed his shirt. Her hands gently followed over the natural plane of his muscles, smoothly gliding over his chest causing him to shiver.

She knew she shouldn't compare, but she supposed it was natural. Jack had been a lover from heaven. He'd been naturally lean, yet muscular, with dark hair and light blue eyes. They had learned together, both starting off as completely inexperienced, silly-in-love teenagers. He had been graceful, virile and, to her, perfect. She shouldn't compare…but Cal was something else altogether. He was…wow. His body was more muscular, his skin more tan, his hair lighter, and more sensually disheveled. She had to admit that he certainly knew what he was doing. He seemed, at least in her mind, that he lived to give her pleasure, with almost no thought to himself. It was as though merely being with her, someone so ordinary, gave him the greatest fulfillment and joy. She couldn't understand it, but being with Cal, was nearly indescribable ecstasy.

"I don't want this to sound wrong but..." he began a sentence she was afraid to hear the end of. "You are adorable when you bite your lip that way." She was holding her breath. "I never thought that a woman who has only been with one other man could make me feel like such a ridiculously inexperienced school boy. I know that sounds outrageous..." he hesitated.

She kissed his full lips, "You are crazy. You make me feel things I've never felt before." Her insecurity about her body was slowly disappearing around him; he actually seemed to think she was quite perfect. It was mindboggling. "Do you mind if I take a shower?" she asked coyly. He grinned and shook his head.

His bathroom was the size of her bedroom. It had large windows on three sides of the room that surely would fog up when she ran the shower. Everything was a steely gray granite swirled with veins of white; there were black towels, and stainless steel, this was a bachelor's dream bathroom. She could hear him speaking to her; she peered out of the partly open door. "I know this is a weird question, but do you have any gum? I'm addicted to chewing gum now that I've quit smoking. Apparently, I'm an addict no matter what I do." His smile was what she was addicted to.

"Yeah, it's in my purse, the zippered part." She shut the door and started the shower, which smelled like him. The scent of his body wash was heavy in the air, and strangely comforting, like a warm layer of clothing. While she was busy washing up, breathing in the aroma she so often associated with his skin, he was looking through her purse. She could barely hear him yell over the blare of the water rushing.

"This is a Poppin's bag, Maddy. I mean, you could fit your townhouse in here. How am I ever to find the gum?" Her only response was laughter. "You can tell a lot about someone by looking through their purse," Callie always said. He didn't see how that was possible. Madison was secretive, but her purse was offering him no hidden clues. It was, if anything, too clean and tidy. He reached the zippered pocket and pulled out a pack of gum, but as he was returning it, he realized he'd grabbed a business card at the same time. Normally, he would have not looked, but who would not notice ICE typewritten in big bold black letters on a day-glow orange business card? Intrigued he read the small paragraph below.

ICE

If the woman carrying this card has been recently made single, through the accidental death of her husband, untimely demise due to unforeseen natural causes (or deliberate murder) or has become single due to the fact that her husband was a cheating bastard who left her, then this is an emergency. A new husband must be procured for her promptly. A list of suitable candidates is provided on the other side. (How could he ignore the suggestion to look on the other side?)

The Back-Up List
1. Calvin Hunt (Singer, Songwriter, Sex god)
2. Paul Walker (He's Fast and I'm Curious)
3. Robert Redford (If a Time Machine Could Take Me Back to 1960)
4. Henry Cavill (From the Tudors, wearing a Codpiece)
5. Charlie Hunnam (SOA OMG)

Wow, this was fascinating. Sex god? Madison walked out of the bathroom, fully dressed, rubbing her wet hair with a towel. Could she be more beautiful? He liked the way her shirt fitted every curve, and gave him a hint of how delicious her body was underneath her clothes. Her eyes grew large as she realized what he was looking at, "No, please Cal!" She jumped at him on the bed, but his arms were just too long for her to reach. "Please!" She blew her drying hair out of her eyes, "It's a joke, an embarrassing one at that." She struggled and wrestled with him, while he chuckled, turning his back to her. "Cal," she cried in frustration. She found herself twisted around the side of him, staring at the ginormous tattoo of a crow on his shoulder blade.

"Maddy, Maddy, Maddy…" He was now fully laughing, "This is the funniest thing I've ever seen, did Kinley make it for you?"

She rolled off of him and caught her breath, clutched at her side, where presumably she had a stitch. "Actually, Kin and I both did; we had them made up for everyone in our group. We all have one; it's a long running joke, since high school." She sighed, "This is humiliating."

"Well, I don't know about that. So, Kinley has one of these in her purse too? Please tell me I'm not at the top of her list too, that would be awkward."

She laughed as she finally wrenched the card away from him and smoothed it out on her jeans. "No, it's Gerard Butler," she lied while trying to catch her breath. She would never tell the truth, however, about who really topped Kinley's back-up list. He was laughing again. "Please stop laughing Cal." She groaned and rolled over, probably to get away from him, but he pulled her back into his arms.

"How long have I been on the top?" he teased lightly.

"Of my list?" she arched her dark thin eyebrow playfully.

"Ooh, yes, the list."

"Since I first saw you, about ten years now. Of course we've only had them typed up in our purses for a couple years though. We've all joked about the back-up list for years. Kin and I started it in high school as the back-up boyfriend list. Only then, it was you know, guys who were evidently more in our reach. Now, it's sort of joke because it wasn't like we'd ever meet any of you on the list."

He laughed, he couldn't help himself. "Maddy, I hope you consider me sincerely thrilled that I am at the top of your list."

"You must believe me, I never thought I'd really meet you, let alone date you."

"I believe you." He kissed the tip of her nose.

22. A Warm Welcome to the Family....Almost

Madison was enjoying herself, but every now and again she felt the distinct pangs of guilt. The anniversary, she hated that word because it implied something celebratory was going on, of her family's accident was days away. She'd been dreading it constantly, yet Cal was so distracting, she nearly forgot it at times. His family was wonderful. Her favorite, though she knew she shouldn't have favorites, was Callie. Cal had been correct in the fact that she was very much like Kinley though they didn't look alike. Callie had straight long blond hair, and was at least five feet and eight inches tall, with the same blue eyes Cal possessed. They had that brother/sister resemblance thing.

Madison's first night there ended in having a large family meal at the Hunt's house. Cal's mother and father were there, and so were his siblings, Rory, Michelle and Callie. Rory's wife and son were there, and so were Michelle's husband and daughters, Callie's husband and sons and a dog named Zeppelin, but called Zeppy. Callie had pulled her chair right up next to Madison, "So, what do you think of my brother? Is he 'the one'?" That was so something Kinley would have asked someone she barely knew.

Madison laughed, "He could be." She deliberately remained vague.

"That's the spirit, keep it open." Callie had joked throughout the entire meal, and managed to throw a roll at her son's head, and hit him right between the eyes. "Knock it off Brian, or the next thing I'll throw will be my fork," she called at one time. Madison then was cornered after dinner by Cal's mother who asked her a whole slew of questions. It was an uneasy feeling; the woman seemed to see right through her. She'd gone to bed in Cal's arms that evening, feeling a little nervous about Mrs. Hunt's opinion.

"Your mother doesn't like me, I think." She'd been through *this* before. The first time she'd met Jonathan and Deborah Grey, she'd known they didn't care for her. In their opinion, their son was going to go to college and they saw her as an unnecessary distraction. He'd gone into working at a factory shortly after they were married. Even though he'd graduated and finished college later, it hadn't mattered to them. Jack's parents still hadn't approved, although they'd loved each of their grandchildren. She'd tried for years to make them like her, but it had been a fruitless pursuit. They'd never gotten over the fact that their son had chosen to marry the girl he knocked up his senior year of high school. They were pleasant enough, but there was always the underlying tension she couldn't quite ease. Debbie had only begun to bond with her in the last year, over the loss of her entire family. Debbie, unfortunately, was the only person on the earth who could understand what she was going through. Debbie still didn't care for her much, but there was unbreakable bond there now. Madison was all that Debbie had left, to remind her that she'd once had a son and grandchildren.

"She seemed to like you. Believe me; I'd know if she didn't." He was trying to comfort her, but she *knew*. She'd been a mother once, and she knew that look. It was the look that said, I see you doing something you shouldn't be doing, but I will support you then help pick up the pieces when you fall flat on your face. She fell asleep in a state of anxiety, but he couldn't rest. He bundled up for the cool night air, and took a brisk walk to his parent's house to see if there was any sugar pie left over. He was delighted to see his mother in the kitchen, wiping down a counter. "Any sugar pie left?" He gave her a big lopsided grin, the one that melted her.

"For you, Cal, of course."

"What do you think of Maddy?" he asked as he pulled the plate of freshly sliced pie closer to him.

"She seems like a sweet woman. She's polite, and very beautiful. But…it seems someone her age should have a family or at least a career," she muttered. Oh, so Maddy was right, his mother didn't approve entirely.

"You don't like her?" He knew better than to talk with his mouth full, but he was shocked. Who could hate Maddy?

"No, I didn't say that. I like her. I just think there is something odd, something not right about her. Was she married before? Does she have children? She seems to be rather secretive and vague when I asked her about her family."

"She was married, but she doesn't have any children," he answered.

"It's just that she isn't the usual kind of girl you date, you know the whore type."

"Mom!"

"I know, but it's true dear." She grinned, while pulling up a chair next to him, "Cal, I thought she was younger, she looks so young. She could be in her early twenties… But I was speaking to her and she is nearly thirty-two! I thought she might have been a career woman, but she's just now finishing school to start a career. So, no career, no family? What has she been doing since high school? Something is there that I can't quite put my finger on." She pushed her light blond hair out of her face, and gazed at him intently with her big blue eyes. "I just think she is hiding something."

"She had a painful divorce. She doesn't like to talk about it," Cal defended Maddy to his mother. "I've often wondered if she can't have children. She doesn't seem especially comfortable around them." He thought of how distant she'd been at first, but had ended up braiding his niece's hair, and giggling with both of them as they talked about famous actors they all thought were handsome.

"That might be it, but surely she would have mentioned it to you." His mother's expression was wary.

"I don't know Ma, isn't it a painful thing?"

"Yes, I imagine it would be, but still…" He left shortly after that, and snuggled back into Maddy, who was the most beautiful woman in the world, sleeping or not.

Madison, meanwhile, was having another nightmare. This one was different, but they always ended the same. "Maddy, you don't have to study all the time! Come to the beach with us," Jack pled. She'd been angry, pulling on her pants, getting dressed while they went round and round in an argument. "It's the last weekend of summer; the kids are starting school on Monday. We'll hang at the beach, make s'mores, do a little boogie boarding, make-out under the pier, it will be fun." He'd tried to coax her.

"Jack, you don't get it, I am here all the time with the kids. Why do I need more family time? I need to get things done that I can't while they are here. I'll see you later tonight." She'd actually told him that she didn't need family time. He'd slammed the door, and she could hear him call the kids to get into the SUV. That was the last conversation they would have. He hadn't kissed her goodbye, he'd been too angry. She hadn't wanted him to. She tossed in her sleep, trying to avoid the next section of the nightmare, the desperate vision she held onto, the dream that she had changed everything and had gone with her family to the beach.

≈

Cal grew concerned as he heard her cry softly in her sleep, "Jack, I'm so sorry." Tears were streaming sideways down her face.

"It's okay, I'm here," he whispered as he pulled her closer. Was her husband's name Jack? She sobbed into his chest. Why did it sound so familiar?

"You think you can forgive me?"

"Yes," he told her, wondering what there was to forgive.

"Oh, thank you, thank you." She grew silent as she buried her face in his chest.

He couldn't help that he became more curious about her past when they were together. All she talked about was Kinley, Kate and Megan. Occasionally she would bring up her friend's children, but not too often. She was bewildering to him. He watched her eat breakfast that morning, with apprehension. Should he ask her about Jack? What did she think she'd done that warranted seeking his forgiveness? It was a mystery. He eventually decided to keep it light; he only had a week with her after all. Maybe he could save serious conversations for phone time.

"So, if Kinley is from Vegas how you did two go to school together?" He chewed on his toast.

She smiled, "Oh, she was a troubled child. She caused her mother nearly to have a nervous breakdown. She was always sneaking out, and partying and so young too. Her mother was at her wit's end so she sent her to live with her sister, Kinley's Aunt Maggie. They enrolled her in a private Christian school, hoping it would help tame her. I met her on the first day. She walked up to me and told me she loved my slutty boots. They were just plain old black boots, but I never laughed so hard, I nearly fell over. She was always joking about something. After that, we were inseparable. That was when we were eleven. Can you believe we've been friends for so long?" She smiled at the recollection.

"I can't believe that she was sneaking out at eleven, I waited until I was thirteen." He grinned at her.

"Her mother thought she needed a positive role model. I guess that was me, although I'm not sure how positive I was. We were always getting into trouble! Her aunt wouldn't say anything to Kinley's mother though, she loved Kinley so much."

"Loved?"

"She passed away a few years ago. I was sadder about that than when my father died," Madison admitted with a wry grin.

"Your father? You never mention your parents much. You're not close, I gather."

"Nope, not at all," she paused to moisten her lips. "My dad was not very nice. When I was young, I couldn't wait to move out of my parent's house. I used to dream about getting married, or having an apartment with Kinley. I just wanted to escape so badly."

He never felt that way in his lifetime. Even his friends had basically come from good homes. Sure, they'd had teenage angst and hated their parents for brief moments in time, but never had he sounded as she did. "What about your mother?" Surely, one of her parents wasn't all-bad. But somewhere in the back of his mind he remembered that they were estranged.

"Oh, she's still alive somewhere. She moves around a lot. Last I heard from her she was in Boca Raton." She shrugged as though she was talking about a total stranger.

"Don't you have any brothers or sisters?" He sometimes realized that it was luxury to have a large family. It hadn't always been, but now he was surrounded by people who loved him. She didn't seem to have that.

"I have a sister. She lives in Virginia, I think." Madison picked up her dishes, clearing off her spot at his table and began to wash them in the sink.

He hopped up, "I have a house keeper this is her job. You wouldn't want to take that away from her would you?" He winked at her, and she smiled bashfully.

"Sorry, I'm used to it being just me." She looked up at him, making him lose focus.

"Would you like to go horseback riding?"

"I would." She laughed. "You have horses too?" She should have known. She was thankful that the conversation had lightened up, she hadn't liked where it was leading. He could have gotten around to asking about her marriage. That was a road she was not comfortable traveling, at least not yet. She frowned as she thought that she'd have to tell him, soon, whether she wanted to or not. Things were becoming far more serious than she'd ever anticipated.

23. Traveling to the Edge

She had two days left with him. So far, it had been the best week of his life including the week Murder of Crows won six Grammys. This topped it. Making love to Madison every morning, afternoon and evening had lived up to the hype Rory had touted sex and love to be. The two intertwined, and one seemed lost or hopeless without the other, just like he was without Madison. It was precisely this that caused his heart to stir restlessly. He was in Canada one more week before he and the rest of the band took off for New Zealand. The thought of being away from her after spending six consecutive days in pure bliss was unacceptable.

She was in his arms, sleeping. Every night she'd had nightmares. Wasn't there something he could do? He'd never been so damned helpless before. Last night she'd called for Alex. Certainly, he knew she was hiding something, but the new addition of another name was perplexing. Why wasn't she opening up to him? He was positive she knew everything she needed to know about him, why couldn't she just trust him in return? She sighed contentedly in her sleep, which gave him hope. What if the longer she was with him, the fewer nightmares she would have? He wanted so badly to make them stop for her. That gnawing, niggling sense pressed against the back of his skull…who was Jack? If he had been her husband, then who was Alex?

Her eyes fluttered open and she smiled up at him. It felt like heaven on earth to have her in his arms, to sleep with her, to make love to her, to be with her. Losing that would punch a great hole into his chest cavity, he was certain. "Marry me," he said softly.

She looked up at him, so many expressions vivid in her countenance. There was a hint of a yes, a look of excitement, terror, wonder, love, hope, doom, and sadness. It was a strange mixture, but he could read every one of her micro expressions. She was terrified and flattered, and the damned phone was ringing again. He picked it up when he saw it was his sister, even though it was early in the morning.

"Hey," he started, rather gruffly. Maddy was watching him, nervously, yet smiling as though she were delighted.

"Cal, Michelle had her baby. We want you and Maddy to come over and meet her," Callie sounded ecstatic. "Are you coming or what?"

"We'll be there in a few minutes," he yawned. He hung the phone up and let Madison in on the new excitement in the family. His family adored Madison so much that he found himself sneaking off with her frequently. His nephew Brian would just sit and stare at her, mentioning to everyone that she was the most beautiful woman alive, Cal not so secretly agreed. She got up; still not speaking and dressed quietly. Something was on her mind, and he was determined to find it out. The walk to his sister's home was merely five minutes, and silent still. "Maddy, what are you thinking?" He had to know.

"About what you asked me earlier, were you serious?" she muttered.

"Of course, how could you not think I am serious? I would never joke about such a thing as marriage." He was feeling a bit aggravated.

"Oh." She walked ahead a little. "It's just that, you don't want to marry someone like me. I'm no good for you." She meant it; he could hear it echo through her distraught voice. Her lip trembled, "I can't be what you want me to be."

He stopped her, grabbing her a little harder than he'd intended, "Damn it woman, would you stop speaking nonsense. You already are everything I want you to be. Why would I want you to be any different? Don't you know I'm in love with you?" Cal practically screamed there in the wooded glen, just steps from his sister's house. He felt horror rip through him as she flinched.

Gabe came up upon them, "They called me too, aren't you excited?" He was wearing an easy smile as he came up the trail to them. His tall head was narrowly missing low tree branches as he ducked, which were more than six and half feet above the ground. "Did I interrupt something?" he asked.

"No, we're just on our way to meet the new baby," Cal lied. He knew Gabe was incredulous but he wasn't about to appease his curiosity.

They followed Gabe in, although Cal was agitated and wanted to finish his conversation with Madison. The two of them had never spoken so seriously before. It was hell to endure not knowing what she was thinking and feeling. They went into the room where Michelle was leaning against fluffed pillows holding a red faced, black haired infant swaddled in pink blankets. "Meet your Uncle Cal," she whispered adoringly to her sweet new baby. He smiled as he took the little one in his arms and cooed to her.

"I will be your favorite, don't listen to the others." Everyone in the room began to laugh. "What's her name?"

"Riley," Michelle beamed. From the corner of his eye, he watched Madison stiffen.

"Do you want to hold her?" he asked, trying to be polite, but he watched as her beautiful tan began to fade instantly from her face. Her natural glow became wan, pale. She muttered something unintelligible.

"I want to hold her and speak subliminal messages in her ear." Rory grabbed the sweet little Riley from Cal's arms. "Rory will be your favorite uncle, not Cal," he whispered with a wicked grin. Rory glared at Cal briefly, it was almost a defensive reaction, as though he were guarding Madison from something. What was going on?

"Where's the bathroom?" Madison asked Michelle.

"Two doors down on the right." She grinned up at Madison, "I'm so glad you're here, Maddy."

"Me too." Maddy looked gravely ill as she excused herself from the room. Gabe left after her. Cal shrugged, thinking they'd come back soon.

~

She was going to be sick. She sat on the sofa and put her head down into her hands. The tears were coming rapidly; she was making that stupid choking noise. Marry him? Have a niece named Riley? Oh, Riley, my sweet Riley, she thought. She remembered sitting in her hospital bed watching Jack hold their Riley, telling her how perfect their baby was. She had been perfect. She would have been nine now. She sobbed harder, and felt the light pressure of a reassuring hand on her shoulder. She gasped as she saw Gabe squatting down beside her, handing her a tissue, looking at her as though for the first time.

"I'm sorry, Madison," he whispered gently. She nodded as she accepted his proffered tissue. She gulped air. Before she knew it, she was weeping into Gabe's chest and his arms were around her.

"Would you take me to the airport? I need to leave. I can't do this." She sounded erratic, confused, but she couldn't have been more certain. She had to leave. This wasn't going to work out and it was no use pretending she belonged to this world, or with Cal. It couldn't work. She was just an ordinary housewife, without a husband or children. The anniversary of the accident, and she is offered to hold a baby girl named Riley? How could God be so cruel? She didn't understand. She rose and walked out with Gabe's arm around her shoulder.

"How long have you known?" she asked him, his arm still around her as they walked along the forest path.

"From the beginning. He was different with you. I had to know who you were." Gabe's voice was steady, "I had to know if you would hurt him." Birds were chirping happily in the treetops torturing her with their explicit happiness. "After I knew, I became concerned more for *your* feelings."

"I'm going to hurt him today." She was sick, bending over a bush, retching out the contents of her stomach, which thankfully had been a glass of water. She gulped the fresh air around her. Steadying herself, she stood, "Please help him."

"I will, but let's take care of you first. I'll bring the car around." She was left, standing on the porch. She hadn't even noticed they'd reached Cal's house. She left a note. She wasn't completely evil. She couldn't answer him, and give him the answer he needed to hear. She couldn't be the mother to his children, be the wife he needed. She couldn't do it again, just to lose him. No, she needed to stop it now, before she hurt him any more than she already had, and before she died wallowing in despair and self-pity. It was beyond her capability to cope anymore.

Gabe brought the Jeep back in a moment and handed her the keys. She watched him, his chocolate skin glistening in the glorious sunshine. Was she doing the right thing? What did it matter? She couldn't do anything else. He plopped her bags into the trunk. "Just leave the car at the airport. I'll retrieve it later."

"I can't just take his car." She trembled, the keys clinking together in her grasp.

Gabe pointed to a building in the distance, "See, it's his garage. He and Rory each have around thirty cars a piece. Rory's garage is off in the other direction. I'm telling you, he won't miss it."

"Why are you doing this?" She stared up at the giant man.

His espresso eyes crinkled in the corners, "Cal is…somewhat immature. He's grown a lot since you came along but I'm not sure he's ready to marry you especially not knowing your history. He needs to know, as I am sure you're aware." He pulled a USB drive from his pocket, "I'm going to tell him today, and neither of us will have to say a word."

"I don't know." She bit her lip.

"Go, I'll pick up the pieces and save them for you." She tilted her head in confusion as he continued to speak, "One day you can put them back together." She nodded, if Cal let her, but she couldn't think about it now. She drove to the airport, following the directions from the navigation woman, her heart breaking all the way. There was only one person she wanted to see when she got back, Kinley.

Where the hell had she gone? An hour to go to the bathroom? Was she sick? He walked around, leaving his family he went to search for her. Was it possible she had gone back to his house? He followed the trail. Where had Gabe gone off to? He frowned; the two of them had disappeared around the same time. He got to his home, having walked a little faster than normal and panted slightly as he climbed the steps. He hunched over when he got inside, placed his hands on his knees and tried to catch his breath, when he noticed the note sitting on the table. His heart was pounding faster than it ought; he nervously reached out for it. Cal. That was all it said on the outside. His fingers numbly moved to open it. He knew he didn't want to read it, but he had to.

> Cal,
>
> I should have said goodbye sooner. It wasn't meant to be, you and me. All the time I kept trying to make it work, it was easy, you know. You made everything easy. I don't deserve it. I am not what I seem. I'm broken. I wish I had the courage to tell you face to face. I can't. I'm weak. Please forget about me.
>
> Madison

He sat down, puzzled, and angry. Shouldn't he have seen it coming? She'd given no indication she wanted to break things off. She'd become rather quiet after his haphazard proposal. He admitted he could've been more romantic, but it hadn't seemed so bad at the time. He was rethinking everything. Hadn't she enjoyed their time together? What had he done to push her away? He was furious. He jumped up only to fling a chair across the kitchen with enough force that it broke into several large pieces, splintering wood fragments whistled as they flew through the air.

"Cal." Gabe was standing behind him. He hadn't heard Gabe come in, during his tirade.

"What?" He was aware he sounded like a wounded animal abandoned to die.

"She's gone."

"How astute of you. Did you help her escape?" His temper flared as he stared up at the over seven-foot tall giant of a man. Gabe just nodded. "To the airport?" Cal interrogated, but Gabe stood his ground and let Cal holler at him until he was purple, and until he could think of nothing better to do than to punch Gabe squarely in the chest. "Thanks for being there for me," he shouted in his best sardonic tone. Gabe hardly moved, even though Cal had hit him with enough force to knock over a baby elephant.

"She wanted to tell you," he muttered.

"What the hell? Is she in love with you?" Cal groaned as he pushed another chair out of the way, and walked from the kitchen before he could thoroughly destroy it.

"No, Cal, it's nothing to do with me. There are some things that are too difficult to say aloud." He was flustered; Gabe shoved something small into his hand.

"A USB drive? Are you saying all the answers I need are on a file?" Cal was in anguish, he just needed Gabe to go away, he needed to be alone.

"I am," Gabe told him. "I think she wanted to tell you, but didn't know how." He was gone, the door shut gently behind him. Cal collapsed onto the floor and pulled his ottoman closer. His laptop computer sat undisturbed on the ottoman. He leaned heavily against the sofa behind him. He unfolded the computer, feeling a searing headache coming on. His eyes could barely focus as he inserted the drive. A file popped open, labeled- Madison Grey. He shook his head. All of her secrets were on this drive? What had she wanted to keep hidden from him so badly? Was this the reason she considered herself broken? He tried to focus on the file as he clicked it open. It was a newspaper clipping. The headline read- *Madison Grey is in our Prayers*. Puzzled, he continued reading.

24. Maddy the Runaway

Madison was glad to see Ryan open the door. She truthfully hoped neither of the girls would answer as she was not in a mood to pretend she was happy. Kinley came up behind him carrying two small cartons of Ben and Jerry's ice cream, the kind with the little plastic spoons attached underneath the lids. "You were expecting me?" she asked as she came in out of the sultry summer evening, and stepped into air-conditioned paradise.

"I had a feeling," Kinley teased, and shook her head, "Gabe called."

"Good, you scared me." She sat her purse down on the hallway table. She frowned slightly as she handed Madison her own little carton of ice cream.

"It's my cue to leave, I'm thinkin'." Ryan disappeared, wearing his jeans and a button down shirt. The hall light caught the silver in his golden blond hair as he walked away.

"He's getting old, Kin," she muttered as they found their way to the black kitchen table. Kinley chuckled warmly.

"He is old, Maddy. That's what I get for falling in love with someone ten years older than me." She sat down at the table and smiled. "So, I was supposed to pick you up from the airport tomorrow evening. I know I shouldn't ask, but why are you here? Not that you're not welcome."

Madison scowled, "You didn't have a feeling or a dream about this?" Madison teased.

"Nope, afraid not," Kinley answered, with her mouthful of *New York Fudge Brownie Chunk*. "That would be cool, would it not? I would love it, you would never have to share anything painful aloud, I would already know." She smiled brightly, "What happened?"

"Gabe is very perceptive," Madison dug her small plastic spoon into her own ice cream. "I made a huge mistake not telling Cal," she hedged.

"Right, you know we are all horrible at this, hang on." She reached for her purse on a nearby countertop and pulled it to her, after rifling through it for a moment; she dug out a card and handed it to Madison. "Here it is, the validation card, you will be validated. So, I support you and everything, and I'm on your side, what happened?" Madison smiled.

"I had the best week I've had in a long time." She began, Kinley nodded as she listened patiently. "Then he had to go and ruin it by proposing this morning." Kinley gasped. "And as if that wasn't enough for me, his sister had a baby girl and decided to name her Riley."

Kinley's expressive face would have meant death in a poker tournament. She shook her head and frowned, "All this morning, on this date? Maddy that is awful." It was Madison's turn to nod.

"I had to get out of there, I was suffocating."

"And you still hadn't told him when you left?" Kinley looked terribly concerned.

"No, but by now, Gabe will have told him everything," she cried. Kinley listened as she continued, "I imagine Gabe has told him by now." Kinley pressed her lips together until they formed a tight line. "I wonder how Cal will take it." She didn't wait for a response, "He'll hate me. I've screwed everything up. You would have loved his family. They were everything a family is supposed to be, and his house, oh his house, everything was perfect. Why did he have to propose today of all days?" Madison cried in frustration.

"Let me make sure I understand you…The man who you have fallen in love with asked you to marry him and you ran away?"

"I can't do it again! I can't! He'll want children and other things."

"It might be completely different this time," Kinley pointed out tenderly.

"I'm too scared, Kin. I just can't. Then I was even too cowardly to tell him my secrets. There are so many." Madison stared down at the table.

"Why didn't you just tell him? What am I missing?" Kinley looked at her with sympathy.

"It wasn't easy, and it never seemed to be the right time. Then there's the small unavoidable fact that I've never had to tell anyone. Everyone already knew. It was fodder for gossip, in the newspapers, on the nightly news, it was everywhere. I never had to say a word." She sighed, "I just couldn't bring it up."

"I guess I never thought of that." Kinley frowned again. "Is it too soon?" She'd asked this one before, but Madison didn't know the answer. Some days it would have been no, others it would have been yes.

"That's the frustrating thing. I can't tell! Is there some rulebook I should be following? Is everything supposed to be wonderful? I shouldn't be feeling happy again at all. I'm so guilty, and terrified. I have always admired Cal, and you and I always joked about the dumb back-up list. Then it happens. My actual, real-life husband dies and I get the top guy on my back-up list to propose? What kind of crap is that? It's too...it's not supposed to be that way!"

Kinley just sat in silence, listening, which is what she needed. "You have nothing to feel guilty for," she spoke sincerely.

"I do. I should have been with them."

"We've discussed this before, Maddy; it wasn't the way it worked out. You can't undo it, or go back for another chance. Life is giving you this chance, and you are just going to throw it away."

"Please Kin, don't. I need you to understand, not to throw my decision back in my face," Madison implored.

"Forgive me, Maddy. I do support you and love you," she answered softly. "I don't want to see you suffer anymore." Kinley reached across the table and squeezed her hand. "Like I said, I'm worried for you, and for Cal." She looked away, her thoughts taking her to another place as her eyes gazed steadily out of the window over the sink. "He's got to be feeling awful right about now."

Cal thought about the things he'd been reading. He walked silently to his mother and father's home. The lights were dimmed, and he could see a bluish light flashing ever so often, reflections of the television. Darkness extended its fingers, casting eerily long shadows across the land, and crawled up onto the porch he stepped up on. His mother was in the kitchen, as always, pulling steaming hot chocolate chip cookies out of her oven. Even those reminded him of Madison.

"You look terrible," she said, not turning toward him, but lifting cookies onto a plate with her spatula.

"I can always count on you to cheer me up," he murmured darkly.

"Cal, I've been talking to Rory, and I want to apologize." He lifted his head up to look at her, "Now, I know what was different about Madison. I'm so sorry." She slid the small plate of cookies across the bar to him, as a peace offering.

He nodded. He could see the words, like a flash of light, still when he closed his eyes.

Jack, Jonathan, Riley, Alex and Jackson Grey were killed this evening when a trucker fell asleep at the wheel. They were 1.2 miles from their home. August nineteenth....

He shook it away. She'd lost everything. But he didn't know what he was feeling. Four children? It seemed impossible. But the pictures...they all looked so much like her, and her husband. He was genuinely jealous of a dead man. It had been easier when he'd believed that the man who hurt her was some stalker, or twisted ex-husband, but this guy was dead. There is no way to compete with the dead. Dead people are notoriously perfect. Then, his sister had to name her new baby Riley. He'd been putting things together all afternoon. Kinley's daughter had mentioned that her friend Riley had been killed in an accident that took her whole family. She, Riley, was Madison's daughter.

Should he call her? He didn't know what to do, or even how to respond. He didn't know if she could love him after all she'd been through. He stared down at the plate of untouched cookies.

"Talk, I'm listening," he heard his mother's voice. He looked up again.

"I don't know if I'm mad at her, or if I feel sorry for her," he grumbled. "I don't know what to feel."

"It was wrong of her not to tell you, but I can see why she didn't." His mother had an expression of irony on her nearly ageless face.

"How can you understand something like that?" Cal complained angrily.

"Because, Calvin, if I lost your father, I would be insane. If I lost Rory, you, Callie and Michelle, I would be *certifiable*, you might as well lock me up." She poured him a small cup of milk before continuing, "It would be heartbreaking to talk about it, think about it, and beyond agonizing to pick up the pieces and move on. My heart goes out to that woman. I can see me in her. Two boys, two girls, one set of fraternal twins. It freaked me out a little."

He'd never seen the similarities. "She could have told me."

"Maybe, but I can't judge. You are only thinking of yourself. I hate to be the one to point this out to you, but while you are sitting there moping, Madison is all alone." His mother passed him a napkin. "I bet she was relieved you didn't know. You didn't feel sorry for her, or treat her differently, because you didn't know. Maybe that was what she wanted, Cal."

He didn't need this from his own mother. Not now. He left grumbling and slightly irritable. He found himself at home, once again studying the pictures and articles on the USB drive Gabe had brought to him. One was an article detailing a quick settlement from the trucking company, speaking of an unnamed amount. He could only assume with five people involved, it had been millions of dollars. There was a picture of Kinley, her arm around Madison, leaving a courthouse. This was how Gabe and Rory knew she wasn't a gold digger. She had to be a millionaire; she never needed his money. He clicked on the next picture. The smiling faces looking up at him had no idea that their lives would be cut short. It was a copy of the Grey family Christmas card Maddy had sent out the year before last. He imagined he'd never know how Gabe had gotten a hold of it. She looked up at her husband Jack with that adoring expression he'd so longed to see for himself. He traced over the computer screen where her face was. Her children were beautiful. This is what she'd lost. He realized she was a different person now; this wasn't even the Maddy he knew. He heard the door creak open and looked up to see Rory holding two frosty long-necked bottles filled with amber liquid.

He minimized the file, tucking it away, his background was the picture Kinley had taken at the concert where he'd met Maddy for the first time. He studied the picture. He was smiling, his arm around her. She smiled too, her large loose curls spilling over her shoulders. But...he noticed something now that he'd never seen before. Her smile did not reach her eyes. She wasn't leaning into him the way most fans did, she was slightly pulling away. He calculated it, six months from the time of the accident. He studied her face more carefully, Rory looking over his shoulder. He recalled not being able to see what she was thinking, she'd been dead inside.

"Thought you could use this" he handed Cal a bottle. How had he known?

"Cheers to the enabler," he muttered before swigging down a large gulp of beer. "Cal, why did you put your arm around her waist? You know we don't do that? We always put our arms around shoulders when we pose. You're such a creeper." Cal chuckled hollowly, choosing to ignore the comment, he brought back the pictures of her family, while Rory merely glanced over his shoulder. He sensed Rory's curiosity.

"Is that her family then?" Rory peered over his shoulder, while Cal nodded grudgingly. "I didn't know she had four kids. Oh, look at the twins, they're a beautiful family." He sighed wistfully, "Jen and I always wanted more, but I guess it wasn't in the cards." Cal knew after Matthew was born, Jen had endured several miscarriages. It wasn't something they ever talked about with anyone.

Cal looked up at him; this wasn't something Rory discussed, ever. He didn't know what to say in return. Yes, Madison had a beautiful family but he didn't want to talk about it anymore. He slammed his bottle down, bringing Rory out of his self-induced trance. "Why would she leave like that?"

"It was probably too much to take in at once. A new baby girl with the name Riley on the anniversary of her family's death...it must have been shocking."

"And a marriage proposal on that anniversary too..." Cal interjected before taking another large gulp.

"Ouch," Rory grimaced. "You proposed?"

"Yep, and I guess I have my answer." He scowled. "I never imagined it this way. I thought the woman who finally got me to propose would want to marry me just as much as I wanted to marry her. I've never been so wrong." The pain eating away in chest made him contemplate third degree burns. Numb, but in writhing agony, and even though the flames no longer touched the skin, the burning would continue to devour the charred flesh. Yes, this was heartbreak in the third degree. What had Madison's been? He shuddered to think about it.

"I don't know," Rory drew out his words deliberately. "She's in love with you, that much was clear."

"Please." Cal clicked on a new picture. "She never looked at me like that. I would have noticed." He saw her looking up at Jack with devotion and love in her eyes. He'd never seen her eyes light up like that, had he?

"Yes she did. It was obvious to everyone; she loves you. I think you should call her." Rory drained his bottle of beer and placed it empty on the coffee table.

"I have called her. She's either ignoring it, or not home."

"Call her cell."

"I called her home, I called her cell. I can't do anything else, Rory. What if she needs her space?" He could picture her in her little townhouse staring at the phone and refusing to answer it.

"It would be a shame to let her go," Rory answered sullenly. "We all think the world of her."

"I didn't want to let her go! I want to marry the woman! I just can't understand this. If anyone could give her anything she wants, it's me."

"Don't take this wrong little bro, but I don't think you can. And…if you ever tell anyone I am this deep, I'll kill you and feed you to the bears. Listen carefully; I noticed the way she looked at you, but it was only hidden glimpses. Pain would appear on her face immediately afterward as though she were betraying someone. My guess is that she feels guilty for loving you and so soon after everything has happened. She doesn't want to be in love and she doesn't want to replace her family. She just wants them back, but now she has a new complication, she wants you too." He swallowed, "Cal, have you ever considered the fact that maybe you can't give her what she wants? Her family back…and maybe she's scared because you want to marry her, and maybe you want a family, and maybe that terrifies her because she's afraid she can't give you what you want?" he asked it in a question as though he may have been doubting it.

Cal stared at his brother and distinctly felt that in his lifetime he'd never been hit harder in the chest. The wind was knocked out of him. He tried to breathe but it was difficult. He'd been called out on being self-centered twice tonight, and both times they had been right.

25. Souvenir Day

Everything was useless without Madison. Knowing he'd be seeing her soon had been enough of an incentive to keep going, but now he had no drive. How had she done it? How had she gone on alone? He thought there was a good chance she was still alive somewhere, although it wasn't much comfort. Still it was better than knowing she was lying in a grave somewhere. He thought of how hard it must have been for her, and how difficult it still must be on a daily basis. He was struggling with just the loss of Madison, when she'd lost five people she loved in a single tragic moment. His loss was nothing to hers.

Shawn, the pretty boy in the group had made a mistake the other day. He'd been speaking to Rory, sharing his concerns, when Cal had happened upon them. "If he cancels on us, when we have forty concerts to go, just because of *some* woman…" Cal had never realized how derogatory the word *some* could sound. Shawn was now walking around with a black eye, or more purple with a greenish hue around the edges. Shawn's wife had let him have hell shortly afterward. She'd told him she'd leave him if he didn't stop being a jerk, "That would give you some empathy," she'd yelled. Cal would have laughed if he thought it might have helped.

He moped around, brooding, pouting. They were on the private jet together, off to New Zealand. How could he perform when he felt like this?

It had been over a week since he'd heard her voice. Sure, he'd heard it on her voicemail, but that was just a modern day torture device as far as he was concerned. There was a large empty pit where his stomach had once been, and a crater where he swore his heart used to be. He could hear Shawn and Rory playing chess, Chris was sleeping, and Gabe was typing on his laptop. He slipped off unnoticed to the back and decided that he couldn't take anymore. "Hello?" It was so good to hear a voice on the other end of the phone, even if it wasn't Maddy's.

"Kinley," the pain of speaking her name reminded him of being garroted.

"Cal? I've been so worried for you." She was? "It's so good to hear from you."

"It is?" He could feel his brows lift in astonishment. "I just thought you wouldn't want to hear from me again," he muttered in anguish. Enough small talk, "How is she?"

They both knew the 'she' he was referring to. "She isn't doing so well. She's locked herself up again." If he understood correctly, Maddy must have shut herself away after the accident. "You know about Jack and the kids now, don't you?" He loved the way she asked. Something in her voice seemed to be telling him that if he didn't know, she was fed up and about to tell him herself.

"I know what little I read in the newspaper articles and the obituary notice," he admitted with a sullen air. Wouldn't it have been different if he'd heard it from Maddy?

"Well then, what would you like to know?"

His heart was leaping; he had so many questions. Where to begin? "What was Jack like?" Yes, that was a good first question. It was safe to ask Kin.

"Maddy had known him for a long time. But, I first met him in junior high. We went to school together all those years. He and Maddy didn't start dating until we were in high school, he was the quarterback on the football team, and she was a cheerleader. He was always a sporty guy; they did a lot of things together. They went out riding quads, boating, had the jet skis and camped in the trailer. He was a fun, outdoors kind of guy. I loved him like a brother, he was a good man." He could hear her voice choke up.

"Was he like me?" He'd noticed the physical differences between them. Jack seemed to be built differently, leaner, more GQ. Cal always looked like he was too big to be allowed, until you saw Gabe next to him, that is. He wanted so badly to be everything different from Jack. He didn't want Maddy to like him because he reminded her of her dead husband.

"No, you're not alike at all. She likes that." He could feel the tension in his chest ease subtly.

"I want her to be telling me this. I want Maddy to feel like she can tell me anything. I won't push her away; I want to hear all about Jack, even if it hurts. I want to hear about her children and what they were like. I want her to confide in me when she is having a hard day, or missing them. Why can't she just see that I love her?" he nearly cried in frustration.

"Cal, she was happier with you than she has been in a long time. She feels guilty for being happy. She is miserable, and dare I say it, somewhat masochistic. She is punishing herself; she thinks she should have been in the car that day. You could give her all that you want; maybe you can say everything you just told me, on a message. She listens to them, all of them."

"She does?" He felt a weak stabbing, dull throbbing in his chest as something moved in the crater where his heart had been.

"Yes, of course. She loves you, she doesn't want to love you, but she does."

"Why doesn't she want to love me! Damn it! Here I am willing to die for her…" He struggled to find the words, realizing immediately that he'd chosen poorly.

"Don't die for her; *live* for her." Kinley spoke softly, "She's afraid, because everything was taken from her so quickly. It doesn't matter that you're rich or famous, it only matters that you are human and can be taken from her too. She doesn't want to hurt you. She's actually grieving herself to death right now. I have been your advocate. I will do what I can to get her to call you."

"You would do that?" He had that mocking hope slide like a needle into his chest.

"We're having souvenir day today so afterward I'll talk to her. I've been trying to persuade her to come out for a week now," Kinley said.

"Souvenir day?"

"We all went on different vacations, me, Maddy, Kate and Megan. At the end of every summer we exchange gifts."

"You are the funniest bunch of women I have ever met." He laughed, his laughter sounded dead in his own ears. "I need to be going, please let me know what I can do."

"I will," she answered before hanging up the phone. He pressed his face against the small round, cool window and sighed. He'd never been a depressed kind of person. He'd always been upbeat and positive, optimistic, his mother said. He closed his eyes and sat back into the reclining seat. He didn't see how this was going to work out, but he was sure glad Kinley was in his corner.

∾

Kinley had made up a big lunch of homemade bread, chicken fettuccine alfredo, and a scrumptious salad. Everyone around her laughed, while she ignored them and picked at her food. "What did you bring us from Canada?" Megan asked. She ran her perfect fingernails, white tips, through her platinum hair and smiled.

Madison picked up a large bag. The four of them had started souvenir day forever ago. The rule was, pick out something you want for yourself, and if you can afford it, buy four of them. She had been in such a hurry to leave Canada that she'd picked up four small maple-leaf shaped (plastic) jars of maple syrup. She knew her friends would think it was the lamest thing ever, but she'd done better in England. She pulled up her other bag from London. Kinley had a bag from London as well. Kate's bag was from Hawaii and Megan's was from New York.

She passed around the maple syrup and each of her friends laughed. She smiled weakly. Megan and Kate didn't know what had happened. "Were you in bed the whole time?" Megan teased.

"She probably picked these up in the airport," Kate chortled.

Kinley grinned, "Now show them what you got for them in England, the ingrates."

She pulled out four small boxes and passed them around. Everyone admired the intricate patterns of blue and white before pulling the lids up. Inside were china tea-for-one sets, in blue and white. She also passed out boxes of English tea to her friends who liked these presents considerably better than the syrup. "This is much better. We can't buy this at Costco," Megan smirked. She threw a cherry tomato from her salad that landed in Megan's hair. "*Oooh.*"

"You next," Kinley told Kate. She was trying to keep it going.

Kate grinned and pulled out little jewelry boxes. "You all are going to think this is lame, but I did my best. I thought it was awesome." The little black velvet boxes were in their hands, and simultaneously as they had before, they opened the boxes. White gold rings with pearls were nestled inside.

"I love it," Madison said as she slipped it onto her finger, "It's perfect."

"They had this place where you pull a pearl out of an oyster, I didn't know what else to get, but I know the rule. If I like it, then all of you will too." They all admittedly like the rings.

"You next Kin, I want to be last." Megan covertly grinned. Kinley nodded.

She pulled out boxes wrapped in silver paper, sealed with a red waxen seal over the white ribbon. Each of the women round the table opened up a pair of blue and white porcelain candlesticks. "These are beautiful." Madison smiled as she twisted one of the candlesticks in the light. "And they match the tea sets."

"You two didn't shop together?" Kate asked.

"Nope, I bought these when I was giving Maddy some *alone* time." Kinley smiled to herself. She pulled out a box of candles from her bag and gave each woman two. "Beeswax, they were the most treasured candles back in the day." Was Kinley blushing? She'd get to the bottom of it later.

Megan hummed a few bars of some random melody, and pounded lightly on the table in a mock-drum roll. She pulled out her large shopping bag that had NYC written in bold red letters. She pulled four designer purses from her bag causing every woman to gasp at the beauty of them. Real leather, large silver clasps, all black so they would match anything. Each one was different from the others. "Please tell me these are not real," muttered Kinley.

"No, they can't be." Kate poked at her new bag then let her fingers follow the softness of the leather. She opened the bag, "It has a serial number."

"Those can be faked though," Madison interjected.

"Would you all stop speculating? They are real," Megan announced.

"How did you afford these?" Madison did not believe her, but she was certain Megan had a good story.

"You will not believe this. I was dying to tell you all. I won a shopping spree when I was there, at Barney's of all places. Actually, my hub won it, but he had no idea what Barney's was. He won it at his business luncheon. It was the top prize for the number one sales rep, my man. I went shopping. Don't worry, they were on sale," she added as if it would make them all feel better. "I bought me two, a brown one too." She grinned, "And we bought my sweetie a suit, and some great shoes and me a couple of outfits, and few things for the baby."

"I'm happy for you!" Kate smiled. "Thanks for sharing the joy. That must have been some shopping spree."

"It was," she sighed as she sat back in her seat. "I win the best gift prize this year," she told them.

"We don't have a best gift prize," Kinley replied.

"We should," Madison laughed loudly.

When everyone had gone, Madison sat on Kinley's red sofa clutching the purse. "Can you believe Megan?"

"You would have done the same thing, you know it," Kinley told her.

"Whatever happened to those bags we bought the day before the accident?" Madison had wanted to ask before now, she'd sometimes thought of that wonderful night, but immediately hated herself for it.

"I took them back the following week. We have store credit. Are you ready to go get new bags soon?"

"Yeah, let's go next week. We can't ever have too many bags." Madison watched Kin smile at the idea of it. Kinley came over to her with a cup of iced tea. "I'm glad you're out of the house again."

"I..." Madison stared at Kinley, unable to speak.

"He called me this morning. It was about time too." Kinley took a sip of her iced tea.

"Cal?"

"No, Paul Walker. Of course Cal," Kinley teased lightly.

"What did he say?"

"Does this feel a bit high school to you?" Kinley teased again. "He said a lot of sweet things. I think you should talk to him."

"But what if he doesn't want me anymore? I just don't think it can work." Madison had been thinking of very little else since she'd left Canada. Why did she do this to herself? She ached for Cal. Now there was a new hole in her heart, next to the old one, which would never heal. She resembled a slice of Swiss cheese. She hadn't meant for it to go so far. She imagined that was how druggie people began. Oh, I'll just take this little bit, who cares if I come down later, it feels so good to fly! But later always comes, down always happens. She was alone again. It would always be that way in the end.

"He wants you. He wants to listen to you, hear everything from you. He wants to be there for you," Kinley told her. "He's crushed. And…Maddy, don't take this the wrong way, but I don't want to be in the middle any more. I feel *awkward*."

"Sorry, Kin. I will, I'll call him. I didn't mean to crush him. I swear I didn't. The timing of everything is so wrong. Why couldn't I just meet him a year from now? Surely, it would've been better."

"You know I'm no good at the comforting thing but, I don't think a year from now would be any better. You are going to hurt from this the rest of your life. You are going to be dealing with the pain, it's never going away. You might as well have someone in your life that makes you happy. That is the best you can do, to go on with your life and fill it with things and people who make you happy. The sadness will always be there, you might as well balance it out. No one can live with just sadness, Maddy."

Madison listened intently. "What you say makes sense, it does. But I can't make the guilty feeling go away."

"You're going to have to try. You have done nothing wrong."

Madison decided to change the subject, "Did *you* do something wrong?" Kinley, being a redhead, was fair and could blush better than almost anyone. Every part of her face was aflame. Madison had stumbled onto something. "I refuse to leave until you tell me."

"I didn't," she stammered, "it's not..." Kinley gathered her composure. "I got caught in the rain the day I was shopping in England. I was lost and wet and..." Where could this be going? "I ran into Rory." There had to be more to it. "He offered to take me shopping on Portobello Road."

"Why were you blushing?"

"I had a really nice day with him."

"*Day*? You didn't do anything did you?" Madison found herself smiling at her friend's agitation.

"No, of course not. I just shouldn't have been with him for the entire day, is all." Kinley smoothed her curls back, "Not like he'll remember or anything. I guess I feel guilty because it felt really nice." She cleared her throat, "Now, back to you, are you going to call Cal and end his misery?"

"I will, you know I will."

Madison loaded her new things into her car and drove home to contemplate the points Kinley had made. In her mind, Kinley made perfect sense. But her heart did most of the thinking in these situations and it didn't seem to be able to grasp the concept of moving on. She fell asleep on her sofa, crying a river, sobbing until her eyes closed from the absolute exhaustion of it all. She knew what she must do; she had to find out if it was right to be with Cal. She had to ask Jack.

26. Jack Stops By

She found herself standing at the grave. A monument of ten feet, solid gray and black granite towered before her. The name Grey was etched deeply in black, and underneath was a family picture. It was beautiful now that it was finished. She crossed slowly to the massive headstone and stared into the faces she missed. Her hand ran along the slightly rough surface of the granite, and she leaned forward until her cheek felt the coldness of the stone. The day was overcast; clouds blurred the view of the sun. The scent of rain permeated the air, humidity hung thickly, weighing down the leaves on the trees and individual blades of grass. Was Jack here? Were the kids here? She couldn't tell. Shouldn't she be able to feel them?

She used to think that if something happened where death separated them, they would still find a way to communicate. Now, she just felt idiotic, standing here staring at the headstone. He wasn't here, who was she kidding? She still felt the inclination to talk, to pour her feelings out as the first droplet of rain brushed her hair. "Jack, if you can hear me, I need you, I need to know something. I have another chance, to love and be loved. But I'm scared, so scared." Her tears felt inclined to match the rate of the rain, trickling down her nose. "Please if you can hear me, give me a sign let me know what to do" she cried.

There was nothing. Jack had never been able to sneak up on her. She tried to explain it, but there was a feeling associated with Jack. She could *feel* him sneak up on her. She could feel when he was in bed with her, and when he was in the house. He was a presence. She couldn't have explained it to him to make him really understand. Now, she waited to feel that presence that meant Jack was there with her, but it did not come. She was feeling foolish again. "I can't keep going on like this," she whispered. Her phone was ringing. She pushed her hair out of her face, as strands clung to the places where her tears had traveled. It was Cal. She looked up at the sky. Was this a sign? Did signs even exist?

"Hello?" She choked out a strangled 'hello', and silently cursed herself for sounding so desperate.

"Maddy," he sounded relieved.

"Cal, can you forgive me? I didn't mean to…" But she was unable to continue speaking. She found a bench and sat down, feeling the moisture of spent rain drops soak into her jeans.

"Forgive you, for what? For feeling overwhelmed? I'm sorry, Maddy. I didn't know what you'd been through. I didn't even know how to feel or what to think when I found out. I do want you to know that you can trust me. You can tell me, or not tell me whatever you want. Just please don't go away."

She swallowed back the new tears and nodded even though she knew he couldn't see her nod. "I'm at the cemetery right now, visiting." Madison looked over at the teddy bears, flowers, notes and other stuffed animals propped up against the base of the headstone. She had been glad when the makeshift shrine had moved from her house and the place where the car had been totaled. A cross was still there in the median, erected by the city. Her children's friends still visited the grave, and flowers found a home here.

"Maddy, tell me something. Tell me you don't want me to go away, that you still need me in your life like I need you," his voice was pleading.

"I still need you. I don't want you to go away," she admitted.

"What else do you need? Do you need me to listen? I can do that. Tell me what to do to help you through this. I know you have Kinley, Kate and Megan, but you have me too, you don't need to shut me out." His voice had a hoarse, raspy tone to it. Somehow, it was staunching the ache in her heart, not truly healing her, but soothing nonetheless.

"Thank you," she whispered. "I need to go, or I'll be soaked in the rain."

"Can I call you later?" he asked with a note of uncertainty in his voice.

"Yes. I need to talk to you. I have so many things to apologize for."

"I have no need of apologies, Maddy. I just need to know that we're going to be okay somehow." She didn't feel as though she deserved his sweetness. She choked on a fresh wave of tears, grieving, pitying herself.

"I think we'll be okay," was all she could muster before running to her car.

She went home to her darkened depressing townhouse, which had never really become her home. It was still so much like a display of who she wanted to appear to be, rather than who she was. There were no family pictures, nothing personal, just like a model home in a sea of cookie cutter houses. She dropped onto her leather sofa and pulled her shoes off. Madison toppled over and closed her eyes. The well is dry, she thought, no more tears. Her mascara was long gone, smeared away with the silver-gray eyeliner she'd been wearing. She heaved a sigh and floated away into a dream.

"Maddy?" Jack's voice. She bolted up and stared at him. There he was standing in her townhouse. "This is a nice place," he mentioned casually. She blinked several times, willing her eyesight to adjust, as he stood there arms akimbo grinning at her. He had a smile that took up his entire face, and made everyone near him want to smile too. Right now she was fighting herself, wrestling a pillow, trying to get to him. She wrapped her arms tightly around his waist, determined not to let go. "It's all right," he spoke soothingly.

She shivered, "I miss you so much, there are too many things to say. Don't leave, please don't leave," she managed to croak out. She was weeping again. It felt so good to be in his arms and so comforting to smell his skin.

"Maddy, wasn't there something you wanted to ask me?" He hadn't said he wouldn't leave.

She looked up, tears shimmering in her eyes and nodded. It was only a dream, she knew it, and yet she couldn't stop herself from looking at him as though he were real. It certainly felt real, but when she awoke later without him, she would tell herself it was only a dream, even though it would feel like she'd lost him all over again. "I'm scared," she stated simply.

"Scared of what?" Oh, she missed his lips. She reached up and ran her fingers over them before she stood on the tips of her toes to feel his kiss. She had to be dead, because this was what heaven must feel like.

"Everything. Am I supposed to be alone, or move on? Am I moving on too quickly? If I do, is it an insult to your memory? How do I do this? Is Cal even right for me? I mean he is the first person I dated after you…you…"

"Died," he grinned, "continue."

"He is such a womanizing, man-whore, and I feel foolish doing whatever it is I am doing with him. Then there's the fact that I'm even dreaming this dream. I must be on drugs. I'm talking to my dead husband about my current boyfriend." She was getting herself worked up. Jack pulled her closer and kissed the top of her head. "Do you even want me to move on?"

"Maddy, my angel, you are so beautiful, especially when you cry. Listen to me, I love you and want you to be happy. I *need* for you to be happy. Are you more afraid of my disapproval, or the fact that Cal is likely to hurt you with his womanizing ways?"

When he said it like that…She didn't know. She looked up into his blue eyes, seeing them framed in dark lashes, "I don't know," she admitted sadly.

"I'm waiting for you here, but it's going to be a while," he mentioned delicately. "You don't need to be alone. Cal loves you, and you love him."

She sobbed even harder. It was something everyone around her seemed to notice. "No," she cried.

"I'm not the most observant man, but I think you do."

"I can't be discussing this with you," she moaned. "It's too weird."

"Talk to Kinley then, or Kate, or Megan." He shrugged nonchalantly.

"That's not what I mean," she growled.

"Come here, I only have a little while, and I don't want to argue with you." He led her to the sofa and sat down next to her. She rested her head against his chest, "Maddy, I'd be lying if I weren't jealous that some living breathing man could hold you while I am forced to be away from you.

And…Calvin Hunt of all people," he laughed. "But, Maddy he is here and I am not. If you must concede to let me watch the kids until you get to be with me again, then I must concede to let Calvin Hunt take care of you while I can't be here holding you."

She shook her head, "I can't do it again."

"The kids miss you," he changed the subject. "I miss you. Go to sleep, Maddy." He kissed her lips leaving a burning feeling, something like peppermint, behind. "I'm here." As though she were drugged, she could feel herself slipping away. She was pleading inside of her head, begging not to be separated from him again. She couldn't do it, but the harder she fought, the more it beat her down. Deeply, she sunk, floating in a sea, tranquilly drowning in its' depths until she awoke with a start. Staring at the sofa next to her and the empty spot where he had been sitting.

27. Finally Facebook Friends

Not that she was truly convinced that Jack had been to visit her, but now she was a bit unnerved. She snuggled down into her blankets and awaited her call from Cal. Kinley left her a message on Facebook, which she logged onto with her laptop computer balanced on the top of her thighs. She navigated to the page and smiled. Kinley had finally posted the picture of Madison and Cal from the night she'd first met him. There were dozens of comments about how great she looked. Some guy friends wrote statements riddled with jealousy, while girlfriends were jealous for other reasons. Her favorite comment was from an old friend who wrote, "Was he more delicious in person?" She had to reply that pictures could not do him justice. His friend request was still sitting there. Ben A. Longtime?

Was she ready to take that tiny leap of faith and let him in a little more? She nervously clicked on the 'accept' option. He would be able to glimpse her through the narrow window of Facebook. She changed her profile picture to the one a worker in Disney World had taken for them; Cal and Madison were posing with Mickey Mouse. She remembered the boy taking a picture for Cal, and then one for her. She smiled as her phone rang fifteen minutes later. "Maddy, you accepted me at last!" he sounded thrilled.

"Where are you?"

"Sydney." He seemed preoccupied. "Love the picture you chose." He was scrolling, looking over her page. She awaited his response. He would soon realize why she hadn't accepted his friendship. Pages and pages of 'hope you are doing better today' and condolences over her loss were all she had for a year now. He was silent, perhaps contemplating, while she held her breath, anxiety ridden over his response. "Thank you," he finally said.

"You want to know me, flaws and all?" She hoped he would say yes, but would have understood it if he didn't.

"Yes." He was pondering something seriously, "Maddy you have a beautiful family." He was looking at her family pictures.

"Thank you," she answered him softly. "I should have told you."

"Perhaps," he agreed tentatively, "I would have been a little more sensitive to you. I feel awful about some of the things I said. I didn't mean to make you run away."

"You didn't. I ran away because I'm weak. I couldn't handle anything more. I was too happy with you. It felt wrong. I was too sad seeing your sister and her new baby. It hit me hard." She didn't want to give anymore. She still felt the need to hold back; there was still something there that she just couldn't quite trust about him. He was in Australia; he could have been doing anything with anyone. His song lyrics were always nagging at the back of her mind, haunting her, making her wonder what Cal really was. Was he the man he was when he sang? Was he the man he was when he was with her? She couldn't tell. His public persona was a bad boy, untamable, wicked and egocentric. The Cal she knew, or thought she knew, was vastly different.

They sat up chatting until he had to go and get ready for a concert. Had she made a mistake letting him in a little deeper? She wanted things to be great, but her heart wasn't certain she was ready for this.

≈

Miles away, Calvin Hunt sat on a box backstage at a venue in Sydney. He was exhausted having traveled to hell and back. Hell, he wasn't certain he'd returned yet. She still seemed to be holding something back, though he wouldn't swear his life on it. He idly plucked the strings of his guitar while backstage; an entire city seemed to be bustling to be ready for the concert. So, this is what that stupid 'money can't buy happiness' statement meant. He had all the money he needed and then some. He couldn't buy what he wanted. He couldn't buy her trust, her love and devotion. He couldn't buy her. She was happiness epitomized and he couldn't really have her because she wouldn't give herself completely to him. She always seemed to be holding back. He was reluctant to walk away from her. He had never been good at quitting anything.

Rory walked by then reversed, "You look as though you're contemplating quantum physics." He was too much sometimes.

"No, although Maddy is just as complicated. I can't figure her out."

"I thought you guys were working out, what's going on?" Rory asked as he took a seat next to Cal on another box.

"It's like she's still holding back. Here I am trying to twist myself around backwards to please her, and it's not enough. I don't want to walk away, in fact, I don't think I can."

Rory gave him a skeptical glance, "You are twisting yourself around?"

"Yes," Cal answered, flustered and annoyed.

"*Um*, okay." Rory began to get up, but Cal pulled him backward by his collar.

"What are you not saying?"

"I'm tired of being the deep one in our relationship little bro. It's all me next to the man who is as deep as a tide pool." He had that superior attitude going on that Cal couldn't stand.

"What makes *you* so deep?"

"Here's the deal, you are an idiot," Rory grumbled. "You're not twisting your life around. You are on tour doing your own thing like you always do, making a little room for Madison. She is the one putting her life on hold for *you*. She keeps having to pick up and follow *you* around. She is the one adjusting, losing herself, fighting a normal schedule so she can date her 'rock star' boyfriend. It's her making all of the sacrifices, not you." Once again, Rory had him. He hated Rory when he got all self-righteous like this.

Cal just punched him in the arm and stalked off.

28. Damn Kinley and Her Prediction

Cal had been gone for four weeks, and wouldn't be back for another four. She listened to another album from Murder of Crows, their first album. She sang along with Cal, "Remind me again why I keep you around." The lyrics always made her smile. Smiling was something she was doing a lot more of lately. It was Cal. She could feel herself letting go a little more each day. She was humming to herself through the bridge when her door opened and Kinley walked in with a small grocery bag. "Are we going to lunch?" Madison asked feeling famished.

"Definitely," Kinley dropped the bag onto the sofa. "I'll drive; you look like you're about to fall asleep."

"Good idea," Madison agreed. "I just haven't really adjusted since we came back from England. You seem to be just fine."

Kinley grinned widely, "Yes well. You can take a nap when we get back." She drove to Fuddruckers, still their favorite burger place. They sat at their favorite red and white striped surfboard table after placing their orders. Madison sipped on a milkshake.

They talked about school and the last few classes Madison needed to complete her Bachelor's degree; Kinley had hers already. She sipped on a *Diet* Coke; her body was craving the caffeine. Would she ever regulate her sleeping schedule? Between school and Cal she wasn't sleeping at nights and spent half of her days taking naps. Kinley had been worried for a while, but now seemed to be accepting it, taking it in stride. "Can you believe that we've been back from England for six weeks? I loved England." She gazed wistfully out the window. "It was so green and alive there."

"It was fun, Kinley. Was the highlight of your trip the day with Rory?" She shouldn't enjoy goading Kinley so completely. She couldn't help it. Madison loved watching her blush and stammer. She rubbed her eyes, "Do you mind taking me home I have to take a nap." She'd been on the phone all night again with Cal, discussing everything that came to mind. She now knew all about his childhood and some of his silliest moments in life. She liked knowing things about him that she couldn't find out in *G-String Magazine*, or read in a tabloid. She was missing him more than she cared to admit. She needed to take a nap so that she could speak all night to him once more. There were things in her life to look forward to again. She hated that much of her joy centered on Cal, but was close to the point of just letting all of her inhibitions go. She knew she needed him. She did love him. She was saving it for the right time. She had to tell him in person, not on the phone.

Kinley took her home, as she slumped over in her seat with exhaustion, "I don't think I've seen you eat so much in a long time."

"That is not right, Kin. We never point those things out to each other. I can't believe you'd say such a thing." Her feelings were on edge as she walked into her house feeling somehow fatter thanks to Kinley.

"I'm sorry, Maddy, don't be upset. I have to go, but I left you something on your sofa. Don't be mad. You'll see what I was getting at. Call me." She was gone, after rattling off. Madison shrugged and picked up the little grocery sack. What was Kinley going on about? She pulled the small box out of the bag and felt her knees give way as she landed with a thump on her sofa. Pregnancy test? She had a good mind to give Kinley a call and yell at her. But she swallowed the lump in her throat.

She got up and went to the bathroom, and pulled out the innocuous looking stick. She had to go anyway. Kinley, stupid cow. Her nose twitched as she watched the colored line spread across the stick. Her heart was seriously thinking of making a break for it, through the rib cage and her skin, and out onto the bathroom floor. What had even made her do this? And, the infernal woman had gotten a new kind of test. The word *Pregnant* appeared as though written by the devil himself. She heard screaming coming from somewhere, yes; it was inside of her own mind. NO! This couldn't be happening.

She quickly picked up her cell phone, all the while staring at the foul word on the stick. "How did you know?" she blurted out.

"You and I have been on the same cycle since going to Valencia Christian Jr. Prep, and let me tell you, you are late. Besides, you are tired, eating way more than normal, and being all sentimental and *gooshy*."

"Is *gooshy* a word?"

"We can add it to our dictionary with *unrewardable*, *debitor*, and *bestower*," Kinley laughed. Madison, however, was not amused. "You are aren't you?"

"You know I am."

"What were you thinking? Didn't you use protection? Lord knows you probably have some disease or two by now," Kinley stated matter-of-factly.

"I…we did use protection," Madison stammered.

"In England?"

"No." Madison felt her heart sink into her stomach. "I guess it was a little spontaneous," she muttered. "Oh, I feel ill."

"Don't you remember that you're Fertile Myrtle? That was why you had Jack snipped all those years ago." Madison groaned in reply. "It's been six weeks. You should be getting sick soon."

"This is crap." Madison's head ached as she leaned back and closed her eyes. "I can't deal with this."

"Everything will be okay," Kinley offered.

"No, it won't," she cried. "This is terrible." After she'd hung up with Kinley, she chucked the annoying stick into the wastebasket. Damn it. How would she tell Cal? Well it was still early, maybe it wouldn't work out. Kinley would have been crushed to hear such a thing. She'd suffered from several miscarriages and would not like the hopeful attitude Madison was taking toward the idea of miscarriage. What would he think? Would he be happy or upset? She realized with chagrin, that she didn't know him well enough to know if he wanted children or not. Did he still want to marry her? Would he want to marry her just because he'd knocked her up? What would his family think?

She sat down on the edge of her sofa, balanced at attention, poised for defense. She hadn't changed diapers in years. The twins had been four, almost five. She knew she was still basically young enough but she felt old when contemplating starting over again. Potty training, *ugh*. What if she couldn't love this child as much as she'd loved the others? Would she be a good single mother? Would she want to marry Cal so that she wouldn't have to be alone? No, she did actually love him. It was true; she loved him so much that she nearly squealed when she knew he was calling. She loved him, the Cal she knew.

She didn't know what to do. She didn't know if she could do the whole 'kid' thing again. It was the recurring thought drilling into her skull. How could she be a good mother when she was a fraction of what she had been? She wondered if she could find a roundabout way of talking to Cal about it. How could she sound unsuspicious? If she brought up kids and marriage would he get the wrong idea? Would he be happy? Or would he be nervous about it? He'd wanted to marry her before, but they'd never discussed having children. Children might not be what he wanted. The other band members had families. How did that work out for them? She silently cursed herself. She wasn't ready for this, and didn't know how to make herself ready.

29. International Incident

Cal just wanted to go home. Maddy wouldn't come to him. He'd tried nightly to convince her to travel some more. She and Kinley were back in school and so were Kinley's daughters. He thought she could stop clinging to Kinley already, but she didn't seem to be following his logic. She had *him* now. There was more. While he found it impressive that she wanted to finish her education, he secretly, selfishly wanted her to just forget about it and concentrate on him. Rory had told him he was a self-centered ass. It was true, he decided. Lately, he'd given up on trying to get Maddy to come visit. He was now focused on one thing and that was getting back to her.

Shawn, Chris and Rory were playing a high stakes poker game in Rory's hotel suite. He'd just folded, tired of pretending to be interested. It was still in the morning where Maddy lived. He couldn't remember what day it was there, or if she had school. He walked to his suite with Gabe next to him, discussing something he wasn't even paying attention to. He was distracted not depressed. He felt anxious to leave Japan and go home. "Did you hear that?" Gabe muttered as he took a defensive stance. Did leaning your ear to the side actually make you hear better? He'd have to ask. He was about to tell Gabe he hadn't heard anything when they heard a bone-chilling scream.

He looked around, while Gabe reminded him of a golden retriever, positioned with his ears alert, ready to pounce. He held his fingers to his lips to shush Cal. Cal frowned at this. Another scream and a loud crash. There were too many doors, where was it coming from? Gabe walked a little way ahead, his lips pursed and eyebrows lowered in deep concentration. From behind Cal, a door burst open and a vase hit the wall beside him, glancing off in thousands of minute pieces. At least he thought it had been a vase once upon a time. What the hell was going on? He shouldn't have looked, but his idiotic senses had never been tuned in on the 'self-preservation' level.

A woman, wearing nearly nothing came streaking out into the carpeted hall, stepping on the glass, trying to get away, but a man had her by her long black hair two seconds into her escape. They were speaking in what he could only assume was Japanese, and the woman looked hysterical. She pulled away, while the significantly larger man twisted her arm behind her. This all happened so quickly that he hadn't even thought about Gabe. The man pulled his fist back, but Cal injected himself into the mix, feeling the bone crushing punch throw him backward. The woman was still screaming, clinging to what little scraps of clothing she had. Before the man could react to hitting Cal instead of his intended target, Gabe had the angry stranger's arm pinned behind his back and his face smashed against the wall. Gabe was shaking his head at Cal as if to say, idiot.

People were spilling out into the hall from all directions, even though this was supposed to be a supremely private floor. Cameras were already clicking, they weren't paparazzi, they were fellow guests, also known as traitors. The woman stared up at him, trembling and threw her arms around him. She planted, what could only be the wettest kiss he'd ever been on the receiving end of, right onto his lips. Tears and blood soaked her skin, as she held onto him repeating something he couldn't understand. Rory came along, with Shawn and Chris following close behind him. "We missed something. I can tell."

"You always were the more observant one," Cal grinned.

"I know," Rory teased. Gabe was speaking Japanese on his phone, all the while still pinning the man against the wall. Gabe spoke Japanese? Chris looked over at the man and shook his head.

"Isn't that the game show host we were watching earlier?"

Shawn shrugged, but then decided to look more carefully. "You're the one guy; do you choose truth or dare." He stared at the tall Japanese man, who wore an Armani suit and an indecently smug expression.

"She's just a hooker. I paid to slap her around a little." He didn't seem at all aware that this was something out of the ordinary. "It's no big deal." He spoke perfect English, his words rolling off his tongue with ease. "Just let me go." His eyes darted to Gabe, "Your big friend can tell the police that I got away."

Gabe growled, "Shut up." The man shivered slightly.

The minor incident took hours to wrap up. The police wanted to question him and Gabe. They wanted written statements signed. They wanted autographs. Cal would be late for his concert. He knew that Rupert would love to have Sludge play a few more songs. The story was out, everywhere, in every paper in Japan. Calvin Hunt, lead singer of Murder of Crows, saves a life. He needed to wrap his mind around it. Gabe was the one who deserved the credit for slamming that nut up against the wall. By the time he fell into bed the next evening, he realized with a grunt that he hadn't talked to Madison.

Had she heard anything where she was? Or was it just a Japan thing? He'd have to call her later and hope she understood. His eyes rolled back into his head as he passed out with all of his clothes and shoes still on.

∾

She had planned on telling him, at least until she'd turned on her computer. He hadn't called, and though it was a first, she had been ready to make excuses for him. Madison paced back and forth. Too many thoughts were flying through her mind; a virtual windstorm of hateful barbs was pitting the inside of her skull. Kinley had tried the usual comforting words. *Any idiot can work photo shop.* But the damned picture was real. It was as real as anything she'd ever seen. There beneath it was the caption *Calvin Hunt Outside His Hotel Suite With Unknown Woman*. Madison's skin was writhing; thousands of red ants could have been marching across it the way her skin prickled beneath her rubbing fingertips.

She was so stupid! Oh yeah, *you're the only woman I have ever brought here. Ha*! I've never brought home anyone to meet my mother before. Because you couldn't bring a whore to meet your mother, she felt like screaming! She slammed a pillow onto her bed and paced some more. Stupid. Fall for his lines, fall for his charming act! Fall for his spontaneous lovemaking and his kisses from heaven. She pivoted on her heel, what had she been thinking? Rage surged through her veins, taking over where blood should have been. Kissing a whore outside his hotel room? Probably thought she'd never see it. So, that was why he didn't call, he was a little busy.

She was invested, even though she didn't want to be. It made her sick, literally. She was heaving over the toilet, wiping sweat from her brow as it beaded up along her hairline. She had been through worse. She'd lost her entire family. She could handle this. But when she looked into the mirror, she began to crumble. He'd worn her down with his words of love. He'd said he loved her. How many women could say the same thing? Lindsey Bell. She cried; gut wrenching sobs into the sink as she heaved again. Damn Calvin Hunt the icon and the man. She pushed her long black hair out of her face and very carefully closed her eyes to mute the wave of dizziness she'd encountered.

Should she even speak to him? Just to give him a piece of her mind? She crawled into bed only to find herself panting on her side. She knew Kinley would be over soon. She buried her face into her pillow. She was a grown woman. She should have known better. She saw all of the signs, knew what he appeared to be, and then questioned the reality of it all. If it looks like a snake and bites you, why should you be surprised? She thought to herself.

The doorbell was ringing. She got up grudgingly to answer it, wishing all the while that Kinley would just use her key. It wasn't Kinley. It was Mandy. "Hi, I brought you a house warming present. It's close to your birthday too. I thought you might need some cheering up. " House warming? She'd been here a while. Madison stood aside and let her in, feeling a chill wind sweep across the threshold with her. Madison smiled her fakest sweet smile and sighed.

"Thank you." She stared at the large gift-wrapped box without even the slightest inclination to open it. It had a cheerful looking house painted onto the wrapping.

"I hope you don't have a cappuccino maker." Mandy practically sang as she smiled, her bright red lipstick seemed cheery and out of place in

Madison's world. Thanks for letting me know what it is before I open it, she thought wearily.

"Nope, I didn't have one. Thank you."

"*Um*, there's something else." *Ah*, the real reason for the visit, Madison thought. She gestured that Mandy should continue, "I found a box, in a little cubby, and…" Jonathan's secret hiding place, he often kept things in there he hadn't wanted his siblings to find. There must be sodas and candy, and it wasn't really what she wanted to think about. She'd honestly forgotten all about his little hiding spot; it pained her to think of it. She needed to lie down.

"Please, Mandy, I don't want it," she barely got the whisper out.

"But…"

"Seriously, do me a favor, and keep it, okay? Kinley put the things I wanted to keep in storage, so…" Madison was growing faint; she didn't need this, not now. Couldn't Mandy just go away already? Mandy nodded but seemed to inherently disagree with Madison's request as though contraband candy was an important keepsake.

"Are you feeling okay?" Mandy asked, finally glancing over Madison in her pajamas, even though it was one in the afternoon.

"No, I think I have the flu," she muttered. She wished Kinley could have been there to see the look of horror spread quickly over Mandy's face.

"I'd better be going," she murmured, reaching into her handbag for hand sanitizer. She muttered to herself all the way out to her car, and still seemed to be chattering away, maybe on her Blue Tooth, as she drove her *Beamer* down the street and out of the complex. Madison at least had something to laugh about. Kinley pulled up not a moment later.

"Was Mandy just here?"

"Yep, she brought me a house warming present, a cappuccino machine."

"You don't drink coffee," Kinley told her, as if she didn't know.

"I know, I was thinking EBay."

"How did you get rid of her so quickly?" Kinley asked, as she sat down on the sofa. "I have got to know your secret." Madison shared the story. "The flu? Who knew? I'll have to remember that one."

≈

He could hear Rory calling to him, in the sea of his misery. "Cal! What the hell? We're supposed to be leaving now!"

"I know," he groaned in despair. "Silence is golden? Who said that? What a crock of shit."

"Mom, now get your ass up." Rory was pulling him to his feet. "If she were here she'd be washing your potty mouth out with soap and praying for your soul."

"I don't wanna do this, I don't care what Mom thinks she's not even here." Cal wanted to wallow, why wouldn't Rory just let him?

"Fine, I'll just give her a call then, shall I?" Rory teased.

"Not a fan of you right now, Ror, not a fan," Cal mumbled. "Can't you just take my place tonight? You know all the songs…you'll be fine."

"I told you, Cal, your man-whoring ways were going to catch up with you. I knew this was going to happen. Now, you've gone and screwed up the one good thing you ever had."

"I don't want to hear I told you so…" Cal whined.

"Too late, said it, can't take it back now." Rory was enjoying this a little too much. "Have some nice reflective time, did you?" Ror escorted Cal downstairs into the lobby, lecturing him all the way down. Rory was shoving him out to the limo, where Gabe stood, parting the screaming fans, ushering them into the waiting car.

"What is your problem, Cal, we should have left ten minutes ago," Shawn asked as he popped open a water bottle.

"He's a little broken hearted." Chris clucked his tongue, "Poor baby. He's not used to being the one who gets dumped." They were laughing at his expense, something he probably deserved. His teeth were practically grinding together as he stared out the window, his jaw tensed, his cheek muscles pulsated. Finally, he put his face into his hands and sighed deeply, "Dude, I think she really broke his heart," Chris added in a loud whisper to Rory.

"Guys, how do I fix this?" he asked them all, imploringly.

"Search your soul," Shawn offered.

"That will take him just a second," Rory snickered.

Gabe was watching him from the corner, "What about sending her some flowers, lots of 'em. It can be something of a peace offering." The guys were all nodding in agreement. What could go wrong with flowers? It was worth a shot.

30. Breaking Up Is Easy To Do...On Facebook

"Maddy!" Kinley called to her, pulling her from her deep reflective state. "Hello? Maddy, are you in there?" Kin's voice was sing-song and an octave higher than normal.

"Yeah, I'm sorry, I was just remembering my last great GNO, and thinking about all the things that happened up until this point." She closed her eyes, "I'm tired, Kin, and I don't want to do this anymore. I'm done with love. I feel so stupid." She really did, and there was nothing Cal could say that would change it. "Past performance, future predictor."

"I've always hated that saying. People can change, Maddy," Kinley, ever the voice of reason, pointed out.

"Whatever, Kin, we knew what he was when we met him. Why would he want me so badly? Was I something he could conquer, and now that he has, I've become another notch on his bedpost?" She stared out of the window, fighting back the onslaught of tears.

"I believe you are mistaken..." Kinley began.

"We've read the magazines, we've seen the exposés, and you really think that I- little old me- was the one who made him suddenly monogamous? Really?" Madison fumed.

"Yes," Kinley answered firmly. "You're different from every other woman he's ever met, he's intrigued by you, he's in love with you. You have your own opinion, your own views, you don't say what he wants to hear- he respects it, you know?"

"How can you explain what he did?" Madison asked her pointedly.

"Well…"

"You can't and neither can I; it hurts too much." Madison didn't want to talk about it anymore.

She'd had flowers for days. Finally fed up she tossed them into white garbage bags. She had been a moron. Kinley, who was feeling guilty, helped her to pack away the red roses, by the bagful. "This is crap," she muttered under her breath.

"Yeah," Kinley agreed. She hadn't said too much though.

"Will you go with me to my appointment? I just don't want to go alone." She sat down and pushed her hair out of her eyes, and straightened her ponytail.

"You know I will." Kinley fumbled with the many bags, "I'll be right back."

She turned her computer on, and checked her Facebook account. Great, Cal was on. She went to click out, when he began the chat, "*Aren't you going to talk to me at all…let me explain?*" she mumbled underneath her breath. This would not break her. She would make it through. She'd taken something from him- his sperm. At least she still had that. She focused positively on the baby. She now thought of the little one as a gift, a blessing. She would refocus and put all of her energy into being a good mother. She was given a second chance even if Cal hadn't wanted to take it with her. She glowered at the screen.

Kinley walked in, dusting off her hands, "Are you on Facebook?" She went to help herself in the kitchen, "Do you want something to drink? Water?"

"Yes, I'd love some. Cal is trying to talk to me right now," she grumbled.

"Answer him. Tell him." She sat down next to Madison, handed her a water bottle and stared at the screen. In a rage, Madison's hands flew to the keyboard. *"You're a cheater, how can you explain it away?"* She fidgeted when she saw his words pop up. *I know it looks bad but they aren't releasing the whole story. Would you answer your damned phone already? I love you so much, don't do this to me!* To you? His words irritated her.

Her answer gave her a small bit of smug satisfaction. *Two Words, Lindsey Bell.*

She could practically hear his sigh from Canada. *I didn't cheat on her either. Let me explain.*

"He will be getting a little note in his in-box." She heaved a sigh, "*Dear Cal,*" she narrated as she typed. "*Please stop sending me flowers and trying to contact me. I am fine, I just should have known that you are what you are, and I couldn't hope that you would change for me. Please let me move on. I need time to heal, and you are only postponing it. I'm hurt. I can't believe you did what you did, knowing everything I have been through. Please stop. Maddy.*" She pressed send and clicked the computer off. "That should tell him how I feel without being too weepy."

"I am all for the new improved 'survivor' Maddy, but maybe he has something to say that will make sense."

"Kin, don't. You know I feel like a foolish little girl who fell for the bad boy's lies. I should have known better. I'm a grown woman. They sounded too good. I can't believe what an idiot I've been. I was too vulnerable, and I'm not going to be anymore."

"But..." Kinley protested. "Don't you think you ought to tell him, you know, about his baby?"

"He doesn't deserve to know." She frowned at Kinley. "I need to eat, let's get out of here. It stinks like roses."

Somewhere in his mind this was not how he imagined things going with Maddy. He actually hadn't done anything! But he couldn't prove it. He was seriously considering suing the moronic guest who had taken his picture. The context had been lost in translation. Now as he sat reading his letter from Maddy, he couldn't breathe. Was there a giant sitting on his chest, refusing to let the air in or out? He pressed his hands into his hair, and against his eyelids. Damn it. He picked up his laptop and threw it. The top unhinged, the screen shattered, lettered keys popped off and flew in every direction. That felt better. He'd never been known to have a serious temper, but since he'd met Maddy, he'd become unhinged just like the top half of his computer.

He scanned the horizon, watching one of nephews ride by on a quad, followed by one of his nieces. He had to admit that the pictures out there looked bad, really bad. There was one where he was resting his head on top of that poor girl's head. He'd been trying to comfort her, and look what he got for his troubles. Did the Good Samaritan get an ass beating for his trouble? The 'no good deed' thing was true. He frowned as he looked out of the window and watched Gabe walk up the drive. Gabe walked in with some mail, possibly from fans. "Your computer is broken," Gabe told him.

"Yeah, I know," Cal moaned.

"You should try harder," Gabe replied.

"I'm giving up, Gabe. That's it. She just wrote to me and asked me not to try and contact her anymore." Flustered, he fell back on the sofa and put his hands over his eyes.

"She's worth the fight you should just give her a little more time. That's all." Gabe dropped his letters onto the ottoman.

"I'm done Gabe. Done. No more." He rolled over, offering his back to Gabe and shoved his face into the pillows on his sofa. His muffled voice never reached Gabe, "Please God, help me."

His phone rang, stupid ring, it was him singing. He thought it was funny at first, but now everything humorous had lost meaning. He answered grudgingly, "Hello?"

"Calveen, eet is On-Ree." Cal sat up.

"Henry Dalibert?" He wanted to make sure, but how many On-Rees did he know exactly?

"Precisely mon ami. Ah have called to schedule zee final feeting." He sounded it out inside his head…fitting…oh, the AMA's.

"Let me get my calendar," Cal mumbled, fidgeting with his blackberry. He'd been to America recently to pick out a suit for the American Music Awards. He'd been so close to Maddy, but he didn't know if she'd want to see him or not. Seemed like he guessed correctly.

"How about two days bee-for zee award show?" Henry Dalibert asked. He usually didn't call clients personally, but Cal thought he secretly liked him. Cal scheduled the appointment, and looked onto his calendar. Two months, that was it? His guts wrenched as he looked down at the calendar. He'd only known her since February, but how his life had changed. He was being forced to live without her? How could this be? He'd done everything right? Hadn't he? He shook with sorrow. What would his life hold now? It was even emptier than before. Yes, before he'd known he was missing something, but couldn't quite figure out what it was. Now, he knew what he was missing. It was a poisonous dose, slowly draining his life away. He didn't know how to react or respond. He'd have to get his mind sorted out and soon.

He began to play his guitar when inspiration struck him. There was nothing like heartbreak for writing a song. "You lied…" he sang. He laughed a horrid, jaded cruel laugh, that was not him, but it felt great. He pulled his notebook over to his side and penned a few of the chords down, and then some random insulting words. Broken, he wrote the meanest lyrics he'd ever written, to go with a beat that would kill and chords that would enthrall the masses. Maybe he would call it Ode to Maddy…

31. Fitting and Not

"Nothing fits!" Madison howled to no one in particular. She felt the familiar rush of bubbles, which was actually a baby kicking, fluttering inside of her. "It's not your fault," she rubbed her stomach. "It's mine, I shouldn't have eaten an entire loaf of Kinley's bread." She tugged at her jeans and frowned at herself in the mirror. She felt huge. Kinley had pointed out that she was still so tiny that there was nowhere for the baby to grow but out. And...she was out, poking out there for all the world to see. Her neighbors couldn't have cared less...but old acquaintances were beyond curious.

She dragged herself out to a maternity store reluctantly and began to look around. As she pulled things off the rack, her heart sunk when Mandy Murphy walked by and did a double take. "Madison Grey, is that *you*? Shopping in a maternity store?"

"That's what pregnant people do, Mandy, when their clothes no longer fit them." She only wished Kin had been here to hear it. It seemed to lose some of its zing with no audience, not even a sales girl. My snark is back, she thought.

"But how are *you* pregnant?" Mandy had no shame, never. Her two-toned hair was twisted up into a chignon; her business suit was tailored and perfect, her too long nails resting against the side of her bag. Madison couldn't stand her.

"Well, I do believe you already know how it works…you see, when a man and a woman…"

Mandy cut her off, "*I know*," she replied scathingly, "how *that* works. I'm talking about a widow who hasn't dated anyone publicly. I mean it's been a year since your family was killed, and you're already knocked up?" No tact either. It was utterly heart breaking that Mandy looked so perfect on top of it all. Her cornflower blue eyes were startling with the dark heavy black eyeliner and bright glittery shadow. Her one consolation was that Mandy's makeup looked as though she'd stopped by the side of the road in a bad neighborhood and had a hooker fix her up. She clung to her Coach bag and just grinned her saccharine sweet grin at Madison.

Madison grinned back, painfully. "I don't tell *you* everything I do, Mandy."

If the statement cut her, she did not appear to be wounded. "Whose baby is it? Anyone I know?" She started looking at Madison's designer bag distractedly. "That is an excellent knock-off," she added.

"First of all it's the real thing; secondly the baby is Calvin Hunt's." She might as well say it because no one would believe her anyway.

"What's gotten into you? I realize you lost everyone you love, but you don't have to become a habitual liar! I mean first Kinley teasing me about Murder of Crows, now you…Fine, if you don't want to tell me, then don't! I think this whole mess has given you a midlife crisis- you're running around buying townhouses and Porsches, designer bags and who knows what else, and getting yourself knocked up like a teenager. I don't even know who you are anymore." Her heavily made up eyes narrowed as she gave Madison her best withering glare, which wasn't very good to Madison, and turned on her heel, amusingly offended by the actual truth. Madison shrugged and turned to pick out more clothes, she had to buy something.

≈

Calvin Hunt found himself in the back of a limo headed for Beverly Hills, one of the stores his designer owned and operated. He was singing at the top of his lungs in the back, to whom else, the Bee Gees. "How do you mend a broken heart?" he wailed. Gabe just stared at him and shook his head, before answering his phone. Gabe flipped his music off but he still went on singing mournfully. "No Rory, he's singing the Bee Gees again. Yes, *I know*." He shot Cal a weary look. "No, we're pulling up now."

Cal stared out the window as people walked by. No one even cared about a limo here. No one stared curiously or tried to peer inside as if someone couldn't see them. The chauffer opened the door and Gabe stepped out first, "Okay, we'll meet you for lunch afterward. Right, bye then." He pushed a button, ending his phone call. They walked into Dalibert's, floating along on tiles imported from Mexico. There was a Mexican theme going on, something like an old Mexican Ranch, but it reminded him of Zorro, rather than a place where someone designed clothes. Henry Dalibert came out with his arms spread out and put his arms around Cal in somewhat longer lasting embrace than Cal cared for. He kissed him on the cheek, which made Cal smile.

"Hi, On-Ree," he beamed.

"Calveen." He grinned with every one of his shockingly white teeth. Henry was an older man in his fifties, with salt and pepper hair and a look of charm and grace. His own black jacket was double-breasted and reminiscent of movies with James Cagney. "Come een to zee back." Cal followed Henry who was speaking but Cal wasn't really listening. He was thinking of that damnable Rory and his damned know-it-all advice.

He'd caught Cal singing his 'Ode to Maddy' song and clapped him on the shoulder. "Cal, Cal, Cal…" His name in threes was irritating when it was Rory, or anyone else for that matter. "Plenty of men have had their heart broken. A real man never calls the woman a 'bitch', but he becomes introspective and wonders what *he* did wrong. Study yourself Cal and learn from your own behavior."

"Yes Master Miyagi, should I wax on and wax off now?"

"Seriously, little bro, have you thought about it if the roles were reversed? What if she was wearing next to nothing, while kissing a man in a photo? What would *you* have thought?" Rory had a momentary look of pain on his face before erasing it. Damn Rory again. He would have been pissed off. "It's not her fault that she took it wrong. Hell, you have your reputation leading the way, it was an easy assumption. Not to mention the whole reality show fiasco, *Lindsey Lovin'*?" He was angry with himself lately, and Rory hadn't helped him. He'd analyzed everything, gone over it all and realized that he *was* a self-centered ass. The only way to forget was to quit being sober, which he'd done a great job of lately. Now he just needed to find a whore who could help him forget the rest, at least for a while.

Speaking of whores…Lindsey Bell just walked in and was giving him a naughty little smile. "Cal, it's been a long time."

"Too long," he answered.

"I always hope we'll run into each other. We should get together." The implication made his blood rush.

"Most certainly," he agreed, casually.

Henry was back and handing him a suit, "Try this on Calveen." He bowed out and went to try the suit on. In his imaginings, he always had Maddy on his arm. She was there, wearing some frivolous creation in black that clung to her like a Virginia creeper, in all the right places. Her svelte figure would be the envy of Hollywood goddesses who starved themselves to look like she did naturally. He let his head fall against the dressing room panel; he had to let her go. It was no use trying to recall how angelic she looked, or how sweet her soul had been. He had to forget. Maybe Lindsey would help him to block it all out.

He walked out, and turned around for Henry, who was gesturing to do so with his hand in a twirling motion. "Excellent." He walked up closer, examining the suit, seeing if it fit in all the right places, which it did. "I surprise eeven myself sometimes." Henry chuckled, "Eez perfect, no?"

"Perfect," Lindsey Bell added, "Cal, who are you taking to the awards?"

"I don't have a date." He gave her his best sideways grin.

"You do now."

She was no Madison, but she'd do in a pinch.

32. Cal's Dedication

Madison pushed back her sleeves and stared up at the man on the ladder in front of her yard. She'd gone a little crazy buying Christmas decorations, even though it wasn't Thanksgiving yet. She needed some cheering up, so she'd called her friends over to watch the American Music Awards with her. She wanted to watch them, just not alone. Murder of Crows had been nominated for two awards. She wanted them to win. She wasn't bitter; they deserved to win. Kate's husband Jared strung white icicle lights along her home, while she beamed. The baby was restless. She arched her back hoping to take off some pressure.

She massaged her growing bump and muttered to herself, "Sorry about that chili dog at lunch."

"Lights are hung," Jared announced. She gave the gruff man a big hug and smiled up at him.

"Thanks J-man."

"No problem," he grumbled. "Where does your ladder go?" She pointed into the open garage. He flipped the switch and the lights sparked there in the in between, not light, not yet dark. Her eyes glittered as she looked up. "Are you coming in?" he bellowed.

"Just a minute," she yelled back, and he closed the garage door. She would not have to be alone tonight. She turned to walk in, but a large hand grabbed her shoulder delicately. She turned; ready to strike, "Gabe, you nearly gave me a heart attack. What are you doing here?"

"I came to check on you." He was staring, as all people did, at her small bump. "Is that...*Um*, how far along are you?"

"Yes it's Cal's," she complained. "I'm not the usual girl he goes out with I expect, there are no other guys."

"No, you are one of kind," he told her as he walked her up to her front door. She shivered, wishing she'd brought out a hooded sweatshirt. "He doesn't know."

"I don't need him to know. I can take care of myself." She was defensive and just a tad bit rude, but it was how she felt.

"I never said you couldn't take care of yourself, Madison." His usual stoic expression smoothed over with a look of great sadness. "He would want to know, I think."

"It's not necessary," her words were clipped, icy like the wind. "How is he?" she softened. She didn't want to seem overly concerned, but she missed that stupid man.

His eyebrows raised in what could only be astonishment, "He isn't so good, if you want to know." He straightened up; the giant of a man had to be over seven feet tall. "I did come for a reason. I know you two are both dealing, but you're suffering. I want to help. I brought you something. I needed to place it in your hands myself. Promise me you will look at it," he begged, his large nearly black eyes seemed to quiver. She gulped.

"What is it?"

He handed her a USB drive. "Okay." She waved her hand, "Gabe what am I do with this?"

"Just promise me you'll look at it."

She was unwilling to promise; she had guests waiting for her. She had to get him to leave, "Yeah, I promise," she mumbled. His face broke into a rare smile and he thanked her profusely. She wondered what Gabe was up to. Had Cal sent him? She'd wager that he had no idea Gabe had come to see her.

"Hey, are you coming in?" Kate asked as she wedged the door open. "It's freezing out here. I know your lights probably look great, but come in already." She nodded and followed Kate into the warm house. Candles gleamed, and the scent of delicious food wafted out to meet her. It felt good to be surrounded by those she loved. The men were talking sports, snacking on hot wings and drinking down beers. Her friends were in the kitchen gossiping about a new teacher but they stopped when they heard her coming.

"Isn't that your ex?" Jared asked loudly.

They all turned to look at the large flat screen television. Cal, damn he was gorgeous. He had Lindsey Bell on his arm. She was the anti-Madison. She had long golden locks of perfectly straight hair, blue eyes, full pink lips, and she was tall. She wanted to turn away, but it was a train wreck she couldn't stop looking at. Cal's arm was around the skinny waif's waist. He was talking, answering questions of the interviewer. She just stared at his mouth; the way it moved still held her fascination. Her eyes were filling up rapidly, nearly overflowing, when she made an excuse to leave the room.

She pulled herself together, and came back in, ready in hostess-mode. "Dinner is served!" she called out, all the while feeling her heart shriveling up inside of her body.

~

Calvin Hunt hated these award shows. He maneuvered Lindsey through the chatting crowd, and occasionally stopped to greet people he hadn't seen in a while. Lindsey clung to him, but didn't seem all that interested in what he had to say. "Cal, have you prepared a speech in case you win? I did," she admitted, smoothing a stray strand of hair into place.

"Of course we'll win. Who can compete with us?" Maddy would have known he was kidding. Lindsey playfully slapped his arm. He hated that.

"Don't be silly," she teased. Her voice was annoying him. They found their seats; Rory was sitting there with Jen. Shawn and Chris hadn't arrived yet. They scooted past Rory and Jen, down the row and took their seats. "Isn't this great? We're so close," she giggled. Lindsey looked like a 'cheap' version of Jen he decided.

"Cal, I still think we should sing your new song," Rory leaned over and whispered so that only Cal could hear him. Cal just shook his head. He couldn't pour his heart out like that, not when it was so badly broken. It would be too noticeable. "Why? It's damned good, probably the best you've ever written."

"Did you write me a song?" Lindsey overheard, and was now batting her long fake black lashes his way.

"No, Rory isn't talking about *anything*."

Rory sat back and began whispering back and forth to his wife. "Cal, Rory is right," she said.

"Not you too Jen," he mumbled. "Let it go you two." Sometimes he couldn't stand her.

Chris came in with Meredith on his arm, and Shawn with Candace. Now all he needed was for all of them to gang up on him. But, the awards show was starting, music was playing, and ushers were sending people to their seats. He leaned back; uncomfortable, too hot, and wishing he'd drunk a case of beer before this night of torture. The night waned, it dragged, he clapped and pasted on his fake smile. He barely noticed when they announced the first category Murder of Crows had been nominated for. He grinned, planning to clap for whoever really won, but Taylor Swift had just read- Murder of Crows for favorite Pop/Rock group or band. He was standing; people all around him were shaking his hand.

Walking up to the podium, he stared around, shocked and filled with dismay. Rory grabbed the mike first, "Thank you to all of our fans, we love you, and to Jen." He raised his award into the air amid cheers of jubilation. Each of them took turns thanking the fans and their wives. He sincerely wished that somewhere Maddy was cheering him on. He was last; his palms were sweating. He didn't usually get nervous. He cleared his throat as the audience members stared at him expectantly.

"I'd also like to thank the fans..." he muttered before clearing his throat again. Damn he had to take a piss; he stared straight into the camera, "And thank you to the love of my life...thank you Maddy." He lifted the award, the clear phallic pyramid shaped contraption on a black base. Whispers filled the crowd, he heard things like- who is Maddy? Isn't his date named Lindsey? Didn't he cheat on her before? Wow, he's such a dick. He sat back down and smiled as Lindsey threaded her arm through his. Her gown was sleeveless on one side. Maddy had worn a shirt like that the first time he kissed her. Lindsey scowled when the cameras moved away. "You thanked another woman with me here as your date?" Her voice was acidic, "Why didn't you bring *her*?"

"We broke up, now drop it," he hissed under his breath. Lindsey was an odd woman. She became friendlier the meaner he became. She made no sense to him, whatsoever. Madison had never made sense to him either, but she'd been a puzzle he'd actually wanted to solve. He couldn't have cared less about what made Lindsey tick.

When the next presenters went on stage, he noticed his brother, Shawn, and Chris, along with their wives were all shamelessly watching him. Rory pulled him into a headlock and ruffed up his hair. "Awesome, little bro, now can we sing the new song?"

"Why not, I'm feeling reckless tonight." Did he need permission from someone....who cared?

Twenty minutes later, he was standing on the stage waiting for whoever it was to announce the band and the curtain to rise. He could hear the voice, a man speaking, "You're about to hear a new song, never recorded, obviously never released. You are all the first to hear it tonight, please welcome to the stage- Murder of Crows!" Screaming from the audience rumbled the stage beneath his feet. He turned to Rory giving him a look that said- I don't think I can do this- but Rory just nodded and pulled his Fender bass guitar against his body.

Cal looked down at the strings of his guitar, carefully placing his fingers and playing the introduction. Somewhere behind him, he could hear Shawn strike the opening chord on his Gibson, closely followed by Rory on his Fender; finally he heard the light beat coming from Chris's drums. He had never had such anxiety about sharing a song, pushing it away; he took a breath and moved his lips closer to the microphone. He closed his eyes and thought of Maddy. "*Instinctively, I always viewed the world- somehow black and white with shades of gray. Colors were unheard of – if not unnatural- I never knew there was another way.*" He took a breath, "*It's seeing what you're, used to it's just rational. It humbled me- when I began to see. Everything around me was one-dimensional. I was a prisoner trapped inside of me...*" He let the note fill the air, people were already applauding and screaming for more when he got to the chorus, "*Breathing you in, tasting your skin, touching your lips and I am so in love with you, none of this can be real. I'm seeing things around me as they may have always been; being near you helps me see just what I feel..."*

The rest of the night, people mentioned the new song. Everyone loved it. But had Maddy? He wondered where she was. Was she out tonight with someone new? Was she watching him on the television? Or was she over him? He couldn't guess. That song had been for her, every damn word. Lindsey was wrapped around him as he left, "Come party with me Cal?" She looked up at him grinning, "I can cheer you up."

"What makes you think I need cheering up?" he asked.

"Everyone can see it. She did a number on you, this *Maddy* person." She said the name as though it were something dirty. He plucked her arm from his and smiled grimly, "I'm just telling you, I think I can help you feel better."

"I don't know..." He frowned as he looked up at the cloud filled sky. His limo pulled up to the red-carpeted curb. Gabe was striding toward him as he started to climb into the waiting limo; he had a look Cal had seen before, determination and purpose. "Where have you been?" he growled at Gabe.

"I had some errands to run." Always the secretive type, Cal thought angrily.

"I have to talk to you," Gabe began.

"Get in," he told Gabe, feeling more irritable than ever.

He gave directions to the driver for Lindsey's party. He didn't want to go, but he didn't want to wallow in self-pity either. He needed to get out, "I'll go with you," he told her.

"Good." She touched up her makeup while glancing into a small oval mirror.

Before he could get out, Gabe grabbed his arm and held him back, "I need to talk to you, Cal." Cal could not mistake the urgency in his voice. Lindsey was hovering outside in her sapphire blue gown that sparkled in the glow of thousands of lights. "I need to talk to you *alone,*" Gabe put a heavy emphasis on alone.

"What? Can't it wait?" he snarled, feeling angry but unable to name a cause as it had come on suddenly.

"It's about Maddy."

"Is she hurt?" he asked, panicked.

"No, not *exactly,*" Gabe began, tilting his head to the side as though he were thinking of the best way to word whatever he had to say. Cal could feel his stomach protesting; he didn't want to hear it.

"Okay, then…"

"Cal, come on, it's effing cold out here," Lindsey whined in a very un-ladylike manner.

"Just a minute," he barked. "You know what Gabe; this evening has been hell for me. I can't think about Maddy right now. I'm going to a party and I'm going to forget all about her. I'm going to get wasted until I can't think of her anymore." He slammed the door, and thought for once, he wasn't going to show Gabe just how curious he truly was.

33. Hating Lindsey

"It was a horrid publicity stunt," Madison argued with Kinley as they walked into a clothing store named Britta's Boutique. Megan had recommended it because Britta apparently had a small selection of designer labels for pregnant women. "Aren't you going to say anything, Kin?"

"Nope, you're hormonal and you might rip my head off. It's a loaded question. You're a mean pregnant woman, Kevin." Kevin was the name of their pregnant, mean, and nasty alter-egos. Kevin said whatever he wanted.

"It's not a loaded question," she bit off as they walked over to the rack at the left hand corner of the store.

"Is too. Oh, no it wasn't a publicity stunt. I think he is the sweetest man in the world, it's obvious that he still loves you!" she began to say, and Maddy was about to pounce onto her and bring her down to the floor. Kinley held up her hand as if to say 'wait for it'. "Yes, I totally think it was a publicity stunt, he's such an ass! I can't believe you were dumb enough to fall for such a loser." She shrugged while picking up a cute red shirt, "Either way I am a jerk. I can't come out winning. Kevin doesn't like to lose."

"You wouldn't have to add the dumb part!"

"It would be implied." Kinley shook her head. "I don't know about this one." She held out a pink shirt against Madison's tanned skin.

A sales girl was making her way over to them, "Can I help you find a size?"

"We're good." Madison smiled politely while Kinley ignored the girl. She was obviously in a mood. The girl continued to hover and listen to their conversation, "What about this one?" She held up a yellow shirt for Kinley to view.

"Yeah, I like it." Kinley grabbed it and threw it over her arm.

"I can take that for you and start a room if you like," the girl offered. She was a plain looking girl, ponytail, no makeup, going for the natural look. Kinley handed the lanky girl in the True Religion jeans, the shirt and went back to looking through the clothes on the rack. Within a moment, the sales girl was back, listening again. Madison and Kinley were both getting annoyed.

"Oh look, pregnant lingerie. How interesting," Madison called Kinley over. She could tell Kinley was about to ask who she thought she would wear it for, but Madison was determined to get rid of their eavesdropper. "If you were my lesbian lover, would you like to see me in this one, or this one?" She held up a solid red teddy and a transparent black teddy.

Kinley picked up on the improv moment and went with it, "I don't know, are we going for sexy, slutty, or bad girl?"

"Ooh, I don't know," Madison replied. "What look would *you* prefer?" Their conversation had the much-desired effect of privacy as the girl gave them a wide berth, clearly not wanting to intrude on whatever was going on. "Finally," Madison muttered under her breath. "I thought she'd never go away." Kinley chuckled. But Madison was about to become the nosy one. The sales girl had turned a television on in the corner of the store, as it hung up on the wall for everyone to see. It was an interview with Cal's date from the music awards. Lindsey Bell. Kinley gestured toward the television by leaning her head in the general direction of it.

"Great," Madison huffed.

The woman, a reporter they cared very little for, named Stacey Houston was interviewing Lindsey. "First let me congratulate you on your win for favorite female artist. Did you sense that it was coming?"

"I did. I prepared a speech; my agent said he would have died of shock if it hadn't been me," she giggled, sounding completely shallow. Madison and Kinley exchanged looks.

"I have to ask, it's what the viewers want to know...Were you upset when Cal Hunt dedicated his win to Maddy? And do you know who this 'Maddy' is?"

Lindsey Bell ran her fingers over her jeans; her body stiffened but her smile never wavered. "Well, he is *my* boyfriend now," she said, licking her lips before she continued. "Maddy is his *ex*-girlfriend. I can't say who she is...I mean her real name might not be Maddy at all." The girl chuckled and so did the interviewer. "I would like to thank her, whoever she is." The girl made herself sound magnanimous as she pulled herself up to sit straightly in the high-backed chair.

"Why is that?" Stacey Houston was clearly intrigued.

"Well, having his heart broken has made him a better person. I really like how thoughtful he's become and how sweet he is. He wrote his new song for me, you know. He only thanked Maddy because she helped him to write music before, she was his muse if you will, but *I* am his new muse." She grinned, her veneers nearly blinding the millions of viewers. Madison walked to the edge of the store, fuming.

"I don't know what to think." She shook her head, puzzled. "I thought he'd written the song for me...I'm such an idiot! Will I ever stop falling for the lies?"

"Let's get out of here," Kinley suggested eagerly.

"Yeah, let me pay for this first. I don't want to try anything on."

∾

"She hasn't called me, and still won't answer my phone calls. I've been de-friended on Facebook. I don't know what else to do!" he screamed at Rory who was still telling him not to give up.

"There's got to be something...She must have heard your song," Rory offered. "Have you tried calling her friend- what's her name- *um*, Kelsey?"

"You mean Kinley, yes! She told me she's *forbidden* to talk to me!" Cal whined.

"Sure, *Kinley*…forbidden? Wow, what a strong word." Rory smiled at his despair.

"Yes, I know!" Cal fumed.

"Yeah, and maybe she heard that I wrote it for Lindsey Bell, along with everyone else. I swear if…" he couldn't finish.

Gabe interjected, "If you just let me tell you something about Maddy…"

"Stop," he held up his hand in return, "I don't want to know whatever it is." Cal scowled. "You've probably been in touch with her somehow and she's probably told you to tell me off. I know you'd do it too. I just can't take another thing, Gabe Ausua, so please? *Huh*, for me?" Gabe nodded, but sighed. He hated it when Gabe sighed. He was having a breakdown. Christmas was coming and he'd be surrounded by all of his lovey-dovey family members. Everyone was married…everyone but the playboy Cal. They would all exchange presents and he would be there, just him, just like every other year. He groaned, "I just need to be alone right now."

Rory and Gabe left him. He thought of the after-party he'd attended with Lindsey Bell at a club downtown in LA. The memory wreaked havoc in his mind, blazing blinding trails through it, carving out its' own special niche. She'd given him a lap dance. He'd struggled to sit there and let her. Why hadn't he wanted her or the dance to continue, for that matter? He couldn't stop thinking of Maddy. He'd taken her back to her hotel suite, drunken idiot that he was. His lips had found her lips easily enough. And she'd unzipped her dress and dropped it to the floor with alacrity.

She smelled so good, and tasted sweet. One of his hands had settled on the back of her thigh, squeezing her ever so fiercely, while she squealed. He'd gnawed on her neck, realizing this was not going to work. She wasn't Maddy. He'd lost it, yanked his zipper back up and left. He'd made excuses about a meeting he had, even though it had been 4:30 in the morning. It hadn't felt right at all.

He couldn't think clearly. His mind blurred like white noise was going off endlessly inside of him. He'd been drinking a lot. He could hear Maddy asking him why. He'd yell at her inside of his mind. Because I can't have you! That's why! But she couldn't hear him. She was miles away, contented to give him messages through his bodyguard. Well, fine, he wouldn't accept it then. He'd move on, he would. He just needed time. He teetered back and forth between hating Maddy and needing to beg on bended knee for her to come back to him.

There was more. He hated knowing that he'd lost Kinley's friendship too. She was funny and he'd enjoyed talking to her. He'd conspired with her, and there was nothing in the world like conspiracy for bonding people. He wanted to call her up and ask her to smooth everything over. But he didn't dare. He could imagine Kinley yelling at him, asking him why he'd had the nerve to call her. He was losing his mind. His family was concerned, but he didn't care. He couldn't allow himself to care. He felt antsy, as though unseen creepy creatures were constantly walking over him. He couldn't sleep, let alone eat. He was to be found playing on his guitar, or working out in his home gym. He'd stopped going by for mother/son visits, and was now becoming a recluse.

He didn't want to be here, or anywhere. Although, he didn't exactly feel suicidal, he began to empathize with people who had felt that way. He struggled inside, trying to figure out what he could have done differently. He didn't understand regret. He'd mocked it before, taunted it. Previously regret had no hold on him. He needed a vacation from his regret now. Regret was a stupid emotion. He didn't need it, because there was nothing he could do with it. It was a damned hood ornament, completely useless.

When the phone rang, he decided to answer. It was Lindsey Bell, darling diva of the stage and silver screen. She now also had an AMA under her belt for recently breaking into song. She wasn't Maddy, not even close, he kept futilely reminding himself. One would have thought that when he brushed her away that Lindsey would have disappeared but she was tenacious. "Cal, I would like you to come visit me for your birthday. I'm planning something big for you." She sounded excited. Well, a birthday party did sound rather better than sitting around moping and feeling sorry for himself. What harm could it be? It was a couple of weeks away.

"Sounds great," he said not meaning to sound as aloof as he did. "I'd like that. Where do I meet you at?"

"I thought we'd do something at Pandora's Box in LA."

He'd been there before. It could be fun. "Okay."

"Let's get a suite together, Cal. I'll make you forget that *Maddy* person."

"I'll get my own suite, thanks," he answered tersely. She seemed to shrug this off.

He didn't know what to do. He didn't want to spend any more time with Lindsey. She just wasn't his 'cup of tea' or 'drink of beer' either. She was someone he could easily forget. He made plans with her anyway. The more he thought of everyone around him staring at him with those 'I feel sorry for him' faces, the more Lindsey Bell's offer sounded provocative to him. It sounded positively inviting next to the idea of blowing out candles on a birthday cake for his folks. His family had adored Maddy and weren't about to let him forget it. Lindsey, on the other hand, would do her best to make him forget Maddy had ever existed.

34. It's a...Confucius

Kinley sat next to Madison in the tiny room. Madison was propped up on a paper-covered bed, her stomach exposed down to her pelvic bone, grimacing as the cold-to-the-touch liquid jelly globbed onto her flesh. Unpleasant as it was to have an ultrasound when you are pregnant at any stage, she was here to find out the sex of her baby. Kinley sipped on a large diet soda; the sound made her have to pee. The woman conducting the exam pushed the scanning device deep into Madison's belly, causing Madison to want to hit the woman.

"You are burning this on the DVD I gave you?" Kinley asked politely.

"Of course," the technician muttered as she drew the wand in circles. "Oh look there is the profile." The three women stared at the flat computer screen and grinned. Madison looked at her child and still couldn't believe it was really in there. It was an it until the sex was known. She'd been calling it a 'he', but it was just a wild guess. She didn't care what she was having. She was just grateful to have this little one in her life.

It felt odd not to have Jack here. But there sat Kinley, waiting for the moment. "Have you decided if you wish to know what the sex of the baby is?" the technician asked.

"Yes, I'd like to know," Madison answered. Kinley looked over at the screen with renewed interest after having an elbow pointed out.

"You are having a girl, Mrs. Grey. I'm sure your husband will be pleased." Madison didn't know whether to laugh or cry. Should she tell the woman she was unmarried and that her husband wasn't the father but her ex-boyfriend was and he didn't even know about the pregnancy? That sounded a little too whorish even to contemplate. Kinley would have said, "Hurry up and call Jerry Springer." No, she just smiled through newly shedding tears, but wiped them away with determination.

Kinley must have been giving the woman a look which puzzled her, "I'm so sorry…are you two…partners? I didn't mean to offend…"

"Sisters," Madison lied with a smile. Kinley was glaring at the woman who was now scarlet. They only laughed when they got out to the Porsche. "Why would she ask that?" Truthfully, they'd been asked before. She assumed it was because they were clearly closer than regular friends, and if they weren't sisters, they must be…something else. Madison had a wild theory. She figured she had meant to be Kinley's sister, if not twin, and there had been some sort of cosmic mishap, which involved either Kinley running on K-time, or Madison getting into the wrong line. Madison had concluded it was Kinley's fault. She was habitually late by fifteen to thirty minutes, without fail.

They had a fun time at lunch bouncing names off each other. Kinley had suggested the name McKinley and not for the first time. Madison just shook her head. "It would be too confusing. What about Aristotle?"

"He doesn't deserve to have a girl named after him. We girls are superior," Kinley giggled.

"Yes, it's true. Confucius?"

"Now that is some moniker. What were his parents thinking?"

"Bertha or Agnes?" They'd thought of the ugliest names possible, and then some popular ones, but nothing sounded right. She'd dropped Kinley off, feeling rather, well, chipper. She came into her home and thought about moving again. Perhaps she'd get a place with two bedrooms. The one bedroom would work for now, with a bassinette in the corner. She sighed contentedly as she pictured where she would put it. She would have to move eventually, even though the place was growing on her. Her daughter, how lovely that sounded, would go to the best school and have the best of everything.

She thought of finally having the opportunity to decorate a nursery. She'd never quite managed to do it before. Her phone was ringing; she picked it up with a distracted air, too busy concentrating on her new daughter, "Hello?"

"Hello, is this Madison?"

"Speaking," she answered. Was it a survey? No, there was something familiar in the voice.

"This is Grace, Grace Hunt."

Damn it! Why was Cal's mother calling her? How did she have her number? She sat down. "Are you still there?"

"Yes, I'm just surprised that's all." Madison didn't really know what to say.

"I apologize. I must have seemed cold and indifferent to you."

"Yes, a little," Madison confessed.

"I like that you tell me the truth. It's refreshing." Grace Hunt paused, "I only found out about what you'd been through later. I'm truly sorry for your loss." Madison thanked her, noting that it was not a hollow condolence, but sincere. She had the ability to tell the difference at this point.

Still, why was she calling? Madison tried to get comfortable, which was becoming harder to do. Had Gabe told them all about her pregnancy? She grew stiff, "I was wondering if you watched the awards show recently." Okay that was a pretty innocent question. Nothing like, I heard my son impregnated you and do I get to meet my grandchild and be part of his or her life?

Madison took a deep breath, "Yes, I watched it. It was beautiful." It had been.

"He wrote it for you."

"I heard that girl Lindsey Bell say that he wrote it for her. Why would she lie?" Madison was confused. Had he really written that song for her? No, it couldn't be. She didn't feel like being introspective and trying to find out what she was doing wrong here. She'd rather just blame him, even though she knew it was petty.

"Wrote it for that little slut? I think not."

"Grace!"

"Well, it's true. He is miserable since you left. You know he is innocent of whatever it is you think he has done." Grace sounded very matronly at the moment, but somehow love was seeping into her voice. Madison felt loved, as she never had even by her own mother. It was strange, and she wanted to deny it.

"There are pictures," she answered sadly. "Don't you know I wish I could believe you? You know what I've been through. My heart has already been through so much. I don't have the strength to do anymore." She rubbed her stomach as she felt her little girl move.

"It's not the way it seems. Didn't you look at that USB drive like you promised Gabe you would?"

Oh, it was coming back to bite her in the ass! She thought of that little drive sitting in a drawer upstairs. She hadn't thought about since she'd placed it there. It was literally out of sight out of mind. Gabe must have informed on her to Grace. It made her want to laugh as though she had secrets worthy of a spy. "I confess, I haven't had the time," she lied. Oh she had time, the time of an insomniac.

"That is a poor excuse when what's on that drive could exonerate Cal, and free you from your self-inflicted prison." Grace was nearly crying, "He is in love with you, and even if you can't admit it, you love him too." She thought of the lyrics to Cal's song- I was a prisoner trapped inside of me.

"I do love him, so much I ache from it. It physically burns." She hadn't meant to lose control, but the hormones had more to say about it than her mind did. "I love him with every breath in my body; it's why it hurts so much. I wanted to trust him, to know that everything he said to me wasn't just some line. But how can I believe what you say, what anyone says when I have a picture of him hugging a prostitute outside of his hotel suite in Japan? I can't believe anything but my own eyes. I'm sorry Grace. I wanted it to work."

"Sweetheart," Grace didn't sound angry but she was persistent. "Even your eyes can deceive you." Madison wasn't sure how to process this information. What did that mean precisely? "You have a look at that USB drive and call me back. Will you do that? If not for Cal, for me? I may not be important to you, but I would consider it a personal favor if you would just look. I knew you wouldn't believe the words of his mother. But maybe, *this* time you can believe your own eyes."

This part of the conversation was going into a bizarre direction. "Okay, Grace, I'll take a look at it and call you back. It might be a couple of days."

"I can wait." Grace hung up the phone leaving Madison slightly curious but not enough to get off her butt and see the thing that was so important on the USB drive. It was probably doctored, to persuade her. The thought of seeing those pictures again was far too painful. She couldn't do it. Madison shook her head as she drifted off into an uneasy sleep. It was a nightmare, but not one she'd had before. Cal and Jack were arguing over who could take care of her better. She'd ended up yelling that she didn't need either of them. She was just fine on her own. She knew even in the dream that this was a lie. It was the lie she told everyone. Only Kinley seemed to see through it. She said she needed no one, no father for her unborn child, no man to hold her at night. But it was a lie. She needed Cal like she needed the air to breathe. She was a fish, flopping on the ground, lost without oxygen, unable to see anything for what it really was. She needed oxygen to think clearly and oxygen was Cal. She didn't want to need him. What she wanted was to be independent and embrace it, but it was all a façade.

35. Eating Crow Blows

Madison was craving Kinley's homemade French bread, with dipping oil. Kinley brought it over wrapped in a plain brown paper bag, still warm, straight from the oven. "That smells so good," she muttered before tearing the end off of the bread. "Have I ever told you that you are the best friend ever?"

"It is implied, love you too," she answered sweetly. "I'm gonna use your bathroom." She disappeared leaving Madison alone with the hot bread. She rummaged through her cupboard for the dipping oil Kinley made for her on a previous occasion, and was busying herself trying to ebb the tide of pregnancy cravings. Kinley's disappearance didn't alarm her at first, but after fifteen minutes, she was admittedly annoyed. She'd told Kinley all about the bizarre phone call from Grace and was dying to talk about it some more, but she was taking her sweet loving time.

"Kin, where are you? Did you drown in there?" She took the corner, and discovered the bathroom door wide open while the bathroom gleaming white was empty, "Kin?"

Madison waddled up the stairs, cursing all the way for getting two-story and found Kinley rifling through her drawers. "Finally," Kinley muttered to herself as she pulled out a USB drive, the very one Gabe had given Madison.

"You could have asked, you know," she laughed from the doorway.

"Damn it, you scared the hell out of me." She clutched her chest and sat down on Madison's bed. "I didn't know if you'd say yes. You know how you are. Up one minute, down the next, raging ball of hormones. Kevin could bite my head my off, or start crying or something. I thought it would be best if you didn't know."

"You might as well." Madison shrugged. She wasn't offended; she'd known Kinley far too long to be offended. Kinley pulled Madison's laptop across the bed to her, and sat it onto her lap. She ran her index finger over the built in mouse pad. "See anything yet?"

"A file labeled, 'what really happened' for Madison." She clicked onto the file and scanned it with her eyes. Madison had known Kinley for what seemed like forever, and she'd never seen such a startled look on Kin's face. "This is not good. It's bad in fact, very bad and not in the way you think."

Madison didn't move from the doorway, her body stiffened in response. Did she want to know anymore of Cal's foul deeds? She just didn't think she could handle another thing. She loved him, but one can fall in love with someone who is wrong for them. It happens every day. Kinley was shaking her head, biting her lip, more like gnawing on her lip in extreme agitation. Her auburn curls which had been pulled up onto the top of her head, were bouncing while she shook her head back and forth. Madison couldn't take the suspense; she sat down next to Kinley who passed the laptop over rapidly. "Look."

Madison hadn't known what was on the USB drive, and hadn't thought of what to suspect might be there. This was not what she anticipated at all. The girl who had kissed Cal, wearing next to nothing, was facing the camera with her face already showing telltale signs of heavy bruising. Her lips on one side were huge, and bleeding. Her nose was bleeding. Her eye was beginning to swell. It was the other side of her face, the side she hadn't seen. There were more pictures. There was a man being led away in handcuffs, police officers were speaking to Cal and Gabe. She could feel individual veins in her neck recede and let the blood from her face flow back down into her body. She scrolled down and read the headline, *"Famed Rock Star and Body Guard Save Young Girl from Crazed Game Show Host."*

The most revealing picture shook her to her foundation. The girl had her arms wrapped tightly around Cal's neck and was kissing him. It was the same picture she had seen here, only when she'd seen it, the picture had been cropped. The only part she'd actually seen was their two faces locked at the lips. The whole picture was far more telling. Cal's arms were outspread in a 'what the hell' kind of pose. He had been taken by surprise, he was stunned. She had been so mean to him. She read past the headlines, down into the story, and moaned in despair.

Calvin Hunt, lead singer in the band, Murder of Crows was walking to his hotel room late Saturday night, followed closely by his bodyguard Gabriel Ausua. The two happened upon an incident involving a young prostitute, who is not named, and game show host, Hara Katsumi famous for his show, Truth or Dare. The young girl was being brutally beaten. Mr. Hunt stood in between Mr. Hara and took the brunt of his punches in his chest. When asked why he did this he replied, "I just did what anyone would have done."

His bodyguard, Mr. Ausua was able to stop Mr. Hara from further assault and detained him until police arrived. Mr. Hara and his wife were unavailable for questioning.

There was more, but she didn't need to read it to see that she had been completely heartless to Cal. She stared at Kinley in disbelief. "I screwed up, Kin. I really did. I misjudged him." She was crying. Kinley grabbed a box of tissue and sat back down. "What am I going to do? I have no excuse, I have to call him. No, I'll call his mother first and apologize to her. What am I going to say? How am I going to fix this? Even if I don't get back together with him, I have to make this right."

"Nothing and I mean nothing, tastes worse than crow," Kinley muttered. "At least you don't have to eat an entire murder of crows."

"I would rather die than do this," she howled. She knew it was hormones, but she couldn't stem the flow of tears. "This sucks." She blew her nose into a tissue. "It blows."

"Yep," Kinley agreed. She, being the executioner, handed Madison a phone, "You know, I'd like to meet his mother. I think I'd like her."

"You would," Madison groaned as she wiped up her tears, which she knew would soon be flowing again, and looked through her recent calls. Alan Hunt. That had to be it. She frowned as she placed the call. It was only a couple hours ahead of her time; she hoped Mrs. Hunt would be home. But then again, she could have used a voicemail message right about now.

"Hello?" It was a soft voice; it was probably Mr. Hunt.

"Hello, you may not remember me, this is Madison Grey. I'm calling for Grace." She made it sound as polite as she could.

"Maddy, why it's good to hear from you. Grace it's Maddy calling you back." Her stomach was rumbling, "Here she is, sweetie." Did Mr. Hunt have to be so freaking nice? It was bad enough.

"Hello, Maddy dear." She was nice too; they both knew why she'd called.

"Mrs. Hunt, I am so sorry." She was already crying again. She couldn't get through a sentence without sobbing, "So sorry." She sounded horrific. "I didn't know."

"It's okay sweetheart." So, like a mother, forgiving the undeserving. "We didn't want you to know so you'd feel terrible. It's okay."

"It's not. I broke his heart."

"What did he expect, living the life he was living? It's a natural assumption. I would have thought the same thing you did. His reputation precedes him." Did the woman have to be so damned nice and understanding? Her own mother would have berated her for being a moron. Madison sobbed quietly while listening to Grace Hunt speak. Her stomach was now planning an uprising. "Please call Calvin. He needs you."

"I will. I don't blame him if he doesn't want me back," she cried.

"What are you thinking? Of course he wants you back. He'd be a fool not to."

"Did he say that?" Madison asked in doubt.

"Sweetie, he mourns the loss of you. He mopes around here. He tries to look cheerful in case someone catches him on camera. He is lost. You should see him."

"So, you don't actually know if he still loves me." Madison let herself fall backwards onto her bed. Kinley was staring at her, concerned, nervously twisting a curl around one of her fingers.

"Did you know your children, Madison?" Grace asked.

"Yes, implicitly."

"I know my Calvin. He loves you; he doesn't have to say it." She cleared her throat. "Can you fix this, Madison? I hate to see either of you needlessly suffering." Madison gave her the *uh-huh* answer. "Good because I'm counting on you. He is having his birthday tomorrow, and Lord knows where he is. Please find him and save him from himself." That was the strangest request she'd ever been given. She knew it was his birthday tomorrow. Kinley had already planned a girl's night to distract her from thinking about it.

"I will call him, and do whatever it takes to tell him, even show him that I love him," Madison said. Kinley squealed and clapped silently. By the time she'd hung up the phone, Kinley was crying and hugging her. "Kinley, what is wrong with you?" she gently pealed her friend from her.

"I am so happy."

"Nothing has worked out yet," Madison pointed out pessimistically.

"Oh, but it will, I can feel it, my women's intuition is kicking in," Kinley gushed. "Now you can get past all of this immature stuff."

"Kinley Brooke, I have not been immature, I've handled myself with the utmost dignity." Madison sat back up, keeping her posture straight.

Kinley snorted, "Oh please. I'm going to break it off on Facebook and ignore you? I'm going to trash all of the roses you sent? I'm going to…" Only Kinley could call her out like this and get away with it.

"Enough," Madison held up her hand in surrender. "You might have a small point. But you should really stop snorting…it's unbecoming."

Kinley laughed in reply. "Oh I am so happy for you Maddy," she squealed and hugged Madison, who was not comforted at all.

36. It's My Birthday and I'll Get Drunk if I Want To

Cal recalled that as a child he would look forward to his birthday. He loved that it was near Christmas. Most people didn't like that sort of thing. His brother Rory had been jealous. "It's no fair Mom, he gets his birthday and Christmas, and so does Callie," he would pout and whine. Both Cal and Callie thought it was excellent. This year, however, he wasn't having a very good birthday. Since he'd become something of a celebrity he'd had some wild parties. This one included. Lindsey had gone all out.

He'd thanked her, but his thankfulness was hollow. How was it that he could be so close to where Maddy was and still feel as though he were a trillion miles away? He stared out of the window. He was on the top floor, looking through solid walls of glass out onto the city of Los Angeles. "Whatcha thinkin' bout?" Lindsey had asked. "Are you wondering what I got you for your birthday? You can unwrap it later, when we're all alone." She tried to be seductive, but he just felt it was awkward. He smiled to let her know he was listening, but he turned to look out the window. She walked away and began flirting with someone else.

"Cal!"

He heard the voice of an old friend, Nick Davies, a fellow singer. Nick sang with an alternative band named Foul Ball. He clapped Cal on the shoulder. Apparently, Nick had a few drinks. Cal hadn't even touched one.

His mind wanted to wallow in misery, rather than erase it all, drown his sorrows, so to speak. "Hi Nick. How's it going?"

"Cal, it's been too long." Nick swayed slightly and clung to Cal's leather jacket for support. "I liked the song you sang at the AMAs. Classic." His breath reeked of booze.

"Thanks." He smiled politely.

"Who is the 'Maddy' girl you were talking about? And if you are so in love with her why the hell are you wasting your time with *that*?" He pointed by holding his lager and gesturing in the general direction of where Lindsey was standing. "She is not inspiring, unless you're singing your princess song." Nick shrugged. His untidy black hair spilling all over his head, his mouth lopsided in a sheepish grin, he was incorrigible. His pale white skin looked sickly underneath the purple overhead lights, and his black nail polish gave him the look of a walking corpse.

"You're right; she is not inspiring in that way at all. Maddy is someone who is lost to me." Saying it made it feel somehow more real and utterly, bewilderingly painful. He stared out of the window again. He thought of how normal he felt to be near her, how soothing and peaceful life was when she was around. He missed their nightly talks and the times he'd spent with her. Gone were the bitter feelings he'd been cherishing. Those felt pointless.

"Where is this 'Maddy' girl anyway?" Nick asked, slipping into a drunken stupor as he gazed out at the city lights.

"She is about thirty minutes from here," he answered softly.

"Then why are you still here? Go get her already." How was this drunken man making so much sense? Here he was thinking clearly, when he barely made it through a sentence without slurring. He was pointing out the obvious and Cal was standing there slack-jawed. "What?" Nick inquired. "Go get her," he repeated. Cal didn't know what to say. He looked up to see a ginormous cake being wheeled toward him. People were crowding around singing Happy Birthday. He was the center of attention. He couldn't move, rooted to the spot, Lindsey sang to him the loudest. Why was he focused on Gabe leaning against the wall? He just wanted to leave. How could he when the whole party was for him?

"I don't know about this." Madison stared at her stomach, feeling humongous. "I am a leviathan, a massive whale. I can't let him see me like this."

"Whatever," Megan told her, while chewing on a new piece of peppermint gum. "Most people are not so small when they are preggers…you look fantastic."

"I suppose I look okay but he won't be expecting this," Madison protested. "It will be shocking."

Kate had been listening to the radio when a DJ announced that Lindsey Bell had a Twitter thing going on. He called her 'Twitter-pated'. He'd thought he was clever. She was telling everyone she knew that she was throwing a party for her 'boyfriend', one Calvin Hunt. According to Cal's mother, this was not so. He was in Los Angeles at an exclusive club downtown- Pandora's Box.

"I can't go to a club and expect to get in while I'm *expecting*. Besides, he's bound to be in private room, we won't get in there at all," she cried in frustration. "This is a bad idea altogether."

"What if we take you to his hotel room?" Kate asked. "I'd bet Lindsey Tweeted about that!" Kate turned to the others, "Well, what should we do? We have to do something!"

"Call Gabe," Megan suggested. "Yes, you still have his number don't you? Call him; you can always get him on the phone. Isn't that was Cal said?" They all looked at each other. This felt like a good move. Madison nodded, but all the while was feeling her skin lose heat. She wouldn't have been surprised if ice crystals had started forming a layer of frost over her body.

She reached for her phone. Some girl's night out this was turning out to be. She searched through her list of contacts and found him somewhere in the middle, under Gabe. Trembling she pushed send, feeling her pulse come and go in spurts. She was in a haze; this felt exactly like she was going to throw-up. She'd called Cal earlier only to get his voicemail. She'd forgotten how nice his talking voice sounded. Should she just let it go? Walk away? She somehow couldn't, not without letting him know how sorry she was. If she put the 'ball in his court' she could rest easy…right?

She hadn't left a voicemail. It hadn't seemed appropriate. What should she have said anyway? *Uh,* sorry I didn't believe you, I'm a loser?

Her heart nearly stopped when she heard Gabe answer the phone, "Hello?" His voice was unusually loud and so was the background noise. He was in the club with Cal. "Hello?" She heard his low rumbling voice call out again.

"Gabe?"

"Yes, who is this?" He was in a mood.

"Maddy," she replied, her hands were actually shaking. Her lips could barely get into the right shape to push her words out. This was stupid, so stupid, why was she doing this?

"Maddy!" he sounded thrilled. Okay. "You looked at the USB drive, finally?"

"Yes. I'm so sorry that I didn't do it sooner," she mumbled. She was so bad at this. She pushed a stray lock of hair away from her face, "Gabe, I…"

"What should we do? Do you need to know where he is staying? I'll have him to his room in a minute, if that's what you need. You two need to work this out, and I can help you," she now was crying again. Damned hormones. She needed to gain control.

"Yes, I'd like that." She nodded to her friends who were all looking anxiously excited for her. She still wasn't certain about how the thing would play out. Would he take her back? Would he accept her apology then walk off with his arm around that bimbo Lindsey Bell? She took down the information from Gabe, during which she felt a panic attack coming on. She was sure she would start hyperventilating. Anaphylactic shock was setting in.

Her friends were cheering as she got off the phone. Her friends were excited but she couldn't be. She had to get to Cal and let things work out the way they would. Her friends would wait for her no matter how it all ended. They would comfort her if she failed to win him back. They would cheer for her if she won his heart and decided to stay in his strong embrace. They were her family now.

"I'm driving," Kate called out. "I'm the fastest. Megan's the most distracted, so we'll get lost, and Kinley's car is the oldest." Kinley smiled knowing it was true. They all laughed.

Kate drove quickly, just as she'd promised. That Hemi engine was living up to the hype. Kinley sat in the back with Madison, watching her with concern as though she might suddenly and spontaneously combust. Kinley appeared to be tuned into her apprehension. Out of the corner of her eye she saw the silver SUV turn the corner too sharply. They were a block away from his hotel. She closed her eyes, not wanting to see it. But she heard it. The crashing of two gargantuan cars splintering, shattering, crunching of metal. A stabbing pain ripped through her abdomen, as she heard her friend's screams shrilly punctuate the cacophonic symphony. Her head was hurting even more, which was saying something.

"Maddy?" Kinley's voice swam to her against the current of the sea of blackness. She couldn't answer; she couldn't move, not even an eyelid. "Maddy!" her voice was urgent. "She's not responding!" Madison could hear the panic in Kinley's voice, but couldn't soothe her. She couldn't reach out and tell her it would be all right, because she couldn't speak. She couldn't comfort her when she didn't know if it really would be okay. "Call the ambulance!" Kin screamed. The pain in her abdomen spread its' scorching tendrils over her stomach, up over her ribcage and centered in her sternum. It hurt to breathe. It hurt to think. She needed to rest; she couldn't worry about Kinley now. She could feel a moan escape her throat before it closed off completely and she succumbed to the familiar shroud of darkness.

37. Called Out

Cal drummed his fingers on the dashboard of Gabe's rented *Prius*. He had scrolled through all of the different screens on the navigation screen. He now knew the intimate workings of the car thanks to the screen with diagrams of the engine. He knew what percentage of electricity and battery power had been used. He knew how much gas was left. He knew what was on the radio, it was not good. He either had to listen to himself sing his song to Maddy, Christmas music, rap, or Mariachi bands. He decided to turn off the radio. Gabe didn't have his iPod or any CD's. They'd been sitting in traffic for over an hour. Some idiot had gone off and had an accident a mere block from his hotel, and they'd driven right into it.

He was now singing his own little version of 'The Little Drummer Boy' while drumming his fingertips over the dashboard. Gabe had been dialing a number repeatedly, and following up with a frown. His lips were drawn tightly in a firm line as Cal went to open the car door. "I wouldn't recommend getting out Cal, you'll be mobbed. I'm stuck here in this damned sardine can and will be unable to push the crowd away." Gabe took a deep breath. "Damn the both of you," he finally said after sitting in near silence for a moment.

"What?" He was pissed. He'd had enough of Gabe's secrets and it was apparent that he knew things that he had not yet shared. "What are you not saying? How did we both manage to piss you off?"

"I know things," he replied angrily. "Things that could have solved this whole stupid immaturely handled mess the two of you have created. Neither of you will let me speak. If we had been in a room together, this would have been solved weeks ago. But no, you two want to act like damned teenagers. If you had listened to me the night of the awards, this would be over by now. If she had listened to me, or at least looked at the USB drive I gave to her, this would be over. But no…you two are stubborn, immature, idiots."

"I don't think she'd like being called an idiot Gabe," he teased with a smirk. Gabe had reached the end of his tether.

"I would tell her like I'm telling you."

"Okay, what revelation do you have for me…wait you saw her? That was where you disappeared to? You were visiting Maddy, giving her a USB drive? With what?"

"You're really too observant," Gabe mocked. "I wanted her to know what really happened in Japan. I say it wasn't her fault for believing the worst of you. But it was her fault for being so damned stubborn and not looking at the drive while she had it in her house the entire last three weeks. Isn't it? And it is your fault for not letting me give you a vital piece of information that would have made you realize how ridiculous you're being. You would have known how superfluous and shallow your irritations had been. But no, again you wouldn't ever let me speak. Never."

"I'm listening now. And you are driving me nuts. Will you just tell me what it is!" His phone rang. He looked down and hit ignore, not even to see who it was.

"You'd better check that."

"Not now Gabe," he was slowly losing his temper. "I've had you calling me out on my shit for the past ten minutes…you'd better tell me what the hell you've been keeping from me."

"Fine." Gabe's arms folded over his chest. A horn honked in the distance. Flashing lights from police cars began to move. Gabe was able to put the car into gear and move, finally. "You're going to be a father."

"What?" he'd blurted in astonishment. "That's impossible. No, that can't be. We always were careful."

"Even in England?" Gabe asked bluntly as the car rolled forward. "It's about damned time," he grumbled. Cal looked over at the old silver *Trooper* smashed beyond recognition. A black Dodge *Magnum's* side was battered while the other side looked as though nothing had happened to it. Cal shivered; relieved it hadn't been him in that car. He was distracted. England. It had been so spontaneous, so beautiful. He hadn't even stopped to think of consequences. He frowned as the memories caught him up to the present.

"How did you know about England?" he sat pondering.

"I can do the math."

"You saw her and she was…" He motioned a hand over his stomach into a little bump. "With my…"

"Yep. She was cute too. Couldn't tell from the back, then she turned to the side. She's the cutest pregnant woman I ever saw."

Cal swallowed. He wasn't certain of how he should feel. He should be angry, furious that she hadn't told him. But he couldn't restrain the smile from spreading ear to ear across his face. "I'm going to be a father." It wasn't a question, but more of a statement of certainty. "She knows about what really happened in Japan? And she called?"

"Yes, I believe so." They pulled up to the hotel. A valet ran to assist them. He was in awe, wandering vaguely as though the participant of a hallucinatory dream. He listened to Gabe inquire at the desk. He'd called ahead to make certain that Maddy would be waiting in Cal's room. Cal only began paying attention when he heard the desk clerk clear his throat and tell Gabe that no one had stopped by.

"That can't be," Gabe mumbled more to himself.

They walked up to the room. "Did she tell you if the baby is a girl or a boy?" he questioned Gabe on the way up in the elevator. Gabe followed him to his room, frowning, concentrating. He shook his head in the negative. Cal needed to see her. Where was she? Maybe she had been stuck in the traffic jam too. He threw himself onto the sofa while Gabe settled his massive body into an armchair. "Relax G; she was probably stuck in that traffic back there. She should be here soon. Imagine me, a father." He was smiling as he tucked his arms behind his head. "Me."

"That wasn't her car back there was it?"

"*Nah*, she drives a little red Porsche. But I'm sure you knew that already."

"Yeah, I guess." he frowned, creasing his face with his furrowed brows. "Something isn't right. She's not answering her phone."

Cal pulled out his phone. "Call Kinley then. I think I have her number in here somewhere. I didn't..." But his blood froze solid before he could finish. Four missed Calls. Callie in the morning, his mother, Maddy and the last one was from Kinley. He searched through his calls. The one he'd ignored was from Kinley. His throat tightened sparking a chain reaction for his chest to follow. He dialed Maddy first. Straight to voicemail, it sent him. He dialed Kinley's number, waiting impatiently as a Christmas carol was being sung to him by Michael Bublé.

"Hi?" Kinley sounded wrong.

"Kinley?" It couldn't be her.

"Cal, you called." No, that was definitely crying going on. He could feel his heart shut down. Never had he felt such a strange, alone, frightened feeling. "I don't know how to tell you."

"Tell me, Kinley. Were you all stuck behind the accident?" he asked while his hope diminished rapidly with each sob from Kinley.

"No, we were the accident. You saw it? We were in the black Dodge."

"No." It was a faint 'no' that escaped his lips without permission. "And Maddy?"

"She's..." Kinley was crying, choking on her tears as his body grew colder and numb. "She's in surgery now. Internal bleeding."

"And the baby?"

"They didn't say," Kinley wept. "I'm so sorry."

"Where are you? I'm coming over there now."

"Cedars Sinai," she answered. "We were all pretty banged up. Kate and Maddy got the worst of it." He thought of the driver's side of the car, smashed in. Kate had been driving and Maddy had been sitting behind her. He pictured the car, and closed his eyes in unbearable agony. How flippantly he'd thought earlier that he was glad it wasn't him, only to be confronted with how shallow he was yet again. They were people, actual people he knew.

"I'm on my way."

"It's past visiting hours. They sent Kate and Jared home, and released Megan already."

"And you?"

"They couldn't make me leave if they sent in a special ops team, or the National Guard for that matter. I'm here."

"Then you shall have me by your side," he told her.

He turned to Gabe, who was already standing, holding his key in his hand. "Let's go." He'd been listening. Cal nodded solemnly as they got up to leave. He'd never felt so completely helpless before in his entire life.

38. The Lack of Hospitality

He hated that the word hospital sounded like hospitable, when there was nothing hospitable about hospitals. He walked in wearing a navy blue hooded sweatshirt (it was chilly even though it was LA) and a hat and sunglasses. His shoulders were slouched. Gabe stood tall next to him, and looked quite menacing although he was only wearing a polo shirt and khakis. He slumped into a chair in the waiting room. He wasn't even certain he was in the right place. Gabe was at the desk asking about Maddy. Cal could hear the bass voice carry across the emptiness of the waiting area. "Madison Grey?" He heard the receptionist ask. He heard the clicking of her keyboard echoing over the tile.

"She's in surgery. Would you like to wait?" She sounded incensed, at the end of her rope. Gabe grumbled something unintelligible before he came back over.

"Call Kinley, she's somewhere in here," Gabe told him as they sat down.

He dialed the number, and decided that he was not in the mood for hearing Christmas music, "Hello?" She sounded exhausted.

"It's Cal, we're here in the emergency waiting room."

"I'll be right there." And like in television and the movies, she didn't say goodbye but hung up on him. He stood and paced until she arrived another minute later. Her left arm in a cast, her hair was clipped up and auburn curls were spilling out from the area of her crown. Her makeup was smeared; she was not looking quite like she normally did. She frowned as she looked at him. He watched her scrutinizing glare, "Cal?"

He nodded. "You look like a criminal." She walked over to him and he hugged her. She leaned against him, probably from fatigue.

"Kin, what happened to your arm?"

She looked up at him; her eyes were not sparkling as usual, full of mirth. "I put my arm in front of Maddy. Instinct, I guess." She shrugged. "You think I look bad you should see Kate. She got the full brunt of the airbag. Megan was too far back. She's gone home with Doug now. So, it's just me and Maddy here. They will probably be back tomorrow." They walked over and found a pair of uncomfortable looking chairs to sit in.

"Doug?"

"Megan's husband." She shrugged heavily as though her shoulders weighed more than the rest of her body. He put his arm around her feeling a brotherly kinship with her as she leaned against him.

"Where's Ryan?"

"He's on break so he took the girls to Idaho to see the grandparents. I was supposed to fly out tomorrow, but I won't be. I can't leave Maddy." She laughed, not happily though. "He'll be flying back soon. I told him to stay. I don't need him flying back here too soon. I'll never hear the end of it from my mother-in-law."

"Tell me what happened," he urged her to speak. Gabe just sat there, arms across his chest, his head leaned back as though he were sleeping, but Cal knew he was listening to every word.

"Some idiot went to his office Christmas party tonight and got wasted. He thought he was fine to drive. I shouldn't call him an idiot. He's dead. It's rude to speak meanly of the dead." She frowned. "He came barreling around the corner and plowed into us. I threw my arm in front of Maddy. The doctor told me that it may have saved the baby. I don't know. He was probably just being nice." She was out of it. "Kate looks like she was beaten, and Megan looks okay. Me, I'm fine. Maddy had some internal bleeding. They told me the baby seems to be fine. But you know if Maddy doesn't make it, then the baby might not. I can't live with that."

He had the distinct impression that Kinley was blaming herself. "It's not your fault." Yep he was right. She was now wailing, sobbing. He looked about helplessly, but Gabe was on it, getting tissue from the receptionist's desk.

"I never told her. I know she suspected but I never told her."

"What are you talking about, Kin?" He didn't understand her but he wanted to- desperately.

"I knew they were going to die. It seemed too farfetched for a whole family to die, but I knew." She pulled away from him as though she didn't deserve to be hugged. She took a deep breath. He assumed she didn't want him to see her like this. She was wiping tears away quickly, taking a deep breath, and trying to appear as normal as she could. "We'd better go back. The doctor will come and let me know when she's out of surgery." She held up a beeper. "I've been getting updates."

He had barely understood what she'd said. What did she mean? She knew that Madison's entire family would die? Maybe she was loopy from pain medication. Well, when someone has been through trauma it could make them sound a bit, well, deranged, couldn't it? He followed her through the maze of hospital hallways until they were at a more comfortable area. There was a table with a coffee maker, and cups on the white paper tablecloth. He moved to get himself a cup-black. He grabbed Gabe a cup too and offered one to Kinley who politely refused.

Another couple was sitting there, both looking extremely anxious. With his back turned he could hear the woman whisper, "I think he's a gang member." Cal smirked. So that's what people thought he was? He turned to see Gabe stifling a laugh. "Let's walk around," the woman who looked concerned, asked her husband. He nodded. They both gave Cal a wide berth as they moved away.

"You know, I'm going to move the car. I'll be back," Gabe muttered, leaving with his Styrofoam cup emitting steam, nestled in his gigantic hand.

"I need to know something." Cal sat down in the chair next to Kinley. She looked up, but didn't let him ask, she just smiled.

"Yes, she still loves you."

"How did you…"

"I'm perceptive, even though I'm on some good drugs at the moment." She smiled to herself. "She's worried; you might not want children. She's worried you might not want to see her again." Kinley looked away as though it were all too painful.

"How can she think like that? I love her more than anything. I've never loved anyone before, beyond my family. I've never felt like this. I realize I'm a bit old to experience first love, but here I am. Better late than never," he paused. "When Gabe told me tonight that she was pregnant...I felt like my love was growing. I can't describe it. I want this baby more than anything. I want both of them."

Kinley's eyes filled with tears. But he continued, "It makes everything we've been through seem, nonsensical somehow."

"I agree," she sighed. A man in the long white coat came into the room. He had a dark complexion and even darker eyes, but they were filled with a glow. Kinley got up anxiously, her exhaustion falling away.

"Mrs. Brooke?" She nodded. "Your sister is doing well so is her baby. She is resting." He gave them a room number. "She should be waking any time now. You should be there when she wakes. I don't wish for her to be alone." Kinley nodded again before thanking him.

They walked in silence to the room. A nurse was coming out; she was a haggard looking woman, with graying hair and deep-set grooves instead of minor wrinkles in her skin. "Visiting hours are *long* over."

"I was just in a car accident. I'm here with my sister; she just got out of surgery," Kinley told her politely.

"I don't care who you are, or why you're here." The nurse frowned. "You need to come back during visiting hours."

Kinley looked exhausted, but she was trying to reason with the hag, "The doctor told me she was out of surgery and to go to her, so if you'll excuse me..." Cal and Maddy had talked about everything under the sun, including the fact that Kinley had been more irritable than normal. Maddy had shared with him the fact that Kinley had told a few people off in recent months. Madison knew Kinley was grieving too, causing her fuse to be shorter than it had ever been. She usually will put up with a lot before she snaps, Maddy had mentioned. He watched as she reached the end of her tether.

"Do you have to be a bitch to work here? Or is there a bonus for being extra bitchy to patients?" Kinley asked while the woman's only reply was a gaping mouth. "You can go now. I'm done listening to whiny bitchy people who actually have no power to do anything. If you want me to leave you're going to have to call security. I'm not leaving for them, and I'm certainly not leaving for you," she told the woman flatly. Cal smirked. Wow.

"You shouldn't be here," the woman argued her words seemed to have left her.

"That the best you can do? Well it looks like you shouldn't be here either. You are missing a bedside manner, and a pleasant face. Why don't you just go and bully someone who will listen to you. Because that person isn't me."

"You have no right." The woman was indignant, but clearly not in possession of the gift of good retorts.

"Get out of my way, or I swear I'll mow you down." Kinley glared at her. "I'm not in the mood; the painkillers are wearing off." Kinley was done playing around, apparently.

"Well!" the woman huffed in anger before stalking away.

"I have a feeling we haven't seen the last of her," Kinley growled before walking into the room." I shouldn't have chewed her out like that." Kinley seemed to regret it instantly. "It's going to get me into trouble, I just can't believe her. Am I supposed to let Maddy wake up all alone?" He followed, realizing that his mouth was still hanging open as it had been when he'd witnessed the verbal rally. There was a tiny woman in the bed. Her dark hair was pulled back, rather untidily, but it never looked lovelier to him. With her back turned to them, she appeared so helpless and small. "She doesn't look prego from here does she?" Kinley was smiling, happy to see Madison. They walked around to the other side of her. She was still so beautiful, and vulnerable looking. Her right arm had an IV inserted in it. He looked at the little bump.

"She's the prettiest pregnant woman I have ever seen," he whispered in awe.

Kinley nodded. "I think so too." She reached out and touched Maddy's hand. "Maddy, can you hear me? Cal is here." Madison's breathing was deep and even. Her lips curled into a smile. "I swear she can hear us." Cal pulled up a chair and settled down, pulling off his hat, dark sunglasses and letting his hood fall. "Oh look, it is you," Kinley laughed hollowly. He grinned.

"There they are." The frazzled looking nurse stood in the doorway, a triumphant gleam in her otherwise dull gray eyes. A security guard was with her.

"You...you...are..." she spluttered as she stared at Cal.

"The baby's father," he finished the nurse's sentence in a completely unexpected way. Both the guard and the nurse were staring now, completely unabashed.

"Calvin Hunt," the guard finally spit it out. "Wow." He turned to the nurse. "They can stay as long as they want," he told her flatly. "It's nice to meet you." He walked away leaving the nurse to only stare in bewilderment. She tried to speak several times, but ended up just stalking away.

"I hate to see what kind of hell I would have had to raise had I not had my famous friend by my side." Kinley grinned at him. "It's good to have you here Cal. By the way, happy birthday."

"I think my birthday was yesterday," he muttered, "But thank you."

"Maddy was dreading it. I was supposed to go out of town with my family, but I didn't think she'd do so well. I planned a girl's night out for your birthday, so it would distract her," Kinley admitted.

"She does still love me? She was dreading my birthday?" He sat back, stunned.

"Of course she was." Kinley looked over at her friend, her hand still resting on top of Maddy's, "Cal, she just read the article yesterday." Kinley was bringing it up. He nodded. "She felt horrible."

"It's my own fault," he owned it. "If I were a better person, who never had such a scandalous reputation, she couldn't have so easily believed it. I wish I'd been worthy of her trust, but I have to earn it. If it takes the rest of my life, I will earn it."

"Do you promise?" Maddy whispered hoarsely. Her eyes fluttered open.

"Yes, with all my heart." He leaned over from his chair while Kinley moved her hand.

"I think that it's my cue to go."

Kinley sure knew how to clear out in a hurry.

39. Belated Birthday Gift

"Can you get Kinley back here?" she asked. She couldn't swallow her mouth was dryer than a front yard in Vegas during a drought. She pictured a Joshua tree withering in the extra arid weather. He hopped up…what an ass that man had. She would have whistled if she could have. Madison's head was swimming in a sea of drugs, but the drugs were beginning to wear off. She hoped it wouldn't be bad for the baby.

Kinley was sitting next to her, "What do you need Maddy?"

"I need to pee, and although I love him, I'm not super comfy with Cal helping me to pee." She grinned up at him. His heart was confused. Should it beat until it wore itself out, or just stop from the shock of it all? She'd never said 'I love you', but he held out. Kin had mentioned that she loved him still, but he had taken it with a grain of salt. He just smiled at her as he watched Kinley help her out of bed, hold her up, and wheel the IV stand behind her. "Is this the most uncomfortable thing you've ever done?" she laughed at Kinley. He watched with apprehension, noticing her legs shaking uncontrollably beneath her.

He could hear their girlish laughter coming out of the restroom. When they came back, he couldn't help but think how sweet they were together. Kinley, who had seemed beyond the point of exhaustion, was suddenly wide-awake. He helped her slide back into bed, just watching her.

He thought his memory had been accurate. He could remember every word of every song he'd heard in his life, even after hearing it once. He remembered melodies, lyrics, faces, names, things he'd read. But he hadn't been as accurate as he'd thought. Even in a hospital gown, Madison Grey was beautiful. How was it possible that she was more beautiful than his memory could recall? How indeed? He didn't know how to act, what to say around her.

"I can let you two be alone now," Kinley told them.

Madison nodded as she watched her friend walk away. "She told me you hugged her. That was sweet." He was pouring her a glass of water out of a small beige plastic pitcher. She coughed as he handed her the little ribbed plastic cup. She sipped.

"Kinley is funny when you hug her." He smiled at her, deliberately keeping it light.

"Did she get all stiff on you?"

"Yeah, how did you know?" He laughed as her eyes crinkled in the corners.

"She hates hugging," Madison giggled. He'd missed the sound of her laughter.

"I think I knew that but forgot somehow."

"She said you were really sweet." She leaned back against her pillows, seemingly worn out from the small conversation and the exertion of going to the restroom and back.

He didn't want to beat around the damn bush anymore, "You said you love me."

Her eyes closed, "God help me but I do." He pulled his chair closer to her and put his hand on hers. Her eyes stayed closed, but her lips curled up in a sweet smile, "I have missed you." He studied her face and watched a single tear leave the corner of her eye and travel over the softest curve of her cheek, down over the edge of her lips. He leaned even closer and kissed her softly on the cheek where just seconds ago the tear had been. "I'm so sorry, Cal. I don't even know how to tell you or what to say. You saved that girl in Japan, and I misjudged you. I am such an idiot. You never gave me reason to doubt you." He touched her face, but she wouldn't open her eyes. She sniffed softly.

"Didn't I? I never had a spotless reputation. I never deserved your absolute trust," he admitted. He kissed her lips, letting his lips linger ever closer to hers. This felt so right.

"I don't want to cry in front of you."

"Why? You're beautiful when you cry. You're beautiful."

She sniffed again. He watched her silently struggle to keep the tears inside. "It's not all I have to apologize for." This was painful for her. Still her eyes remained closed. He longed to see them opened.

"Whatever do you mean?" he couldn't help but tease her, and hope she'd open her eyes and look at him. "Are you talking about the child you kept a secret from me?" It had the effect he wanted. Her eyes flew open, and she began to cry, muttering something about being horrible and evil.

He held her in his arms. "It's alright."

"It's not. I didn't…" she just wept, and whatever she was trying to say remained unsaid. He brushed the tears away with his fingertips. "I'm…" He touched her lips and shook his head.

"I don't care anymore. It all seems ridiculous now. I almost lost you." He pulled her closer, "Don't leave me again."

"I won't," she answered, "I love you Cal." He felt his chest tighten, his jaw lock. He'd waited so long to hear her say those words.

"I love you, Maddy." He just wanted to look at her. "Can you tell me one thing?" She nodded. "Are we having a girl or a boy?" He hoped she knew. He'd never really been much for surprises. It had been a surprise to find out that he was having a child, and he'd nearly lost her again afterward. Yes, he'd had enough surprises for the day.

"You said *we*…" she sighed contentedly. Her dark chocolate eyes, rimmed with tears, had to be the loveliest eyes he'd ever seen. "*We* are having a girl."

Why did this news make him happier than anything ever had? He couldn't stop smiling. "A girl." He shook his head. "This is the best birthday present ever." She stared at him in shock, but smiling all the while. "No really, it is. Have you any names picked out yet?"

"No." She frowned. "Kin and I have joke names picked out, like Connie." He grimaced. "We took Philosophy together. Confucius or Connie for short. Don't you like Confucius Hunt?"

"What about Hildegard, since we're picking out ugly names," he teased back. She laughed hard, grabbing her stomach.

"That hurts." She frowned.

"May I?" He held the edge of her hospital gown. She had one on backward to cover her back. He grinned as she nodded. He lifted her gown and looked at her beautiful stomach. He let his fingers run over it. Deep bruises were forming. He laughed as he noticed that it was the exact shape of Kinley's arm. He kissed her stomach. He noticed that there was a bandage over her swollen abdomen. "You are beautiful."

"You keep saying that, Calvin Hunt, you are such a bad liar."

"I mean it."

"Yes, I know. But I think you must be on drugs or delusional. I am hugely fat right now. I mean…you are seeing me like this." She ran her hands through her hair, suddenly self-conscious. "I am huge," she stated again. "Look… I even have *tharms*." She wiggled her arm as if to show him.

"What is a *tharm*?" He stared openmouthed at her, blinking, confused.

He heard a voice from the vicinity of the door, "Thigh arms." Kinley was laughing.

"You eavesdropper," Maddy yelled out.

Kinley walked in. "I was out in the hall pacing when I heard my beautiful friend complaining about her '*tharms*' and I couldn't help myself."

"*Tharms*?"

"Didn't we tell you?" Kinley began, "we have our own words we make up. Someone, poor nameless soul, is out there without having gotten the credit for naming cankles." She shook her head as if this were even sadder than world hunger. "We have a list, it's ongoing."

He looked at her, humorously puzzled, "What's another word? I find this intriguing."

"*Bondish*," she said with a straight face.

"*Bondish*?"

Maddy was laughing. "It's like James Bond." She cleared her throat, "You know, Mr. Hunt, when you were at the American Music Awards, you looked very '*Bondish*' in your suit." She sighed.

"Wasn't he hot?" she asked Kinley. Kinley nodded. He just laughed.

"Are all women like you two?" He had no idea.

"I don't think so," Maddy replied. Kinley was shaking her head.

"But *all* women like us," Kinley responded with a hint of sarcasm. He laughed. But when he turned, he could see Madison was trying to hide the fact she was in pain. It hadn't escaped him that she was rubbing over her bandages. "I'm getting the nurse." Kinley looked as though she were about to do something extremely unpleasant. "She hates me, she won't be pleased." She left.

Cal adjusted Madison's gown, giving her more cover. "You missed a good fight."

"Did I?" She shook her head. "Did Kinley tell a nurse off?"

"You could say that…it was more of a verbal slaying," he chuckled. "Wow."

Madison laughed while clutching at her side, and looking miserable through her laughter, "You will have to tell me all about it later. I'm going to talk to her about calming down her redheaded temper a bit." She looked up to the door. A nurse was standing there, obviously filled with disapproval for guests visiting in the middle of the night. But she was torn, because she recognized Cal and didn't want to let him have any dissatisfaction.

"Are you in pain?" The nurse was a gruff woman, irritated, and frowning.

Madison was nodding.

"On a scale of one to ten?" The woman was covering Madison with a sheet. Madison's teeth were chattering without control. Madison wondered aloud if the scale could go up to eleven, which made Cal bristle. "We have to be careful for the baby." She glared at Cal, plainly chagrined, thinking he was some irresponsible father. Maybe she blamed him for the accident. She took Madison's blood pressure and checked her chart. Fussing over her, she finally pushed a needle of something into Madison's IV line. Madison smiled and uttered a thank you. The woman grudgingly said 'you're welcome' before leaving the room. Kinley didn't come back in until she was gone.

"I'm going to call Ryan. I promised I'd call when you woke up." She hugged Madison.

"You hugged me?" Madison choked out, "You *must* have been worried."

"You have no idea." Kinley shot her a sideways grin before she left.

Madison reached over for Cal's hand and squeezed it. "Stay with me, Cal. Don't leave." Her eyes were closing. "That was fast," she yawned.

"I won't be leaving you again," he whispered. He touched her face, and swept her hair aside. He chuckled to himself. *Tharms*? He smiled when she'd told him he was '*Bondish*' at the music awards. She'd been watching. He leaned against his chair and smiled. Strangely, it had been both the worst birthday and the best birthday he'd ever had.

40. Filling in the Blanks

Cal found Gabe curled up, fast asleep, well as curled up as a man that huge can be, in the leaned-back front seat of the rented *Prius*. He stood over him with some crappy hospital coffee, knocking on the window. Gabe yawned and stretched, which wasn't working out so well in that cramped little car. It was Gabe's own fault. The *Prius* wasn't the only *green* car around. Cal handed him his coffee when he opened the car door. Droplets of dew decorated the windshield. The frost-filled air misted as Cal's breath hit it, "Why didn't you go back to the hotel?"

"I thought you might need something. Damn, I have a crick in my neck." He turned his head all the while making tiny cracking and popping noises. "How is Madison?" he yawned. Gabe's dark eyes narrowed as he sniffed the coffee, and took a sip. "*Ugh*, this is terrible."

"Well, it's the best I can do. If you want something better, I hear there's a Starbuck's inside."

"That sounds much better." He sat the seat upright and cracked his knuckles.

Cal couldn't stop himself from smiling like an idiot. He just kept grinning, the kind of grins which took up his entire face. Gabe followed him in, cracking more joints as he walked, and they parted ways for Gabe to find a better cup of coffee. He breathed in the medicinal smelling morning air as he walked back to be with Madison. He'd left to give her a bit of privacy with the doctor. When he returned, Maddy was sitting up, staring at a small container of Jell-O with disdain. "I hate Jell-O," she told Kinley, who was not listening, but sleeping.

"I don't think she can hear you," he told her from the doorway.

Madison turned to look at her sleeping friend, "Oh. She was awake just a moment ago."

Cal sat down on the edge of her bed; they both watched Kinley, who had her good arm tucked underneath her cast. "What did the doctor say?"

"He can't find anything else wrong with me but they want to monitor me for another day or so. I just got off the phone with Megan and told her not to come back. Kinley won't leave until they let me leave, I suspect. But, then again, she might not be able to get home. Kate *was* our ride out here."

"I have a feeling that your friend Kinley is a resourceful woman who could get home if she wanted to." He touched Madison's face. He loved watching her close her eyes in a cherishing smile. "I also suspect that she is fiercely loyal, and will not leave because of you."

"I believe you are right. It's like you know her better than anyone else, well, besides me and Ryan." He was still fighting back laughter as he thought of the nurse Kinley had verbally thrashed the night before. She was a feisty little thing. "What are you doing for Christmas?" she asked as she smoothed her blue-green hospital gown out over her tiny bump.

"I don't know. Whatever it is better involve being with you. Do you have plans? If so, you can squeeze me in somewhere. I'm not very big and quite portable," he told her with mock seriousness.

"I was planning to spend Christmas with Kinley and her family, they are my family too." Madison put a smile on her face, "We have all of these silly traditions. I don't know if a big rock star such as yourself would be interested in silly little holiday traditions with the regular folks."

"You cut me to the core woman. I want to be where you are, even if we are bobbing for apples in an ice-lake with a hole cut in the ice."

"Creative. But no, we sing Christmas carols while we hunt for mistletoe in the mountains nearby. We bring thermoses filled with Kinley's homemade hot-coco and go sledding and skiing and snowboarding. Kinley has her annual Christmas party, and we eat until we can't move. The holidays are wonderful here. Don't you have any silly traditions?"

"Yeah." He leaned back as she made room for him to sit next to her. "We play in the snow a lot, and there's hot-coco too. My mother opens little packets of hot-coco, you know, the kind with dehydrated marshmallows in them. I can't say that I've ever had homemade hot chocolate."

"Don't let Kinley hear that," Maddy smiled.

"I won't." he lowered his voice accordingly. "*Um*, let me think, we have snowshoe races and we take a big family portrait every year. Oh, and my mother gets us each an ornament, and we open new pajamas every Christmas eve. She always gets us new pajamas. I'm now thirty-two and I will still get some pajamas. Probably flannel." He didn't mind sharing all of this with Maddy. Somehow he knew he could tell her everything, no matter how mundane.

"Cal, will you spend Christmas with us?"

"I would love to."

"What about your family? Won't they miss you?"

"I know they'll be happy for me." He held her hand, feeling giddy and a tad euphoric.

"Stay with me, in my home," she offered. He turned to look at her and found himself captured, a prisoner lost somewhere inside of her chocolate brown eyes. He kissed her lips, honey sweet, refreshing, rejuvenating.

"I wouldn't be anywhere else."

"Not even in a five-star hotel with a spa in your room and room service?" He loved her face, he found he could look at her all day and never tire of it. He shook his head in reply. "Very well, then maybe the least I can do is throw in a free massage." He laughed.

Waiting around was something akin to torture for Cal, who didn't care for sitting around doing nothing. He wasn't sure how much he could talk about with Kinley in the room, but to give her credit, she disappeared quite often. He couldn't imagine where she would go to, but he was glad for the moments alone with Madison. He also had the feeling that Kinley couldn't leave Madison's side. It didn't matter if Cal was there now, which concerned Cal. He realized sadly that Kinley had been there when he had not. He would have been if not for the colossal misunderstanding. He could see Kinley's unconditional love for Madison which never failed to touch his soul. He imagined his sisters would be the same way.

Just when he'd had enough, the doctor came in on the morning they could leave and made a follow-up appointment while ticking off the symptoms she should be concerned about seeing. Cal thought the symptom of 'death' seemed pretty self-explanatory. If one dies, something might be very wrong. Madison woke Kinley who smiled contentedly at the idea of taking a hot bath in her own home. "Stupid cast," she muttered. "Well, I will make it work."

Cal informed Gabe that they were leaving and asked him to come and pick them up in front of the hospital. They dropped Kinley off first, who barely spoke on the drive to her home. Madison could picture her locking the door behind her and falling into bed, clothes and shoes still in place. Kinley did not do well with exhaustion. Gabe was informed that Cal would be staying with Madison. He frowned slightly as he digested the information. Finally, he decided to get a hotel room around the corner from Madison's townhouse. Madison offered him the sofa or a guest room at Kinley's but he kindly refused. Cal was secretly grateful. He just wanted to be alone with Maddy, and fill in all of the blanks.

Blank filling is what they spent the rest of the day doing. There they were, lying in bed, and nothing sexual was going on at all. Either he was losing his touch, or…never mind. "You know what I missed most about you?" she asked him, while they both stared up at her ceiling fan. He couldn't imagine.

"My love making expertise?" he asked, grinning. She tossed a pillow at his head.

"I was referring to our nightly talks on the phone. Every night we used to talk until I exhausted myself. There were times where I fell asleep clutching the phone. Not comfortable, but very nice all the same."

"Me too." He maneuvered onto his side and rested his head against his knuckles while supporting himself on his elbow. "This has been the laziest most fulfilling day in my life. How is that even possible?"

"I don't know." She just turned onto her side and smiled to him. The doorbell rang. As they were expecting her favorite Chinese take-out, he told her he'd get the door. He skipped two and three stairs at a time. He hadn't been this happy since, well…he'd never been so happy. He opened the door, wallet ready, but quickly he was confused. An older woman stood before him and she was carrying what looked like a gift basket with red and green ribbons along the handle. She smiled pleasantly at him then frowned slightly with a puzzled look on her face.

"I'm sorry; I think I've got the wrong house." She was moving back, glancing upward at the now dimly lit house numbers, "Wait, are you a friend of Maddy's?" she asked delicately.

He looked her over. She was petite with dark hair which had touches of silver threaded through it. Her eyes were cool blue, but deep and fathomless like the nearly bottomless open waters of the ocean. Her skin was creamy, ivory, with hints of wrinkles at the edges of her eyes and lips. "This is Maddy's house," he offered, "won't you come in?" Who was this woman? Why did her eyes cause him to feel such despair?

Maddy came cautiously down the stairs, but froze when her eyes landed on the woman, "Debbie?"

"Hi sweetie. I was just dropping off a Christmas gift. I'm sorry. I didn't know you had company." Her voice echoed through Madison's soul, pinging off anything that might be painful to think of. She could hear that voice in her mind laughing with her children, speaking to Jack. She self-consciously smoothed her hands over her abdomen, which was exactly where Debbie's eyes had gone traveling to.

"You…you…" she began to speak to Cal. He was used to this kind of thing, where people started to recognize him and couldn't quite get hold of their speech, but something was clearly different here. She couldn't keep her eyes on him; instead she glared at Madison. "I'm interrupting something. I should go; there is your Christmas present on the bar. I can see myself out." She turned to leave, but Madison bounded across the room and touched her arm, pulling her back. She looked faint. Cal, all the while remaining in the dark.

"Debbie, I'd like you to meet my boyfriend Cal."

"We've met." She looked down at her shoes.

"I'm not like you, Debbie. I can't do this alone any longer. I need my friends to lean on, and I need Cal." Debbie nodded curtly as Madison spoke.

"It's just heart breaking to see Jack replaced so soon," she cried.

Cal suddenly joined the realization of what was really going on. He stepped in next to Maddy and put his arm around her waist, pulling her protectively toward him. Letting instincts take over, he thought of his own mother and began to speak softly, "Debbie, may I speak?" She nodded, resigned, defeated. "I could never replace your son. On all accounts he was a good man, a good husband and father. I have never been any of those things, yet," he added the yet hesitatingly. "Those are big shoes to fill. My only desire is to make Maddy happy. I want to be here for her. The loss of your son is still a huge thing for her. She's not over it and I have serious doubts to the fact that she ever will be. Loving her as your son did, I know with all of my heart he wouldn't want her to continue on in misery. He'd want her to be happy. I can't take his place. He possesses it still."

Whatever she'd been expecting to hear, this clearly wasn't it. She nodded, listening, slowly taking it in. "Maddy," she turned to Madison, "I don't want to be selfish and hold onto you any longer. I," she blinked away her tears. "I want you to be happy, too. I know it's what Jack would have wanted. He's a good man, this one, don't let him get away." She stood and brushed the tears away with the backs of her hands. "Take care Maddy."

Madison nodded as she snuggled into Cal's side. He held her as the woman left. Her mother-in-law. Former, he reminded himself. There seemed to be such coldness between them. He held her tightly against his chest, feeling her cry. Madison, at that moment, knew somehow Debbie had released her, given her silent permission to move on and to be happy, if grudgingly done so. And somewhere inside of her she knew she probably wouldn't see Debbie again.

41. Karaoke? Really?

Maddy was in the kitchen baking what appeared to be thousands of cookies. He stole one off a plate, while he watched her with fascination. "Why are you doing this again?"

"It's a thing you do, you know?" She pushed up a sleeve that was sliding down over her elbow. "Didn't your mother ever do this?"

"Do what exactly? Bake like a fiend? No." He munched on the cookie.

"You know, take plates of homemade cookies around to people?"

"I don't think so." He smiled at her. "You and your friends have so many traditions. I can't believe it. I liked the mistletoe hunting, but cookie giving? Is that a thing you all do?" He couldn't quite figure out the inner workings of the Madison, Kinley, Kate and Megan's circle of friendship.

"We usually sing carols when we hunt for mistletoe. It's a shame no one wanted to sing in front of you, but then again, I couldn't blame them. I don't want to sing in front of you either. I wonder if anyone would sing in front of you at Kinley's party tonight if they knew who you were." She blew a hair out of her face.

"Sing? Don't tell me, karaoke?"

"Totally. We love watching people make idiots of themselves; we've been doing karaoke parties for ages. Some people are bad and they know it, which makes it fun, others are bad and they don't know it, which can be just as entertaining. Some people are really good, like Kinley, for instance. She can sing, but she won't." He watched her bend over, admiring her from all angles was his new favorite pastime as it were; she pulled another batch of cookies out of the oven and replaced them. "There that's the last one."

"Kinley sings? How good is she?"

"She was enrolled at Julliard but some things came up. McKenna, to be precise. Kin's amazing, but she keeps it a secret. One can only imagine why. It's a good thing no one knows or they'd never make fools of themselves on the karaoke."

"I will be in disguise. No one need know that I sing either. Kinley and I can keep our secrets together." He shrugged. "It might be kind of funny."

"That's how Kinley is."

He watched her carefully, loving the way she wiped the counters down, and hummed to herself. He hated to compare but she was as different as she could be from Lindsey Bell. Lindsey wouldn't have been caught dead in a kitchen, actually working or otherwise. He loved Maddy, her independence and her spunk. He moved into the kitchen with her and held her in his arms. He'd been dying to make love to her, but she was full of excuses. It was something that needed to be overcome somehow. He frowned as he thought about it, "Why will you not let me touch you? Are you still angry with me, or is it because of the baby? Or are you in pain from the accident? Please tell me."

"You'll think I'm stupid," she muttered into his chest.

He lifted her chin, "Try me."

"The pain isn't bad anymore…I just hate that Lindsey Bell. I picture you doing things with her and I can't…" She cut herself off, obviously angry, for she hadn't truly intended to say as much as she had. "I know we were broken up…"

"*Ah*, you sound a wee bit jealous, and of Lindsey, of all people." He was grinning widely.

"*Ugh*, you slept with her. I can't bear the thought of it."

"I did." She blanched. "A very long time ago. However, the last person I slept with was you," he admitted proudly.

She was shocked; it was clear. "You, but, you…"

"Always so eloquent, are you?" She whacked him with a dishrag. "Maddy, being with you was like flying. Why would I go slumming after I'd been with you?"

"I…" She bit her lip, "It looked like the two of you were getting on well. I mean, she threw you a birthday party and you went to the award show together."

"You watched the award show didn't you?" he asked, still holding her in his arms. She nodded "Did you hear me thank Lindsey Bell for anything? I don't recall doing so, I believe I said thank you to Maddy, not Lindsey." She leaned against his chest.

"Now that you mention it…"

"I also have in my recollection, singing a song I wrote for you. I can't imagine Lindsey inspiring anyone to write a song, at least not *that* one." Cal closed his eyes. If he could just freeze this moment, holding onto her, breathing in the scent of her hair, and her skin. He let his fingers form a trail over her hair, skimming the surface of her silky tresses. "I just ran into her and she asked me to go with her. There was nothing there. Nothing."

"And the song was really for me?" How could she doubt it after everything?

"Yes." He kissed her lips, feeling his knees fail him. "Won't you do something for me?"

"Anything." She gave him a sweet smile. "But I want you to do something for me, too."

Now, *this* was intriguing. "Anything," he answered, feeling completely honest about it. He *literally* would do anything for her. "You first," he offered.

"Sing the song to me again," she asked him. He brushed a dab of flour from her cheek. That had to be the sweetest thing anyone had ever asked him to do. He couldn't stand the way he melted into a puddle whenever she spoke to him. All she had to do was look at him and his feet began to rethink standing. His legs trembled whenever she kissed him. If she'd noticed these little weaknesses she never mentioned it. He led her over to the sofa and pulled her close. Her head just beneath his chin, he sang to her. He felt the way her hand glided over his chest. How was it that she could make him feel invincible, and impervious to weakness of any kind, while at simultaneously she weakened him? He'd never figure it out.

When he finished singing to her, she wiped tears out of the corners of her eyes, "I think I burnt the last batch of cookies." She grinned sheepishly.

They attended Kinley's party later in the evening. People milled about chatting. The aroma of food, even outside her house, invited him in. It seemed to call to his stomach. She'd prepared a homemade Mexican feast. Her table was piled high with tamales, tortillas, salsa, rice, beans, shredded beef, shredded cheese, stacks of lettuce, bowls of tomatoes and onions. His mouth watered in reply. "Now, how do I introduce you to people?" she asked quietly as she began dishing food onto a red plate.

"Your boyfriend Cal?" he asked her. He followed her by picking up a green plate and placing a tamale onto it.

"Sounds good." He waited for it, watched for it, and when it finally happened, he could have been knocked over by Kennedy's little finger. It was the expression he'd desired to see above all else. She looked up at him as though he were the only person who existed in the world, or maybe the only person whose existence she cared about. It stunned him momentarily. "Are you okay?" She laughed heartily.

"I don't think so, but it's not necessarily a bad thing." They found a place at a table crowded with couples. Kinley was there laughing at something someone had just told her.

"You, Max, are as sweet as a rosebud." She grinned. Madison smothered her laughter in the sleeve of his shirt, while she leaned into his arm. "Oh, hi Madison and Cal. Everyone," Kinley cleared her throat, "this is Maddy's new boyfriend Cal."

He heard greetings pour over him from all around the table. "Guess we didn't need to worry about it," Maddy told him. Hands were reaching across the table. Everyone was so friendly, and they didn't even know he was famous.

"What were you laughing about?" he asked Madison in a whispered voice, once the interest in the new guy at the table began to fade.

"Once a long time ago, we took a Cinema Appreciation class. It went toward art credit. We had to watch Citizen Kane." She took a breath, all the while keeping her voice very low. "Ever seen it?" He shook his head. "Don't.

All the way through the movie, you keep hearing the word or phrase, if you will, rosebud. It was the most boring movie we have ever seen. When something is boring, we work rosebud into the conversation." He shook his head in silent laughter. Kinley was a wicked little thing.

Christmas music, the Rat Pack, was playing in the background, while Kinley busied herself cleaning up, taking people's plates. He'd never seen anyone with a cast work so much. Maddy hopped up to help. He looked over as the front door opened and a short woman in extremely tall shoes walked into the room, her hair dark underneath layers of blond, it had been puffed up a few inches. He didn't have to speak to her to know what she was. She walked over to Kinley, carrying a cylindrical gift box made for wine. "Merry Christmas, Kinley." She turned toward Maddy, "Maddy," she added somewhat stuffily.

Cal held his breath while Maddy introduced him to the *ice queen* he knew this woman was, "Mandy, this is my boyfriend Cal."

"Oh," she seemed to relax, albeit very little. "This is Calvin Hunt?" she smirked. How did she know? Maddy smiled at her. "She told me she was knocked up by Calvin Hunt when I ran into her last. Clever."

He didn't like Mandy, and strongly suspected that Madison didn't like her either, but she was reaching out her hand to introduce herself properly to him, "Amanda Murphy, but Maddy and Kinley call me Mandy." Madison smirked. He thought this must be another one of Madison's and Kinley's inside jokes. "It just kind of stuck." She let out a shallow laugh, as she brushed her white-blond bangs back from her face and tucked them behind her ear.

"It's nice to meet you," he lied.

"Well, it's good that you are helping Maddy move on." He could feel his jaw tighten as he looked over at Madison with concern. Madison just smiled at her. How did she take it? He wanted to pick the woman up and toss her out onto the lawn. He gritted his teeth, hoping she was done talking, but she wasn't, "It's great, you're helping her move on, in more ways than one." Her eyes traveled over Madison's swollen abdomen. That's it, he thought, I'm gonna toss her out onto the lawn, or I might miss and let her fly into the street.

Madison never ceased to surprise him, and she was not letting him down now, "The sex is fantastic. I mean, he does things that make me scream." Madison kept her face straight, but Kinley was fighting back the laughter. "I can barely keep myself from sneaking away right now with him. Honey," she looked up at him, dramatically fluttering her eyelashes, "want to go to the guestroom with me?"

"I…" Mandy Murphy was seemingly struck dumb, her overly made-up eyes blinking.

Kate walked in with her husband. Kate looked as though she'd been beaten up, and her husband looked as though he could have been the one to do it. He was tall and built like a GI Joe action figure, only life sized. His dark hair was buzzed short and altogether he was quite intimidating, even to Cal. "Good Lord Kate, what happened to you?" Mandy-foot-in-in-her-mouth Murphy exclaimed.

They all watched Kate, wondering how she would handle it. "*Unrewardable,*" Kinley said to Kate.

"Did you add it to the dictionary?" Kate asked. They appeared to be speaking in code. Kate got a wicked gleam in her eye. "Mandy, I was in a car accident the other night. But let's forget about that. When can we play volleyball again? Let it be soon."

Mandy nodded, while Kinley had to turn around to laugh into her kitchen sink. Madison waited before Kinley turned back around. Mandy walked away to speak to someone else, oblivious of the fact that no one seemed to like her. "I am going to nominate Kinley for sainthood."

"Please, I'm not even Catholic."

"I think Catholics everywhere would be able to overlook the fact. There are homeless people at a shelter right now thanking God above that Mandy didn't volunteer tonight." Madison turned to Cal to explain, "Kinley invited her here to a party instead. Don't you think Kinley should be sainted?" He laughed in response.

"You women are evil," Ryan walked by and whispered to them. "Why did you invite her Kin, I can't take it. She just told me I'm looking old," he muttered before stalking away.

Maddy, Kinley and Kate just laughed. "Why don't you three say something to her? She's awful," Cal asked them.

"Go ahead," Kinley offered. "Get as mean and blunt as you like. She won't even notice. It's really unfortunate. I have no idea if she is just as dumb as a stump or if she is purposefully obtuse. It doesn't matter because whatever you do, she will always think you like her." Kinley lowered her voice even more, "Wait until you hear her sing." She winked before walking away to set up the karaoke.

Megan squeezed in next to Maddy for a moment, while Kinley and Kate worked on setting up the karaoke. "Who is Ryan's friend?" Cal caught himself looking over at Ryan who was talking in the corner. His companion was a beautiful blond in a tight red dress.

"Some lady from work," Maddy answered. "I think Kin told me her name was Sally, she says she's going through a rough time right now." Madison shook her head.

"I don't like her," Megan growled low enough for only Madison and Cal to hear.

"I know me either."

Kate came back and began filling a plate of food up, piling it so that it all overlapped, before she handed it to her husband. He grumbled a thanks before walking away to sit down. "He hates coming to these things, but Kin is such a good cook, he can't say no."

"Kate doesn't cook," Madison filled him in. "She does love take-out though." Kate nodded. That was the moment when a terrible sound filled the room, the sound of silence. He stared as the girl named Mandy took the microphone and sleigh bells introduced a karaoke version of "Sleigh Ride". The woman was pretty, he could give her that, but she had the personality of a barracuda and the singing voice of a tone-deaf rooster.

It took him a moment to realize it, but this was the most wonderful Christmas party he had been to, other than parties with his family. This wasn't an impersonal club scene; it wasn't the dreadful birthday party Lindsey Bell had conjured up. The club idea was supposed to be synonymous with fun, but this was truly, where he wanted to be. He was with Maddy and her quirky bunch of friends, listening to an 'ice queen' sing, or whatever it was, and laughing behind her back at her. Why was this so fun? He had no idea, but he knew he didn't want to be anywhere else.

42. This Christmas Better Be Good

The last three days with Madison had been absolutely heaven. He'd slept with her every night, just slept, holding her in his arms. "What was it?" she asked looking over at him.

"What?" He thought of the party they'd just left and how much fun he'd had being part of her world.

"You asked me if I could do something for you earlier. I wanted you to sing. I guess it was an ADD moment because I forgot to ask you what your request was."

"ADD moment?"

"Yeah you know, you're talking and then suddenly your mind is a million miles away, or everywhere else, other than where it should be. I get so discombobulated during the holidays."

"Discom-what?" He moved closer to her, scooping her up into his arms. She giggled. He trailed kisses down her cheek until he reached her lips. "I wanted you to allow me…" he cleared his throat, "to make you scream like you told Mandy I could earlier this evening." She laughed, burying her head into his chest.

"I never saw the color of your skin change so abruptly. It was as if you were trying to blush while the blood was draining from your face." She leaned back and sighed, looking up at him with that same look of absolute adoration and love. "Cal," she kissed him leaving him breathless, "I just have one question for you."

"Yes?"

"What's taking you so long?"

Even the time she was with him in Canada, which had been some of the happiest moments in his life, couldn't compare to the days he was spending with her. They'd gone out everyday shopping, playing with her friends and their husbands, and doing everything an average ordinary couple might do. Whoever invented the word-bliss- had felt like this. He'd come to this conclusion on the evening of Maddy's annual gift exchange with her friends. He'd thought it to be a serious thing at first, but once he began to see it for the joke it was, he found he'd never laughed so hard in his life.

Kinley was the first to open a gift from Kate, "Oh, Kate, this is perfect!" He peered over her shoulder and was confused by the small box of cards. Were they business cards? He frowned, slightly perplexed. She passed the box to Madison who examined them and began laughing hard enough to hold her side. "Classic isn't it?" She passed the small box over to Cal who stared down at it, slightly bewildered still. The top card read- Validation for a year. Puzzled he removed it and the card below read- Validation Card. He shrugged and passed it over to Ryan who grinned wryly.

"I wish I would have given that to her." Laughter filled the room.

"Yeah, where can I get one of those for my wife?" Doug, Megan's husband, jumped in.

"I hate to admit it but I'm in the dark about all of this," Cal finally stated.

"We are horrible at validation," Megan told him. "We usually say things like 'suck it up' when one of us is having a bad day. Maddy came up with the validation idea. One day when Kinley was being particularly whiney…"

"Hey…" Kinley began.

"Well, you were," Kate pointed out. Kinley nodded begrudgingly.

"I could never get away with saying that," Ryan told Jared, Kate's husband. All of the men nodded.

"Well, as I was saying, Kinley was whiney and Maddy busts out this card and hands it to her. 'You're right, she said, I'm not validating you, so here you go, you've been validated.' We were laughing so hard, tears were streaming. Maddy's card just said- Validation- that was it. So, it was the validation card."

He shook his head as he watched the four friends giggle. Ryan grumbled, "Let's get on with it, I had Cal's name. I am dying to see what he thinks of my present."

"But…" He'd frowned thinking he hadn't gotten anyone a present.

"I took care of it," Madison told him. A bag was passed over to him. He removed the tissue paper bunched into the top. He pulled out a t-shirt, at first it looked like a plain black shirt. What to say? Laughter was surrounding him, echoing in his ears. The men were all smiling and pointing to the front. Jared was laughing the loudest. Doug was bent over in hysterics. Each of the women were puzzled, until Kate moved over to get a better look.

He flipped the shirt around; there on the front read the words- I Made it to the Top of Maddy's Back-Up List. The women were now laughing. He wondered if they all knew about her back-up list thing. But apparently even the husbands were in on it. "You all have back-up lists?"

"Not us," muttered Ryan, "men aren't allowed to have back-up lists."

"That hardly seems fair," he told Ryan.

"Tell me about it," Jared barked. "I wanted to have Angelina Jolie but no…" Kate whacked him across the middle. He doubled over wheezing with laughter.

"So, this is a joke right?" he questioned Ryan.

"Absolutely," Ryan promised him. "All of these gifts are jokes. The real ones are exchanged on Christmas." He couldn't help but feeling less than reassured.

Presents were passed around like strange homemade coupons for 'me time' and 'I'll clean one bathroom for you on the day of your choosing' and 'lunch on me'. Ryan got a statue of a white elephant, which everyone seemed to laugh themselves silly over. Kinley explained that every year Ryan complained about their silly white elephant party, and how he hated white elephants. He then came to understand the post-it-note secured to the elephant's gargantuan belly. "Don't be a hater, Ryan." Even Ryan was laughing. They all enjoyed each other's company so thoroughly. And somehow, he seemed to fit right in with them.

Christmas morning came, no snow, something he'd never seen before, and Madison lying beside him. Pregnancy made her glow. Making love to her was yet again, a new and wondrous experience. It was not what he was used to, but he could see himself becoming used to it. She breathed new life into him, gave him reasons to be a better person. Then there was the baby. She was this person he was falling in love with, who he couldn't even touch. He'd started a new tradition of singing to her at night. Madison would run her fingers through his hair while he sang to her stomach. She swore the baby knew it was her father singing. The idea of being a father was captivating.

She was getting clothes on, brushing through her untidy hair, which he loved. "Maddy, I was wondering if I could give you my gift before we saw Kinley and her family." He was nervous. This hadn't worked out so well the last time he'd tried it. He couldn't stop trying. The idea of living a life without her in it…well, it wasn't an option. She nodded.

He got down on one knee. "Cal?" He pulled out the box, trembling, knowing she could refuse as she'd done it before. But she wasn't moving away, she stood still, her eyes glittering with joy. He cleared his throat, "Please be my wife." His hand quaked as he opened the box and showed her the ring that Ryan had helped him pick out. She threw her arms around him, but he maintained his balance. She was kissing him; that had to be a good thing, right? He hoped.

"Yes, yes, a million times, yes." He could finally relax; he closed his eyes and breathed her in. Maddy leaned back. "Why, Cal, you're trembling. Were you afraid?"

"So afraid," he hated to admit.

"Don't be." She ran her fingers through his hair. He removed the ring and slid it onto her finger. "It's beautiful."

"Ryan told me if we go on a cruise I should make certain that you wear a life preserver anytime we are out on deck. He said you might sink like a stone wearing that thing."

"You know, he's right. I think." The diamond was emerald cut, set in platinum. It was huge. She had no idea how many carets it might be. She held it up to her eye. "It's bigger than my iris." She grinned at him. "I wouldn't have cared if it were a plain old band, I love you Calvin Hunt. I just want to be wherever you are."

"You mean it don't you?" he asked while she nodded in reply. "What about your life here? I want you to finish school and whatever else makes you happy. I want it all for you."

She stared as she sank backward onto the edge of her bed. "I finished in the first week of December."

"I'm so happy for you, Maddy." He smiled.

"Thank you, Cal." She looked down at the ring upon her finger. "I can't believe how happy I am." Her eyes glanced up at him. "Do you want me to live in Canada?"

"I want to live wherever you want. Here, if you want. But maybe somewhere bigger. This is a bit small. I should think the baby would like her own room. We might keep *her* up at night."

"What about living here and in Canada? Is it possible?"

He smiled as he stood up and picked her up so that her feet were dangling a foot over the floor. "I love the idea of it. I don't want to be too far away from my family, but I'd hate to take you away from your friends. They are your family just as much my family will be."

"What if they don't like me?" Why was she suddenly feeling insecure about it?

"They love you. They were all furious when you went away. Everyone just knew I'd done something. I've never brought anyone home for my family to meet, so they were all becoming attached to you. They wondered what I'd done to screw it up."

"But you didn't do anything. It was all me. Didn't you tell them I was broken?"

"You're not broken." They fell onto the bed together.

She touched his lips, "Not anymore."

They would spend Christmas with Kinley and her family. He walked in without a disguise on, and found Kinley's parents sitting there. Her mother was snuggled into Kennedy, watching some awful kid movie, and McKenna was talking animatedly to her Grandfather about a video game.

All the presents were still under the tree. He smiled when he read his name on a large, yet flat, white box with burgundy ribbon. It looked like clothes. What on earth? He hoped it wasn't another back-up list reference. There was another box for him too. How funny.

"Oh, I forgot the presents in the trunk of the car." Maddy turned and ran out of the house. Kinley's parents looked up at him.

"You must be Cal." Her mother was older and just what he pictured a grandmother to be. She was sweet, short and round, with a cheery disposition and large glasses perched upon her nose. Her graying hair was cut short and curled around her face. She hugged him. "Welcome to the family dear."

"How…" he stuttered.

Kinley walked out into the kitchen with a stack of waffles teetering precariously on a large platter. "Ryan didn't know her ring size so he had to call me, I'm afraid I let everyone know. My happiness for Maddy could not be contained."

"But…." His hand was being shaken by Kinley's father who had to be nearly a foot shorter than he was.

"You did ask her this morning didn't you?" Ryan asked him. He just grinned. Maddy was walking in with a small skyscraper of presents, towering over her head. He nodded.

Kinley ran over to her and helped her by taking some of the presents and placing them under the tree. "Merry Christmas, Maddy." Kinley gave her a little sideways hug.

"Kinley, I am going to add that to the other tally marks in my diary. I think you've hugged me now a total of eighteen times in our lives." Everyone laughed. Kinley was flipping her hand over and examining the ring. *Oohs* and *Ahhs* came from every direction as Ryan made a face that seemed to say- I told you so.

Kinley's parents, it turned out, were more Maddy's parents than not. They loved her, hugged her, and showered her with presents too. Kinley's parents, who he now called Mr. and Mrs. Michaelson, had even brought presents for him. He unwrapped a Guinness t-shirt from Kinley, a watch from Kennedy who thought he would like it, an iTunes gift card from McKenna, and a travel pillow and blanket set from the Michaelsons. They knew he traveled a lot, but didn't have any idea of who he was. This alone was entertaining. The presents were all so thoughtful; it made him feel like choking up.

Breakfast was divine. Everything about this morning was marvelous. He had a fiancée and a whole new family. He and Madison gave Kennedy a new snowboard, a suit and a pass. She cried out of thankfulness. It was a contrast, indeed, to his nephews and nieces who would have expected gifts to be overpriced. Kennedy sobbed her little heart out. They gave McKenna a new iPod and a substantial iTunes gift card. It turned out that hers was used, and beaten up. She cried too. When it came to Kinley, he'd gone *slightly* overboard. He didn't know if he'd done the right thing for her and Ryan. It hadn't gone unnoticed that while everything they had looked nice, it was old. Their cars were no exception. She drove and older model SUV, with fading paint, but it was in great condition. Ryan seemed to love his rundown old pickup truck. He hoped they wouldn't be insulted. He handed Kinley a box.

"Don't be upset with me," he muttered. Gabe had helped him before he'd declared himself useless and flown back home. Cal had bought a new car for himself, having no idea how long he'd be here. Kinley turned the small box over in her hand. "It's for you and Ryan. I hope you are okay with it. If you don't like them, you can return them. They assured me."

Kinley lifted one eyebrow then lifted the lid from the box. Inside was another box, this one small, but not jewelry small. She opened it, but closed it again, "You did not do this." She looked at him. Ryan grabbed the box from her and opened it, staring down in disbelief. "Cal, you…you…"

"You don't even know if you like it yet," he told her. Ryan was ignoring them all, everyone was staring, he got up, slid across the wooden floor in his stocking feet and threw the door open.

They could all hear him yelling, "Woohoo!" from the driveway. Maddy grinned, having only found out about his secret that morning. He'd had it delivered at the same time they'd arrived. Kinley ran outside after her husband. The whole family was now coming out to see what all the fuss was about. There in the driveway, parked for all the neighbors to see was a brand new set of Lexus cars, one was an SUV, in white and the other was a sportier looking white car. Both of them were something out of a commercial with large red bows on the hoods.

"Cal." Kinley had unshed tears in her eyes. She looked down at the sets of keys in her hand. "Thank you." He hugged her, even though he knew she would hate it.

"Maddy, you knew about this?" She eyed Madison suspiciously.

"You know I couldn't have kept that a secret if I'd tried! He did it all on his own. I only found out about it this morning." Ryan came back and wrapped his arms around his wife, and kissed her.

"Thanks man." He shook Cal's hand while he squeezed his wife. "I'm afraid the things we got you aren't quite even." He gave Cal a sheepish smile.

"Yeah, I owe you both so much more," Cal told him.

When they finally made it back to Maddy's place, stuffed with turkey, exhausted from chatting, playing video games and jumping on the trampoline, they dropped onto the sofa. "I can't believe you got them cars." Madison smiled, "Who does that?"

"It was over the top, *huh*?"

"Totally," she sighed, "but, no two people deserved it more." She twisted around until she was facing him. "I haven't given you my present yet."

"You didn't have to get me anything," he said sincerely.

"I gathered that, but I wanted to do something." She had a tiny tree on the coffee table. He finally noticed the box sitting next to it. He picked it up, and tilted his head. "It isn't expensive or anything. I just wanted to show you how much I love you."

He tore the paper away and pulled the lid from the box. Flannel pajamas were inside, with a Christmas ornament tucked into the shirt. "You actually listen to the things I say?"

She just smiled, "I can help you change into them if you like."

"Now, *that* would be a present."

43. Finding Maddy

Maddy was off to the store while Cal looked up his email on her laptop computer. He heard the key twist in the door and glanced over, to his surprise it wasn't Maddy, but Kinley. "Hi." She walked over and sat down with a space in between them on the sofa.

"Good morning," he told her, but something about her wasn't right. "Maddy is out for the moment."

"I know." She was staring down into her lap. "She told me to come over and talk to you."

"Oh," he stared at her, "Kinley what's wrong?"

She reached out and placed a set of keys in his hand. "I just can't accept this. I've tried to reason with myself all night, but I can't do it."

"And Ryan's car?"

"It's up to him, I guess." He would have laughed if she weren't so serious. She wanted to give her gift back, but Ryan clearly disagreed. He thought of how his sister would have acted if Michelle's husband Wyatt gave her a car. He tried to picture Callie married to a schoolteacher, struggling to make ends meet, but incredibly happy.

"I can't take it back," he told her frowning, "I got it for free."

"What?" He pictured comic book punctuation when she said this...

"I did." He sipped on a cup of cappuccino. "You see, when you are famous, people do the weirdest things for you. As if I needed a free car, let alone two of them." The beauty part was that he wasn't lying too much. He had paid for the cars, but they had been severely discounted. "You see, I strolled in there and was looking at cars for you. I intended to buy you one, and so what if I had. Elvis used to do it all the time. I mean, I'm no Elvis, but still, I really am doing all right financially speaking." He seemed to have to mention this fact a lot to everyone Maddy was associated with.

"Cal, you can't be serious."

"Completely. They were stunned to see me walking around. The sales crew was going crazy. I should have worn a disguise I suppose. But, I had Gabe with me."

"Cal, are you making this up just to make me feel better?" Her expression was dubious.

"Not at all. I promised to film a couple of commercials all in exchange for two cars. Now, don't say you wouldn't have done the same thing. Believe me, being paid to appear on camera is not such a hard thing for me to do. So, I did it all for advertisement sake. I feel like a whore, I tell you, but you are worth it, Kin. I would have paid for them if I'd had to. But, seriously I signed a few, twenty-three to be precise, autographs, had my picture taken with a few people and will appear in some commercials." He took another sip of his cooling coffee.

She stared at him, "But I shouldn't accept such a thing. I..."

"Kinley, growing up, my dad did construction and my mom stayed at home with us kids. I remember when we didn't have much. I also remember our car breaking down and my parents worrying themselves sick over what they were going to do."

"You noticed our cars?"

"Yes," he sighed, "Kin, are you close to Maddy?"

"She's like a sister to me," she answered loyally as he knew she would.

"Then you're practically my sister too. So, what's the problem?"

"I can't reciprocate the gift with equanimity," she told him; he noticed her shaking as she spoke.

"Do you like the car?"

She reluctantly answered, closing her eyes, "So much. And I needed a new car."

"Yes, I noticed. But you would have had me pretend I didn't see."

"I feel so…like a charity case or something." She had tears burning in her eyes as she hastily wiped them away with her still gloved hand.

"You're not in my debt because of this," he spoke plainly, but she was shaking her head in disagreement. "You're not, I tell you. I am the one in your debt." This seemed to stun her out of her embarrassment. "I can never, not in my lifetime, hope to repay you for what you've given me."

"I did nothing," she replied.

"Not true. I wouldn't have Madison in my life without you. Think about it."

She grinned, again, grudgingly. "I don't see it," she replied flatly.

"Oh, I think you do," he laughed, "you are going to keep that car and love it." He teased, "Because I will film a commercial for you to have it." She nodded. "Kinley…" She looked up at him, chocolate brown eyes, so beautiful, but so different from Maddy's. He loved this woman, not as he loved Madison, but as he loved Callie. He couldn't have described it to anyone, not a soul, but he felt so wonderful having his life filled with new people who loved him and thought nothing about what he could give them. She'd never asked him for a single thing. She just wanted her friend to be happy, and fought hard for it, even harder than he had. Madison was lucky to have her.

Madison walked in carrying a bag of groceries. "Ryan told me what you got him."

"I'm afraid I quite forgot about it until later. The cars completely took it out of my mind. You know, Maddy, it was an ADD moment." He absolutely loved how they had phrases for everything.

"He wouldn't take the car back would he?" Maddy asked Kinley.

"Nope." Kinley smiled up at her, "But, I think it's okay." Madison sat down next to her. "You're not going to hug me are you?" Kinley groaned.

"*Nah*, we're good. I can't believe you got him King's tickets."

"He really wanted them. I squeezed it in." Kinley settled down on the sofa. "Besides, he gave me the best gift in return."

Cal was curious, "What did he give you?"

"He told me that I don't have to go with him." Kinley beamed. Cal and Maddy laughed. "Thanks for talking with me, Cal."

"Don't you want to see what I found at the store before you go?" Madison asked, clearly bemused by something. Kinley raised a single eyebrow as Madison handed her a tabloid magazine. Cal moved closer and whistled as he read the headline.

Is This Calvin Hunt's Maddy? Underneath the questioning headline was a picture shot with what may have been a cell phone camera. It was fuzzy, but Cal's face was somehow recognizable. He was leaning over someone in a bed. It was Madison of course, but her back was to the camera, and she was lying on her side. His face was weary with concern, his hand on her arm. Beneath the picture was a small typed line- *Nurse gives full details.*

"I knew there was a reason I didn't like her. I could feel it in my bones." Kinley swore as she rubbed her cast.

"It's only a matter of time now," Cal told them.

"For what?"

Madison and Kinley stared naively at him, awaiting his answer. "Did they just put that rag out?"

"Yes, fresh off the presses," Madison answered but she still looked up at him with the face of an inquiring angel.

"They will learn who you are. Someone has paid her by now, for all of your information. You won't be able to leave your house. I'm surprised your phone isn't ringing off the hook."

"I got rid of the house phone," she replied, looking nervously about as if one might suddenly sprout out of the wall. "But, oh, my cell phone, I turned it off when I went into the bank." She rummaged through her purse and found it. "Oh no."

He nodded. "I'm shocked they didn't find out sooner." He put his empty mug down on a coaster. "This isn't good." He looked over at Kinley, who was now up looking out of the window.

"Did you notice anything strange while you were out?"

"I didn't." She looked guilty. "I'm so sorry, Cal."

"It's all right. No worries." He joined Kinley by the window. Rows of cars were outside of the gated community. Men and women were standing there with cameras. "Just think…they don't even know I'm here. Not really. They just want to find out if you're the mysterious Maddy."

"Damn it." She sat down. "Someone did say something odd to me. I shrugged it off. I didn't think about it…" He smiled at her, urging her to continue. "Are you having a baby? A little man asked me. I told him I was. He was looking at my ring-mighty big ring for such a little lady. A rich man fall for you? Ooh, and I answered, something like that. He said congratulations and walked away. It was weird, the kind of encounter that gives you shivers up the spine."

Cal laughed, "It's funny how you look so guilty."

"Aren't I?"

"No. Those people live to be nosy and get paid handsomely for it. It's not a big deal. Really. I feel like announcing it to the world." He wrapped his arms around her, "This is Maddy, the woman I love. I'm going to marry her, and we're going to have a daughter, and I couldn't be happier." He laughed, shocking Kinley and Madison who now both looked pale and ill. "The only thing holding me back is that I haven't told my family yet. I wanted to surprise them, you know, tell them in person. I really didn't want them to find out this way."

"Do you think they know about this in Canada yet?"

"Probably," he admitted.

"He's like royalty up there, or so I've read," Kinley finally spoke. "Well, at least they don't know anything about me."

"Don't bet on it." He grinned wryly.

"Don't tease me, Cal."

"I love teasing you, Kin, but I am not teasing at the moment. They probably know all about you. I've never seen a group better at conjecturing and following the teeniest trail of breadcrumbs," he sighed. "Don't worry about it. You don't have to say a word."

"Okay." She frowned. "I have to go." She turned, "Maddy, what about the thing you wanted to do?" Madison shook her head as if to say 'not now'. Was she keeping something from him again? "Think about it, if you need my help." She said goodbye before heading out into the chilled air.

They watched Kinley, and she frowned as two cars followed her. "They do know about her."

"Either that, or they strongly suspect some connection. Those people can piece together things like you wouldn't believe." She leaned against him, filling him with a sense of peace and security.

"You really wish you could tell the world about me?" He nodded. "I don't understand you, Cal. How could you fall in love with someone so ordinary? Someone like me."

"How could you, someone so perfect, fall in love with me?" he asked her back.

"Perfect? Hardly," she scoffed. "The question is, how can anyone not love you?"

44. Good-Bye For Now

She stared up at the motionless white blades of the ceiling fan, following the deep gray shadows it cast, with her eyes. She couldn't sleep. Maybe Cal was used to this sort of thing- the unqualified invasion of personal space, but she wasn't. "Are you asleep?" She heard his voice reach out to her in the darkness. She turned and looked into his eyes. "I knew it." She gave him a quizzical glance, which he answered as though it were a question spoken aloud, "Because you," he grinned, "don't take this wrong, but you weren't having a nightmare."

"Oh, I thought they were going away." He moved closer to her.

"They are happening with less frequency," he uttered as he touched her face tenderly.

She looked back up, studying the shadows. "Kinley mentioned there was something you wanted to do. You now feel hindered because of the nosy idiots camped outside. What was it?"

"I was going to have a hard time telling you anyway, but now I am worried."

"You're all alone in this until you let me in." He kissed the very tip of her nose, which always sent shivers coursing through her body. He was right. She bit her lip, like she always did when things were not quite what she thought they should be.

"First, can I ask you a question?" He nodded. "What are we going to do?"

"About that…"

"Did I ever tell you I love the way you say 'a boat'?"

He tickled her side, "Seriously, I want to take you home with me, if you don't mind. It's an impregnable fortress. We'll be left alone there."

She thought about it. "When can we go?"

"As early as I can get Gabe back down here with the private jet." He rolled over onto his side and propped himself up on his elbow. "Do you want to go right now?"

"As soon as possible." She turned toward him. "I just know this is only going to get worse."

"Where's my optimist?" He kissed her lips, leaving behind the pleasant tingling feeling she usually associated with fake cinnamon candy.

"I have to tell you something." She was biting another hole in her lip. "I want to say goodbye."

"To who, your friends?"

This was the thing she'd been dreading. She hadn't told him, not knowing how he would handle what she needed to say. "No, not exactly." She didn't want to say it.

He must have sensed it, because without warning, he pulled her into his arms, and pressed his lips against her ear. "Your family," he said knowingly. She nodded, feeling that damned knot coming back into her throat. "Whenever you want to go, we'll come up with a plan. I can be there, or not," he added the not with a little hint of doubt in his voice.

"No, I want you there." She could feel his muscular body relax.

"Good, because I really wanted to be there."

"You do?" She couldn't figure him out sometimes.

"Yes." He held her until the sun began to come up. She reached over for her phone, somehow knowing Kinley would be awake and began typing out a text. Within moments she learned that Kinley had been receiving phone calls non-stop. The press wasn't certain she was "The Maddy" mentioned at the awards show just yet. She was the number one suspect. She told Kinley about wanting to say goodbye before leaving for Canada, which they would be doing quickly. Kinley did not answer again for several minutes. Tension was building, her jaw was clenched; she couldn't seem to relax.

Finally another text came; it was from Megan, not Kinley.

They know about Kate, but not me yet. I guess I'm not good enough of a friend...LOL...so be ready and I will be there in twenty to take you and Cal to the cemetery...may I suggest a disguise? C U Soon!
-Meg

Maddy texted her back and told Cal. He was up, pulling his dreadlocks onto his head. He studied her and asked her if she had a beanie. She did. She ran and put her black beanie on and braided her hair into pigtails. They both put on huge black sunglasses. "It feels like we're spies."

Megan was there, yawning, leaning against the side of the house. "You don't think that those vultures are camped out at the cemetery do you?" she asked as they followed her to the car. Cal honestly didn't know, and sincerely hoped not. The men and women encamped along the security fence didn't pay them any attention as they drove by.

~

Cal hadn't known what kind of grave to expect. The cemetery near his home was an old one, crammed with historic looking headstones dating back a hundred years or so. This cemetery was one large rolling hill after another. All of the headstones were in the ground; little rectangles set into the earth were all that remained naming the individuals in the ground beneath them. Megan drove over the final hill and his eyes felt inexplicably drawn to the hill's top. There was a monument of sorts up there, and no one around it for miles. "I'm staying in the car."

He watched Maddy carry a red gift bag up with her. He didn't dare ask, it felt a little too personal still. He followed behind her, the monument looming into view, with the sun rising, pink, peach, coral, purple and blue just behind it. The wall of granite had the name Grey in the center, with an oval tipped onto its' side beneath that. As he moved closer, he viewed a family portrait; a terribly happy family stared back at him. Maddy was there, a tall man's arms drawn around her. His dark hair, and pale skin, made his extraordinarily bright blue eyes stand out. Their four children surrounded them. His sight traveled over the unique headstone and found six individual pictures set in upright ovals with names and dates. He shuddered as his eyes fell over the picture of Maddy with her name and birth date hyphenated into emptiness.

He walked over and leaned against a nearby tree. He felt the silence falling over him like a thick, heavy blanket. He watched her place five individual red boxes underneath every name but her own. She stepped back to look, and very quietly she moved closer until she was leaning against the monolith. "Jack." His heart shriveled a bit when she spoke her dead husband's name. Her hand traced over his picture, "I'm doing like you said. I'm happy. I still miss you, but I'm going to be all right." He could hear her fervent whisper as though it traveled right into his soul. He wanted to look away but he couldn't. He watched as she pressed her lips to her fingertips and transferred her kisses onto the pictures. "Good-bye for now," she said. Then she quietly let her head fall against the headstone. She stayed there, leaned against that cold impersonal wall which represented a warm and very personable family. She stayed until the ache became more than she could withstand.

She walked over to him, "I'm ready."

They began walking back down the hill, "Can I ask?"

"What's in the boxes?" He loved how she seemed to know his thoughts.

"Is that too impertinent of me? My mother tells me I'm impertinent all the time."

"No." She grinned. "They're empty. It's just my love, and hugs and kisses." He wrapped an arm around her waist and kissed the top of her head, which was covered by her beanie. It was one of the sweetest things he'd ever heard.

45. A Warm Welcome to the Family...No Really

Her own mother had been distant, formal, and thought of her as something that was in the way, rather than a child to be adored and treasured. She'd promised herself so long ago, that now she hardly remembered, she would always be a good mother. Her father had been aloof and cruel, the type of man who laughed at the expense of others. His joy came in other people's awkwardness, anxiety, embarrassment, humiliation and sorrow. She'd been thrilled when he died. He was a tenacious hateful man who held onto her for the sheer joy of making her miserable. Once he was gone, she'd been set free, by her mother as well.

She'd been a teenager forced to marry, she'd been able to make a life for herself. Madison Leblanc would have her own family and it would be wonderful. It had been wonderful. Sure, the Grey family had ups and downs like normal people, but she had given her children all of the love she could give them. She had no regrets on that count. None. She'd been a good wife too. She knew she had. She'd been devoted and loving, and when she thought of it, especially after the accident. She couldn't have done more. She could have expected more from Jonathan and Debbie Grey but that had been a fruitless relationship from the start. Never had she felt more unwelcomed. She'd been determined she would be a great mother-in-law and welcome the lucky people who married her children with open arms. Those dreams had been taken away.

It seemed she could somehow renew them, through this new little one. She moved her hands absentmindedly over her abdomen as she stared out of the window of Cal's jet. Who owns a jet? Who gives away cars at Christmas? Who does anything the way Cal does? She snuggled into him. Why did he look so damned happy whenever she looked up at him? He could have anything he wanted, and he had wanted her? It still awed her. Sometimes she just wanted to shake him and ask him what he thought he was doing with her, when he could have any supermodel he wanted. But she was too thankful. Not only was he gorgeous, but he was precious to the very core of his soul. He was rare, and beautiful, and for some unknown crazy reason, he loved her.

"Have you ever had someone say something to you that made absolutely no sense whatsoever, but you can't stop thinking about it?" His mind was moving in a different vein of thought altogether.

"The woman Mandy from Kin's Christmas party quite frequently does that to me," she laughed.

"It was Kinley, not Mandy."

"Kinley said something strange to you?" This wasn't terribly shocking.

"Well, she *was* on drugs at the time," he conceded. He looked out the window out into the Manitoba Province he'd called home his entire life. His heart lightened as he was finally feeling the release of tension he'd been storing the last few days. He watched her carefully, laughing, because she was waiting for him to speak up and spit it out already. "She had a dream about your family and what happened. She blamed herself for it."

"I thought she might have." Madison closed her eyes. She'd tried numerous times to get it out of Kinley but she'd never worked up the courage to ask. She's suspected Kinley had been feeling guilty about it. "The thing is, she has the dreams whenever someone is going to die. Anyone we've ever known, she'll dream about it. She's never been able to stop it from happening though."

"She wasn't kidding around?" He let a low whistle escape his lips. "Has she tried to stop it before? I mean, they're just dreams, how accurate can they be?"

"Kinley's dreams are extremely accurate. It's like she is a fly on the wall, seeing the person's last day play out before her. Every single thing she dreamt seemed to be some sort of Godly countdown until the person has to go."

He nodded. "That would be a horrible burden." He didn't want to think about knowing things like that. He imagined Kinley knowing about Maddy losing her family in a single instant. He would have hated to know ahead of time, and not be able to stop it. But, he wasn't certain how much of it he believed.

"I never thought of it that way." She seemed thoughtful. "I always think of it as God's gift to Kinley. She gets to know what no one else knows. No, she can't stop it, but she can spend precious moments with the dying people and tie up any loose ends. Don't you see, she has insider information and can make the most of the person's last moments here on earth."

"She is kind of psychic then?"

"*Nah*, she just has the dreams. I can't believe she told you. Only Ryan and I know about it." Madison bit her lip while wondering if she would ever be able to work up the courage and ask Kinley what had really happened in the last few moments of her family's time on earth.

They rode in a limo home; he enjoyed watching the countryside roll by, while he thought of everything Maddy had told him. He was glad the roads had been cleared. Snow drifts were up to ten feet along the sides of the deserted streets. Crazed fans and paparazzi had known they were coming and had bombarded them, even in this weather. Gabe slept, his head bobbing on his chest as the limo hit little bumps in the road. He'd tried to shield Maddy from everyone, covered her up, so no one could truly see her. Her identity was now an overnight sensation. He hadn't thought when he'd dedicated his music award to Maddy that it would even be a big deal. He just wanted to get the message to her somehow, and had hoped she'd been watching. He only wanted her to know that he loved her.

It had made a big mess of things, but she didn't seem to be blaming him. What would his family say though? There had been rumors flying since Nurse Ratched had decided to become an informant to the tabloids. He truly hadn't thought about Maddy's identity being a mystery in need of solving. There were crowds gathered around the gates surrounding the vast acreage of his family compound. They'd had to move closer together, the more famous his group became, the more people wanted to know the dumbest things.

He'd found himself on the cover of a magazine once, eating a muffin. The entire story had been about what coffee he'd drunk, the muffin he'd eaten and the napkin the reporter was able to save from the depths of the trashcan and sell on EBay. When the gates closed, he could feel Maddy relax a little, "Is this what you go through? It sucks."

He laughed and so did Gabe. They did have to drive a short way to his parent's house where everyone was waiting for his official announcement of what they now all suspected. His family was outside waiting when the limo pulled up to the first main drive on the extensive property belonging to his family. "Welcome home!" His mother was the first to put her arms around Maddy and welcome her into the family. "Madison!" So, she now knew she was about to be a grandmother again. He'd been dreading, yet fantasizing about how she might take it. She hugged Madison again, this time even tighter, "Oh, sweetheart, you are glowing. Isn't she the most beautiful pregnant woman we've seen since Michelle?" The biting cold made him want to continue this reunion inside.

Chatter spread through his family. They were all congratulating Cal and Maddy, coming up and hugging them. Rory clapped him on the back, "Good job, little bro." He gave him something of a sideways manly hug.

"You must be famished," his mother began, as she put her arm around Maddy's waist and steered her into the house.

"Grace…" Madison said sheepishly.

"There is no Grace here Madison, there is only Mom."

She smiled sweetly as she looked back at Cal. Debbie had never asked her to call her mom. Somehow, she knew, she'd come home.

46. Life in the Eye of the Hurricane

The eye of a hurricane could not have offered a better vantage point of the ongoing storm around her. After every member of the Hunt family had examined her ring, and asked her a thousand questions, she thought the chaos would simmer down. It had only begun. The whirlwind spinning around her involved a bridal shower thrown by future sister-in-laws Callie and Michelle and shopping with her soon to be mother-in-law, Grace.

"You don't have to take me shopping," she'd muttered somewhat self-consciously.

"Nonsense. I'm going to be your mother-in-law and the grandmother of your child. I can't wait." She was too excited. It was giving Madison a little more compassion for Kinley, who she secretly thought had acted silly over receiving a car for Christmas. This was only baby clothes and furniture, but she felt awkward and undeserving. She wore a hat, gloves, and a covering jacket while they shopped incognito, in the frosty city of Winnipeg. Everywhere she turned there were pictures of Cal, Rory, Shawn and Chris, practically the royal family of Manitoba.

Magazines everywhere speculated on the existence of "Cal's Maddy". Some headlines asked the question- Does she even exist? Will the final member of Murder of Crows tie the knot? The phone calls had dwindled to a few a day for Kinley. The reporters were moving onto a marriage/affair scandal involving hockey player, Dan Murtagh. She couldn't have cared less. In Canada, however, the mystery of Cal's secret love was still the latest thing.

"Have you thought about the name Katie?" her soon to be mom-in-law asked as they shopped for adorable little girl clothing. She hadn't.

"I want something, more," she frowned, "different I guess."

"Be careful how different. I'd read Rory's name in a romance novel and thought it sounded so manly. Then they come out with a television show years later where the main girl is named Rory. He was furious…still can't mention it to him without starting a war."

"I'll keep that in mind."

~

The baby shower came and went. People, some of them famous, she'd never so much as spoken a word to, were hugging her and telling her congratulations. All the while, Cal's family was embracing her as one of their own. Kinley's family had been this welcoming, but she'd always had the secret hope that Jack's family would embrace her one day. They hadn't.

She and Cal began to plan a wedding- a private affair, as it was possible to have. She planned on flying Kinley, Kate and Megan up, along with Kinley's brother, mother, father and sisters. Despite the fact that she'd been considerably careless with the whole birth control thing, she did want to be married before the birth of their little girl.

The joke names had begun to fly around the Hunt campfire. Confucius Hunt was now the most common one. They'd been thrown names like Gertrude, Dandelion, Goldilocks, and Felix, which didn't sound remotely girlish. But then again, neither did Confucius. Her only peaceful moments were stolen. She and Cal found themselves sneaking off many times during the day, just to breathe, it seemed. In one of those brief stolen moments, Cal's phone rang, and he decided to answer it.

"Hello Mark." It was an annoyed, even patronizing greeting if Madison had ever heard one.

She pressed her body tighter against Cal, loving the way his muscular frame seemed to have been made for her. She fitted with him as though she'd been the missing piece in a matching set. She felt him wriggle closer to her, letting his hand slip underneath her shirt and caress her growing stomach. "I know Mark, it's just that," annoyed he groaned, "I have an idea." He sounded cheerful at the prospect. "I need to let you go and discuss it with Maddy."

She could hear the voice on the other line, a deep baritone speaking voice, "There is a *Maddy*?"

"Yes. I'll call you back." He pressed the button ending the phone call. Her hand slid underneath his shirt and her fingers seemed to sink into skin quickly distracting him from whatever he was thinking earlier. "He's going to be angry if I make him wait, but what do I pay him for anyway?" His soft lips found hers.

"Who is he?"

"My publicist." He wasn't interested in speaking about Mark Young.

Cal held onto her tightly and rolled over until she was sitting on top of him. "I could look up at you all day," he told her. She smiled, her eyes glittering in the dusky light.

One of her fingers traced along his jaw line. He grasped her hand and kissed the inside of her wrist, lightly outlining a vein with his tongue. "You taste so sweet." He pulled her closer burying his hands in her hair pulling her lips onto his. "Would you mind if we got a wedding planner? I'd rather spend my days doing this than picking out coordinating napkins." He let his hand follow the natural curve of her neck.

"I'm in complete agreement with you," she told him.

With the weight of planning a wedding lifted from her shoulders, she felt carefree, and for the first time since she'd met Cal, she could just be left to fall in love with him. "Why did you notice me that first night we met?" she asked him one night while enfolded in his arms.

"You threw your head back laughing. It caught my eye. You owned me from that moment on." He grinned. "I wonder what caught your eye with me," he muttered, musing aloud.

"Your eyes. I love your eyes. *Every* woman loves your eyes." She laughed. "You are just some delicious eye-candy, Cal. The best part is that your physical deliciousness isn't all there is to you, you are so much more."

"So, what keeps you around, Maddy?" He knew it wasn't his money, or his secluded home. He didn't need to think quite so shallowly when it came to Maddy. He tried to let his mind wander, but he knew she would say something completely unexpected.

"You are humble."

"Humble? I always picture poor people being humble."

"You know it has more than one definition." She smiled. "The one I think of you is, unpretentious, real. You're also introspective, and if you notice a flaw in yourself, you try to fix it. I've never met any man like that before. You don't flaunt all of your money or possessions; you don't make people feel bad for having less than you. You've always fit in with my friends even though you have so much more than any of us. You are my angel man." She spoke softly, "Yet, you have a strong will and don't give up easily. You didn't give up on me, though you probably should have."

"I couldn't," he answered with all of his sincerity. "Knowing you were out there somewhere and weren't with me, it was pure hell on earth. I can't believe all of those nice things you said about me. I had no idea you felt that way."

"I love you Cal, because of who you are, not what you can do for me, or because you're famous. I love you for the reasons I named. I couldn't not love you if I tried. What I can't figure out, on a daily basis, is how you can love me. I just can't wrap my mind around it."

He kissed her neck, "You are unselfish, funny, witty, brave, intoxicatingly beautiful inside and out." He kept kissing her, now he was down to her collar bone. "And there's such a long list that if I go on with it that we might miss our own wedding."

"That wouldn't do." She let her head fall back, enjoying his lips on her skin.

"I love you, Madison. I can't wait to say Madison Hunt."

"I can't wait to be Madison Hunt."

47. Cold Feet

Cal couldn't remember ever dreaming about marrying someone. To him, that was a girl thing, planning weddings out in their heads, finding the man who fit the fantasy. He just knew that when he met 'the one' whoever she was, he would know. He had known, somehow, even looking back, there had been something different about her from the very beginning. She was utterly captivating. *She* hadn't known right away, which wasn't exactly in the plan. Weren't both parties in love supposed to know at first sight? Wasn't there music that would play and fireworks to ignite when the passionate first kiss happened? She hadn't seemed aware; in fact she had been in denial about loving him at all. He was never happier than when she'd admitted to loving him in return, there in her hospital bed.

He loved seeing her near her friends. If she had been a diamond, the setting of her friends merely enhanced her beauty and charm. He found her constantly running to them, wrapped up in a warm blanket over her jacket, to tell them about the littlest things. Kinley and her family were squeezed into his guesthouse, which felt irrational because his home was more than big enough for everyone to fit. Kinley insisted that he and Maddy have their privacy. He could be thankful, he supposed. He did adore the way Maddy would run out back and skip toward the guesthouse over the rugged terrain, with something new to share with Kinley. Kate and her family were in yet another guesthouse, with Megan and her husband.

He didn't think he could stand such complete happiness, he was certain he would explode and leave behind a terrible mess. Maddy kept telling him that she thought something had to go wrong because it isn't possible for so many things to go right in one person's life. He kept reminding her that there were two people falling into this category.

The day of the wedding arrived and he was not at all thinking what he would have imagined himself to have been thinking in the past. He thought in the past that he'd have cold feet…well, he did, only physically because Manitoba was freezing in early January, it was a snow covered wilderness. He'd had crews working tirelessly on removing much of the snow, and the guests were being flown in by helicopter. He should have flown everyone to the south of Italy. It had to be warmer there.

He'd imagined himself feeling trapped or anxious. He *was* anxious, anxious to marry Maddy. They'd pulled off the planning of the wedding in less than a month. Madison had insisted it be quick, as she was growing bigger daily, and was afraid she wouldn't fit into her dress. He adored the way her body was changing. He wouldn't have thought he'd be capable of that either. He just hadn't known how love could transform him, reinvent him, make him feel so…alive.

The snow had been cleared away in time, but frost clung to imported vines and the portable building made out of sheer material. Rory was calling it the 'lean to'. When twilight fell, the lights on the 'tent' came on, they were twinkling white lights. It looked like a scene that fairies had conspired to create. He was standing up at the front, next to the minister who he'd known since his youth. Father Thomas smiled benevolently at him. "She's a lovely woman," he'd mentioned to Cal. Cal couldn't agree with him more. Rory was whispering in his ear, "What he really wants to say is, Cal couldn't you have waited to get her pregnant until after you were married? Sinner." Rory walked back to the tent set up for the wedding party after his quick congratulations. Cal was ready.

~

Music played, where it came from, he'd never know. Maybe fairies were in charge of both lights and music. He was grateful for the little heaters placed around the inside of the tent. Kinley walked up the aisle, her arm entwined with Rory's, and they parted, he noticed Rory glance back at her. His palms were sweating and he was rubbing them on his tuxedo pants. Kate walked up the aisle with his nephew Brian, they were indubitably mismatched. Megan had her arm threaded through his nephew Matthew's arm. Matthew, who was fifteen, dwarfed Megan, and funnily enough, they didn't look bad together. His sister Callie came next with her husband, then Michelle with her husband, holy crap could any more people come in front of Maddy? Ring boy, his nephew Phillip and flower girl Kennedy…this was getting old. Did he have to have such a big family? Finally, the right music played.

Maddy walked up the aisle, gliding on the arm of Kinley's father, Mr. Grant Michaelson. McKenna held the long train, which had rose petals falling off of it. Her hair was twisted up, and every few steps he caught a hint of something sparkling in her dark tresses. Her gown was white empire-waisted, and she barely showed. She just looked superbly radiant, she glowed more than the moon, stars, twinkle-lights, or flickering candles set around everywhere. The chill in the air subsided with her entrance. Wisps of curls escaped from underneath her simple veil, while her ruby red lips eased into a smile, just for him.

Father Thomas started the ceremony, and he'd never felt more impatient, not ever. He knew he must have been holding his breath for what felt like several minutes, when Father Thomas told him he could kiss the bride, he was able to exhale. A party broke out all around them. They were introduced as Mr. and Mrs. Calvin and Madison Hunt. He had to admit, it did sound quite nice. He danced the night away with his new bride, hating to share her, but he did when he needed to.

He was allowing himself to be completely self-absorbed but something unusual caught his eye. Rory had been mostly acting like himself, but there were moments when he let his guard down a little and Cal could see past the lie. Something was bothering him, clearly, but what? Cal would have to investigate later. What caught his eye at the moment was the way he looked at Kinley as he spun her around the dance floor. There was something not quite right there. It was almost as if...never mind. This was *Rory* he was thinking about.

The night seemed to go on and on. He knew the party would continue without them, once they left. Which could not be soon enough for Cal. "I need to put my feet up, I am exhausted," she whispered in his ear as they danced yet again. He nodded, knowing he did not fully understand but also not exactly envious of her carrying around a small growing child. She couldn't ever just pop her stomach off and set aside while she stretched out. They left in a hail of flying, floating bubbles. He'd arranged for a horse and carriage to take them to his house.

"Madison, it was fun marrying you." She giggled as she leaned into his arms. She felt chilled to the bone, as he let his hands run over her smooth skin. She begged him not to carry her over the threshold, even though she wasn't heavy in the slightest. They fell laughing into bed, collapsing onto each other.

"My feet are killing me," she moaned, pulling her shoes off and heading for the closet where many of her things now had a home.

"You could have kicked them off right here." His eyes traveled over her, taking in her beauty, his soul's constant ache for her was growing. "I can't wait until you come back." He flipped the lights off as he went, watching a smile start in the corner of her mouth and spread to the other side of her exquisite lips. He held her, unzipping her dress, slowly almost to the point of torturing himself, and let it drop to the floor in a nice satin heap. "You're beautiful." He let his lips touch lightly upon her skin, his hands began slide over her back. His lips traveled over her silken skin, down from her lips, furthering the journey over her neck, following the tilt and curve, kissing her as his fingers moved nimbly while he finished undressing her.

He didn't think life could be any sweeter until there in the semi-darkness he heard her whisper, "Oh Cal, I love you."

48. Everything She Ever Wanted

She wasn't sleeping again, but Cal's ceiling was far more interesting to look at than hers had been. It sloped upward at an angle and half of it was made of glass. It was a window to look up into the heavens through; large beams of wood supported it. She was secretly glad the snow had been cleared away to reveal the celestial scene above her. It was really spectacular. It was hers too now, she considered, she was married. The sun was beginning to rise somewhere so that there was a large colorful clash of clouds, sky and light hues happening in front of her. Madison was unable to turn her mind off; thoughts were flooding, raging rampant through her as though they were a great tsunami or tidal flood.

"Madison?" Cal yawned. He seemed so far away at the moment in the overlarge bed with voluminous sheets. She crawled over to him. "That is so sexy," he murmured.

She snorted, "Now I know you love me."

"It's something you should know, but what has reinforced it, pray tell?"

"No one thinks pregnant is sexy unless they are in love," she told him flatly, before fluffing the blankets and pulling herself closer to him. "I feel huge."

He let his hand rest on her stomach. "It's definitely sexy." She shook her head. "And… it lets me be creative." She poked him in the side, before placing her head in that spot seemingly made for her. Her eyes were closed but she wasn't sleeping. "What has you up so early?" He yawned again as if to point out *how* early it really was.

"I think we're going to have a problem here."

"I know what you mean. We can't name our child Confucius no matter how elegant it sounds," he teased her. She laughed, but also gave him a look that said 'that is not exactly the direction I was headed in, but funny nevertheless.' "I know…" he sighed, "You are worried about where we are going to live."

"Exactly. I love it here, but I miss Kinley, and Kate, and Megan."

"They are in the guest houses right out back."

"You know what I mean, you tease." She kissed his bare chest sending electrical impulses sparking through his torso. "I love having them here. Everything feels right having them here, but they are going to leave soon, and I will be lonely when you go back to work." He had mentioned songwriting, and a few projects he was involved with.

"I know, I was already thinking about all of this. What should we do?"

"I wish I knew," she answered sadly.

"Do you want to go back to California?" He didn't mind going back. In fact, the idea sounded rather exciting to him. It was better to be a little away from his family for a while than to pull her away from hers, especially as she was still a little too fragile. He could fly anywhere he wanted; he could commute. Eventually, it would get old, however. They would have to come up with some long-term arrangement.

"So much." She fidgeted. "But I don't expect you to conform to me. I must fit into your world, not the other way around."

"I have no idea what that means," he grinned, "but if you want to go back to California you just say the word and we are back in California."

"I believe you mean what you say." She frowned, "*Your* family is so close. It's what I've always wanted." She burrowed down, snuggling closer to him, not letting him see the agony in her face.

"It is?" He lifted her chin and kissed her, "Maddy, does your mother even know that you are married?"

She laughed, "I wouldn't think so."

"I cannot imagine not telling my mother I was married. She would kill me."

"My mother will not care. There's the difference."

"Doesn't it hurt?" He lovingly caressed her face, letting his fingers tangle into her hair.

"Not anymore." She shrugged. "It's funny but it hurt so very much before, then Kinley goes and says something in her little quirky way and puts it all into perspective for me."

"I have to know," he muttered.

"I even remember where we were. We were sitting by Megan's pool, sunbathing, she was reading some grotesquely long book, and out-of-the-blue she says, 'you know, it kind of sucks that your mom is such a crappy mom.' That was random, even for Kinley."

"How weird, no offense to Kinley, but it's a strange thing to say."

"I suspect whatever she'd just read had made her think of it, and if she'd left it there, I would have shrugged it off and gone back to reading my magazine in peace. But she didn't leave it there, she said, 'You know it's crap how you can't control what your parent's do, but what you can control Maddy, makes up for everything.' I admit I was confused, but she explained. 'You can control being a good mother, which you are. Your children have one of the best mothers in the world. You are loving and good to them, everything your mother wasn't to you. You didn't become like her, you broke the cycle and became better than she was. You didn't let not having a family get you down; instead you created your own family. I'm not just talking about Jack and the kids, but us. We're your family.' She said that about her, Kate, and Megan. It was a moment for me. That silly little Kinley changed my outlook on everything that day."

"Did I ever tell you how much I like your friend Kinley?" She shook her head. "No really, she is the funniest little thing. And she loves you."

"I know she does. I love her, in a non-lesbian way of course."

"Married to me and feeling the need to clarify…" he said to no one. She pulled him into a passionate kiss, "Wow, what a way to wake up." He put his hand on her stomach and felt a little nudge. "That wasn't you was it?" He sat up, pulling the covers away. "Was that you, little one?" Another nudge confirmed his suspicion. "That is so weird." He put his mouth up to her stomach, "But so cool."

They decided to get up and grab some breakfast, which turned out to be his mother's freshly baked cinnamon rolls. Someone had mysteriously dropped them off. "These are heaven, just what the baby wanted," Madison told him.

"I'm glad she likes them."

"Hey guys," Rory was hunched over gazing into the opened stainless steel fridge. "Do you have any butter? I am out." Cal knew something was amiss; Rory was in his shirt from the previous evening, and his tuxedo pants were rumpled as though he'd slept in them.

"We were just married last night; a little privacy may be in order," Cal glared at him.

Rory pulled out a stick of butter. "I think you all have had privacy before." He pointed to Maddy's stomach. Cal threw a cinnamon roll at his head, and was sad to see Rory duck just in time. Cal briefly wondered if Rory needed to talk to him, but finding him with Madison, had come up with another plan. He'd talk to him another time; he was in no hurry.

"Have you thought of any real names yet?"

Cal considered this for a moment, "I like Brooklyn Julia, what about you, Maddy?"

She was beaming, glowing. He could have sat there all day, admiring her lovely face, "Brady Julia. Funny that we came up with the same middle name."

Rory was laughing, doubled over, practically wheezing. "What has gotten you so amused Ror?"

"You guys kill me…" He was trying to control his fits of laughter, "Oh…so…funny."

"Do you see it, because apparently I am missing something here."

"Me too," Maddy answered looking a little nonplussed.

"You're going to name your daughter BJ Hunt? BJ Hunt!" he howled, practically crying.

"Your brother is an ass," Maddy told him as she took a bite of her cinnamon roll. "Would you mind terribly if I said something to stop him?" Rory wasn't even listening, he now had tears leaking from the corners of his eyes as he doubled over, taken away in his hysterics.

Cal stared at her; this was something he had to see. He didn't much care what she did, even if it involved kicking Rory in well-deserved way, which would deliver the most pain. "Rory, we didn't want to tell you before, but now we have you alone, I think we should. Don't you, Cal?" Rory straightened up and looked at her. Cal agreed with her but had no idea where this conversation might be actually headed. "I love your name; did I ever tell you that?" Rory looked alarmed, frightened. Suddenly, he and Cal both knew where it was headed and Cal had to do everything in his power not to collapse into an intense fit of roaring laughter. "We are going to name her Rory after *you*. It will make such a pretty girl name, don't you agree?"

Rory scowled, "Touché, little sister, touché."

"Why, I thank you my good man. Now, if we name her Brooklyn or Brady you may never call her BJ or so help me, we *will* call her Rory." Cal laughed; his sides were aching. "I'll change that child's name in the middle of her seventh year if I have to."

"I never saw this side of you before." He stole a cinnamon roll from their table. "But I like it. Cal you've got yourself a fine woman there." He tipped his nonexistent hat to her. "Good day newlyweds. I shall not bother you again. Not right away…in any case."

After Rory left, he considered their earlier discussion. "You know I can postpone my projects until after the baby comes." He watched her face light up, "And we can move back to California in the meantime. I want you to be near *your* family while you are going through all of this."

"Do you mean it, Cal?"

"Absolutely." She jumped up and he pulled her into his lap, kissing her lips, feeling how light she was, even though she was carrying their tiny child inside of her. He couldn't remember a time in his life when he'd been happier. This was one of those moments he would always remember.

49. First Impression

Where had the time gone? After having such a horrid courtship, married life had been living a dream. He'd always pictured it all a bit differently, but he'd never known how short his imagination had fallen. It was April fifth already? It just didn't seem possible. But here he was, seeing his wife underneath a tent of sorts; he was wearing scrubs and a surgical mask. Maddy was having a Caesarian, which was enough to make him nauseated. He admittedly would never have made a great doctor.

There she was, held by the doctor, quite suddenly too. She was screaming. He loved it. Here she was, feisty little thing, inherited his lungs…oh she was beautiful. Someone was cleaning her up, and the doctor was beginning to put Maddy back together. She just stared up at him smiling as though her body hadn't been nearly cut in half. He was about to ask something, or say something when he became completely distracted. Maddy would have said he'd had an ADD moment. A nurse was handing him his baby. She was so small. Was she too small? Must not be if they are handing her to me, he thought.

She just stared up at him, as though she knew him. He loved her, it was instantaneous. Her light hair, and bright blue eyes, and perfect little lips. Maddy's lips. Madison was watching him, he wanted to speak, but words weren't coming out. He couldn't think of anything to describe this moment, the way he felt, the things he was seeing, the people he loved most in the world, in this very room. He just reached out and touched her face; she seemed to know exactly what he was thinking, she just smiled.

In her recovery room he paced anxiously until their little one could be with them again. She was having tests run or some nonsense. "They'll bring her back soon," Madison encouraged him. She laughed.

"I can't believe I feel this way. I thought I loved her before I met her, but now it's just taken over my entire body." She just closed her eyes, which prompted him to kiss her eyelids. "This will inspire a great song. I can feel it."

He sat next to her bed, and watched as she fell into a light sleep. It began to hit him in a way it never had before; she'd had children and lost them. The thought of losing her and his new child was terrifying beyond any fear he could be faced with in this lifetime. Maddy had grown in strength just sitting next to him. His admiration for his wife couldn't have been measured. She'd lost everything and fought hard to survive the devastation. She was his hero or was it heroine?

A nurse brought their baby inside and smiled at him before placing her in his arms. "She's beautiful," the nurse said. He hoped Kinley wouldn't tell this one off, anyone who thought his baby was beautiful was good in his book.

"Her name is Brooklyn," Maddy told her. He looked back, not realizing she was awake watching them. The nurse excused herself, shutting the door with a light click behind her.

"Are you sure?" he asked.

"It makes me think of Kinley Brooke." She smiled up at him. Her dark brown eyes were lively as she grinned at her little girl. He placed the baby in her mother's arms, and watched as she winced slightly.

"Should I grab someone? Are you in pain?" He was getting ready to leave, but she reached out and pulled him back. He looked down at his baby, "She's a mini-Maddy."

"I rather thought she had your eyes," Madison muttered before bestowing a kiss on her new baby's head.

He just watched his new little family, and thought of his old life, how unrewarding and shallow it had been. He thought of the person he'd been before and compared him to who he was at this moment. He was two different individuals. So much of his life had been altered in the last year, and for the better. "I love you Maddy and little Brooklyn." With a kiss of absolute affection and adoration, he welcomed his sweet baby girl into the world then turned to kiss her mother. Life couldn't get any better, could it?

~

Madison sat in her hospital bed contemplating many things, but mainly it was the epiphany she'd had that left her in a contemplative state. She'd looked into those deep blue eyes and felt something strange and absolute hit her quite abruptly. Brooklyn had been quietly, peacefully gazing up at her mother and though she did not cry or communicate in a way most adults would understand, she seemed to be telling Madison something through a higher level of communication. You can be happy now. It was a simple thing; one thing anyone else would have understood and accepted. It was nearly impossible for Madison to allow herself to let her happiness devour her. She felt she had an obligatory duty to fulfill by holding on to much of her sorrow and never truly allowing herself to feel the thoroughness of her joy.

Today, in a flash of a moment, she'd given herself permission, but more importantly (and she'd most likely only share this with Kinley later) she felt that her children had been reaching out to her. It was as though Brooklyn had brought her a message from the great beyond. Her children wanted her to feel joy and they fully endorsed it. She hated recalling it but somehow it felt apropos to the situation at hand. Riley had caught her crying over something. She couldn't remember the thing that had brought her to tears but only that Riley couldn't bear to see her cry. She'd thrown her arms around Madison and wailed, "Please don't cry, Mommy." She hadn't been able to see her mother upset, it was as though her entire world were in jeopardy. They haven't changed, they still can't bear to see me cry, she thought, even though they weren't with her any longer.

"What are you doing?" Kinley stood in the doorway watching her. Madison had absentmindedly been folding her stomach in half.

"It's that post-pregnancy fat, you know, the moldable stuff you can squish into pants and form it as though there was play-doh underneath your skin."

"Yes, I do recall how it works. You're lucky it will all disappear by tomorrow. Curse you, Maddy." Madison laughed as Kinley sat down in the seat next to her. "So, where's this baby you won't tell me the name of yet, and where's your adoring husband?"

"They will bring her in soon, any minute now. I told Cal to go home and get some rest. He will be back any time."

"You're too kind," Kinley mused. "He has no idea how it's going to be, does he?"

"You mean midnight feedings and colic?"

"That would be precisely what I mean." Kinley's brown eyes twinkled with amusement.

"One of us might as well get rested up. Although, I suspect he'll want to hire a nanny after the first week." She looked away, thinking, wondering if she should say something. She'd been pushing it away for too long. "I had another nightmare last night. I'm still having them. I thought they would leave, but I can't make them stop. At least I don't have them every night like I used to."

"Maddy, I'm so sorry." Kinley kindly put her hand on Madison's hand. "If there's anything I can do..."

"There is something you can do. I think I know the reason I'm still having them. I don't know what happened that night, not really. I know the gist, but my mind keeps trying to fill in the blanks. I know if you tell me about your dream, that I will know what happened."

"How did you..." Kinley's voice faltered, "I never said..."

"Kinley, anyone who ever died near us, you always knew beforehand. Of course you knew about my family."

"I didn't believe it."

"Why, all of your crazy death dreams come true. It's like you were there."

"I never had so many people die in a dream. There has only ever been one at a time. I thought I was losing it, and that it couldn't possibly be real," Kinley muttered, looking down at her hands folding and unfolding them nervously in her lap. "I do have lots of dreams that don't come true," she added.

"Will you stop blaming yourself Kinley Brooke? It's not your fault, any more than it was my fault," Madison assured her.

"I know I couldn't have stopped it. But heaven knows I wanted to probably more than any other dream I'd had. Even more than Aunt Maggie. I love those kids, and Jack. I miss them every day." Kinley was crying. Madison couldn't bear the thought of losing Kinley's kids; the idea alone was too much.

"You can lie to me, tell me they didn't suffer. I want so badly to believe it that I will believe you. Make my mind rest at ease. Please Kinley, do this for me."

"I don't have to lie Maddy, if my dream was accurate."

"They are always accurate, scarily so," Madison told her. Couldn't she feel the tension? She had to know. She'd never had the gumption to question Kinley regarding her unusual visions, not about her family.

"I'll tell you." Kinley wiped her tears away with a tissue she stole from Madison's bedside, "Your children were asleep. All of them."

"Even Jonathan?" she asked with hope weighing down her voice.

"Yes, even Jonathan. I can see him still, his iPod in his hand, his ear-buds firmly in place. I can see Riley, her little head leaning on a stuffed animal she was using as a pillow. There had been a movie on, but it put them to sleep, one by one. Alex's head was leaning kind of funny and Jack was worried that she'd get a cramp in her neck. He turned; I can still see it so clearly. His arm was up on the passenger seat, he was twisted around. He leaned back and was fixing Alex's head when the truck crashed into them. He never saw it coming and neither did the children. It was rather instant, *explosive*." Tears were streaming, makeup running, and Kinley's pale complexion was now splotchy.

"You promise?" Madison swallowed the lump in her throat and brushed her tears away.

"I do, Maddy, it was instantaneous. It was the absolute worst dream I've ever had, but also the most comforting after the fact. I know they didn't suffer."

Madison leaned back against her pillow, her eyes closed in relief, "You have no idea how happy you've made me."

"*Happy?*" Kinley questioned her.

"I know it seems like a misplaced adjective but I've had an enlightening day."

Kinley didn't question her anymore, as though it were too personal for even her to pry into. A nurse was wheeling in a little bed with a baby swaddled in a pink blanket. Kinley popped up to look at her. Madison couldn't help but smile at Kinley's reaction. "She's beautiful. You and Cal do good work together…I hope this won't be your last venture into the child creating business."

The nurse, a woman in her mid-forties, smiled at the baby before she matched up the mother/daughter bracelets and handed the baby carefully to Madison. She must have sensed that she should leave right away as both women had blotchy faces and swollen eyes. "Kin, I have something else to ask you." She passed the baby to Kinley, who took her with enthusiasm, snuggling her as she sat down across from Madison.

"Ask away, my dear friend," Kinley whispered, gazing into the beautiful face of Maddy's little baby.

"Do you miss *me* as much as I miss you?" Anyone else would not have understood, but Kinley needed no explanation.

"So much." Kinley was crying again, holding little Brooklyn tightly as she wept. "Do you think we'll ever be ourselves again?"

"I hope so," whispered Madison. "You have been fighting with way too many people lately."

"I know." She gulped. "I fight with Ry all the time too. I am miserable. I am depressed. I can't sleep, I hardly eat. I don't know what to do with myself. I don't have much patience, and I feel highly defensive over you. This isn't how it's supposed to be, Maddy. You are the one who is always a little more dominant, and I am kind of the follower. Our relationship is all skewed. I don't know how to put it back. I don't know who I am anymore." Kinley was stroking Brooklyn's hair, before planting a soft kiss on her forehead. "She is too beautiful for words."

"Kin, I love you." Kinley smiled through her tears, "We're going to be ourselves again, I think."

"How?"

"We definitely need our senses of humor back," Madison suggested.

"Yes, I feel mine for moments only then it seems to vanish. I try to put myself out there, but I am unsure. I come across mean rather than funny. There is a harsh edge to me that wasn't there before. I'm trying Maddy, I swear." Kinley was done being emotional, wiping her tears away, she took a deep breath through her nose. "Seeing you happy again, it's really been the thing that is helping me. I think you may be right. We'll be back to normal, someday, maybe not completely normal but something like it." She cleared her throat, longing for the seriousness to fade away, "Wow, she is so beautiful. I wasn't kidding. You and Cal do some seriously great work together."

"You sound as though we were a team of sculptors," Madison laughed.

"Eat your heart out, Michelangelo." Kinley let the baby lie on her chest. "What's your name baby girl Hunt?"

"Brooklyn Julia," Madison told her, admiring the back of her little girl's head.

Kinley looked up at her and smiled, "It's perfect."

"Cal picked it out, but it made me think of my friend Kinley Brooke."

"I like it." Kinley kissed the top of her head, "Are you going to let yourself be happy about this?"

"I am," Madison told her. "It's like she's telling me it's finally okay."

"It's nothing any of us could have said sweet Brooklyn." Kinley snuggled into the baby. Megan and Kate were walking in. "It's about time you two got here. But, I'm not complaining, I got to hold little Brooklyn first." Their personal conversation was officially over.

"Brooklyn, I like it. We thought you'd be running on K-time," Kate said as she grabbed the baby from Kinley. "She's adorable. I hope she keeps the blue eyes."

"Me too," Madison sighed. "Cal has the most gorgeous eyes."

"Except for *Rory*, don't you think, Kinley?" Megan teased.

"Yeah, Rory does have some gorgeous eyes," Kate added.

Kinley groaned, "Can you guys stop? First, Ryan, now you." Kinley smiled. "He was awful at the wedding, and he hasn't been able to let it go."

Madison laughed. While Cal had been at the top of *her* back-up list, Rory had been at the top of Kinley's. Ryan had moped around the wedding and the reception the entire time. "He's the guy *huh*? So, when I buy the farm, he's next in line? I think he's checking you out."

Kinley had pointed out that in most cases the back-up list was meant as a joke. It wasn't like we were ever going to meet any of those men on the list, she'd pointed out angrily. Leave it to Maddy...she'd said. *He's* married; happily, I might add...Kinley had protested. Ryan had not been able to let it go. I saw him when he danced with you; Ryan had brought it up several times. Kinley would always laugh it off. Madison suspected that Ryan had a small point but doubted anything would ever come of it.

"Doesn't Rory have the same eyes as Cal?" Megan asked, not letting it go.

"We do." Cal walked in with another vase of roses, "Why?"

"No reason," Kate replied rather too quickly. His eyes narrowed in a scrutinizing expression as he looked at each woman in turn. He bent over and kissed Madison sweetly.

"I'm not even going to ask." Cal shook his head in silent laughter.

"Good," Kinley fumed. Madison knew that the last person she wanted to know about her back-up list aside from Rory Hunt was Cal. While she told him nearly everything, she suspected Kinley would not appreciate him having access to that knowledge. Knowing Cal as she did, he would probably tease Kinley. No, it was best to leave it alone. Madison smiled as she looked around the room. There she was, surrounded by her 'family', next to the man she loved, and looking out to see Megan now taking Brooklyn into her arms from Kate. Inexplicable joy filled her soul, and she thought, surrounded by laughter and teasing, and love, could life possibly get any better than this?

50. The Interview- a few months Later

"Are we going to read it yet?" Kate asked with enthusiasm.

"We can't. Kin isn't here yet. She's running on K-time *again*," Megan groaned. "But…this does give me a moment to ask you something, Maddy. Why is Cal renovating the kitchen already? You've only been here a few months and the kitchen was just fine."

Maddy shrugged. "He says we're going to live here for a while and I might as well make things the way I want. I wanted something different. I'm kind of excited actually."

Kate added to the conversation, "But it's kind of wasteful."

"No it's not, I'm donating stuff. It's all good," Madison responded.

Kinley came in, arms full with her towel, bottled water, her bag, "Oh my gosh, Maddy. They've done so much since yesterday! It is looking so good in there. I can't believe how much they've done in a day! Wow! I can't wait to see the kitchen when it's done. It's going to look amazing." She began to lay her things out, "Sorry I'm late, guys. Kids had an award assembly. Did I miss anything?"

Cal walked out into the backyard, carrying the *G-String Magazine* they were all anticipating seeing. It was not available to the masses yet. "Kin!" He smiled. "Did you bring it?"

"Yes." She smiled back, pushing a stray curl away from her pale face.

"What did you bring him, Kin?" Kate asked curiosity over taking her.

"Yes, Kin, what could you possibly offer a rock star?" Megan playfully added.

"Bread," Cal answered them as Kinley pulled a full loaf of French bread out of her bag, wrapped tightly in clear plastic wrap. "And I don't have to share?" She shook her head as he smiled even bigger. "Yes!" He squeezed her in a sideways hug, "Love ya, Kin."

"Love you too, Cal." She dropped onto the lounge chair next to Maddy, "Where's my Brookie?"

"Sleeping in the playpen," Madison told her as she pointed over to the sleeping baby snuggled into the blankets in a playpen off to the side of her.

"You guys ready?" He pulled the magazine out and flipped through the pages, "Wow, Kin look how beautiful you look."

"Cause I'm airbrushed," Kinley told him matter-of-factly.

"No you're not!" he countered. "*Um*, okay," he cleared his throat, "I began this interview, the most peculiar interview I've ever given, in the quaint little home of an ordinary housewife."

"Ordinary, my ass," Madison grumbled. Kinley giggled.

"I have discovered that this housewife, Mrs. Kinley Brooke, is the closest friend of Madison Hunt née Grey, who as it turns out is the 'elusive' Maddy we have all speculated about since the night of November 23, 2008. It was the night that started an obsession for many of us in the media. Calvin Hunt, *that's me*, lead singer in the band Murder of Crows announced to the world that he was in love with someone he called *Maddy,* that would be you." He winked at his wife. "The American Music Awards suddenly became interesting. People everywhere sat up and took notice that his date was named Lindsey."

"The dumb cow," Megan said with a smile.

"Had he made a mistake? Hell yeah, I did. Who was this Maddy person and why wasn't she on his arm walking up the red carpet? Many people, such as myself, wanted to know," he read as Madison snorted.

"I was hugely pregnant, wouldn't have gone anyway."

He rolled his eyes and continued to read, "I was contacted by Calvin Hunt's publicist and assured that if I wished to know *anything* I could contact a woman named Kinley Brooke, who knows all. But will she tell all?" He leaned over, arching his eyebrow, "Will she? Let's see," he read on, "I learned Madison Hunt had a past I wouldn't wish upon anyone. She had been, by all accounts, an average housewife too. On the night of August 19, 2007, however, it all changed. She was married for nearly thirteen years to a man named Jack Grey. They had four beautiful; yes count them, children together. Her entire family was killed that evening when truck driver Luis Sandoval fell asleep at the wheel. He was killed too. It is a tragedy from which one can never fully recover. It was for this reason Madison's friends conspired to cheer her by taking her to a concert. This concert was Murder of Crows and the tickets were VIP. These were some seriously good friends." He read through this part almost quickly, not wishing to cause anyone pain, especially Maddy.

He turned the magazine around for everyone to see the picture Kinley had taken on the night they'd first met. It was like being in kindergarten having a story book read to you. "It was destined to be a magical evening. These women were invited backstage. The moment Calvin Hunt met Madison Grey, sparks flew. He actually let her walk away, Kinley Brooke confirmed, he had to find us by tracking down who bought the tickets. It was sweet really. Oh, Kin." He grinned and continued, "This began a relationship to be envied by women around the world." He looked at Maddy, "You're welcome. He soon was flying Madison and her friends out to see concerts in places such as Las Vegas, Orlando, and even London." The girls all let out simultaneous *oohs* and *ahs*.

"Through it all, Calvin and Maddy remained close. I *wish*, I see you skimmed over the details, Kin," He laughed. "They talked on the phone frequently, flew back and forth between Canada and California. He eventually spent Christmas with Madison and her friends. Kinley joked about how he attended her Christmas party in disguise and many people were furious with her later when they found out."

They all giggled as they said in unison, "Mandy."

He smiled. "His family wanted them there for New Years so after Christmas they flew to back up to Manitoba. I see you also left out the part about paparazzi chasing us out of town." Kinley shrugged. "They married in

January, to the delight of her friends and his family. I tried to delve for more, especially when it concerned rumors of a pregnancy and a rushed marriage, but Kinley Brooke isn't speaking." His voice went all high and Southern as he imitated Kinley, very badly. "It's funny but when you're in the center of things, you just don't hear the rumors. I told her the rumor was that Calvin and Maddy are expecting a Calvin Jr.- Kinley just smiled and commented that rumors are nothing we can rely on."

Every one of the girls clapped and giggled, as Cal bowed. Maddy gazed up at him with that loving look he'd always hoped to see. Now, he saw it many times daily. He was easing into his life as a husband and father, finding the peaceful days he spent in happiness, the best he'd ever known.

Epilogue- Return to Cal's Wedding or
Rory Opens Pandora's Box

Rory was beyond angry. Livid didn't quite sum it up either. He felt anger on top of crushing agony. A few months ago he'd received a manila envelope with pictures of his wife getting a whole different kind of work out from her personal trainer, while he was on the road in England. The letter was succinct- I thought you might want to know- signed, *a concerned friend*. He did want to know, but he'd been in pain ever since. To think- he thought he'd never known such pain and he'd been naïve to think it couldn't possibly be any worse. Another letter had arrived, delivered to him anonymously once again, only this one caused him greater anguish. This one told him years of grieving had been for no reason. It could have been from anyone as there a large group of people in town for Cal's wedding.

His *concerned friend* had rotten timing, this much was certain. Today was Cal's wedding day, he was already dressed in his tuxedo, but he was about to lose his mind, hunched over the edge of his bed as he sat with his head in his hands. Years ago, he and his wife had a son, shortly after she had miscarriage after miscarriage. He'd buried those lost little ones in tiny wooden boxes just at the edge of his yard where the wilderness nearly crept in. Now, he stared at the medical transcript copies in his hands and realized he must have buried empty boxes or were they? He was a fool. He'd been conned by his wife, the one person he should have been able to trust. She'd shed tears, sobbed into his arms countless times, weeping despondently about wanting to have more children with him.

It had been a deep and everlasting source of grief and despair and it hadn't even been real. It said here, in black and white, she'd had a tubal ligation done just after giving birth, and had hidden it from him. Years of fertility treatments, miscarriages, prayers, and it had all been a lie. He didn't know how to feel. Cal was immersed in bliss while *his* heart had been ripped from his chest. Cal wouldn't welcome him dumping his heart out at this time. Jen came in, but he couldn't look at her. He wasn't sure he could look at her ever again. "Rory, are you ready?" He shook his head, unable to speak. "What's this?" He allowed her to pick up the paper, examine it, and turn it over in her graceful hands. "Where did you get this?"

"You see the signature, he wasn't exactly forthcoming," Rory muttered into his hands. "Why, Jen? You could have told me you didn't want any more children. I would have understood." Was he lying? Would he have understood? They'd talked for hours about having a big family, how it had been one of their dearest dreams. Now, he realized it had been his dream alone.

"I can't believe someone would do this to me!" she cried, instant tears appearing in her cool blue eyes. "Rory, you have to listen to me…"

"I'm not going anywhere." He felt dizzy, sick in his heart. "I have all day, but I hardly think the person who sent this is to blame." He wasn't about to let her pin her deeds onto the messenger. She grimly frowned, as she began to explain, delicately.

"I thought it was the best way, *the only way*. You wanted a big family, and I wanted you to love me. I didn't want to disappoint you." Jen was pacing in her black evening gown, swishing as she moved, wringing her hands, "You would have wanted to adopt, to do anything. My supposed grief allowed me to be done, when you would've kept going. I couldn't be what you wanted, and I couldn't destroy your dreams." Her words sounded rehearsed as though she'd dreaded this moment. He didn't put it past her. This was far worse than her telling him outright that she didn't want more children. That would have sucked, but the elaborate hoax and cruel lie hurt far worse than anything he could have imagined.

"What did I bury, what, Jen?" His voice rose as he lifted his head.

"Nothing." She shifted uncomfortably in her evening gown.

His mouth went dry. The boxes weren't empty; he could see it on her face. "What did I bury?" His voice rose again, this time filling the entire room from the ceiling to the tiled floor. Her cerulean eyes were outlined in black, they narrowed dangerously, murderously. "What did I bury, Jen?"

She stared him down, "You need to let it go," she calmly told him.

"I refuse to let this go!" It was eating him alive, a cancer spreading through his soul, cankering his feelings for her until it would consume all of his love and leave behind nothing but hatred in its' place. He began to walk away, pulling his jacket with him. "If you won't tell me, then I'll have to see for myself what I have been grieving over all of these years."

"Can't we discuss this later? You'll be late to your own brother's wedding." She was trying to coax him as she followed him down the winding, sweeping staircase. "Please, baby."

"Once again, what the hell did I bury? What was I crying over as I put it in the ground?" he barked as he made his way to the garage. "What have I been grieving for?"

"The ground is frozen, Rory, you can't do this!" Panic filled her voice. "You need to stop this now!" she shrieked.

He turned on his heel and screamed, "Tell me!"

"Damn you, Rory, you need to leave it alone!" He'd incensed her but he didn't care. In the backyard, in a little wooded sitting area, he would find the boxes. There would be snow but he'd clear it away. "Stop!" She picked up an antique vase she loved and threw it, sending it through the air. It grazed his shoulder as it hit the wall and shattered. "Rory, I'm serious!" She was losing it, breaking down in front of him.

"So am I." He reached the garage, the chill was unbearable, and he pulled a pair of work gloves on and grabbed a snow shovel and a pick. She stepped in between him and the door. "Move out of my way, Jen," he grumbled. She was pulling the snow shovel out his hands, clawing at him, tearing at his sleeves, he pulled away. "What the hell is your problem?"

"It's too cold you won't get to them!"

"Good, then I can give you a chance to remove them, get rid of the evidence. I don't think so. You're hell-bent on keeping me from doing this which tells me those boxes aren't empty," he yelled. She began sobbing, when he didn't stop, finally she broke out into an ear piercing scream, so high, he nearly covered his ears. The wailing and shrieking continued; she was something like a toddler having a meltdown. She took anything in reach, shredding, throwing, destroying, but he did not relent. She could shriek all she wanted; he was done. He would find out even if he missed the wedding. His face froze in anger, "You're insane."

She was pulling at his jacket, fighting him, "Why are you doing this to me?"

"To you?" he called back to her as he left the garage and walked with long strides across the frozen ground. He found the statues of angels he'd placed to mark the graves and began to shovel. "You must be joking."

"We're going to miss Cal's wedding!" she squealed, teetering, her teeth chattering as she followed him into the snow.

"Like you care. You don't even like Cal and you care for Maddy even less." He huffed as he shoveled deeper.

"They've probably disintegrated; I doubt they're still there." She was wailing, eyes puffing up, red and swollen, gnawing on her lip with agitation.

"Cedar boxes? I don't think so, they're fine," he grumbled as a droplet of sweat ran down his neck. This revelation seemed to upset her more than anything, knowing decomposition couldn't hide her sins.

She was clawing at him again, trying to wrest the pick from his hands. "Leave me be, Jen." He pried her grip easily from his arm. The ground was harder than he'd anticipated, like hard plastic, but he was strong and determined and the graves were shallow. She ran into the house, screaming at the top of her lungs, until he thought her lungs would burst. Yet, a moment later she ran back out again, trying to appear calmed down.

"Rory, please, I beg you." She was in agony, twisting her hands; her hair loosened from the elegant chignon and began to fray.

He paused, leaning against the handle of the pick, taking a deep breath of the too-cold air; it hit his lungs like a hammer, "Are you going to force me to keep digging? You don't seem to realize that I will chisel away at the ground until my fingers bleed. I don't care if I miss the wedding; I'm going to find out what the hell you did to pull the wool over my eyes."

"Fine! They're just baby birds! I had no choice! Will you let it go?" He unintentionally dropped the pick letting it make a unique mark as it sank into the snow. He turned to look at her in disbelief. She was catching her breath, which formed a foggy mist in the air, she was looking absolutely wild. "They were just dead baby birds, wrapped up in gauze and…" He grew more nauseated as he let it settle in. He couldn't get the information to sound right to his brain. Where exactly had she gotten dead baby birds? Had she killed them herself? He finally got the nerve to really look at her, she was positively manic. "I know what you're thinking. You're wondering about the beaks." He stared at her without being able to speak; this was not even close to what he'd been thinking, "I removed them in case you looked, I covered them in blood…" He felt the nausea swell inside of him as he blinked in astonishment. Whose blood? "You might have looked! I couldn't take any chances!" She was crying, weeping as she leaned against him, he pulled her back. She'd also wept over those wooden boxes, quite convincingly too.

"Dear God, you let me believe we lost three children. You allowed me to grieve and despair over tiny birds in little coffins? What kind of monster are you? " His rage was rising into his throat. "Jen, we need to get a divorce. I can't live with you; I can't even look at you." Who had he married? If she'd told him she wanted a big family and then did unspeakable things to get out of it, he could only guess at the other things she lied about. She'd cheated too. Was nothing beneath her? Even killing baby birds to keep a ruse going?

"Please, Rory, you're the most kindhearted forgiving man I know. Can't I do something? I love you. I didn't want to lose you, and I've dreaded this. But now, it's out in the open, can't we rebuild? Start from scratch? I have always loved you, that's the honest truth. I'd do *anything* to keep you." Would she keep their son, Matthew, from him? Would she destroy him for leaving? He inhaled deeply. This would clearly require much thought.

"At this point, I think we can hang on until Matthew is older," he whispered, afraid of his own anger. He went inside to clean up, leaving his tools in the snow. He splashed cool water over his face as Jen swept her hair back up and pinned it down while standing next to him. "We'd better go," he mentioned hoarsely. How would he witness Cal's happiness without thinking about his own misery? He wanted this for Cal, hell, he wanted it for Maddy. They deserved to be happy. But…did he deserve such misery? Couldn't the letter writer have waited one more damn day? He could hear

Jen following him down the hall and to the garage. His car roared to life in the darkness, as the smell of her perfume gagged him. He knew he'd forever associate the scent with this vicious memory. How could he make this work when she'd made him fully hate her? She'd killed his love in a single blow.

He was startled by the way she'd become composed after her psychotic break. She'd have to put on a show and make it good. "Please, Rory, speak to me?" she whined. He just knew he was going to throw-up.

"I can't." He drove to Cal's house, parked his car and walked down toward the white tent, putting on his false smile as he walked. He pulled her arm into his, wishing he could leave her then and there. He dropped her off in her seat, gave Cal a quick congratulations and joined the wedding party in the other tent. They'd rehearsed this whole thing, he knew he'd be walking up the aisle with Kinley, but he had no idea how drop-dead gorgeous she'd look in her bridesmaid gown. The deep blue material looked like dark water, the way it flowed around her, she looked like a water nymph, a goddess, her face was glowing. "Hello, it's nice to see you again." She always made his heart pound wildly in his chest. If only he could find a way to avoid her better. What a contrast she was to Jen. What a breath of fresh air...

"It's nice to see you too, Rory. I don't know how you live here, it's so cold." She bit her lip, looking up at him, "aren't you freezing?" There was something sweet and sincere in her countenance, something Jen did not possess. They were standing in a separate tent, stocked with heaters, but the tent was stubbornly holding onto that Manitoba biting chill.

"I'm fortunate to have a jacket, while Maddy has left *you* exposed." He grinned, wishing he could wrap her up in his jacket, which might be crossing the line. Hell, who cared, "Would you like to wear my jacket for a moment?"

"Who says chivalry is dead?" she asked him, her bright eyes glowing. He gulped as he draped it over her shoulders. She took in a deep breath, "oh, and it smells so good too. Thank you."

"You're welcome, fair maiden." He bowed, and winked at her. She was stunning, her skin as white as the surrounding virginal snow, her smiling lips were like red rose petals, her brown eyes deep and alluring. He had to stop. He paced in a corner away from her, not speaking to anyone until he had to. He smiled kindly at her when she handed him back his jacket, telling him it had done the trick, but he noticed her perfume, a flowery scent had been left behind on his collar. She took his arm, as he walked her up the aisle, and for some stupid reason, he turned and glanced back at her. Idiot, he thought. He knew he was trying to rationalize wanting her after the terrible betrayal he'd suffered at Jen's hands. She's married, and so are you, he thought to himself.

He watched Cal light up like the little lights sprinkled all around them when Maddy walked up the aisle. She glowed, and so did he. They radiated happiness, and he wanted it to last for them. He needed Cal, needed to tell him, needed to get this miserable information off his chest. What could he do? Would Cal think he was a moron? His mind replayed the grisly scene for him over and over. It was making him physically ill. The party came about quickly, regardless of his pain, heaters kept the warmth going, and music blasted into the cold night air. He danced with Jen because it was expected, and she whispered into his ear, "Please, Rory, don't give up on us?" He couldn't respond. He'd been contemplating everything; he was still wondering what other things she'd lied about. Had she even wanted Matthew at all? He twirled her around the floor, while he casually glanced over at Kinley, who seemed to be having a lively discussion with her husband who was hunched over to her height.

He thought back to the day he'd spent with Kinley in England. It had been a mistake because it had been wonderful. He shouldn't have spoken more than a few words to her, because she'd somehow captured his curiosity. He wanted to ask her all sorts of questions, he wanted to know her, but it was a bad idea. She looked as though she might be happily married, which was a pity, because he definitely wasn't. He'd thought *he* was, but that mirage had been obliterated. He eyed Kinley with something akin to hunger. Jen was watching him, "So when did you start liking redheads?"

"*Please*, Jen." He was annoyed that she'd seen through him.

"If you leave me," she whispered softly, yet viciously, "I'll destroy you and whoever you leave me for. Matthew might not even be safe." He gulped. He'd never been more terrified in his entire life. "Just remember that, Rory. You have no idea what I'm capable of." He believed her. She turned and looked back at Kinley, "I'm taking the car you can find your way home." He nodded as she sauntered away, leaving his insides searing, his mind reeling, his heart numb. He could sleep at Cal's tonight; Cal would never know. Matthew wouldn't be going home tonight. Maybe she just needed a break, to wind down.

His eyes flickered back to Kinley who was standing there, eyes glittering with joy. What would it be like to be with someone like her? He shrugged it away, not good to think about it. But…he was under her spell, in a trance he made his way across the floor, past one couple who were making out, and found Kinley looking radiant as she did every time he saw her. "Would you care to dance?" He'd located her husband talking to their friends beside the punch bowl, two glasses in his hands.

"I'd love to."

He took her hand and led her out to dance, it was a song Murder of Crows had made famous, "In Your Arms Tonight", one of the few songs he sang lead on. "You are looking lovely tonight." He smiled as he spun her around. What a nice distraction from his traumatizing day.

"That is a huge compliment coming from a man married to a super model. I shall treasure it always." She smiled, reminding him of the moment she'd first caught his eye, from the stage at one of their concerts. He was a horrible person, no better than Jen, feeling despicable and ashamed. He had to extricate himself from this situation. He pulled her closer but not too close. Cal was watching him, scrutinizing him; he smiled at his brother but placed his attention back on Kinley. He tried to look innocent as Cal could easily see through him.

"Have you warmed up?" he asked politely.

"Sort of, but I fear I will be drinking hot chocolate all night. My husband might want to kick me out of bed when I stick my freezing feet up next to him later." She grinned, and he secretly began to let his mind wander down a dangerous path.

"I'm sure he'd never do such a thing." Rory smiled benignly, knowing *he* wouldn't kick her out bed for anything. The song ended too quickly, forcing him to let her walk away. He'd crossed the line and would not cross it again. He'd steer clear of Kinley, no matter what it took. It would take a miracle to save his marriage; he didn't need a beautiful distraction. Could it be saved after something like this? He disappeared, removing himself surreptitiously from the crowd, until he felt the cool embrace of the wilderness. His favorite footpath had been cleared for Maddy to visit Kinley in the guesthouse behind Cal's glorious mansion. He slipped unseen into one of Cal's many bedrooms. With any luck, he could slip out in the morning unnoticed. He was such a fool.

For more about Cal, Rory, Madison, and Kinley please visit our website -

thebackuplist.blogspot.com

Look for the sequel

THE LIST OF POSSIBILITIES

Coming soon

The Shout-Out Pages

First of all we'd like to thank our husbands and children. Jeff, Mike, Zach, McKayla, Makenzie, Regan, Britney, Dylan and Kenley, we love you all very much and couldn't have done this without you. However, the constant interruptions and whining often made us lose our train of thought. So, thank you… we think.

Thank you to our friends who read our book chapter by chapter, and to those who gave us positive feedback, which we feel helped us write a great story. We love it.

Thank you sooooo much to Ciara Sullivan our agent who wears many hats wonderfully, especially the pointy wizard hat! Thanks to the folks at Perfect Fit Publishing for their support and general awesomeness! An extra special thank you to Ruby Lowe and Cillian Cubstead for your amazing 'mad skills'. We bow down at your feet. We know what this book looks like without the help of your 'super powers'. It wasn't pretty…but we still loved our ugly baby…We like her a little better with her glorious face lift. The cover design is lovely, Ruby. The title page art is fabulous, Cillian, so thanks for taking a tiny break from drawing comic books for us.

This one is for the haters…We want to thank Nickelback, yes, Nickelback for providing hours of musical enjoyment, and inspiration. We gave them a giant present when we saw them in LA, yes, Chad, you're welcome, for the gigantic boat cover. May your boat always be protected. This book was not based on Nickelback, but we do love our Canadian rock stars.

And finally, it must be mentioned, we'd like to thank the members of the Academy and all the little people for this magical moment…sniff….

About the Authors

Miriam and Amber have been friends for quite a few years now…because Amber walked up to Miriam and told her she loved her slutty boots, on a Sunday morning at church. They've been friends ever since. They decided this was too funny not to write into the book *somewhere*. They started The Back-Up List in 2009; it has given them many hours of amusement. Writing these books has given them nearly endless laughter, which they love above all things. Some of their whacky real-life stories have been written surreptitiously into the books, although they'll never tell you what they are. The Back-Up List is their personal joke, and yes they do have cards in their wallets (thanks Molls). They both live in Southern California with their families, and they enjoy going to Disneyland, the beach, and fun GNOs.